Edyth stared blindly through the window, as they passed through the gates set in the high walls that surrounded the workhouse, infirmary and fever hospital complex. They reached the bottom of High Street and drove under the railway bridge into Tumble Square. She rapped her cane on the roof in Taff Street and shouted, 'Drive home via Mill Street, Catherine Street, Gelliwastad Road and Bridge Street, and drive slowly in Mill Street.'

'Yes, Mrs James,' came the coachman's muffled reply.

Edyth removed a lavender-scented handkerchief from her handbag and held it over her nose and mouth as she studied the dilapidated terrace that backed on to the river. The heat of August had abated, the evenings were growing shorter, and people were taking their winter coats out of mothballs to prepare for the winter, but the stench of sewage, rot and decay was still overwhelming. She saw the sign over Owen Bull's shop and imagined Sali and her child living within those mouldering walls, breathing in the foul air day after day.

'No more!' she promised herself fervently. No matter what the police said, or what 'rights' Owen Bull claimed as Sali's husband, there was no way that she was going to allow her niece, or Mansel's son to return to that slum to live in those foul conditions with a man she regarded as a murderer, even if the police didn't. Not while she still drew breath.

Catrin Collier was born and brought up in Pontypridd. She lives in Swansea with her husband, three cats and whichever of her children choose to visit. Her latest novel in hardback, *Winners and Losers*, is also available from Orion.

By Catrin Collier

HISTORICAL

Hearts of Gold
One Blue Moon
A Silver Lining
All That Glitters
Such Sweet Sorrow
Past Remembering
Broken Rainbows
Spoils of War
Swansea Girls
Swansea Summer
Homecoming
Beggars and Choosers
Winners and Losers

CRIME
(*as Katherine John*)

Without Trace
Six Foot Under
Murder of a Dead Man
By Any Other Name

MODERN FICTION
(*as Caro French*)

The Farcreek Trilogy

Beggars and Choosers

CATRIN COLLIER

ORION

An Orion paperback

First published in Great Britain in 2003
by Orion
This paperback edition published in 2004
by Orion Books Ltd,
Orion House, 5 Upper St Martin's Lane,
London WC2H 9EA

A CIP catalogue record for this book
is available from the British Library.

ISBN 0 75285 923 4

Typeset by Deltatype Ltd, Birkenhead, Merseyside

Printed and bound in Great Britain by
Clays Ltd, St Ives plc

www.orionbooks.co.uk

For John, for thirty-eight years of unconditional love and for believing in me, even when I lost faith in myself.

ACKNOWLEDGEMENTS

I apologise in advance for the length of this acknowledgement but I would like to express my gratitude to everyone who helped me research this book and so generously gave of their time and expertise.

All the dedicated staff of Rhondda Cynon Taff's exceptional library service, especially Mrs Lindsay Morris for her ongoing help and support. Catherine Morgan, the archivist at Pontypridd and Nick Kelland, the archivist at Treorchy library, for not only guiding me through the records but also helping me to compile maps of Pontypridd and the Rhondda Valleys as they were in 1900.

The staff of Pontypridd Museum, Brian Davies, David Gwyer and Ann Cleary, for allowing me to dip into their extensive collection of old photographs and for doing such a wonderful job of preserving the history of Pontypridd.

Professor Dai Smith of the University of Glamorgan for sharing his knowledge of the Tonypandy Riots with me and his account of the riots in Wales, in the chapter, 'A Place in South Wales' in the book, *Wales, A Question for History*.

Deirdre Beddoe for her meticulously documented accounts of women's lives in Wales at the turn of the century.

The fascinating period photographs Gareth Williams has posted on his Internet site, *A Tribute to the Rhondda*, which also gives an in-depth account of the Tonypandy Riots.

D. J. Rees for his book *Pontypridd with Ynysybwl,* a compilation of old photographs of Pontypridd.

Don Powell for his book *Victorian Pontypridd.*

Professor Norman Robbins, whose definitive history of pantomime, *Slapstick and Sausages*, gives an account of the 1894 pantomime *Babes in The Wood* featuring Baron Ystrad Rhondda, in which the robbers are sentenced to sit on Cardiff City Council for the rest of their lives.

Father Mark Rowles of SS *Gabriel* and Raphael Church, Tonypandy, for his help in detailing the exquisitely beautiful church as it might have been in 1910.

The people of Tonypandy and the Rhondda, who helped me and offered me so many cups of tea when I was walking around the streets trying to envisage Tonypandy as it was at the time of the riots. They have to be the friendliest, most hospitable people on the planet. Never once was I asked who I was, or what I was doing.

My husband John and our children Ralph, Ross, Sophie and Nick and my parents Glyn and Gerda for their love, support and the time they gave me to write this book.

Margaret Bloomfield for her unstinting friendship and help in so many ways.

My agent, Ken Griffiths, for his professionalism, friendship and making my life so much more interesting than I ever thought it could be and his wife Marguerite for her hospitality and warm friendship.

Absolutely everyone at Orion, especially my editor Yvette Goulden for her encouragement, inspiration and constructive criticism, Rachel Leyshon my eagle-eyed copy editor, Sophie Mackrell my publicist, Juliet Ewers, Sophie Hutton-Squire, Jenny Page, Dean Mitchell and all the editorial, sales and marketing teams.

And all the booksellers and readers who make writing such a privileged occupation. And while I wish to acknowledge all the assistance I received, I wish to state that any errors in *Beggars and Choosers* are entirely mine.

Catrin Collier, February 2003

NOTES

I hope I have not caused any confusion or offence in allowing my characters to occupy actual houses that existed in Pontypridd in the early twentieth century.

The Williams' family owned Danygraig House in Taff Street for several generations, it was demolished in 1910 and the present YMCA, among other buildings, erected on the site.

Gwilym James is based on the Gwilym Evans' Department Store. In the early 1900s the site of the store in Market Street was occupied by a general warehouse, which sold clothing and household goods to the public.

Ynysangharad House and estate were bought by public subscription and donations from the Miners' Unions funds in the early 1920s. The land was laid out as a public park and named the Ynysangharad Memorial Park, as a tribute to the men from the area who lost their lives in the First World War.

Ynysangharad House was used as an NHS clinic until it was demolished, like so many other fine old buildings in Pontypridd, in the 1960s.

The Horse and Groom was demolished in the 1960s, the New Inn in 1981, Pontypridd Police Station in Gelliwastad Road during recent years. Mill Street is no longer the main road to the Rhondda but a cul-de-sac. The cottages and shops I housed Owen Bull and his butcher's shop in were demolished and others built on the site between 1910–1912.

Penuel Chapel and its burial ground were situated behind the fountain in Taff Street. The chapel was razed to the ground in 1967 and the burial ground excavated. The remains of those buried there were transferred to Glyntaff cemetery with the exception of James James. His remains and later Evan James's were interred beneath the bronze memorial in Pontypridd Park, to the father and son who wrote the Welsh national anthem, *Hen Wlad Fy Nhadau* – Land of My Fathers.

In the mid-1890s a farmer in Llanerchymerdd, Anglesey, remarried after the death of his first wife. His bride refused to allow the children of his first marriage to continue to live on his farm, so sixteen-year-old Ruth Jones and her two brothers, thirteen-year-old Owain Glyndwr Jones and twelve-year-old Harry Glyndwr Jones walked from North Wales to the Rhondda Valleys in search of work. They settled in Tonypandy where Ruth went into domestic service and her brothers became boy colliers. Harry Glyndwr Jones was my grandfather and although I only met him twice, I am proud to be descended from a miner who took an active part in both the 1910 and 1926 strikes.

CHAPTER ONE

A tinsel and candle bedecked Christmas tree soared upwards from the ground floor stairwell to the balcony in the foyer of the Empire Hall theatre. Beneath it stood a trestle table covered with a red tablecloth. Sali Watkin Jones, her two brothers, sister and the family's housekeeper, Mari Williams, were busy arranging pyramids of paper cornets containing boiled sweets on it when the door banged open and Mansel James strode in, followed by a train of errand boys carrying large cardboard boxes.

Mansel returned Sali's smile and directed the boys to set the boxes down on to an empty table next to the theatre's closed box office. He lifted his hat and inclined his head. 'Miss Watkin Jones, Master Geraint, Master Gareth, Miss Llinos, Mrs Williams, compliments of the season to you all.'

'And to you, Mr James.'

Sali's formal greeting contrasted oddly with that of her two younger brothers who ran to Mansel and proceeded to 'pretend' box with him. One of Gareth's punches flew wide and hit Mansel on the chin.

'I yield. I've taught you too well,' Mansel pleaded, adopting a pained expression as he rubbed his jaw. He opened one of the boxes in an attempt to distract the boys. 'I promised I'd check the contents, but only because I knew I could trust you two to do it for me. There should be eight hundred assorted sixpenny toys, for the knockdown price of fifteen pounds, as negotiated by your father with Mr Hopkins.'

'You want us to count them all?' Gareth gasped, horrified by the prospect.

'Only if you're up to it,' Mansel replied gravely.

Geraint, who knew Mansel's ploys well, untied the string on a second box. 'Bet I finish before you, Gareth.'

'Bet you don't.'

Mansel crossed to where Sali was standing. 'I am not the only businessman in town to complain that your father spoils his workers and their children at this time of year to the detriment of every other employer in Pontypridd. I don't think he realises that our staff expect, no, *demand* the same generous treatment.'

'Father says that Christmas only comes once a year.' Sali set the last cornet from her box on the table. 'I assumed Mr Hopkins would deliver the toys.'

'He was busy so I volunteered.'

'The owner of a toy shop was busier than the owner of a department store two days before Christmas?'

'Would it make you happier if I admitted that I bribed him into allowing me to make the delivery because I wanted to see you?' he flirted outrageously.

Disregarding Mari's knowing smile, Sali inspected the toys her brothers were counting. 'Mr Hopkins really did send us an assortment this year,' she commented, eyeing the array of tin mechanical toys, spinning tops, bags of marbles, card games, jigsaws, doll's tea sets, boats, miniature rag dolls, teddy bears, scrapbooks complete with envelopes of coloured scraps, and, for the older girls who had been press-ganged into helping with the babies, wooden brush and comb sets. A gale of high-pitched laughter echoed from the auditorium.

'It sounds as though your father's colliers' children are having a good time. But then so they should with buns and pop supplied courtesy of the management, free admission to *Babes in the Wood* and . . . ?' Mansel sat on the edge of the table and looked quizzically at the paper cones Mari was still arranging.

'Boiled sweets,' Geraint explained, muttering numbers under his breath as he foraged in his toy box.

'I dread to think what this lot is costing your father and that's without the free chickens he handed out to every worker for their Christmas dinner and the party he hosted for his colliers in the Horse and Groom last night. I heard they drank the pub dry.'

'I didn't realise you were an admirer of Scrooge's philosophy before the ghosts of Christmas converted him,' Sali mocked.

'Father said the colliery has had a good year and it's only fair he share his profits with the workers who made it possible.' Geraint repeated his father's standard explanation for his generosity. 'Hear that booing? The evil robbers have been caught by Robin Hood and Maid Marion, the Babes rescued and Baron Ystrad Rhondda has promised to take everyone to Ilfracombe on holiday to celebrate.'

'You've seen the pantomime?' Mansel directed his question at Geraint, but he was still staring at Sali.

'Father booked a box the night Gareth and I came home from school and Llinos came with us.'

'Not you?' Mansel asked Sali.

'I'm too old for pantomimes.'

'No one is too old for pantomimes. I'll book us a box.'

'When?' she enquired. 'My father's Christmas ball is this evening, our family Christmas Eve dinner with all the aunts and uncle tomorrow, and we could hardly go on Christmas Day, even if the theatre was open, which it isn't.'

'Then I'll book it for Boxing Day.'

'You're hosting Aunt Edyth's party, remember?'

'So I am.' He dismissed it carelessly. 'We'll have to make it Wednesday night.'

'I've accepted an invitation to Harriet Hopkins's party.'

'So have I, but we don't have to go.'

3

'And what would it look like to the rest of Pontypridd if you and I sneak off by ourselves?'

'Like we find Harriet Hopkins boring.' Mansel made a face. 'She's a nagging busybody. The last time I saw her, all she could talk about was her precious Bible Circle and the desperate need for young men to volunteer their services to lead the boys' discussion groups.'

'A very worthwhile cause.' Sali had difficulty keeping a straight face.

'Miss Llinos, you and your brothers would like to see the pantomime again, wouldn't you?' Mansel called out.

'They would not,' Sali answered for them.

'You really intend to go to Harriet Hopkins's tedious party? And it will be tedious. There'll be parlour games of the spin the plate variety,' he lowered his voice to a whisper, 'and no postman's knock. And she'll sing. Something ghastly and Victorian like "Come into the Garden, Maud."'

'It would ill-mannered not to turn up after accepting her invitation.' Mansel's prediction was likely to be accurate, given Harriet's previous efforts, but Sali refused to join in his criticisms.

'Then I'll go with you, but only on condition you promise not to leave my side all evening.' Mansel's words were swallowed by a deafening burst of music.

'This bit is funny.' Geraint pushed open the door to the back of the stalls and he, Llinos and Gareth crept inside the darkened auditorium. Mansel felt for Sali's hand under cover of her skirt, and pulled her after them.

Two robbers in clown make-up, black-and-white striped jerseys and red baggy tights were sitting, tied back to back, in front of the closed curtain. Maid Marion was standing centre stage in a glittering gown of Lincoln green hung with spangles. Sali blushed as a well-endowed female Robin Hood stepped up alongside her, in a pair of knickerbockers that skimmed the top of her thighs, revealing what seemed like yards of leg.

'I sentence you robbers to a fate worse than death.'

4

Maid Marion's clear young voice rang out above the heads of the hushed audience. 'You will sit on Cardiff City Council for life.'

'Grand Finale is next,' Geraint whispered in Sali's ear, as laughter rent the air. 'We'd better go back and help Mari prepare for the attack.'

'For me?' the small girl asked Sali in wonder.

'For you.' Sali handed her a rag doll dressed in a sailor's outfit. 'Don't forget to go along to that lady and gentleman to get your sweets.' She indicated Mari and Geraint.

'Thank you, Miss Watkin Jones.' The child, who was dressed in a dark frock and white, ruffled pinafore, clutched the doll, curtsied and moved to the table Mari was manning.

'I thought that queue was never going to disappear.' Mansel peered into the box. 'How many toys do you have left?'

'About fifty, which Father expected.' Sali closed the box. 'The coachman will take them to the orphanage along with some other things tomorrow.'

'So you're finished here?' Mansel smiled hopefully.

'Miss Sali, the coach has arrived and you only have two hours to dress before the ball.' Mari boxed the remaining sweets.

'You haven't even five minutes to spare?' Mansel helped Sali close the toy box.

'Apparently not.'

'Keep all your dances for me tonight?'

'No,' Sali retorted.

'I only want to make the other boys jealous.'

'At the cost of my reputation.'

'All the waltzes?' he pleaded.

'Maybe,' she murmured softly, as Mari called her a second time.

'This dress is nothing but hooks.' Mari tore a fingernail

5

as she fastened the cotton underbodice of Sali's evening dress. 'Breathe in and stand still.'

'I'm trying.' Sali gripped the cheval mirror to steady herself, as the housekeeper heaved the boned back over her spine. She held herself, tense and rigidly upright, lest she lose her balance and accidentally step on the ruffled lace skirt of the dress that lay heaped on a sheet around her feet.

'At last.' Mari fastened the last hook and lifted the skirt carefully to Sali's waist before hooking it on to the bodice and handing Sali the silk cord that held the long train. 'This is beautifully worked lace. You are going to be the belle of the ball.' Mari lifted the cream satin and lace bodice from the bed, slipped it over Sali's arms, hooked the back and pulled it down to cover the waistband. She frothed out the layers of lace on the sleeves, low-cut décolletage and the hem, finally smoothing the lines of fine gold baby ribbon threaded through the lace borders. 'Definitely the belle of the ball,' she muttered, as much to herself as to Sali and her younger sister Llinos, who was sitting on the bed playing with Sali's ivory and lace fan.

'You say that before every party, Mari, but there are far prettier girls than me in Pontypridd.' Sali studied her reflection critically in the mirror. She held no illusions about her appearance, but she was not displeased with what she saw. A slender young girl of middle height with an abundance of rich, chestnut hair pinned in an elaborate style, a small, neat nose, large grey-green eyes and a determined chin. She smiled and a dimple appeared at the corner of her mouth.

'Gloves,' Llinos reminded, handing Mari a pair of cream satin, elbow-length evening gloves.

Sali held out her arms and Mari rolled them over her fingers, wrists and arms.

'Jewels.' Llinos opened the white satin-lined case and picked out the heirloom sapphire and diamond hairpin, bracelets, necklace and ring that had belonged to their grandmother.

'Miss Harriet's maid told me that Miss Harriet wears six hairpieces to pad out her evening hairstyles. I told her straight, my Miss Sali's hair is that thick and long, she doesn't need to wear a single one.' Mari pinned the diamond hairpin to the side of the elaborate bouffant hairstyle she had taken over an hour to create. 'Look at that, perfect.'

'You don't think it's too elaborate for a family ball?' Sali asked anxiously, turning her head.

'Not for tonight.' Mari fastened the twin bracelets over Sali's gloved wrists, fastened the necklace around her throat and slipped on the ring.

'Scent?' Llinos unscrewed the silver cap of the blue and silver glass bottle that held Sali's favourite essence of violets.

'What would I do without you, muffin?' Sali took the bottle.

'Let me, or you'll stain your gloves, or even worse your dress.' Mari intercepted the bottle, removed the rubber stopper and upended the bottle on her forefinger. Dabbing carefully she applied scent to the back of Sali's neck, behind her ears and sprinkled a few drops on her hair. 'Where's your hanky? We can risk staining that.'

Sali handed over a scrap of silk and lace.

Mari placed a dab, then screwed the cap back on the bottle and set it on the dressing table.

'Grandma's fan.' Llinos flicked it together and Sali smiled as she took it.

'Well, you're as ready as I can make you. And if I do say it myself, you won't disgrace your father when you stand next to him in the receiving line,' Mari announced.

'I don't see why I can't stand in the line,' Llinos grumbled. 'Geraint is, and he's only four years older than me.'

'And when you're four years older, Miss Llinos, you'll be able to stand in the line too,' Mari said ruthlessly in an

7

attempt to stamp out Llinos's envy before it became any more apparent.

'And by then I'll be an old withered spinster.' Sali hooked up her train and tried a twirling dance step.

'That, I doubt,' Mari countered.

'Here's your card.' Llinos glanced at it before giving it to Sali. 'Aren't you terrified that no one will ask you to dance? If I have a single line left free at my first ball, I'll die of shame.'

'Then it's just as well that you're not going to the ball, Miss Llinos, because no girl is engaged for every single dance at a ball. Except perhaps your sister tonight,' Mari amended. 'Looking the way she does I wouldn't be surprised to see the men queuing up as soon as they come through the door.'

'That's nonsense, Mari, and you know it.'

'I know no such thing.' Mari combed the hair from Sali's brush, curled it round her finger and placed it in the hair tidy. 'Right, now you're finished, I'll go along and see if I can help Alice with your mother.'

'Do you think you'll be able to persuade her to come downstairs?' Sali asked.

'I'll do my best.' Mari pursed her lips disapprovingly. Gwyneth Watkin Jones's 'delicacy' was famed from one end of Pontypridd to the other and the 'good days' since the birth of her youngest son Gareth ten years before, had been marked by the occasions when she had relinquished the day bed in her boudoir, for the drawing-room sofa. 'You run along, Miss Sali, you don't want to be too late to greet your father's guests.'

'It's horrible being the youngest. I'll never be old enough to go to balls,' Llinos muttered petulantly.

'You can watch from the landing,' Mari consoled.

'It's not the same.' Llinos crossed her arms and glared at the housekeeper.

'It's no good looking at me like that, Miss Llinos. Everyone would quite rightly look sideways at your father if he allowed you to go gadding around downstairs tonight at your age. But if you go along to the nursery, I think you'll find an early present for you and one for Master Gareth on the table, along with some cakes and Christmas biscuits.'

Llinos frowned. 'What's the present?'

'I'm not saying anything,' Mari answered mysteriously.

'Please, Mari,' Llinos pleaded.

'Now, let me see.' Mari stared at the ceiling. 'Didn't someone say something about wanting a puppet theatre . . .'

Llinos shrieked, jumped off the bed and darted out of the room.

'Your father spoils her and Gareth something awful.' Mari picked up the sheet she had laid on the floor to save the skirt of Sali's dress from dust, folded it and put it away in the bottom of the wardrobe.

'No more than he spoils Geraint and me.' Sali checked her reflection one last time.

'The difference being, you're so sweet-natured you deserve it.'

'I was just as difficult and awkward as Llinos at her age.'

'No, you weren't.' Mari watched as Sali went to the door. 'If you didn't look so perfect I'd risk hugging you.'

'I'll give you a thank-you hug for making me look like this later.' Sali walked on to the landing in time to hear the first knock on the door.

'I know we're early, Harry, but I couldn't contain Mansel a moment longer. He's been like a jack-in-the-box that's outgrown the box since he came home from the store.'

Edyth James waited until Harry Watkin Jones's butler, Tomas, removed her fur evening cape before offering her cheek to her nephew.

'Thank you for coming so early, Aunt Edyth.' Harry watched Sali walk sedately down the staircase. 'You look very beautiful,' he complimented.

9

'The dress is beautiful,' Sali corrected. 'Thank you for buying it for me.'

'Thank your aunt, she was the one who suggested it as an early Christmas present.'

'In that case, thank you, Aunt Edyth. You have exquisite taste.' Sali kissed Edyth and held out her hand to Mansel.

'Steady,' Harry warned, as Geraint charged down the stairs at speed, fastening his gold cufflinks.

'Am I late?'

'No more than usual, Geraint.' Mansel shook Harry's hand.

'Harry, Mrs James, Mr James, children.' A tall, gaunt, dark-haired, sallow-faced man entered the house, removed his overcoat and handed it to Tomos.

'Morgan,' Harry greeted his wife's brother. 'Thank you for accepting my invitation.'

'I won't stay long, Harry. It isn't done for a minister to be seen on such frivolous occasions, but I called out of respect for Gwyneth.'

'She will be downstairs shortly.'

'Then she is well?'

'I believe so,' Harry replied tersely. He disliked his brother-in-law intensely, not least because he felt that he encouraged his wife in her fanciful notions of ill-health.

'Sherry, sir, madam?' Robert, the footman held out a tray.

'As you well know from my previous visits to this house, I never indulge in strong drink,' Morgan replied curtly.

'Thank you, Robert.' Edyth took a glass.

'Thank you,' Mansel took a second.

'Why don't you three bright young things go and tell the orchestra what to play while Harry and I receive the guests?' Edyth suggested.

Harry hesitated for the briefest of moments. 'Go ahead, Sali.' He knew exactly what Edyth was trying to engineer and hoped that she wasn't reading too much into a relationship he had been monitoring since Sali's eighteenth birthday.

'You can't take them all,' Sali protested, as Mansel James pulled her into a corner of the deserted library and proceeded to write his name against every single dance on her card.

'Who says I can't?' His blue eyes twinkled with mischief and he continued to scrawl his signature.

'There are other boys—'

'Are there?' He stood in front of her, effectively imprisoning her in the corner.

'I was going to add "who are coming to the ball".'

'How can someone who looks so lovely be so hard-hearted?'

'I am not,' she asserted.

'No?' he questioned with mock gravity. 'You refuse me your dances after stealing my heart in the summer. You disappear back to college in September for nearly three months leaving me in purgatory . . .'

'That I don't believe. I heard you took Harriet Hopkins to the Market Company ball.'

'Only because Aunt Edyth insisted I couldn't go without a partner. And I only danced one dance with her. I didn't hold hands. Not once. Or,' he lifted his eyebrows, 'try to kiss her.'

'You promised you wouldn't say that word again. Not after what you did last summer.'

'You said you were going to forget about it.'

Sali's fingers wandered to her lips. She could no more forget the first kiss Mansel had given her – the first she had ever received – than she could forget her own name. But before she had time to recall all the emotions he had evoked, he bent his head to hers and kissed her again. A soft, gentle, warm kiss that made her spine tingle and tinged the room with a soft, pink haze.

'Marry me?'

She stared up at him.

'Tradition demands that you give me an answer, not gaze at me open-mouthed.' He gripped her hands in his. 'Please say yes. There is an alternative, but I'd prefer not to think about it.'

'Mansel . . .'

'You don't love me?'

'You know I do.'

'Then I can speak to your father?'

'Yes. Please.'

'Remember your dance card is full.' He kissed her again, and then he was gone.

'Sali, where have you been?' Harriet Hopkins accosted her as soon as she walked into the large drawing room that her father had ordered to be cleared of furniture to make room for dancing.

'Checking the supper buffet arrangements with the housekeeper,' Sali prevaricated, glancing around the room. Neither her father nor Mansel were there and, although she knew that they could be in the library watching the card players, or in the small drawing room drinking tea with her mother and the 'ladies', she sensed they were closeted in his study. It was desperately unfair. Her whole life depended on the outcome of their interview and she wasn't even allowed to be present.

The orchestra struck the final chords of a waltz and the dancers applauded politely before moving off the floor.

'. . . If he's half as dangerous as they say, I'm surprised your father invited him into his house.'

'Who is dangerous?' Sali asked Harriet in confusion.

'That man?' Harriet nodded towards a tall dark man who was talking to a middle-aged matron on the other side of the room.

'Mr Evans, my father's deputy manager in the colliery?' Sali said, surprised. 'Why on earth should he be dangerous?'

'My father says he's working class, has extreme political views and shouldn't be allowed in polite society.

Oh, quick, he's coming this way, pretend we haven't seen him.' Harriet turned aside and feigned great interest in an oil painting of the old bridge hanging on the wall behind her as the band struck up a polka.

'Miss Watkin Jones, may I have this dance?'

Sali barely glanced at Lloyd Evans, as Mansel stood in the doorway and beckoned to her. 'I am sorry, Mr Evans, I am engaged—'

'With me,' Mansel interrupted. He held out his arm to Sali. 'Your father would like to speak to you, Miss Watkin Jones. He and your mother are in the study.'

'Miss Hopkins.'

Harriet giggled nervously as Lloyd Evans switched his attention to her, and Sali saw her simpering and blushing as he led her out on to the dance floor.

Sali gripped Mansel's arm tightly as he led her from the room. When she had embarked on her teacher training at Swansea Training College two and a half years before, nothing had seemed more purposeful or worthwhile than shaping young lives at the very outset of their academic careers, but as she gazed at Mansel's blond profile she couldn't imagine anything more wonderful than marriage to the man she loved.

'Sali is very young,' Gwyneth Watkins Jones drawled in her painfully languid voice.

'She is two years older than you were when you married Harry, Gwyneth,' Edyth reminded her tartly.

Harry looked across at his daughter. 'You have already accepted Mansel?'

'I gave Mr James permission to speak to you, Father.'

'But you do want to marry him?' he pressed.

'Yes.' She gazed into Mansel's eyes. 'Yes, Father, I do,' she said steadily.

'Then it appears to be a match made in heaven.' Harry slapped Mansel soundly across the shoulders. 'I can't imagine a better husband for you, Sali, or a better friend for Geraint and Gareth. But,' he frowned, 'Sali has yet to finish her education. Are you prepared to wait until the summer to marry her, Mansel?'

'You give your consent, sir?' Mansel could no more stop looking at Sali than she could at him.

Harry took his daughter's hand and placed it in Mansel's. 'Nothing would give me greater pleasure. However, there are conditions. Sali would not be allowed to continue in the college should the engagement become public knowledge. And, although I think it desirable that a married woman should be as well educated as her husband in these modern times, there are those who would disagree with me. So, why don't we hold off announcing your engagement until after Sali has finished her finals and in the meantime go ahead with all the legal arrangements that have to be made. Like the marriage settlement.'

Sali leapt to her feet and hugged her father.

'And no ring, not yet,' Harry warned Mansel. 'Sali isn't allowed to wear anything other than a bracelet watch in college so it will have to wait. You can give her one when she comes home after she has sat her finals in June. We'll hold a ball and make a formal announcement then. Until that time, the engagement will remain a secret between everyone here and my solicitor who will draw up the marriage settlement.' Harry held out his hand. 'I would say welcome to the family, Mansel, but you've been a part of it since the day you became Aunt Edyth's ward.'

'Thank you, sir.' Mansel shook Harry's hand vigorously.

'I dislike long engagements, but I suppose it will give Mansel and Sali an opportunity to arrange all that needs to be organised,' Edyth interposed.

'Long?' Harry laughed. 'How can you call seven months long, Aunt Edyth?'

'I was engaged for three weeks before I married Gwilym, but then,' Edyth turned to Sali, 'fewer things were expected and demanded of women in those days. I agree it's just as well that Sali finishes her education. The wife of Mansel James will have many duties to carry out and for the town's benefit as well as her husband's.'

'Morgan?' Harry looked up as his brother-in-law walked into the room without knocking.

'Forgive me. I presumed the room was unoccupied. I was looking for somewhere quiet to sit. The drawing room is full of ladies, card players are in the library, and the buffet is laid out in the dining room.'

'The morning room should be quiet, Morgan.' Harry pulled his watch fob from his pocket and singled out a key. 'Ladies, Gentleman, it is time we returned to the party.'

He waited until everyone had dispersed before leaving his study and ostentatiously locking it.

'Wonderful ball, Harry.' Edyth James kissed Harry, then Sali. 'See me to my carriage, Geraint.'

'I would be honoured, Aunt Edyth.'

'You taking flirting lessons from Mansel, Geraint?' Edyth tapped his arm with her fan.

'Mr Watkin Jones,' Mansel stood in front of Harry and Sali in the deserted hallway, 'may I take Miss Watkin Jones riding in Aunt Edyth's fields after chapel tomorrow? We have a great deal to discuss.'

'I am sure you do, Mansel,' Harry said dryly. 'You and Sali have my permission to go riding after chapel and you can tell Aunt Edyth from me, that now she has had her way and you two are unofficially engaged, she can stop her scheming. There are no overbearing Victorian fathers or wicked ogres on the horizon to blight your happiness.'

Sali relaxed her hold on the reins and gave her horse his head as she approached the gate. Lancelot cleared it and she reined him in, waiting for Mansel to catch up with her. It was a cold, crisp day with a hint of frost in the air that had hardened the ground, making it easy-going for the horses.

'That was grossly unfair, you had a two-minute start,' Mansel complained after jumping his stallion, Brutus, over the gate and drawing alongside her.

'You should check your stirrups are the right length before you leave the stable.' She leaned forward and stroked Lancelot's neck.

'Back along the lane?'

'Had enough of racing?'

'I'd prefer to talk to you than race after you. We have a lot of decisions to make.'

'Like?'

'What kind of wedding we're going to have, how many flowers, bridesmaids, hymns, where we're going on our honeymoon, where we're going to live, how many personal maids you need . . .'

'Considering I have none in college, one is more than enough.'

'You will need more when the grey hairs and wrinkles start appearing,' he joked.

'By then you will be bald and toothless, so you won't mind having a grey-haired, wrinkled wife.'

'You'll never be old.' He drew his horse closer to hers and laid his leather-gloved hand over hers. 'I looked around the house yesterday.'

'What house?' she asked in confusion.

'Ynysangharad House.'

'Mansel, you've lived there since you were six years old. If you don't know it by now, you never will.'

'Sometimes, you need to take a fresh look at your surroundings. Do you realise there's a whole wing closed off with eight large rooms that are never used?'

'I thought there'd be more.'

'And they aren't small. One would make a superb drawing room, another a dining room that could comfortably seat twelve. Upstairs, there's a room large enough for a master bedroom with two dressing rooms attached. And three other full-sized bedrooms besides.

One of which would make a cosy nursery,' he added, with a significant look.

'You'd like us to set up home in Ynysangharad House?' she questioned, colouring at the mention of children.

'Would you mind very much if we lived with Aunt Edyth?' he asked seriously. 'Not because I'm her heir and due to inherit Ynysangharad House, but because I can't bear the thought of leaving her alone at her time of life.'

'Have you asked Aunt Edyth if we can live with her?'

'No. I thought I'd better ask you first, as you are soon to become my lady and mistress.'

'You know I adore Aunt Edyth.'

'There's a difference between adoring an aunt and living with her.'

'I can't think of anyone I'd rather live with, apart from you.' She smiled and then just as she'd hoped, he kissed her.

'Goodbye, Mother.' The three-week Christmas holiday, to which Sali had looked forward for the entire autumn term, had begun in a whirl of balls and parties, and passed in a flash with too few private moments between her and Mansel for her liking. She had difficulty believing that she was already saying goodbye to her family.

Gwyneth raised her head from the pillows on her chaise longue and offered her cheek to her daughter. 'I still don't see why you have to return to college when you are marrying Mansel James in the summer.'

'Because education is never wasted, Gwyneth,' Harry said firmly. 'Sali is only six months away from qualifying as a teacher and that will be an achievement for her to be proud of.'

Gwyneth fell back on to the pillows. 'You will write, Sali?' she murmured.

'Yes, Mother.' Sali kissed Gwyneth's pale cheek. 'And I will be back at Easter.'

'I hope that holiday won't prove as exhausting as this one. All these parties . . .'

'If you rest now, Gwyneth, you might be up to dining downstairs this evening for once,' Harry said irritably. 'The carriage is waiting, Sali, and your boxes are loaded.' He looked his daughter up and down. In her plain black walking suit, white blouse and boots, she looked a very different woman from the exotic creature in white lace who had graced the ball the night before Christmas Eve.

Geraint, Gareth, Llinos and the servants were waiting at the foot of the stairs. Sali shook hands with the servants, hugged Mari, embraced her brothers and sister, and followed her father to the carriage.

'A little extra in case you need it.' Harry removed two five-pound notes from his wallet as the coachman set off up Taff Street.

'It's very good of you, Father, but I don't need it.'

'You might, keep it safe.' He pressed it into her hand. 'I want you to know the whole family are happy with your engagement to Mansel. Even your mother, although she doesn't show it, and I think Edyth has been planning the match since the day you were born.'

'I'm very lucky.'

'Mansel is luckier. And I'll be on hand to make sure that he'll do everything he can to make you happy.' The carriage drew to a halt in the station yard and Harry waited for the coachman to open the door and fold down the steps. 'Take care of yourself.'

'And you.' Sali flung her arms around her father's neck. 'I'll work hard to make you proud of me.'

'I couldn't be any prouder of you than I am now, darling.' He kissed her. 'Well, well, look who is here.' His dark eyes shone with mischief as Mansel charged up to the carriage window. 'Aunt Edyth said you had business in Cardiff.'

'I do, sir.'

'Then you'll make sure that Sali changes trains safely without losing her luggage.'

'I most certainly will, sir.'

The coachman appeared with a porter. Sali's trunk, hatbox and bags were loaded on to a trolley, and she, Mansel and her father were swept up with the crowds on to the platform. The train was in and a few minutes later she found herself leaning out of the window waving her handkerchief to her father who grew into a smaller, more solitary figure as the train drew out of the station.

'This business in Cardiff?' Sali asked. Mansel had bribed the guard to keep their carriage clear of other passengers.

'Is very urgent.' He sat next to her on the bench seat.

'How urgent?'

'Urgent enough to make me want to hold your hand all the way to Cardiff. But your father warned me that we have to part like cousins. We don't want to make any of your fellow students on the Swansea platform suspicious.'

'My fellow students won't be, but it might be a little difficult with certain other people,' Sali murmured, as the door to the corridor opened. 'Harriet, how nice of you to join us.'

'Yes, how nice.' Mansel gritted his teeth and forced a smile.

'The stupid guard told me that this carriage was reserved. It's quite a coincidence seeing you both on the train. You going to Swansea as well, Mansel?' Harriet took the seat opposite them.

'Cardiff on business. I timed the train so I could help Sali with her luggage.'

'How considerate. But then, if you are only going to Cardiff, what time train are you getting back?'

'The ten o'clock.' He beamed as her face fell. 'I have a gentleman-only dinner in my club.'

'I was hoping to have another chat with you about my Bible Circle.'

'I am afraid it will have to wait until some other time, Miss Hopkins. I promised to help Miss Watkin Jones revise her knowledge of mathematics for her forthcoming examinations.' He turned to Sali. 'Now, what can you tell me about Pythagoras?'

Chapter Two

'Please, Mari, I need to know how Father died.' Sali turned her dry-eyed, anguished face to the housekeeper. 'All Aunt Edyth could tell me when she brought me home from college was that he had been killed in an accident in the pit. Mother bursts into tears or faints every time I go into her room. Geraint, Gareth and Llinos don't know any more than I do and Uncle Morgan tells me to be quiet every time I try to ask him about it.'

Afraid to look her young mistress in the eye lest her own grief surface yet again, Mari brushed an imaginary speck of dust from the back of one of the oak-framed, upholstered, dining chairs. 'Mr James told Tomas it was down to one of the new compressed-air, disc coal-cutters the master had brought in.' She dabbed a tear from her eye with a sodden black cotton handkerchief, before returning it to her skirt pocket. 'Not that any of the miners are blaming your father, mind; there aren't many pit owners concerned enough about the men to put in machines to lessen their load.'

'Did the engine break down?' Sali pressed.

'Mr James said the engineer thought a bearing failed, sparking the engine and setting off a pocket of firedamp. A new seam cut only last week was destroyed in the explosion and nine miners, four of them firemen, were taken with the master. When Mr James called yesterday—'

'Mr James called?' Sali broke in urgently.

'Mr James and Mrs James have been to the house every day, along with most of the town.'

'Then why haven't we seen them?' Sali questioned in bewilderment.

'Your Uncle Morgan gave Tomas, Robert and the parlour maids, strict instructions not to admit anyone, only to take in visiting cards, condolence letters and flowers. They were told to say that the family were too upset to receive anyone.' The housekeeper's disapproval of Morgan Davies's edict was evident from her pursed lips.

'But you saw Mr James.'

'You know Mr James. He could see that Tomas was in a state, so he went around to the kitchen door to ask if there was anything he could do to help. He said he had a letter for you, but your uncle walked in on us before he could give it to me. I told Mr Davies that Mr James had called because Mrs James had offered to lend us her cook for the funeral tea but—'

'Uncle Morgan has taken a lot upon himself,' Sali interrupted bitterly.

'I thought you knew about his orders, Miss Sali.'

Sali shook her head. She should have realised that the absence of callers was down to her uncle. He had taken on the mantle of master of her father's house before she and her brothers had even reached home.

'Mr James spoke to the rescue party that went down after the explosion, not that there was anyone left for them to rescue.' Mari sniffed back her tears and straightened the chair in front of her. 'From the state of the drift, he said the end would have been too quick for any of them to have suffered. Your father, God bless him,' Mari pulled her handkerchief from her pocket again and clamped it over her reddened nose, 'wouldn't have known what hit him any more than the others. And that is why none of the coffins were left open.'

Sali closed her eyes against an image of her father's long, lean body blown apart. His clean-cut, classical features scorched beyond recognition. 'Has anything been done for the men's families?'

'Not that I've heard, Miss Sali.' As Mari wiped her eyes again she wondered when the young miss was going to shed a tear for the father she had so loved and adored. 'But your uncle ordered a fire to be lit in the library this morning. Mr Richards will be staying to read the will after the funeral tea so I expect something will be done for the families then.'

Sali opened her eyes and stared blankly at the under-house parlour maid, who was smoothing creases from a damask cloth she had unfolded over the massive oak table. Turning her back, she walked restlessly to the window and looked right, up Taff Street in the direction of Penuel Chapel. Snow lay over the road and pavements, a thick strip of virginal white where it met the buildings, liquefying to a dirty grey slush, pockmarked with the glossy black imprints of footsteps on the pavements. A criss-cross of narrow lines on the road gleamed dark and icy where cart and carriage wheels had cut through the snow and an old woman draped in shawls slipped, only just regaining her balance as she reached the safety of the pavement.

Masculine voices raised in song, echoed faintly and sonorously through the closed window and Sali tried not to envisage the scene being played out in the burial ground behind the chapel; her father's oak coffin being slowly lowered beneath the frozen ground into the family grave alongside that of her grandfather. It wasn't fair; he should have had so many more years . . .

'It's not right, Miss Sali,' Mari observed, as if she had read her thoughts. 'A good man like your father who always put himself out for others, going before his time when there's those . . .' a momentary hesitation told Sali exactly who Mari meant, 'who wouldn't lift a finger to help a soul in need. Living nasty, selfish lives . . . Polish that spoon,' she ordered the under-house parlour maid brusquely, spotting tarnish on the bowl of a silver soup spoon the girl had set out on the cloth.

'Yes, Mrs Williams.' The maid bobbed a curtsy before scurrying off to the butler's pantry.

Mari cast a critical eye over the napkins the maids had folded into fleur-de-lis. 'Perhaps cockscombs would have been more appropriate for a funeral, after all,' she murmured, more to herself than Sali.

'I doubt the mourners will notice how the napkins are folded, Mari.' Sali looked up at the heavy pewter sky as flakes fluttered downwards filling the air. 'It's snowing again.' She turned from the window and surveyed the long table set for twenty. 'Are the tables laid in the preparation kitchen?'

'Don't you worry, Miss Sali, I've seen to it that there's plenty of warming cawl, ham sandwiches, Welsh cakes and tea for your father's tenants and the miners. They'll need it in this weather.'

'You have rum for the tea?'

'Yes, but don't go telling your Uncle Morgan that,' Mari warned. 'You know his views on strong drink.'

Sali did, but then she reflected, she knew Morgan Davies's disapproving views on everything that could be regarded as mildly pleasurable. As her father had often remarked, 'A benevolent God would never frown on a man who allowed himself a few harmless indulgences after a hard day's work, only warped and twisted ministers who misinterpreted his Gospels.' And although her father had never actually said that he counted his wife's brother as one of God's misinterpreting, warped and twisted ministers, the inference had been obvious – to her.

'Have you made up Mother's tray?'

'It will be ready before we begin serving here.' Mari puckered her lips again. 'Although I'm not the only one who thinks she should receive the mourners, if only for ten minutes. No one will expect her to sit at the table or even come downstairs, but she could at least thank the bearers.'

'You know Mother.'

24

'It's the poor young masters I feel sorriest for.' Mari set a silver salver in the centre of the cloth. 'Having to bury their father at their age. And with Mr Davies the only man left in the family for them to turn to, God only knows how they'll come to terms with such a loss, or for that matter, how any of us will. Your father was the kindest master, the fairest employer, the most generous . . .' As Mari's voice wavered, Sali turned back to the window.

Snow was falling thickly and silently now, coating the gleaming strips of black ice on the road and the grey slush on the pavements. After a full week of living behind closed drapes, Sali found even the leaden winter afternoon light startlingly bright. But now that her father's coffin had left the house, the drapes would be opened every day and the second stage of mourning would begin. Her Uncle Morgan couldn't shut her into the house, or the town out for ever. Condolence visits would be made. And given her mother's insistence on abdicating all responsibility, she and her brother would have to receive the callers. There were some people she longed to see and others, like the chapel deacons, who subscribed to her uncle's view that tragedies were 'God's will', to whom she and Geraint would find it difficult to be civil.

A solitary, black-coated figure appeared through the misty swirls of white flakes; seconds later a tide of men swelled into sight, filling Taff Street from side to side as they tramped through the thickening snowstorm. When they drew closer, Sali saw a mass of tenants and miners dressed in their Sunday suits and flat caps, following at a respectful distance. As the top-hatted crache made resolutely for the house, the workers headed for the opposite side of the street, where they halted. Doffing their caps, they clutched them to their chests and stood bareheaded, silent, waiting deferentially. Sali knew none of them would venture around the side of the house to the kitchens until the last of the mourners had walked through the front door.

'They are coming,' she warned, as Mr Richards, her father's solicitor, opened the gate.

'Tell the cook she can pour the brown soup for the dining room and the cawl for the men into the tureens as soon as she's ready,' Mari ordered the maid, who had returned with the newly polished, offending spoon.

'Yes, Mrs Williams.'

'Ready, Miss Sali?' Mari looked apprehensively at her.

'Yes.' Sali lifted her chin and held her head high as she left the dining room and crossed the hall where the footman, Robert, and two parlour maids were standing, waiting to attend to the mourners' overcoats and hats. Nodding to Robert, she opened the door to the drawing room where the ladies had congregated to mourn while their men attended the chapel and graveside services.

'Sali.' Edyth James beckoned her over to a high-backed sofa. When Sali drew closer she saw that the old lady was holding Llinos's hand under cover of their black crêpe skirts. 'How are you bearing up, child?' Edyth asked, making room for Sali to sit the other side of her.

'I won't be sorry when this day is over, Aunt Edyth,' Sali confessed guardedly, lowering her voice lest the wives of Pontypridd's crache overhear her. She sank in a crackle of stiff crêpe on to the sofa.

'Harry was a fine man who understood Christ's concept of charity. He will be sorely missed in the town, and not only by his tenants and miners.'

'Thank you.' Sali wondered why she found it so easy to accept her aunt's references to religion when she felt either angered or embarrassed by her Uncle Morgan's constant biblical allusions.

'Sherry, Mrs James, Miss Sali? Lemonade for you, Miss Llinos.' Tomos held out a tray.

'Thank you, Tomos.' Sali took two sherries and handed her aunt a glass.

The butler lowered his head close to hers. 'Masters Geraint and Gareth have just walked through the door, Miss Sali.'

'All right Tomos.'

'Llinos is fine with me, aren't you, dear?' Edyth handed Llinos her own bordered handkerchief to blot her tears. 'You see to the others, Sali.'

'Thank you.' Sali took a glass of sherry from the tray for her brother Geraint and headed for the hall.

'Thank you, Mair.' Geraint divested himself of his hat and coat and handed them to the maid who had been ordered to look after the family's outdoor clothes. 'And thank you, Sali.' He looked her in the eye and took the sherry she handed him.

'How was it?' Sali reached out and briefly grasped her younger brother Gareth's hand as he walked past them to join their aunt and Llinos on the sofa.

'The singing was beautiful, especially from the miners,' Geraint said loudly. He lowered his voice as they instinctively headed for the quietest corner of the drawing room, furthest from the fire, 'but Uncle Morgan delivered the service as if he were on an election platform. And he didn't spare us at the graveside. We were there a full hour. The gravediggers looked too frozen to move, let alone dig, when he finally stopped sermonising.'

'I am sorry.'

'So am I.' Despite his apparent composure Sali knew Geraint was as devastated by their father's death as she, Llinos and Gareth were, but nine years in public school had taught him to conceal his emotions. 'The man's impossible. He said more about the wages of sin than the way Father lived his life.'

'That is just his way.' Sali forced herself to be tactful as she glanced around to check if anyone was listening in on their conversation.

'He behaved as if he was preacher, minister and chief mourner rolled into one. Never mind that I'm the eldest son and you, Gareth, Llinos and I thought more of Father than him, or any of our damned aunts except Aunt Edyth—'

'Geraint,' Sali admonished, afraid that one of their elderly relatives would hear him swearing, on today of all days. 'They will all be gone in a couple of hours,' she reminded, dropping her voice to a whisper as Morgan entered the room.

'And then what?'

'We get on with the rest of our lives as best we can,' she suggested bleakly.

'No tears, Sali,' Geraint warned, seeing her bottom lip tremble. 'Remember how Father hated us to show any signs of weakness, especially in front of Uncle Morgan and the aunts.'

'I'll check Mari has everything ready in the dining room.'

'Tell her she can't begin serving quick enough for me. The sooner we get the tea over with, the sooner we can clear the house.' Setting his jaw, Geraint left her and shook the hand of the man closest to him. 'Hello, sir, thank you for coming to pay your respects.'

'Miss Watkin Jones, I was hoping to pay my condolences before the service, but your uncle told me you weren't receiving visitors.' Mansel grasped Sali's hand and pulled her out of the hall into the passageway that led to the kitchens.

'That was my uncle's decision, not mine or Geraint's.' She looked around to make sure they were alone.

'I thought it might be. I know how close you were to your father and how much you loved him. I only wish there was something I could say to ease your pain but I remember how I felt when my parents died and words simply aren't enough.' He gave her a small, sad smile, and for the first time since she had been called into the Principal's office at Swansea Training College to be told her father was dead, she could almost believe that life was still worth living.

'There is nothing anyone can say, Mr James,' she whispered, as Robert passed with an armful of coats.

'When do you go back to college?'

'The Principal told me to take as much time as I like. She said that sitting my finals would be a formality. My work is of a sufficiently high standard to gain me a pass without further study.'

He squeezed her hand as her eyes clouded. 'If you need me or Aunt Edyth for anything, anything at all, day or night, you only have to send for us,' he whispered earnestly.

'I know.' She grasped his hand with both of hers. 'And thank you for your letter of condolence.'

'I wrote another, but I wanted to be sure that you'd be able to read it in private . . .'

'Sali.' Her uncle's voice thundered down the passage. 'Geraint told me you were seeing to the domestic arrangements.'

'I am.' Feeling a need to assert her independence, Sali left her hands clasped around Mansel's. 'Thank you again, Mr James.'

'Please, Miss Watkin Jones, don't mention it.'

'Are you lost, Mr James?' Morgan enquired pointedly, when Sali finally released him.

'Not at all, Mr Davies, I know my way around this house as well as my Aunt Edyth's,' Mansel replied easily, refusing to be intimidated. 'If you'll excuse me, I'll pay my respects to Master Geraint, Master Gareth and Miss Llinos.'

As Sali turned the corner of the passage she glimpsed Mansel looking Morgan Davies coolly in the eye. She lingered just long enough to see her uncle step aside.

The kitchen was comparatively quiet, the preparation kitchen and the dairies beyond it, where the maids had set out tureens of lamb stew, ham sandwiches, Welsh cakes and urns of tea on long tables for Harry Watkin Jones's employees and tenants, was even more crowded than Sali had seen it on the King's coronation day three and a half years before.

'Every single family in the town has sent a representative,' Mari declared proudly as she stood at Sali's elbow.

Sali's eyes were so dry they hurt, but there was a lump in her throat that prevented her from speaking.

'You want the soup on the table in the dining room?' Mari prompted.

'As soon as possible,' she whispered hoarsely.

'Your brother will want to speak to the tenants and miners first.'

'I'll get him.' Sali fled the kitchen. Leaning against the door, she stole a moment to compose herself. As she glanced into the dining room to check the table was perfect enough to suit her eagle-eyed aunts, the hearse drew past the window. She had been forced to accept her father was dead, although she hadn't been allowed to say goodbye to his body, but the empty etched-glass box drawn by eight black, plumed horses brought the shattering realisation that she would *never* see him again in this life. And given the injustice and cruelty of his passing, she was beginning to doubt the existence of a next.

'My father would have been touched and heartened to have seen so many of you here today to pay your respects.' Geraint's voice rang out in the hushed preparation kitchen down the rows of men who had risen from the benches as he, Sali, Gareth and Llinos had entered the room. No one made a sound as they stood waiting for him to continue his address. 'I am aware that some of you will be concerned about the future—'

'Geraint, your guests are waiting,' Morgan interrupted, from the kitchen behind him.

'I have guests here, Uncle Morgan.' Geraint didn't even turn his head.

Sali shuddered when she saw their uncle's face darken in anger. Logic told her she was being ridiculous. Her uncle had no control over their lives and his weekly visits were irksome rather than anything more sinister.

'I will make an announcement as soon as I have spoken

to my father's solicitor,' Geraint continued. 'In the meantime, on behalf of my mother, brother and sisters, I would like to thank you all for your letters of condolence and your presence here today.' He turned to Sali. 'Is there anything you would like to add?'

Sali drew closer to Geraint for support. 'It is a great comfort for us to know how well-respected Father was by his employees and tenants.'

'Your father gave more thought and kindness to the ordinary miner and the people of Pontypridd than any other pit owner, Miss Watkin Jones,' a voice said from the back of the room.

Overwhelmed, Sali took her sister's hand. 'If you'll excuse us.'

'Our deepest sympathy, Miss Watkin Jones, Miss Llinos.' Lloyd Evans, the deputy manager, spoke for all the men.

Sali took Llinos's hand and led her past her uncle, through the passage into the dining room. Owen Bull's squat, corpulent figure blocked their path. Moving obsequiously among the elderly maiden aunts, he pulled out chairs for them, handed them their napkins and made polite small talk that sent them simpering like naïve young schoolgirls. Sali was irritated to the point of wanting to slap his face. Recalling her father's dislike of the middle-aged butcher, who had insisted on being addressed as 'Councillor Bull' since his election to the Town Ward nine years earlier, she wondered why he had been accorded a privileged place at the family table. Then she recalled that he was a senior deacon at her Uncle Morgan's chapel.

When Owen finally took his seat, Mansel appeared at her side and escorted her to the chair she occupied at the head of the table, except on the extremely rare occasions when her mother left her sofa.

'I moved the place names,' he whispered, standing behind her and holding her chair for her while she sat.

'Gareth is one side of you, I'm the other and I've wangled Llinos a place between me and Aunt Edyth.'

'I believe this is my chair now, Uncle.' Geraint took his father's chair at the opposite end of the table.

Morgan stood at Geraint's right hand and waited until everyone around the table had risen from their chairs. 'For this food and all thy mercies, Oh Lord, we give thanks . . .'

Mercies! Furious that her uncle should use such a word on the day of her father's funeral, Sali shuddered uncontrollably for a second time. Then Mansel's hand closed around hers under cover of the tablecloth. The strain of her father's death was affecting her reason. With Mansel at her side and her brother taking her father's place, she had nothing to fear. Nothing at all.

'. . . To my valet, Tomos Edwards and my housekeeper, Mari Williams, the sum of two hundred pounds apiece, in recognition of their long and faithful service and the hope that they will remain at their posts in Danygraig House to serve my family as they have served me. To all other servants in my employ, the sum of five pounds apiece to provide for mourning clothes. To my colliery deputy manager, Lloyd William Evans, the sum of five hundred pounds and a five per cent stake in the Watkin Jones Colliery in recognition of his honest, hard-working service and the hope that he will remain with the Watkin Jones Colliery to serve my heirs as he has served me. To my beloved Aunt Edyth, all of my father's photograph albums. To Mansel James, my silver cigar case, silver pocket watch and chain. To my wife's brother, Morgan Davies, in his capacity as Treasurer of his Chapel, the sum of one hundred pounds to provide for new hymnals.'

Despite her misery, Sali smiled, as Mr Richards paused for breath. The dilapidated state of the hymnals had long incensed her father, but as Treasurer as well as Minister, Morgan had categorically refused to release a penny of the chapel funds to buy new ones, on the grounds that once bought and put into use, they would become as worn as the ones that were falling apart.

'To my wife, Gwyneth Watkin Jones, I leave an annuity of four hundred pounds to be paid yearly until her death, when it is to be shared equally amongst our surviving children. Our home, Danygraig House, 28 Taff Street, is to remain her home for her lifetime, or as long as she wishes it.'

Mr Richards shuffled his papers and looked along the rows of assembled family and servants. Sali glanced at Geraint. He was as pale as Gareth and Llinos but his jaw remained firm.

'To my daughters, Sali Watkin Jones and Llinos Watkin Jones, I leave all of my mother's and grand-mother's jewellery, to be divided between them as they see fit and dowries of three thousand pounds apiece to be paid on their marriage. To my younger son, Gareth Watkin Jones, I leave my gold pocket watch, gold cigarette case, three thousand pounds, the two farms and all the properties I own in the town of Pontypridd with the exception of Danygraig House. The residue of my estate, including my father's gold watch, gold cigarette and cigar case, personal jewellery, Danygraig House and investments in the Watkin Jones Colliery, together with all other colliery and miscellaneous investments and monies I leave to my eldest son, Geraint Watkin Jones in the hope that he will use his inheritance wisely for the benefit of his mother, brother, sisters, the employees of the Watkin Jones Colliery, Watkins Jones tenants and the townspeople of Pontypridd.'

Mr Richards again took a deep breath.

'Should I die before my eldest son, Geraint Watkins Jones's twenty-first birthday, at which time he will assume full control of his inheritance and responsibility for his brother, sisters and mother, I appoint my father, John Watkin Jones, and my wife Gwyneth Watkin Jones joint guardians of my children and my estate. Should my father, John Watkin Jones, predecease me before my son,

Geraint, comes of age, I appoint my wife, Gwyneth Watkin Jones, and my solicitor, Richard Richards, joint guardians of my children and my estate.'

Sali heard Mari stifle a sob in the ranks of the servants behind her. Llinos was crying, large, soft silent tears that splashed down on to her black crêpe skirt, staining it white.

'Thank you, Mr Richards.' Morgan stepped up alongside the solicitor. 'The servants are dismissed.'

Furious that his uncle had dared to give an order to the staff, Geraint rose from his chair and nodded to Tomas. The butler bowed and Mari curtsied acknowledgement. They stood either side of the double doors as the staff silently filed out. When the last one had walked through the doors, they followed, closing the doors quietly behind them.

'Am I to take it, sir, that the colliery will continue to function under a new manager?' Sali knew that Lloyd Evans was only twenty-five years old. He was the son of a collier, yet had the demeanour and bearing of a gentleman. Her father had recruited him from a mining school where he had studied engineering and promoted him from overman to deputy manager after only a few months, telling Geraint that if he was interested in taking over the colliery he would learn more about modern mining methods in a five-minute discussion with Mr Evans than any number of theoretical lectures from academics.

'I have yet to discuss the matter with Mrs Watkin Jones, Mr Evans,' Mr Richards replied.

'I'd appreciate it if you would reassure the miners that their jobs are safe, Mr Evans,' Geraint said. 'I know I can never fill my father's shoes, but I intend to assume his responsibilities.'

'Not before you have finished your education, Geraint,' Morgan reproved.

Sali clenched her fists and prayed that her brother

would have the sense to remain silent in front of so many of their relations.

'Mr Richards, I believe it is time for you to explain the content and import of the document you drafted and Mrs Watkin Jones signed yesterday evening.' Morgan looked expectantly at the solicitor.

Mr Richards gave a small, embarrassed cough and laid his hand on an envelope at his elbow. 'Being of delicate constitution, Mrs Watkin Jones has relinquished the responsibilities of guardianship of her children in favour of her brother, Mr Morgan Davies.'

Geraint grew even paler; Sali clasped his arm. She knew Llinos and Gareth were staring at them, but she doubted they understood the full implication of the announcement.

'Can a mother relinquish guardianship of her own children?' Edyth James questioned cautiously.

'It is not common, Mrs James,' Mr Richards prevaricated, 'but given Mrs Watkin Jones's ill-health, understandable.' He pretended to study the papers set out on the table in front of him to avoid looking directly at Edyth – or Geraint, who wasn't even attempting to conceal his fury.

'What exactly does this mean?' Lloyd Evans asked the solicitor.

'This is a family matter, and as such, does not concern you, Evans. You may leave.'

Both Sali and Geraint blanched at their uncle's offhand dismissal. Their father had always insisted that his deputy and any miners who came to the house be addressed formally, and with respect.

'Miss Sali, Miss Llinos, Master Geraint, Master Gareth, my sympathies.' Lloyd went to the door. 'Your father was a great man and the best employer a worker could wish for.'

'Thank you, Mr Evans. I know that my father valued your professional judgement and I look forward to working with you in the future.' Geraint held out his hand and Lloyd shook it.

'I have papers for you to sign, Mr Evans. Would you call into the office in the next day or two? At your convenience,' Mr Richards added.

'I will, Mr Richards. Goodbye.' Lloyd Evans closed the door behind him.

'There are documents and settlements that require family signatures. Perhaps I could return at a mutually convenient time to attend to them,' Mr Richards suggested diffidently, returning his papers to his attaché case.

'Tomorrow morning at ten o'clock,' Morgan replied.

'So soon?'

'Geraint and Gareth will be returning to school on Monday.'

'We haven't discussed our return, Uncle Morgan.' Geraint offered the solicitor his hand.

'There is nothing to discuss, Geraint.' Morgan left his chair. 'If you will excuse me, I must attend to my sister. I will see you out, Mr Richards.'

'The gall of the man! You heard him, Sali!' Geraint paced furiously to the cold hearth of their father's study where he and Sali had retreated to escape the remaining aunts who had taken root in the drawing room. 'Daring to tell me what to do in our father's house! . . .'

'Hush, Geraint, he'll hear you,' Sali cautioned.

'I don't care if he does,' Geraint raged. 'He is only one of two guardians.'

'Mr Richards is employed as our family solicitor. He will never make a stand against him,' Sali reasoned. 'Please, Geraint, in four and a half years, you will inherit everything.'

'If Uncle Morgan leaves us anything to inherit.'

'Gareth has the properties held in trust for him, you own this house, the shares in the colliery and all of father's other shares and property. What can Uncle Morgan do?'

'I don't know.' Geraint halted in front of the fireplace. Resting his hands on the mantelpiece, he stared down at the unlit fire as he set his foot on the coals. 'But what I do know is that ever since I can remember, Uncle Morgan has disapproved of Father and the way we live. And now he is in a position of authority over us and in control of Father's estate, I don't doubt that he'll exercise his power to change things to suit himself and humiliate us every opportunity he gets.'

'Master Geraint's just disappointed that he can't fill his father's shoes right away, Miss Sali,' Mari consoled when she brought up a cup of cocoa after Sali had retired to her room for the night. 'It is only natural. He sees himself as the man of the house, but he's still a boy and he needs to get some more education before he can take over the pits.' She picked up Sali's crêpe dress from the back of a chair, opened the wardrobe and hung it away.

'And you, Tomas and the other servants are going to find it easy to take orders from Uncle Morgan, as you had to today?' Sali watched the housekeeper in the mirror as she removed her mourning cap, jet hair ornaments and brushed her hair out of the chignon she had worn for the funeral.

'As Tomas said when we shared a glass of sherry in the butler's pantry just now, it's not as if your Uncle Morgan lives in the house. Of course it will be quieter with only the mistress and Miss Llinos at home, and it's going to be odd just laying the dining table for Miss Llinos . . .'

Sali opened the drawer of her dressing table and handed Mari one of her own black-bordered handkerchiefs as the housekeeper began to cry – again.

'There are many decisions to be made and changes to be organised, Mari.' Sali left the stool, untied the belt of her dressing gown and dropped it on the footboard of her bed. 'But they will have to wait until tomorrow.'

'It is thoughtless of me to keep you up, Miss Sali.' Mari folded back the bed. 'Drink your cocoa and get a good night's rest.'

'Thank you, Mari.' But even as the housekeeper turned down the wick on the oil lamp and closed the door, Sali knew sleep was impossible. The minute she closed her eyes, her father's face, smiling, vibrant, wonderfully and unbearably, painfully alive, filled her mind and the tears she had managed to hold in check all day, finally flooded down her cheeks.

CHAPTER THREE

At five o'clock, Sali heard the servants walk down the uncarpeted back staircase that led from their sleeping quarters in the attics, to the kitchens. A few moments later she left her bed. The fire had burned low in her grate, but it had kept the temperature in the room high enough to prevent the water from freezing in her wash jug. She filled the china washing bowl and threw in her sponge and soap. It was icy, but the maid wouldn't be up with warm water for at least another hour and there was something she had to do that couldn't wait.

She stripped off her nightgown and soaped her sponge. She winced as she rubbed it over her breasts, but braced herself to bear it. She might be cold, but it was colder for her father lying in his oak coffin under the ground.

After emptying her bowl into the slop bucket and wiping the splashes from the marble-topped washstand, she slipped on her camisole, laced up her front fastening, Coutille corset and brassiere bust bodice, and rolled on a pair of black woollen stockings, fastening them with the corset suspenders. All of her white Directoire knickers and petticoats had been replaced by black, and by the time she finished dressing in one of the plain black serge suits and a black flannel blouse, she felt as though all colour had been drained from the world.

Brushing out her waist-length dark-brown hair, she drew it back, away from her face, plaited it, rolled it into a chignon on the crown of her head and secured it with jet hairpins. She laced on her walking boots, turned back the bed and opened the window. Stopping only to pick up her jet-headed hatpins, she ran lightly down the stairs and opened the hall cupboard, lifting out her woollen winter coat, which had been dyed from light grey to black. After buttoning it, she pinned her hat to her head, drew on her gloves, wound a black muffler around her neck, unbolted the door and stepped outside.

The air was breathtakingly sharp and clear, the sky, still night dark. Snow glistened palely on the rooftops and in drifts that sparkled under the street lamps. Setting her foot forward and her head down, she turned right at the front gate, and walked at a brisk pace up Taff Street towards Penuel Chapel. Within minutes, the high, triangular capped façade of the chapel loomed ahead of her. Opening the barred metal gate, she walked around the building to the burial ground. Someone moved as she approached and she started nervously, until she recognised the massive figure of Iestyn, Owen Bull's simple-minded younger brother, who dug the graves and cared for the graveyard. He had been busy. The cover had been replaced on the grey slabbed family tomb and it was heaped high with carefully balanced wreaths of evergreen and winter roses that reminded her of Christmas.

She called out, 'Thank you, Iestyn.'

He touched his cap and grinned vacantly at her before disappearing around the side of the chapel.

She knelt beside the tomb and scraped the snow from the inscriptions.

Here lie the mortal remains of Henrietta Watkin Jones 1836–54, beloved wife of John Watkin Jones and much loved mother of Harry Glyndwr. Blessed are they that walk in the way of the Lord.

Also the above mentioned John Watkin Jones 1829–1902.

She ran her fingers over the blank spot beneath her grandparents' names and imagined her father's name inscribed below that of her grandmother, who had died giving birth to him, and the grandfather she had loved almost as much as her father, who had died peacefully in his sleep three years ago. She bowed her head and tears trickled, cold and icy over her cheeks. Why did he have to die and leave her?

'I thought it was you.' Mansel James crouched on his heels beside her. 'If you'd rather I went away . . .'

'No.' She fumbled blindly for his hand.

'I'd like to call on you later on today, if I may.'

She turned her tear-stained face to his and he helped her to her feet. His face was pale and hollow-eyed in the muted yellow glow of the street lamps, his blond hair shining as white as the snow around them.

'Of course you may.'

'I thought I heard voices.' Her uncle walked around the chapel and headed towards them. His anger turned to fury when he recognised her. 'Sali, what you are doing out at this ungodly hour?'

'I wanted to see Father's grave.'

'And you, young man?'

'I was walking to my office. I saw Sali and stopped to speak to her,' Mansel answered boldly.

'At this hour in the morning, in darkness? Have you no concern for her virtue or her reputation?'

'I have every consideration for both, Mr Davies.'

'It doesn't look like it to me. Come along, Sali.' Grasping his niece's arm, Morgan frogmarched her away.

'I will see you this evening, Mr James,' Sali called back over her shoulder.

'I think not,' Morgan contradicted, his voice as frosty as the air. 'And I expect my niece to know better than to screech like a fishwife in the street, especially when she is in mourning.' He looked down at her skirt. 'That is not crêpe.'

'Crêpe isn't practical for everyday use.'

'It certainly isn't practical to roam the streets dressed in crêpe, but you are in mourning and as such should remain within the house. I expect you to change as soon as we are indoors.'

'I invited Mr James to call, Uncle Morgan.' Sali tried in vain to free her elbow from his grip.

'And I will leave instructions with the servants that you are not at home. Do you understand?'

Sali understood that her uncle was attempting to control her life. But given her secret, she would rather she wasn't alone with him when he discovered there were some things in her life that were already out of his control.

'You'll see that Mr James gets it right away?' Sali pressed an envelope into Mari's hand.

'I'll send one of the maids to his office.'

'Now?'

'As soon as I reach the kitchens.' The housekeeper pocketed the envelope.

'And there'll be three extra for dinner.'

'Mrs James, Mr James and Mr Richards.' Mari hesitated thoughtfully. 'All three are hearty eaters so I'll ask Cook to roast one of the legs of lamb hanging in the outside meat larder. She was making Palestine soup earlier. Your uncle isn't keen on artichokes.'

'So he says every time he eats one in this house, but there's never anything left on his plate whenever he dines here.' Sali was too preoccupied to worry about her uncle's preferences, the dinner menu, or even if her uncle would dine with them that evening.

'Then I suggest Palestine soup, fried haddock in anchovy sauce, followed by the lamb with potato croquettes, carrot soufflé and stuffing, chocolate pudding and oyster fritters for a savoury.'

'I am happy to leave the menu to you and Cook,' Sali murmured absently. 'Thank you, Mari.'

'You'd best get into that library before your uncle has an apoplectic fit,' Mari muttered, as the library door opened and Morgan bellowed his niece's name into the hall.

'It is good of you to join us, Sali,' Morgan said caustically, as she pulled a chair out from the sofa table where she had done so much of her studying, to join him, Mr Richards, her brothers and sister.

'My apologies, Uncle Morgan, I was giving Mari instructions for dinner.'

'A less wasteful one than yesterday, I trust. Given that this is a house of mourning, frugality should be the watchword.' Morgan made a great show of opening a large notebook. The first page was covered with neat rows of his tiny handwriting. 'I spent an hour after breakfast with my sister, Mr Richards. We discussed and agreed all the changes that need to be made in this household.'

'What changes, Uncle Morgan?' Geraint enquired suspiciously.

Ignoring Geraint's question, Morgan continued to address the solicitor. 'As you are the fellow guardian of my nieces and nephews, I trust you see the necessity for alterations in the family's lifestyle in the light of my brother-in-law's demise, beginning with the implementing of stringent economic measures.'

'The late Mr Watkin Jones left his family well provided for,' Mr Richards ventured guardedly.

'And in mourning.' Morgan's tone was polite, but Geraint and Sali exchanged glances. They realised that in declaring he had already discussed and agreed changes with their mother, their uncle hadn't only assumed the authority of a parent, but also increased the significance and consequence of any decision he made. Instead of being joint guardian to his client's children, Mr Richards had been relegated to the position of one of three.

Despite Sali's warning frown, Geraint sat back in his chair, tossed his pen on to the table and crossed his arms mutinously over his chest.

'First,' Morgan looked sternly at Geraint, 'Geraint and Gareth will return to school early on Monday morning. If I weren't opposed to Sunday travelling, I would send them tomorrow. It is vital their education be disrupted as little as possible. My brother-in-law's plans for their future will remain unchanged. Boarding school until the age of eighteen and after that university.'

'I concur absolutely.' The solicitor nodded agreement, while Geraint continued to scowl defiantly and Gareth looked as though he had spent the entire night in tears and was about to break down again at any moment.

'Llinos will continue to attend the Grammar School as a day pupil, for the moment.'

'Why only for the moment?' Geraint raised his eyes to his uncle's.

'Surely you don't need me to tell you that your mother's health is precarious. She requires rest and quiet, which is impossible in a house with a young girl. I will look for a suitable boarding school for Llinos.'

'I don't want to go to boarding school,' Llinos whispered.

'You, young lady, will do as your elders and betters dictate,' Morgan lectured, 'and you, Sali,' he continued swiftly, denying Llinos the opportunity to make further protest, 'will leave the Training College to run this house.'

'I begin my final examinations in June. That is only a few months away.'

'Your mother needs you to run this house, Sali,' he repeated sternly.

'But Mari is a perfectly capable housekeeper.'

'That I sincerely doubt. On my many visits here I have observed her to be wasteful and extravagant. She needs to be curbed and she won't be, unless she is closely supervised.'

'I really must protest, Mr Davies,' Mr Richards remonstrated. 'The late Mr Watkin Jones encouraged Miss Watkin Jones in her studies.'

'It is her mother's decision as well as mine, Mr Richards,' Morgan interrupted ruthlessly. 'I have already written to the college requesting that my niece's room be cleared and her personal possessions returned here, post haste. Now we must proceed to other matters or we will be here all morning and I have arranged to meet Mr Bull to discuss chapel business in one hour. I am giving up my house and moving in here.'

'Do you really think that necessary?' Mr Richards questioned mildly. 'Mrs Watkin Jones—'

'Is weak and ill,' Morgan reiterated impatiently. 'As the senior male member of this family I would be derelict in my duty if I did otherwise. It would be impossible for me to give my sister, nieces and the servants the attention they deserve if I live elsewhere. Given the state of my sister's health and indeed my own, I have ordered the servants to prepare my late brother-in-law's room for my occupation. It is ideally placed between my sister's room and my niece's, so, if either my sister or I are taken ill in the night, Sali will be on hand to care for us.'

Unable to meet Sali or Geraint's horrified gaze, the solicitor looked down at the table.

'And, as my sister and her family will be living a quieter, and less social life, my sister and I have decided to reduce the number of servants. I will give all but one parlour maid, kitchen maid and stable boy notice this afternoon, along with the footmen. The housekeeper, butler, cook and coachman will remain – for the present. But I have arranged to interview all four this afternoon to warn them that under the new regime, the wasteful, sloppy ways of the past will not be tolerated. You have papers that need to be signed, Mr Richards?'

'Yes,' the solicitor prevaricated, making no effort to extract the papers from his briefcase, 'but before we move on, Mr Davies, is there no way that I can persuade you to reconsider your decision to remove Miss Watkin Jones from Swansea Training College?'

'My sister and I have made our decision, Mr Richards. The papers, if you please.'

The solicitor opened his case and produced neatly tied bundles of papers. Sali took a deep breath and steeled herself. She had never hated anyone as much as she hated her uncle at that moment, but she fought to conceal her disappointment and her rage.

'May I invite Mr Richards to dinner this evening, Uncle Morgan?'

'I hardly think a dinner party appropriate in a house of mourning, Sali,' Morgan reproved.

'I have sent a letter inviting Aunt Edyth and Mr James. Mr Richards has details of the wedding Father planned for me this summer as well as the marriage settlement. I would like Mr Richards to review the documents to see if any changes need to be made to the arrangements.'

'What wedding?' Morgan narrowed his eyes.

'Miss Watkin Jones's wedding to Mr Mansel James,' the solicitor interposed. 'The late Mr Watkin Jones gave his blessing and consent to their engagement at Christmas on the understanding that the wedding would take place after Miss Watkin Jones qualified as a teacher.'

'Something that will not now occur.' Morgan's lips curled upwards.

'No,' the solicitor agreed evenly. 'But as Miss Watkin Jones comes of age in June, it is irrelevant. Because at that date she will be free to marry whomsoever she chooses without reference to her guardians and, on her marriage, claim her inheritance.'

'Mother, please,' Geraint pleaded, as he stood next to her bed. 'Sali only has a few months left in college before she sits her final examinations. She will be back before you know it, then she can keep you company and run the house, if that's what you want her to do,' he added, suspecting that the decision to terminate Sali's education had been entirely his uncle's.

'There is no point in her sitting examinations when she

will never need the qualifications,' Gwyneth Watkin Jones murmured lethargically, intoning her brother's argument, as she clutched a lavender-scented handkerchief to her nose.

'You can't be sure she won't need them. None of us knows what lies ahead.'

'Sali's future is mapped out, thanks to your father who never gave any consideration to my needs or wishes,' Gwyneth bleated peevishly. 'I would never have allowed Sali to become engaged to Mansel James. It is the eldest daughter's duty to stay at home and look after her parents, especially if one of them is in poor health and suffering. As I have been for years.'

'Years during which Mari has run this house perfectly efficiently,' Geraint countered.

'Have you no compassion?' Gwyneth pressed the back of her hand to her forehead. 'I am ill, your father has just died and you come here to argue, knowing how easily I am upset.'

'Mr Richards and I think that Sali should be allowed to return to college.' Geraint had lived too long with his mother's protestations of ill-health to be moved by her threat of upset. 'If you side with Mr Richards—'

'Geraint, how dare you raise your voice in your mother's room?'

'Morgan.' Gwyneth held out her hand as her brother entered.

'Leave now, Geraint,' Morgan ordered.

'I am far too ill to be bothered.'

'Of course you are, Gwyneth.'

'My smelling salts and medication.' She fell back weakly on to her pillows.

Morgan opened the drawer in the bedside cabinet and removed a jar of smelling salts and a green glass bottle. Realising Geraint was watching him, he snapped, 'I'll see you downstairs in the library before dinner, young man.'

Geraint left the room and walked along the landing to Sali's door. He knocked and at her 'Come in,' entered to

47

find her and Mari mothballing his father's clothes and folding them into a trunk.

'I asked Tomas and Mari to bring all Father's things in here,' Sali explained. 'Uncle Morgan ordered his room to be cleared and I didn't want to put anything in the attic without checking if it would spoil.'

Geraint sank down on the bed and picked out a small, leather-covered box from an assortment of hairbrushes, shaving gear, and pomander jars he had last seen on his father's nightstand. Opening the box, he lifted out the gold cufflinks his father had worn with his dress shirt.

'Those are yours now,' Sali said.

'Mine or Gareth's,' Geraint amended. 'We can hardly take them to school.'

'Your uncle asked me to collect and take your father's watches, chains, cigarette and cigar cases and personal jewellery to the library.' Mari smoothed out the creases of one of her late master's silk evening shirts as she folded it into the trunk.

'For Mr Richards to distribute?' Geraint asked.

'He didn't say,' Mari replied tersely.

Geraint left the bed. 'The next four and a half years are going to last for ever.'

'Not quite.' Sali rose to her feet and rested her hand on his shoulder. 'After Mansel and I marry in June, I'll be moving into Aunt Edyth's house. We settled it at Christmas. We will have our own sitting and dining rooms, not that we'll need them, because I can't imagine Aunt Edyth ever interfering.'

'Perhaps your aunt remembers what it's like to be newly married and doesn't want to get in the way when you and Mr James start throwing things at one another,' Mari commented, with a faint trace of her old sense of humour.

'Mr James and I will never throw things at one another,' Sali replied confidently.

'I'll talk to you again after you have been married a month, Miss Sali.'

Sali took Geraint's hand and pulled him back down on to the bed. 'Mansel and I won't be quarrelling, and you, Gareth and Llinos will be welcome to spend as much time with us as you like. Stay every holiday . . .'

'You've already asked Mansel and Aunt Edyth?' Geraint enquired eagerly.

'Not yet, but I intend to tonight and you know Mansel and Aunt Edyth. They'll be delighted to have all of us.'

As Mari continued to pack she didn't have the heart to remind Sali and Geraint that until Geraint was twenty-one, he, Gareth and Llinos would have to ask their uncle's permission to stay even one night away from school or home.

'Goodnight, sleep tight, both of you.' Sali kissed Llinos and almost managed to hug Gareth before he dived away from her and ran ahead of Mari and Llinos up the stairs.

'You'll be in to kiss me goodnight, Sali?' Llinos called back.

'I promise. You too, Gareth.'

'I'm too old for kisses,' he retorted, evincing the hostile attitude he had adopted since he had been told of his father's death.

'Then I'll shake hands goodnight, Gareth,' Sali replied softly. She left the hall and joined Edyth in the drawing room where Mari had set out the tea tray.

'My compliments, Sali, that was very good lamb.' Edyth sat on the sofa and held her hands out to the fire.

'I can't take any credit, Aunt Edyth. Mari says the quality of the meat is down to the care that's taken when it's hung and not even Cook dares to interfere with Mari's organisation of the pantries.' Sali joined her aunt on the sofa and picked up the teapot.

'It was an excellent dinner and, without minimising the work you put into it, proof that Mari is more than capable of running this house.'

'You know?' Sali spooned two sugars into her aunt's cup, stirred it and handed it to her.

'About your uncle's insistence that you give up college, yes,' Edyth confirmed. 'Mr Richards called on me before returning to his office this morning. Would you like me to talk to Morgan?'

'It is kind of you to offer, but it wouldn't do any good.'

'I could appeal to your mother.'

'Geraint tried. All he succeeded in doing was getting a lecture from Uncle Morgan, who has forbidden any of us to enter her room without his permission.'

'Now she won't see her own children! That is ridiculous!' Edyth exclaimed with uncharacteristic anger. 'Your father's single fault was that he was too soft with Gwyneth. Your mother needs a good shaking.' Edyth remembered she was in a house of mourning. 'I am sorry,' she apologised. 'I had no right to say that. Harry's hardly cold in his grave and here I am criticising him, and to you of all people.'

'Please don't stop saying exactly what you mean to me.' Sali set her own cup next to her aunt's on the table. 'At the moment, it feels as though you and Mansel are the only allies I have left apart from Geraint. Llinos and Gareth are too young and upset to understand most of what is going on and when Geraint and Gareth leave for Monmouth on Monday, I'll be alone apart from Llinos. And Uncle Morgan intends to send her away as soon as he can find a suitable boarding school.'

'So Mr Richards told me.' Edyth laid her withered hand over Sali's. 'But you won't be alone, not while Mansel and I are close by, and you have Mari and Tomas.'

'Whom Uncle Morgan has threatened to dismiss if they so much as put a foot wrong. And he means it,' she added. 'He has given more than half the staff a week's pay in lieu of notice.'

'You will only be here until June,' Edyth reminded.

'If Uncle Morgan allows me to marry Mansel.'

'He can't stop you. That is not to say he won't try,' Edyth warned, 'but if you are strong enough to stand up to him, Sali, you and Mansel will be man and wife six months from now. I promise you.'

'You didn't see my uncle's face when Mr Richards told him Father had already agreed to the arrangements and that I would be able to marry without the permission of my guardians after my birthday in June.' Sali started nervously as the door opened behind them.

'You gentlemen didn't linger long over your port and brandy,' Edyth observed, regaining her composure sooner than Sali.

'An after-dinner tradition that has been put into abeyance while I reside here, Mrs James,' Morgan pronounced sternly. 'You know my views on strong drink.'

'Indeed I do, Morgan.' Apart from his close relatives, Edyth James was the only woman in Pontypridd who dared to address Morgan Davies by his Christian name. But then she remembered Morgan as a runny-nosed child in nappies and enjoyed regaling anyone who held him in awe with tales of his boyhood misdemeanours.

'I have informed Tomas that this evening is the last time wine will be served in this house.'

'Until I come of age, Uncle Morgan,' Geraint amended.

'By then I trust that you will have learned to respect the teachings of the Christian faith.'

'Wine is mentioned in the Bible, Morgan. Didn't Christ himself turn water into wine when there wasn't sufficient refreshment to serve at a wedding reception?' Edyth enquired coolly, as if she didn't already know the answer to her question.

'Tea, Mr Richards? Mr James? Uncle Morgan? Geraint?' Sali asked in an attempt to diffuse the tension, but as she poured tea and milk, spooned sugar and passed cups, the strained atmosphere grew even more palpable.

'Have you had time to look over the marriage settlement, Mr Richards?' Mansel gave Sali a sly wink as she handed him his cup.

'Yes, like Mr Watkin Jones's will, it is quite straight-forward.' Eager to discuss business, the solicitor became quite animated, Sali suspected because as soon as his contribution to the evening was over, he could leave. 'The marriage can take place after Miss Watkin Jones qualifies, or on, or after, her twenty-first birthday. And as soon as the marriage takes place, the settlement is to be paid.'

'A wedding is out of the question until Sali has observed mourning for her father. A full year is considered the minimum for a parent. Personally, I think it should be two.'

'Harry would not have wanted Mansel and Sali to wait any longer than June, Morgan.' Edyth deliberately softened and lowered her voice.

'He would have been concerned with appearances, Mrs James,' Morgan snapped acidly.

'Harry was always more concerned with right than appearances, and considered the happiness of his children paramount.' Edyth eyed Morgan over the rim of her cup as she sipped her tea.

'Nevertheless, I think people will, quite rightly, be shocked if Sali dons a bridal gown before the year is out.'

'Then perhaps she should consider marrying in black,' Edyth suggested.

'That is a preposterous idea,' Morgan spluttered.

'If she did, she wouldn't be the first bride in Pontypridd to marry in full mourning.'

'No respectable woman—'

'You don't consider Mrs John Edwards respectable?' Edyth questioned artfully, referring to one of the town's oldest – and leading matrons.

'Of course.'

'Then you can have no objection to Sali marrying in black.' Edyth turned smoothly to Sali. 'Given the state of your mother's health, I would be happy to help you select your trousseau and bridal clothes. We have six excellent dressmakers under contract to the store. But if you prefer, we could go to Howell's in Cardiff.'

'I would prefer to shop in Gwilym James in Pontypridd, Aunt Edyth.' Taking comfort from Mansel's conspiratorial glance, the only thing that prevented Sali from smiling, was the relentless, heart-wrenching pain of her father's death. She did have allies besides Geraint and Mansel after all. And Aunt Edyth, seventy-five years old and so frail she looked as though a strong wind would topple her tiny, wizened frame, was standing up to her Uncle Morgan – and succeeding in overriding his opinions, when everyone else had failed.

'I will ensure that our most capable assistants wait on you.' Mansel opened his cigarette case and offered it to Geraint and Mr Richards before braving Morgan's surly refusal.

'Do you really think it necessary for Sali to marry in black, Uncle Morgan?' Geraint leaned towards Mansel as he struck a Lucifer.

'If I had my way, she would not be marrying until she had completed *two* years mourning,' he thundered. 'But as all of you, including Sali, seem to be hell bent on flouting Christian propriety, it appears my opinion counts for nothing.'

'Not at all, Morgan,' Edyth soothed. 'We value your opinion immensely, and I sincerely hope that, on the day, you will set your disapproval aside long enough to marry the happy couple.'

'It was only a dream, you're safe now, darling.' Wrapping her Welsh flannel robe closer against the chill of her sister's bedroom, Sali smoothed Llinos's hair away from her face as she sat on her bed.

'Why did Father have to die?' Llinos sobbed. 'Why couldn't God take someone else? Rhiannon Davies in my class in school hates her father.'

'Hush, darling, you mustn't say such things.' Sali

curled up on the pillows and pulled Llinos's head down on to her chest.

'Uncle Morgan said it's God's will that Father was taken. If that's right, I hate God! And I hate Uncle Morgan!'

Llinos, you don't know what you're saying.'

'Yes, I do,' Llinos contradicted rebelliously. 'And I won't go away to school whatever Uncle Morgan says. All my friends are in Pontypridd. You are here and Mari's here and you're the only ones left who love me now Father's gone. I won't go away. I won't!' she screamed as her grief boiled into hysteria.

'Please, darling, don't upset yourself,' Sali pleaded, but her own tears fell on to her sister's cheeks.

Llinos tightened her arms around Sali's waist. 'Can I live with you and Mansel after you marry?'

'You know Mansel and I would love to have you, darling,' Sali assured her, 'but it wouldn't be our decision. Mr Richards and Uncle Morgan are your guardians. We'd have to ask their permission.'

'And Uncle Morgan is a mean old crabby face who wouldn't give it.'

A floorboard creaked on the landing outside Llinos's door and a sharp rap was followed by, 'Sali, are you in there?'

'Yes, Uncle Morgan,' Sali answered through gritted teeth.

'It is after eleven o'clock.'

'Llinos had a nightmare.'

'That is no reason to wake your mother and set the entire house in uproar. Return to your room at once.'

'You'll be all right now?' Sali whispered to Llinos.

Llinos nodded, before pulling the bedclothes over her head.

'Sali!'

'Coming, Uncle Morgan.' Sali turned Llinos's lamp down, picked up her own and dropped a kiss on the crown of her sister's head, all that could be seen above the sheet.

Morgan was standing on the galleried landing, lamp in hand, a striped flannel nightshirt flapping around his bony ankles, his feet encased in beaded, backless slippers. He had thrown a robe over his shirt but he hadn't fastened it, and his neck, with its prominent Adam's apple, rose, long, loose-skinned and scrawny, from his pasty chest, reminding Sali of a chicken's after it had been plucked. As he stared at her, she instinctively wrapped her robe even closer to her shivering body.

'Your noise woke your mother and me.'

'I am sorry, Uncle Morgan, but Llinos had a nightmare.'

'That girl has been spoiled and pampered. She has learned how to get whatever she wants by shouting at all hours of the day and night. I'll have no more of it. I'll start looking for a school first thing on Monday. A school that places emphasis on self-control and discipline.'

'Is anything the matter?' Geraint opened his door and joined them in his pyjamas.

'The noise your sisters are making,' Morgan replied abruptly. 'And that is no excuse for you to walk around half naked,' he rebuked, tightening the belt on his woollen dressing gown, which considering his profession, was an incongruous, cheerful crimson.

'If that was Llinos crying, she has been having nightmares ever since Father was killed,' Geraint explained.

'That still doesn't give her the right to wake the entire house. Geraint, return to your room. Sali, go down to the kitchens and make tea. A weak cup with plenty of sugar and milk for your mother, a stronger one for me.'

'Let Miss Sali see to Miss Llinos, Mr Davies, sir. I will make the tea.' Mari, her long, grey hair plaited over one shoulder, a shawl thrown over her nightdress and robe, was standing in the arched doorway that connected the servants' passageways with the main house.

'Llinos is to be left alone. Any more mollycoddling and she'll never learn to sleep through the night.' Morgan glared at the housekeeper. 'And you, Mrs Williams, will not venture on to the family floor again except to check that the maid has done her work, or to clean the rooms yourself and *never* at night. Is that clear?'

'Yes, sir.'

'I will expect you alert and prepared to assume your duties at the usual hour.'

'Sir.' Mari bobbed a curtsy and retreated along the landing, closing the connecting door behind her.

'Tea, Sali,' Morgan reminded.

'I'll get my slippers, it's cold in the kitchens.'

'I am disappointed to see that you left your room in bare feet and risked picking up a splinter. If your foot becomes infected you will be absolutely no use to your mother. It is time you started thinking of others, girl.'

'Llinos was crying.' Sali fought a tide of misery that threatened to engulf her. Her father had always been the first to leave his bed if any of them woke in the night. She recalled the smell of his cologne, the feel of his arms around her, warm, comforting and reassuring, as she sipped the cocoa Mari made whenever one of them had a nightmare, and the serious look on his face as he had listened to stories of bogey monsters that had disturbed their sleep. She remembered the grave attitude he had adopted when he searched their wardrobes and the spaces beneath their beds to make sure that the beasts had been well and truly chased away.

Her sister might be too old for bogey monsters, but she sensed Llinos's imagination, like her own, was all too adept at picturing the burial ground behind Penuel Chapel and the tomb where her father lay.

'Are you being deliberately obdurate, girl?'

Sali set aside her memories. 'No, Uncle. I'll get my slippers now.'

Chapter Four

The hot plate had been opened on the range and a milk pan and copper kettle were already gently steaming when Sali reached the kitchen.

'Uncle Morgan told you not to come down, Mari.'

Mari held her finger to her lips. 'Then we'd best whisper in case he followed you.'

'He could sack you, and Llinos and I and the boys couldn't cope without you,' Sali pleaded.

'I have been making tea for the mistress every time she's had one of her funny turns in the night for the last twenty-one years and I'm not about to stop now. If your uncle asks, he and the mistress are not the only ones who can't sleep, and as housekeeper I'm entitled to a cup of tea to help me rest.' Mari set an embroidered cloth on a japanned tray and laid out a Coalport porcelain breakfast set of teapot, cups, saucers, jug and sugar bowl. 'I had a few minutes' start on you, so he won't be expecting you yet. Make the most of it.' She poured warm milk into a cup and stirred it. 'Cocoa, just the way you like it.' She handed it to Sali together with a tin of Huntley and Palmer biscuits.

'I am sorry about the maids, footmen and stable boys being given notice, especially Robert,' Sali added. 'He must hate us. He's been with us since he was twelve years old.'

'None of them blames you for it, Miss Sali. They know exactly what's going on in this house.'

'Which is more than I do,' Sali mused gloomily. 'My uncle only informs us of his decisions after he's made

57

them.' Taking her cocoa, she sat in the rocking chair next to the hearth. As the kettle began to boil, she handed Mari a blue and gold tin tea caddy from the shelf next to her. It was battered and scratched and bore the words *Lipton – tea, coffee & cocoa planter. Tea merchant by special appointment to Her Majesty the Queen* although the Queen had been dead for four years. 'We ought to replace this with a tin that says by special appointment to His Majesty the King.'

'The way your uncle has tightened the purse strings we won't be replacing anything in this house for quite a while,' Mari observed abruptly. 'There, I've half-filled your mother's cup with hot water, all you have to do is pour in the milk and top it up with tea until it's a sickly shade of pale mushroom. Then you can take the tray in to your uncle.'

'Thank you, Mari.' Sali finished her cocoa, left her chair and kissed the housekeeper.

'None of your sloppiness now, Miss Sali.' Mari pushed her away and closed the hotplates. 'And your Aunt Edyth is right. You mustn't let anything get in the way of you marrying Mr James in June.'

'How do you know about that?'

Mari tapped her nose. 'We servants know more than we let on. Another thing, don't close your uncle's bedroom door when you take him that tea. If you need me for anything, shout. I won't be far.'

'Your tea, Mother.' Sali topped up the cup of hot water with tea, spooned in three sugars, stirred it and carried it from the tray she had set on her mother's dressing table to the bedside cabinet.

'I hope you haven't made it too strong.' Gwyneth struggled to sit up.

'I haven't.' Sali plumped her mother's pillows and set them at an angle behind her back.

'It is in the drawer.'

Sali didn't have to ask what was in the drawer. She opened her mother's bedside cabinet. The top drawer was crammed with an assortment of patent medicines. Bottles of Hughes's Blood Pills, Thompson's Burdock Pills, Jones's Red Drops, Hayman's Balsam and Deakin's Lung Healer vied for space with small porcelain and glass jars of smelling salts, but in pride of place in the corner nearest to the bed and within easy reach of her mother was a green bottle that contained laudanum. Sali lifted it out, along with an eyedropper. Taking the glass from the top of the carafe of water on her mother's cabinet, she poured in an inch of water. Then she pulled the cork from the bottle and inserted the dropper, squeezing the rubber bulb until liquid was sucked into the glass tube. Lifting it from the bottle, she held the dropper over the glass and depressed the rubber bulb four times.

'Six more drops.'

'When I was home at Christmas, Doctor Evans told Father no more than four, and then only if you were very upset.'

'That was before your father was killed. Morgan talked to Dr Evans, told him how bad my nerves were and he increased the dose.'

Sali depressed the rubber bulb six more times, took her mother's teacup and handed her the glass. Gwyneth made a face as she drained it. Sali took the glass from her, returned her teacup and waited until she finished her tea.

'See to the pillows.' Gwyneth settled down and Sali rearranged the bed. Her mother's eyes were closing as she replaced the cup on the tray. 'Make sure Llinos doesn't disturb me again.'

'Uncle Morgan has warned her to be quiet. Goodnight, Mother.'

Gwyneth didn't reply. She was already asleep.

'Set the tray on the table by the window,' Morgan ordered, as Sali walked into the room that had been her father's. She was shocked, both by the distasteful intimacy of seeing her uncle in bed and the changes he had wrought in her father's room in a single day.

The brown and beige floral wallpaper was marked with darker squares where family portraits and her father's favourite paintings had hung until that morning. The furniture had been moved and the head of the bed placed against the left-hand wall instead of opposite the window where her father had set it so he could watch the sun rise in the morning. The tallboy and chest of drawers had exchanged places and the nightstand no longer stood beside the bed but next to the wardrobe. The new positions neither suited convenience, nor the size of the furniture and Sali couldn't help feeling that her uncle had ordered the servants to make the changes simply to announce to the household that he had taken possession of the master bedroom, just as he had the house.

'Pour the tea and set it on the bedside cabinet.'

Sali sensed her uncle watching her as she did as he asked.

'Two sugars.'

'Yes, Uncle Morgan.' Feeling uneasy, she moved to the door.

'Sali?'

'Yes, Uncle Morgan?' She turned and looked back at him.

'Close the door quietly behind you and on no account are you to return to Llinos's room tonight.'

'Yes, Uncle Morgan.'

'And tomorrow I want you to bring all of your and Llinos's jewellery to me in my study before breakfast.'

My study. Sali burned at his presumption.

'Did you hear me, Sali?'

'Yes, Uncle Morgan.'

'It is inappropriate for females to wear jewellery while in mourning. I will take it together with your mother's to the bank for safekeeping.'

'Yes, Uncle Morgan.'

'Goodnight, Sali.'

'Goodnight, Uncle Morgan.' Sali closed the door behind her, and returned to her own room. She stared at the lock as she shut the door and, for the first time in her life, turned the key.

'I know I keep saying it, but it's not right, Miss Sali. A young girl of your station in life shouldn't be treated like a servant, or ordered about the way your uncle orders you,' Mari admonished, as she and Sali packed away the family's overcoats and winter blankets in camphor chests for the summer.

'It's either this or read to Mother, and she never notices whether I'm sitting with her or not these days.' Sali checked the pockets of the cashmere coat Geraint had left behind after the Easter holidays and pulled out a handkerchief and an empty cigarette packet. Llinos's pile of clothes were the largest and Sali recalled the tears they had both shed when her sister had been sent away along with the boys after Easter.

'And we all know whose fault that is.' Mari pursed her lips disapprovingly.

'Ssh . . .'

'Your uncle can't hear us. He's in the library with Mr Richards and Mr Evans . . .' Mari fell silent as Lloyd Evans's voice thundered from the library and rang out into the hall.

'I won't do it!'

Sali left the walk-in linen cupboard, looked down the stairs and exchanged nervous glances with Tomas who was polishing the lamps.

'Then you are no longer in employment with the Watkin Jones Colliery.' Morgan Davies's voice was equally loud, but steadier.

'I'd rather be sacked than cut men's wages below the breadline.'

'You do as I order you, or you get out of this house and the Watkin Jones Colliery.'

'Mr Evans, please . . .' Mr Richards faltered as the library door banged open and Lloyd emerged into the hall.

'Walk out now, Evans, and I'll see that you never work in another colliery in Pontypridd again. You'll get no reference or severance pay from me.' Red-faced and furious, Morgan followed Lloyd. Seeing Tomas, he lowered his voice. 'You are dismissed.'

'Gentlemen, please.' Mr Richards ran out of the library and stood between the two men as Tomas retreated. 'We should be holding the interests of the Watkin Jones Colliery paramount.'

'I am.' Lloyd faced Morgan head on. 'The interests of the workers as well as the owners.'

'The Collieries Company pay their workers less than I'm offering . . .'

'They pay their workers a shameful pittance,' Lloyd interrupted. 'And I'll not advise the men to take your offer and that's my final word.'

'Tomas,' Morgan shouted.

'Sir.' The butler emerged from the servants' passage.

'Show Evans the door.'

'It's all right, Tomas.' Lloyd took the coat Tomas handed him. 'I'm leaving.' He shrugged it on and took his hat, gloves and muffler from the butler before turning back to Morgan. 'Cut the men's wages and you'll have a strike on your hands,' he said.

'I won't have to cut them now that you are leaving. The Collieries Company will do it for me.'

'That's what you wanted all along, isn't it?' Lloyd challenged. 'An excuse to sell the Watkin Jones Colliery.'

'We will get a greater return if it is sold and the money reinvested in the Collieries Company.'

'And your return will be soaked in miners' blood. Enjoy it!' Lloyd turned his back to Morgan and saw Sali standing at the top of the staircase. He tipped his hat to her, walked to the front door and opened it before Tomas could reach it.

'You can't sell Father's colliery!' Sali ran down the stairs and confronted her uncle and Mr Richards.

'Without Mr Evans to run it, we have little option, Miss Watkin Jones,' Mr Richards murmured apologetically.

'Uncle Morgan?' she appealed.

'Women have no right to interfere in things that are beyond their comprehension.'

'Father spent his whole life building up that business for Geraint.'

'Enough!' Morgan bellowed. 'The subject is closed. And as you are intent on going out gallivanting this morning, see to your duties and your mother. And don't you dare discuss this matter with her. The decision to sell has been made and it is irreversible.' He returned to the library and slammed the door.

'What was all the shouting about?' Gwyneth carped, as Sali carried her mid-morning tea tray into her bedroom.

Mindful of her uncle's warning, she answered, 'Uncle Morgan discussing business with Mr Richards and Mr Evans.'

'Oh,' Gwyneth murmured disinterestedly, as Sali poured her tea and set it on her bedside cabinet.

'Are you sure you don't want me to ask Mari or the maid to sit with you, Mother?'

Sali glanced at the clock on her mother's bedside cabinet. The hands pointed to ten. Aunt Edyth had arranged to bring her carriage around at ten-thirty so they could spend the day shopping for wedding clothes. Although she had told her mother of her plans a week ago and mentioned the trip every day since, her mother categorically refused to recognise that she had made an engagement that would take her out of the house. And her uncle had referred to her plans as 'gallivanting' ever since Edyth had mentioned them to him.

From the moment Morgan Davies had moved in four

months ago, he had encouraged her mother to commandeer every minute of her time that he hadn't earmarked
for her 'household duties'. Whenever he caught her trying
to sneak into the library, or her bedroom in the hope of
stealing half an hour to herself, he marched her to her
mother's room and subjected her to a sermon on 'a
daughter's duty'. As a result, her mother now considered
her constant attendance an entitlement and her absence a
deliberate attempt to annoy.

'I am sure,' Gwyneth snapped. Sali plumped up her
pillows and helped her into a sitting position. 'The
servants have work to do and I can hardly disrupt the
entire household simply because my own daughter can't
spare the time to sit with me.'

'This is the first time I have been out in a month and
my wedding—'

'Your wedding.' Gwyneth sighed theatrically. Sali
handed her the tea. 'That is all you can talk about. As if I
need to be reminded that you can't wait to be rid of this
house and me. Am I that tiresome?' she questioned
plaintively.

'Of course not, Mother.'

'Then why this rush to marry Mansel James before
your father is cold in his grave?'

'Father died over four months ago.'

'As if I needed reminding.' Gwyneth lifted her handkerchief to her eyes.

'It is not as if I am moving away from Pontypridd.' Sali
tidied the rows of glass bottles and jars of smelling salts
on her mother's bedside cabinet. 'And as soon as Mansel
and I return from honeymoon, I will visit you every day.'

'And if I die while you immerse yourself in wedding
preparations with your Aunt Edyth? Or during the
ceremony? Or when you are away on honeymoon, what
then?' Gwyneth demanded. 'I suppose it will be too much
to expect you to delay your pleasure to observe any more
mourning for me than you have done for your father.'

Tears formed in Sali's eyes. 'You know how much I miss Father.'

'From the way you behave, I know no such thing,' Gwyneth broke in acidly.

'Father was pleased when I accepted Mansel's proposal of marriage.'

'He wouldn't have wanted you to marry Mansel James at the expense of what little health that remains to me.'

'I spoke to the doctor. He assured me that you are in no immediate danger.'

'And what would he know of my suffering?' Gwyneth settled back on her pillows and stared at the ceiling. 'Lying here, hour after hour, with no one to see to my medicines, and no one to read to me.'

'Mari has offered.'

'She has such a coarse voice. I can't bear her reading and you know how dreadfully my eyes and head ache whenever I try to read myself.'

'Perhaps we should consider the suggestion Geraint made at Easter and look for a paid companion for you,' Sali ventured. 'The last time Aunt Edyth visited, she mentioned she knows a highly suitable lady. A curate's widow.'

'That is just the sort of low person your Aunt Edyth would be acquainted with,' Gwyneth replied.

'Aunt Edyth assured me that she is a lady in every way but her circumstances, Mother.' Sali poured an inch of water into a glass and picked up the laudanum bottle.

'And as a curate's widow she would be an Anglican. Your uncle would never allow her in the house.'

'Would you like me to ask Aunt Edyth if she knows any respectable Methodist widows?' Sali measured out her mother's medication and dripped it, bead by bead, into the water.

'Only if you are also prepared to ask if Aunt Edyth will pay her salary. Morgan has informed me that our budget won't run to the expense of a paid companion.' Gwyneth drank the laudanum and water.

Sali fought an impulse to answer back. Since her Uncle Morgan had taken control of the household accounts, he behaved as if the family were one step away from the workhouse, which was ridiculous given the size of the estate her father had left. But despite Mr Richards's pleadings, Morgan had refused to hand over a penny of her dowry before her marriage certificate was signed and had halved allowances. A measure that would have caused Geraint, Gareth and Llinos considerable embarrassment at their schools if Aunt Edyth hadn't privately made up the deficit. Morgan had also cut Mari's housekeeping to the point where she was implementing economy measures usually only seen in the poorest households in Pontypridd.

'You'll be sorry when you marry Mansel,' Gwyneth hissed suddenly, with a venom that shook Sali's equanimity.

Sali took her mother's glass and strove to compose herself. 'I love Mansel, Mother, and he loves me.'

'And you think I didn't love your father when I married him?'

'Of course not.'

'And look at me now. I can barely drag myself out of this bed to lie on my chaise.' Gwyneth lowered her voice to a whisper. 'Men are beasts and it was your father's demands and the rigours of childbirth that brought me to this. It may be all perfume, poetry and flowers between you and Mansel now, but it won't remain that way. He'll use and degrade you just as your father used, degraded and broke me.'

It wasn't the first time her mother had spoken to her about the physical side of marriage and Sali couldn't bear to listen to any more. 'That was the front doorbell, Mother. If there's nothing else, I'd like to go.'

'Then go, and ignore me and my advice, as you always do.'

'I am neither ignoring you nor your advice, Mother, but it would be impolite to keep Aunt Edyth waiting.'

'I'll die here alone in this bed and no one will care.'

'I'll call Mari.'

'If you must.'

As Sali moved to the door, Gwyneth asked, 'Are you sure you gave me the full ten drops?'

'I am sure, Mother,' Sali answered, although if she hadn't measured her mother's laudanum herself, she might have wondered. A minute or two after a dose of 'medication', her mother usually sank into a stupor for three to four hours, but she seemed oddly agitated and nervous. 'Do you feel unwell?'

'Unwell!' her mother exclaimed scornfully. 'You know that I am always unwell.'

'Would you like me to send for the doctor?'

'How can he examine me without you here?'

'Mari—'

'Please, spare me the embarrassment of a medical examination in front of a paid servant.'

'Would you like me to ask him to call?' Sali reiterated.

'No,' her mother said in a martyred tone. 'But you can give me some more medication.'

'Wouldn't it be dangerous to exceed the dose?'

'Now *you* are a doctor.'

'I don't think you should increase the dose without his permission. Shall I ask him to call tomorrow when I am at home?'

'Who knows how I'll be tomorrow?'

'I'll ask Mari to call him if you feel any worse. Goodbye, Mother.' Sali closed the door and retreated to her own room before her mother could conjure another excuse to delay her.

'My coachman will drive Sali home after dinner this evening,' Edyth informed Morgan briskly, as she accepted his offer to join him in the morning room.

'I assumed Sali would return home this afternoon so she could sit with her mother.' Morgan refrained from making a more forceful protest. During the months that had elapsed since his brother-in-law's funeral, Edyth had become adept at anticipating his disapproval and countering the objections he made to her plans for Sali.

'Surely the maid can sit with Gwyneth for one afternoon.'

'As Sali is so insistent on going ahead with her wedding, my sister is anxious to spend as much time with her as possible while she is still at home.'

'I would have thought that as Sali will be leaving in six weeks it would be better for Gwyneth to become accustomed to another companion,' Edyth advised tartly. She lowered herself into a chair without waiting for an invitation. 'I have invited Mr Richards to dine with Mansel, Sali and me this evening. He has prepared some papers that require Mansel and Sali's signatures. Business – you do understand?' She met Morgan's steely glare.

'I would be derelict in my guardian's duty if I allowed Sali to remain out so late unchaperoned.' Morgan stood between the hearth and Edyth's chair, effectively preventing the warmth of the fire from reaching her.

'Mr Richards has accepted the use of my carriage, so he will chaperone her. As Harry appointed him Sali's joint guardian, he is eminently suited to the responsibility. Wouldn't you agree?'

Morgan nodded ungraciously, realising that once again he had been outmanoeuvred. 'Would you like some tea?'

'No, but thank you for offering, Morgan.' Edyth glanced at the watch she had pinned to her lapel, as much to alert him to the fact that she had been in the house a full ten minutes before he had offered her refreshment, as to check the time.

'You must forgive Sali for being tardy, she is with her mother.'

'And how is Gwyneth these days?'

'Frail, she suffers a great deal.'

'She might find fresh air beneficial.'

'The doctor has warned that the slightest exertion could have an adverse effect.'

'Sali,' Edyth beamed, as Sali walked into the room dressed in her coat and hat. 'Ready for a full day's shopping?'

'Yes, Aunt Edyth.' Sali returned her aunt's smile.

'I thought you had ordered everything you needed on your last shopping trip, Sali.'

'Not everything, Morgan.' Edyth rose to her feet. 'We haven't even looked at accessories yet. And Sali is booked in for final fittings with the dressmaker. Afterwards, I've arranged for us to see china and silver patterns.'

'Have either of you given a thought as to how these extravagances are to be paid for? Sali has her allowance but—'

'There is no need for you to concern yourself about the cost, Morgan,' Edyth countered blithely, as Sali opened the door for her. 'Sali's wedding dress and trousseau will be my wedding present to her, and her household linen, china and silver my wedding present to Mansel.'

'I still think they should consider postponing the wedding for at least another six months.'

'We have discussed your proposal that they do so, at length, and dismissed it, Morgan. When can I see Gwyneth?' she enquired, as he followed them into the hall.

'She is in no condition to receive visitors.'

'Time is pressing. We need to discuss the wedding arrangements. Thank you, Tomas.' Edyth took the gloves and cape the butler handed her.

'Gwyneth is in no condition to arrange anything. Any pressure, mental or physical, could prove extremely dangerous.'

'Quite,' Edyth agreed, fully aware that she was irritating Morgan. 'And that is why I think Sali should be married from Ynysangharad House.'

'Sali can hardly marry from the same house her bridegroom is living in.'

'Which is why Mansel is moving into rooms above the department store.'

'It is a preposterous idea.'

'Don't you think I'm a suitable chaperone for Sali, Morgan?'

'This is her home. Her mother needs her.'

'And when Sali marries, Gwyneth, like all mothers before her, will have to learn to live without her child. But don't worry, Morgan, when Sali moves in with me, we will both visit Gwyneth as frequently as her health will allow and, who knows, having something to look forward to may be good for her.' She handed her cape to Sali so she could drape it around her shoulders. 'As Gwyneth is too ill to receive me, will you discuss my offer to host the wedding with her as a matter of urgency? As Sali's closest female relation after her mother and sister, Mr Richards thinks I would make an eminently suitable hostess for the wedding, but we really do need to send out the invitations next week.'

'You have talked this over with Mr Richards?'

'I would never make plans without consulting and gaining the approval of the family solicitor. Come along, Sali, we don't want to keep Miss Collins waiting. Good morning to you, Morgan.'

'That's put Uncle Morgan in a foul mood for the rest of the day,' Sali observed, settling herself in her aunt's carriage.

Edyth lifted her cane and rapped on the roof. 'Then it's just as well you won't be returning home until bedtime. Now, I suggest we forget Morgan and concentrate on the task in hand.' Her smile broadened. 'Serious shopping.'

'Is my dress ready?'

'As ready as any dress before a final fitting.'

'Then you've seen it?' Sali's face shone with excitement.

'Yesterday afternoon, and before you ask, Miss Collins has been careful to keep it out of Mansel's sight.'

'And?' Sali pleaded.

'I don't want to spoil your surprise.'

Mansel stepped in front of the doorman as his aunt's carriage drew up outside the Market Street entrance to Gwilym James. It would have been a sizeable store in Cardiff; in Pontypridd, it had revolutionised the shopping habits of those who could afford to patronise its well-stocked clothing and household departments. An electric lift carried shoppers and stock between the four shopping floors and attic stockroom. An automated cash system whizzed capsules containing money around the store and over the heads of its patrons, to the delight of children. And the staff, trained, disciplined and closely supervised by Mr Horton, who had managed the store during the years between Gwilym James's death and Mansel's coming of age, and stayed on to assist Mansel, were the epitome of courteous deference.

'Aunt Edyth.' Mansel opened the carriage door, folded down the steps and offered her his hand as he helped her to the pavement. 'Miss Watkin Jones.' A wink belied his formal greeting.

'Mr James, how are you?' Sali made an effort to forget her mother and uncle's fault-finding and the loss of her father's colliery, and smiled at him.

'All the better for seeing you, Miss Watkin Jones. Miss Collins and her staff are waiting for you in the fitting room. After you have finished your morning's shopping I hope you'll both join me in the upstairs rooms for lunch.'

'You've finished refurbishing them?' Edyth asked.

'The decorators left yesterday so I can move in any time. I don't know why I didn't think of renovating them before. We could have saved the cost of a night-watchman if a member of staff had lived in.' Mansel held open the door.

Edyth nodded acknowledgements to the floorwalkers as she entered the store. 'What time do you intend lunching?'

'I thought about half past twelve, but as the meal is cold apart from the soup, it really doesn't matter.'

'Half past twelve sounds fine, however, Sali and I are dependent on Miss Collins.' Edyth headed for the lift.

'Good morning, Mrs James, Miss Watkin Jones.' Mr Horton stationed himself next to the lift cage.

'And good morning to you, Mr Horton,' Edyth greeted him warmly. 'How is Mrs Horton?'

'Sadly ailing, Mrs James, but thank you for asking.' He held out an envelope. 'Your butler redirected a letter from your house.'

Edyth took it and pushed it into her handbag. 'Thank you, Mr Horton.'

'I've arranged for a china and silverware showing for you and Miss Watkin Jones in one of our private rooms, Mrs James.'

'That was thoughtful, Mr Horton, but Sali and I can manage on the shop floor.' Edyth took Sali's arm as they entered the lift. 'I meant it when I said we had some serious shopping to do and it will take for ever if we wait for the assistants to carry everything through to a private room,' she whispered, as the boy closed the cage.

White silk gleamed beneath fairy-tale weavings of the feather-light, starched, antique Bruges lace that covered the bodice of Sali's gown from the high-necked collar to the pointed triangle that ended an inch below her natural waistline. Long sleeves clung, a second skin on her upper arms that frothed out in cascades of lace worked to the same pattern as the bodice, layering the lower sleeves from her elbow to the base of Sali's thumbs. The slim-line, satin skirt covered in a single layer of lace, swept down, foaming into a mass of ruffles on the hem and short train. Lifting the train by the fine white cord attached for the purpose, Sali spun slowly before the cheval mirror. After four and a half months of full mourning, the dress seemed blindingly, surreally beautiful.

'The hat and veil.' Miss Collins snapped her fingers at

her assistant. 'As you see, Miss Watkin Jones, Mrs James, I've used the same lace to trim the hat and make the veil.'

Sali continued to stare at herself in the mirror as the dressmaker pinned on the white, broad-brimmed hat trimmed with frills of lace and white and cream silk rosebuds.

'Before the ceremony,' Miss Collins covered Sali's face with the veil, 'and,' she deftly swept the lace away from Sali's face and over the crown of the hat, 'after.'

'What do you think, Sali?' Edyth asked. Sali's eyes misted over. 'It's beautiful but . . .'

'Your father would not have wanted you to wear mourning on your wedding day,' Edyth declared resolutely.

Overcome with emotion, Sali turned aside.

Edyth turned to the dressmaker. 'This dress is exactly right, Miss Collins, understated yet elegant. It would not look out of place at court. Once the town sees it, you will be hard-pressed to fill the orders that will flood in. Every bride in Pontypridd will be clamouring to buy one of your creations.'

'Thank you, Mrs James.' The dressmaker glowed at the compliment as she helped Sali unbutton the dress.

'Thank you, Miss Collins, and not only for my wedding dress,' Sali added. 'The morning, afternoon and evening gowns are beautiful.'

'It is a pity they all had to be black or grey, Miss Watkin Jones.'

'I am sure Miss Watkin Jones, or Mrs James as she soon will be, will return to order more gowns as soon as she is out of mourning, Miss Collins.' Edyth glanced at her watch as she rose to her feet. 'Would you please arrange for the accessories Miss Watkin Jones has chosen, her trousseau and wedding dress to be delivered to Ynysangharad House this afternoon and send a message to Mr Horton to tell him that we will be leaving the choosing of Mr James's and Miss Watkin Jones's china and silverware until this afternoon? Mr James is expecting us to join him upstairs for lunch.'

'Certainly, Mrs James.'

Remembering her letter, Edyth removed it from her bag as the dressmaker helped Sali to change back into her walking suit.

'Bad news?' Sali asked, as Edyth frowned.

'Inconvenient.' Edyth pushed the letter into her pocket. 'Miss Collins, thank you again.'

'My pleasure, Mrs James, Miss Watkin Jones.' Miss Collins opened the door of the fitting room and bobbed a curtsy, as they headed for the lift.

CHAPTER FIVE

'Harry would have been proud of you for going ahead with your wedding exactly as planned, Sali,' Edyth assured her, as they left the lift on the attic floor and walked past the stock rooms.

'You don't think I am being disrespectful to his memory?'

'On the contrary, I think you are being brave in adhering to his wishes. You don't need me to tell you how delighted your father was when you told him you wanted to marry Mansel.' As Sali brushed a tear from her eye, Edyth murmured, 'Have Morgan and your mother been giving you a harder time than usual?'

'Not really . . . but . . .'

'They've been trying to persuade you to observe a full year of mourning.'

'Two.'

Edyth grasped her hand. 'Only another six weeks to go. Be strong.' She opened the door in front of her. 'Mansel has transformed this room. The last time I was here it was as dark and dingy as a chapel vestry.'

'It's light and airy now.' Sali followed her aunt into a large, comfortable drawing room papered in cream and white striped paper. The green plush-upholstered sofa and chairs were old-fashioned and heavy, as were the round table, upright chairs, and the Turkish rug on the floor was a dismal shade of green, but the scale of the room was forgiving enough to accommodate the furnishings.

'It smells of paint.' Edyth wrinkled her nose as she

inspected the skirting boards and fire surround. Both had been painted cream to complement the wallpaper. 'No one has lived here since Mr Lewis retired six months before Mansel took over. When Mansel was in school, he often talked about moving in here himself and living the high bachelor life, but then,' Edyth gave Sali a sly look, 'that was before you accepted his proposal.'

Sali moved to the window and looked down over Market Square. 'You can see the whole street from here.'

'And Taff Street, the river and the fields around Ynysangharad House from the window on the other side.'

Sali crossed the room. 'I wonder why Mansel never suggested that we move in here?'

'Probably because I told him what it was like when Mr James and I began our married life here.' Edyth unpinned her hat. 'Despite all the builder's promises our house wasn't ready, so we lived here for four months when we returned to Pontypridd after our honeymoon, and in all that time we never had a moment's peace. Even when Mr James gave the staff direct orders not to disturb him, there was always something that needed his personal attention. An important customer demanding that he and no one else wait on them, a wrong delivery that needed sorting, or an errant assistant to reprimand. And if it wasn't this store, it was the Market Company, the bakery, or one of his provision stores. Believe me, comfortable as these rooms may be, you and Mansel will be better off living in Ynysangharad House.'

'I am sure you are right.' Sali helped her aunt to remove her cape and hung it together with her hat on a stand next to the door.

'But, saying that, despite the constant interruptions, we were happy during the short time we lived here.' Edyth looked inward as memories flooded back. 'However, I wouldn't have been for long. No window or view is an adequate substitute for a garden. Shall we look at what Mansel has done to the rest of the rooms?'

Sali arranged her own hat and coat on the stand before opening a set of double doors to her left. They entered a dining room hung with the same paper as the drawing room and furnished with similar, old-fashioned, sturdy pieces, designed more for comfort than elegance. Three place settings had been laid at a square table that dominated the centre of the room. A vast sideboard filled half the remaining space. On it were a spirit-fuelled chafing dish from which emanated an appetising aroma of leek and potato soup, baskets of bread rolls and butter pats, a selection of cold meats, chutneys, pickles and mustards, a cold vegetable salad, an apple tart, a bowl of clotted cream and a drinks tray holding bottles of sherry, whisky and brandy.

'Your Uncle Morgan would disapprove of you eating here if he could see that,' Edyth indicated the tray. 'There's a kitchen, through the inner hall.' She led Sali through a second set of double doors into a tiny, dark vestibule walled by four doors. Unlike the drawing and dining rooms, the kitchen was small. It held a Belfast sink, miniature range, a coal bucket and single cupboard. A scarred pine work table stood in the centre of the room.

'Bedroom.' Edyth opened another door and they glanced into a dark room that had also been newly papered, this time in pale grey. An enormous four-poster, hung with red curtains and covered with a matching bedspread, stood beside a wardrobe that filled an entire wall. The gloom was due to a massive dressing table that had been placed before the only window and blocked out most of the light.

'Bathroom.' Edyth looked into a room scarcely larger than a cupboard that held a washstand, slipper bath, cabinet lavatory, slop pails and four huge jugs of water. 'Mansel really must see about extending the plumbing to this floor. I don't envy whoever has to carry those pails downstairs. Be careful of the walls if you come in here,

Sali. I remember that green distemper; it used to rub off on my clothes.'

'Everything looks fresh and clean,' Sali said, as they returned to the dining room.

'Apart from the furniture.' Edyth smiled at the confused expression on Sali's face. 'It is all right to criticise. I didn't furnish this place; my mother-in-law did. Fifty years ago it was probably the height of fashion, but thankfully tastes have changed. I am glad Mansel's spared no expense in redecorating. It would be a pity to allow the rooms to decay. I haven't been up here for a couple of years but as I recall, the wallpaper was a rather dismal brown in all the rooms the last time I was here. It might be as well if he replaced the furniture as well.' She gave a wicked smile as she glanced at the sideboard. 'How about a small sherry before lunch?'

Sali thought of her Uncle Morgan. 'I'd love one.'

'Given your mother's state of health, if there's anything you're unsure of, or anything you want to know about married life you can ask me,' Edyth offered, as they sat companionably either side of the fireplace in the drawing room. Although it was a warm day, a fire burnt cheerfully in the grate. More cheerfully than at home, Sali observed, recalling her uncle's latest edict to Mari to cut coal consumption. A ludicrous order given that until that morning, they could have ordered all the coal they needed from the family colliery at no cost to the household budget.

You know Mother is finding it difficult to accept that I am about to be married.'

'Yes.' Edyth set her sherry glass in the hearth. 'Please, don't take this the wrong way, Sali, but you do want to marry Mansel, don't you? It's not just something that you are doing simply to break free from your mother and uncle?'

'Of course I want to marry him,' Sali protested earnestly.

'Married life does take a lot of adjusting to,' Edyth

mused, 'But the rewards of a successful marriage more than make up for any sacrifices. Your uncle and I were very happy.'

'You always seemed to be whenever we visited,' Sali concurred.

'That's not to say we didn't argue, especially at first. I remember quarrelling with him on our honeymoon in Swansea. I stormed out of the hotel and spent an hour searching for somewhere respectable to hide, in the hope that he'd worry about me.'

'What did you quarrel about?' Sali sipped her sherry. After months of abstinence it brought an unexpected warm and cheering glow.

Edyth frowned. 'Do you know, I don't even remember . . . Yes, I do – he accused me of putting too much milk in his tea at breakfast. I was mortified that he'd dared to criticise anything I did.'

'And where did you go?'

'I caught the train to Mumbles and walked around Oystermouth Castle for four hours. It was very cold and damp.'

'And did he worry?'

'Not enough to order a search, but he didn't pass judgment on the way I poured his tea at four o'clock. But then, you are so much more sensible than I was at your age. I can't imagine you behaving so foolishly or pouring Mansel's tea any way other than how he likes it. Besides, Mansel is a very different man to his uncle. He is much more sensitive.'

'I love him very much,' Sali burst out solemnly.

'I know you do, darling, and I'm sure you'll be happy together.'

'Mother said –' Sali coloured at the memory of the ugly threats her mother had flung at her that morning. 'She said . . .'

Edyth waited patiently for Sali to finish.

'She said that I would become an invalid like her if I had children,' Sali finally blurted.

'And you believe her?'

'She told me she was healthy before she had children.'

'That depends on what you mean by healthy. Gwyneth always has been something of a hypochondriac. If she so much as cut her finger she'd have hysterics and demand a maid run for the doctor. Her own mother was always imagining herself ill and I think she instilled the ridiculous notion in both Morgan and Gwyneth that women are delicate creatures that have to be constantly nurtured and cared for like hot-house plants.'

'Father told me that you had children.'

'A boy and a girl. Did he also tell you that they died in a diphtheria epidemic just like Mansel's parents?'

Sali nodded in response to the bleak expression in Edyth's eyes.

'When Mansel moved in with Mr James and me after he was orphaned, I had reached a point where I no longer wanted to go on living,' Edyth said simply. 'Grief brought us together and it was Mansel who sustained me when Mr James died. It was his idea you live with me after your marriage, not mine.'

'I know. We discussed it when he asked me to marry him. We both hoped you'd want us.' Impulsively, Sali left her chair and grasped her aunt's hand.

'I think it is more the other way around. You two have given me far more than I have ever given you in terms of affection and consideration. Like most women of my age I have become self-centred and opinionated. I have also developed an alarming tendency to try to force people into doing things I think will be good for them. And before you contradict me,' she eyed Sali sternly, 'ask your Uncle Morgan what he thinks of me.'

'I wouldn't dare,' Sali smiled. 'He wouldn't stop talking for hours.'

'It's good to see you smile when you talk about him.' Edyth hesitated. 'I don't know what Gwyneth has told you, but the physical relationship between a man and a woman can be the most beautiful expression of love, especially between two people who care for one another as much as you and Mansel.' She patted Sali's hand. 'There really is nothing to be afraid of when it comes to love – or childbirth.'

'Thank you.'

'For what, child?'

'Always being there, to put things into perspective for me.'

'I hope I'll be there for you for a while yet.' Edyth rose to her feet as the door opened. 'And when it's time for me to go, I know someone who'll be waiting to take over.'

'So, Aunt Edyth,' Mansel blotted his lips with his napkin before tossing it over the remains of his apple pie and cream, 'was the lunch to your satisfaction?'

'Perfect.'

'How polite of you not to tell me that the soup needed more salt and the beef was overcooked.'

'Let's just say that I like it rarer than you.'

'I ordered a light meal as you have invited guests for dinner this evening. The cook tends to overdo the spread if we have company.'

'Is that a complaint?' Edyth asked.

'Never! I wouldn't dare risk injuring Mrs Plumb's feelings. She might refuse to make me another Welsh cake. Coffee?' He left the table. 'I have everything ready to make it in the kitchen cupboard.'

Edyth glanced at her watch. 'I haven't time.'

'Admit it,' he teased. 'You don't believe that I can make coffee.'

'I am sure that you can make it; whether or not it would be drinkable is another matter. However, I will have to investigate your talent another day. I received this earlier.' Edyth pulled the letter Mr Horton had handed her from the side pocket of her skirt. 'Mr Richards has asked me to meet him at two o'clock. Apparently there are one or two matters relating to the Mining Disaster Fund that need urgent attention. A widow with six children has appealed for money to pay her rent. If the matter isn't settled by the end of the day, she and her children will be taken into the workhouse.'

'You can't help everyone, Aunt Edyth,' Mansel reminded gently. 'Gwilym James has contributed more to the last six Rhondda mining disaster funds than any other store or shop in Pontypridd.'

'I know and Mr Richards knows, but a hundred and nineteen men were killed at the National Colliery in Wattstown alone last year, and thirty-three in the Cambrian at Clydach. Mr Richards has received petitions from the Catholic Priests in the area. Some of the widows and children of those men are in dire straits.'

'The store's charity account is standing at two hundred pounds. You may as well empty it,' Mansel said philosophically. 'But don't give away too much of your own money. There'll be another good cause next week.'

Edyth turned to Sali. 'I hope you don't mind if we postpone the rest of our shopping until another day. Unless that is, Mansel can help you to chose your china and silverware.'

'Me?' Mansel queried in astonishment.

'Why not?' Edyth enquired in amusement, 'After all, you will be the one to use it.'

'What do you say, Sali? If there's time, we could even go on to the jeweller's and look at wedding rings,' Mansel suggested.

'I'd like to.' Sali looked to her aunt for confirmation that she wouldn't be offending propriety by being seen in public with Mansel while she was still in mourning.

'Your uncle couldn't possibly object to you walking around town with Mansel in the middle of the afternoon so close to your wedding day,' Edyth reassured. 'And, as it's a fine day, you could even go for a walk along the river if there's time. Your uncle and I went for several walks there before we married. If I remember correctly, they were quite enjoyable.' She picked up her handbag and left her chair. 'I will send the carriage back for you.'

'There's no need.' Mansel retrieved his aunt's cape and hat from the drawing room. 'I'll walk Sali home when the shop closes. It will still be light and if there isn't time to go for a walk this afternoon, perhaps we could go for one then.'

'So long as you are both home before dinner is served. I left orders for it to be ready at eight.'

'Sali?' Mansel asked, as he draped Edyth's cape over her shoulders.

'A walk sounds wonderful. The winter seemed to last for ever.'

'And not just for you, child,' Edyth said. 'Now remember, both of you, when it comes to choosing your china and silverware, listen to Mr Horton. He has an eye for quality.'

'We'll do that,' Mansel agreed. 'Coffee before we go downstairs, Sali?'

Realising that if she accepted, she would be alone with him, Sali looked to her aunt again, but Edyth appeared to be preoccupied with pinning on her hat. It was a decision she would have to make for herself. 'Yes please, Mansel.'

'Milk and two sugars?'

'You know how I like it.'

'I've made it my business to know all there is about you.' He opened the door for Edyth. 'Have a good meeting with Mr Richards, Aunt Edyth, and don't worry about us.'

'I won't.' She kissed Sali's cheek. 'Enjoy your coffee.'

'So, finally, I have you all alone to myself.' Mansel carried a tray into the drawing room and leered at Sali in a parody of a stage villain.

'We've been alone together before.' Sali cleared a vase from the table, so he could set down the coffee.

'Several times, but only when there have been other people behind the closed door likely to walk in us at any moment. It's a long way down to the stock rooms, and,' he lifted his pocket watch from his waistcoat pocket and pressed the catch, 'at this time of day, all the behind-the-scenes workers are at lunch.'

'I hope they enjoy their meal.' Sali took her coffee and sat on the sofa.

'You could at least pretend to be afraid.' Carrying his cup, he joined her.

'You'll have to do a better Mr Hyde impression than that before I'd exert myself.'

'You've hurt my feelings.' He set his cup on the floor. 'How about a kiss as compensation.' Cupping her face tenderly in his hands, he kissed her gently on the lips. 'I love you, Sali Watkin Jones, and a great deal more than you can ever know.'

'I do know,' she countered seriously. 'The tribulations faced by Romeo when he wooed Juliet are trivial compared to what you've had to put up with from Uncle Morgan.'

'I only wish that I could take the credit for overcoming his objections.' He picked up his coffee and sipped it. 'But all I've done is hide behind Aunt Edyth's skirts. Face it, sweetheart, you are engaged to a coward.'

'One I love.' She sat back as he set his cup aside again and took her cup from her. He kissed her a second time, moving closer to her than before. She trembled as his hand closed around her left breast. The warmth of his fingers percolated through layers of clothing, sending a heady sensation, half thrill, half fear, coursing through her veins.

She shivered and he removed his hand.

'I am sorry if I shocked you,' he apologised.

'No . . . it's . . .' She sensed colour flooding into her cheeks but she forced herself to continue. 'It's just that I'm not sure what's expected of me . . . What you expect of me,' she amended. 'I want to be a good wife to you, Mansel.'

'When the time comes,' he suggested dryly.

She raised her eyes to his. They had never looked bluer or more piercing. 'Aunt Edyth told me that the physical act between a man and a woman can be the most beautiful expression of love.'

'You asked her?' He was clearly shocked.

'No. With Mother being ill and Uncle Morgan being ... well Uncle Morgan, and both of them disapproving of us marrying so soon, Aunt Edyth suggested that I talk over any problems or questions I had about married life with her.'

'And you asked her ...'

'Not about that.' Her entire body burned with embarrassment.

'Then what?'

'Mother said ... you know how she is.' Perspiration trickled down her spine. 'She blames her ill-health on my father ... on having children.' Unable to look him in the eye, she stared down at her lap. He returned their coffee cups to the tray.

'Sali, everyone in the town, except perhaps you and your Uncle Morgan, knows your mother's illnesses are more imagined than real. Thousands of women all over the world have children, manage to be "good wives" to their husbands and still remain perfectly healthy.'

'I know,' she whispered, wishing that they had never embarked on this conversation.

'Yet, you are still afraid of our wedding night?' He returned to the sofa but sat at the opposite end. The gap between them yawned; a symbol of their sudden estrangement as her mother's voice, vicious, venomous, filled her mind.

It may be all perfume, poetry and flowers between you and Mansel now, but it won't remain that way. He'll use and degrade you just as your father used, degraded and broke me.

'I am sorry, Mansel.'

He lifted her chin with his fingers and forced her to return his gaze. 'Aunt Edyth is right, it is the most beautiful expression of love between a man and a woman.'

85

'You know?' she muttered unthinkingly.

Ignoring her question he said, 'If we did a little practising before the honeymoon, it won't come as quite such a shock to you.'

'Uncle Morgan . . .'

'Watches you like a fox watches a chicken penned in a coop.' He pulled her towards him. 'But you are here now.'

'And everyone in the store will have seen Aunt Edyth leave and know that we are alone.'

A knock at the door startled her and she rose abruptly to her feet.

'Come in,' Mansel called, as she turned her back to the room and gazed out of the window.

A young girl wearing a khaki work overall opened the door to the corridor and bobbed a curtsy. She looked from Mansel to Sali and back to Mansel. 'Sorry to disturb you, sir, but I've been sent to clear the food and the dishes.'

'You are not disturbing us.' Mansel left the sofa and lifted Sali's coat from the stand. 'Miss Watkin Jones and I were just leaving.'

The maid held the door open for them. Sali pinned on her hat and Mansel helped her on with her coat.

'Do you think your uncle arranged for her to interrupt us?' Mansel asked, when they waited for the lift to reach the top floor.

'I don't think so,' Sali replied, before she saw his smile and realised he was teasing her.

'If we don't take too long deciding the china and silverware patterns that we are going to live with for the rest of our lives and then leave for the jeweller's, who is to say how long it took us to choose your wedding ring? Or whether or not we stole an hour or two to walk along the river before we return to Aunt Edyth's for dinner. Would you like a stroll?'

Sali knew he wasn't simply asking her to accompany him on a walk. She thought of her Uncle Morgan, his cold, joyless life, and how he drained all pleasure and happiness from the lives of those around him. Then she recalled the pained expression her father had adopted whenever he had entered her mother's room, his long-suffering silences when she had castigated him with catalogues of her ailments. And the expression on her Aunt Edyth's face when she had said, 'The physical relationship between a man and a woman can be the most beautiful expression of love, especially between two people who care for one another as much as you and Mansel.'

It had been obvious that she hadn't been speaking about her and Mansel at all, but on a much more personal level. If only she and Mansel could build a marriage as strong as her Aunt Edyth's and Uncle Gwilym's had been. But no matter how she tried she couldn't forget her mother's warning.

He'll use and degrade you just as your father used, degraded and broke me.

'I'd love a stroll,' she said, firmly relegating her mother's words to the back of her mind.

'Love aside, if I didn't think you'd make me a good wife I wouldn't have asked you to marry me, Miss Watkin Jones.' He offered her his arm as the lift reached their floor and the boy opened the doors for them. 'But then, no man wants a wife who is *too* good.'

'Courtesy of your assistance, Mr Horton, it appears that Miss Watkin Jones has made all the choices that needed to be made.' Mansel studied the mass of china, crystal and glassware scattered over the long counter in front of them.

'I hope you didn't think I was being too forward, sir.'

'Not at all, Mr Horton.' Mansel tapped two cigars out of his gold case and offered the under-manager one. 'In fact, Mrs James recommended that we take your advice on both quality and pattern.'

'I had no idea Mrs James had such confidence in my opinion, sir. Thank you.' Mr Horton took the cigar and slipped it into the inside pocket of his suit.

'If you'd call an assistant, Mr Horton, I think Miss Watkin Jones is ready to place our order.'

'I'll take it myself, sir.' Mr Horton held out his hand to the three assistants who had been delegated to help them. Within seconds an order pad was placed in his palm.

'One seventy-piece Olde Delph, breakfast ware,' Mansel looked to Sali. She nodded confirmation.

'A wise choice, Mr James, traditional but a constant favourite and always acceptable. Never quite in fashion, it will never be quite outmoded either. I assure you that you will never tire of it. Children love the pattern—'

'Thank you, Mr Horton,' Mansel interrupted, unwilling to waste a precious moment of his and Sali's unexpected private time in polite chit-chat with an employee, albeit his immediate subordinate. 'One seventy-piece Diana Wedgwood design for luncheon and everyday use, one white Royal Doulton porcelain dinner service—'

'Banded with silver not gold.' Mr Horton failed to keep the disapproval from his voice.

'And one forty-piece English Poppy design tea service,' Sali added, giving Mr Horton a shy smile.

'A very modern service, Miss Watkin Jones. I only hope you will be as taken with it a year from now as you are today,' Mr Horton cautioned.

'If she isn't, we'll have fun smashing it, Mr Horton,' Mansel chipped in flippantly.

'Crystal, Mr James?' Mr Horton enquired.

'One set of Bohemian, one of fine English.'

'Port, Sherry, Liqueur, Claret, Champagne, tumblers, half pint and quarter pint . . .' Mr Horton glanced up from his pad and Mansel nodded agreement. 'Custards, finger bowls, ice plates,' he continued, 'Quart decanters . . .'

'Two dozen of everything in both sets, except decanters and we'll take four of those in both.'

'Water jugs, pint decanters and Claret?'

'A dozen jugs, four pint decanters and two Claret decanters.'

'Both sets.'

'Both.' Mansel was accustomed to making swift business decisions, but he had never made such speedy personal judgements before.

'Carafes, salad bowls, fruit bowls, oval dishes, vases?' Mr Horton enquired.

'Half a dozen in each size, except small fruit bowls and we'll take two dozen of those in both and a full canteen of the King's pattern silver cutlery.' Mansel opened his pocket watch. 'If you're finished here, Miss Watkin Jones, we can go on to the jeweller's.'

'All to be billed to Mrs James's account, sir?' Mr Horton asked.

Mansel did a speedy calculation. 'The china to be billed to my aunt's account, the crystal to mine, Mr Horton.'

'Very good, sir, Miss Watkin Jones.' The under-manager signalled to the assistants who had been poised, waiting behind the counter. 'I will have the order packed and delivered to Ynysangharad House this afternoon.'

'Thank you, Mr Horton.' Mansel offered Sali his arm.

'Will you be returning this afternoon, sir?'

'No, Mr Horton, I will not. My aunt is expecting us as soon as we have completed our business at the jeweller's. You will lock up and give the night watchman his orders?'

'Certainly, sir.' There was a hurt tone in the under-manager's voice as if Mansel had suggested he would be derelict in his duty.

'I will see you in the morning, Mr Horton.'

'Yes, Mr James. May I compliment you on your final choices, Miss Watkin Jones?'

'Thank you, Mr Horton.'

'Half past two,' Mansel breathed, as they stepped out of the shop into Market Square. 'I've never made so many decisions so quickly.'

'Let's hope we can both live with them.' Sali gripped his arm tightly and they rounded the corner into Taff Street.

'I am not too sure about the Poppy tea service.'

'You should have said!'

'One of the perks of being a man is you don't have to drink tea at home, except on Sunday,' he grinned. 'And with luck, as popular newly-weds we'll receive a lot of invitations out.'

The moment the manager opened the silk-lined wooden box and showed them the ring, Mansel wanted it.

'Do you like it?' Mansel removed the wide gold band, which was engraved with a fine tracery of leaves and embossed with raised daffodils, and felt its weight.

'It is beautiful,' Sali murmured, not wanting to disagree with him, although she would have preferred a plainer ring.

Mansel set aside the trays of rings she, or rather he, had rejected, and studied the ring critically.

'It is the most expensive ring in the shop, Mr James,' the manager warned.

'We'll discuss the price later, Mr Fowler.'

'Of course, Mr James.'

'Try it for size, Miss Watkin Jones.' Mansel slipped it on to Sali's finger. It fitted easily, too easily. When she moved her hand it slid from her finger and fell to the counter. 'Do you have it in a smaller size, Mr Fowler?'

'I am afraid not, Mr James. That ring is a very singular and special one. Handmade, the design is unique to the goldsmith who cast it.'

'Could you make it smaller?'

'Not without damaging the pattern. But it might be possible to order in a similar one.'

'Not similar, Mr Fowler, identical. The cost is imma-
terial. And I want it ready for collection sometime in the
next six weeks.'

'I'll write to them today and make every effort to see
that it is ready in time, Mr James. Shall I send a message
to your office when they contact me?'

'Please, Mr Fowler, and thank you.' Mansel tipped his
hat and opened the door for Sali.

'I feel wonderfully, deliciously free.' Sali pulled off her
hat as she and Mansel left the old bridge behind them
and strolled down the path that bordered the bank of the
Taff. The town was across the river to their right, to their
left lay a dense strip of woodland that bordered the fields
around Ynysangharad House and although the area was
usually busy at weekends, it was blissfully deserted on a
weekday afternoon.

'Six weeks from now we'll have a fortnight of this with
nothing to do but indulge our whims and no one to think
about except ourselves. You are sure about wanting to
honeymoon in Mumbles?' Mansel slipped his arm
around her waist as he led her away from the stench of
the coal blackened river and closer to the trees.

'Very sure. I loved every minute of our family holidays
in Swansea and it will be good to be in a familiar place.'

'And the hotel won't remind you of the times you
stayed there with your father?' he said sensitively.

'Yes, it will, but they are happy memories.' Slipping
away from him she stepped back from the path and
leaned against the trunk of a birch tree, hoping for
another kiss. 'We are alone again, Mr James,' she
reminded him brazenly.

He glanced up and down the path to check before
taking a box from his pocket. 'I should kneel to do this,
but I wouldn't be in a good position to receive your
thank-you kiss should you like it, or perhaps more
importantly, monitor your reaction if you don't. Your
father didn't want me to give you a ring until just before

our wedding, and after he died, your uncle wouldn't allow you to wear any jewellery so I saw little point in discussing what kind of engagement ring you would like. Then it occurred to me that you might like to wear my mother's. And Aunt Edyth suggested that as we are marrying in six weeks, it was high time it came out of the bank vault so you could give your approval or not, as the case may be. Please don't feel that you have to wear it. I'd be happy to buy you anything you wanted.' He watched her face intently as he opened the box.

'Oh Mansel, it's lovely.' She held out her finger as Mansel took the half hoop of diamonds and slipped it on to her ring finger.

'You're not just saying that. You really do like it?'

'All the more because it was your mother's. But do you think I should start wearing it today?'

'Absolutely. And if your uncle or mother dare object, tell them as it's only six weeks to our wedding day, Aunt Edyth ordered you to wear it.' He rested his hands on the tree above her head effectively imprisoning her. 'So, Miss Watkin Jones, may I have my kiss?' Sure of her response, he bent his head to hers.

'I hear footsteps.' She jerked back quickly, hitting her head on a branch. As they looked down the path they saw the soberly garbed figures of Morgan Davies and Owen Bull marching side by side from the direction of the river bend.

'Quick, duck down.' Mansel pushed her back into the bushes. Creeping after her, he took her hand and led her into a thicket. Crouching low, they ran away from the path into the woods.

'Do you think they saw us?' She gasped for breath; her corset stays dug painfully into her ribcage.

'No, because if they had, your Uncle Morgan would have chased us.' Laughing, Mansel took off his coat and tossed it on to the bare ground beneath an oak tree.

'It will get dirty,' Sali warned.

'Then the maid will have to clean it.' He sat on his coat and pulled her down beside him.

'Sssh, they might hear us.'

'They'd need an ear trumpet. They are probably over the bridge and halfway down Taff Street by now, given the speed they were walking.'

'What do you think they were doing here?'

'I neither know nor care. Aren't you warm in that coat?'

'Yes.' Her heart thundered at the implication of his question.

'Then let me help you off with it.'

She turned her back to him and he eased off both her coat and jacket. Folding them into a pillow he pushed it beneath his head before drawing her down. Pressing the full length of his body against hers, he kissed her. Slowly, tentatively, she kissed him back.

His fingers moved to the buttons on her blouse and a draught of air blew across her throat as he exposed it. She shivered as he tugged at the front lacing on her corset, loosening it, he slid his hand inside and cupped her naked breast.

No man wants a wife who is too good.

The words rang out in her mind and she closed her eyes tightly so he wouldn't see her fear – and embarrassment.

She buried her head in his shoulder as he kissed the soft skin at the top of her breast before pushing down her corset and exposing her nipples. She sensed him looking at her and instinctively tried to cover herself with her fingers.

He imprisoned her hands in one of his and pinned them above her head.

'I'm sorry, Mansel,' she said. 'I am not used to this.'

'I would be worried if you were.' He kissed each of her nipples in turn. 'You are very beautiful and I promise you will get used to me looking at you this way because I intend to do a great deal of it.'

He moved away from her and she sat up to lace her corset. But he pushed her back down and brushed her skirt aside. His hand moved up her stockinged leg to her naked thigh and he slipped his fingers inside the leg of her drawers. Shifting suddenly, he slid both his hands beneath her skirt, lifted it and her petticoats to her waist and tugged her drawers down.

'Mansel . . .'

'No one can see. We're almost married.' His voice was strange, husky, and it took all her powers of concentration to suppress her instinct to fight him off.

No man wants a wife who is too good.

They were almost married. Now or in a few weeks, what was the difference?

Tossing her drawers aside, he unbuttoned his trousers and knelt between her legs. She closed her eyes, mortified as he ran his hands over the most intimate parts of her body.

'This may hurt a bit.'

She braced herself, but she wasn't prepared for the pain that followed, or his thrusting that penetrated to the very core of her being.

CHAPTER SIX

'I didn't mean to get quite so carried away, but that was rather wonderful.' Mansel rolled on to the ground, rose to his feet and glanced back at Sali as he pulled up his drawers and trousers, tucked in his shirt and buttoned his flies. 'Are you all right?'

Sali swallowed hard in an effort to control the tide of nausea rising in her throat. 'I . . . I think so.'

'I didn't hurt you, darling, did I . . . oh God!'

She looked down and saw the lining of his jacket that he had spread beneath them and the edge of one of her petticoats were soaked in blood. Tears fell from her eyes as she covered them with her skirt. 'I am all right,' she whispered unconvincingly in response to the stricken expression on his face.

'I should have waited . . . we're in the middle of nowhere . . .'

'I need to dress,' she pleaded, unable to face trying to sort her stained and ruined underclothes with him watching her.

'After what we've just done, don't you think you're being silly, darling? I can help you . . .'

'Please, Mansel,' she begged, choking back her tears.

'I'm sorry. You need time to get used to me. I'll turn my back.'

'Thank you.' She picked up her drawers. They at least were free from stain and in one piece, but if the pain was any indication, she was still bleeding. She rose unsteadily to her feet, stepped into her drawers, straightened her petticoats, laced her corset, buttoned her blouse and retrieved her jacket and coat. 'Do I look all right?' she asked tremulously.

He turned around and studied her critically. 'You look shaky, but your skirt is clean.'

'Your jacket isn't.'

'I'll fold it and carry it so the stains don't show.'

'People will stare if you're only wearing your waistcoat.'

'Let them,' he said, more concerned for her than what people would think of them. 'Here, lean on me.'

'Where are we going?'

'Somewhere where you can clean yourself up and we can be sure that we won't be disturbed.'

The clock on St Catherine's church struck four as they returned to Taff Street. Feeling as though everyone in the town knew what they had done and was watching them, Sali walked slowly, looking downwards as she clung to Mansel's arm. He stopped outside the Taff Street entrance to Gwilym James. Taking a bunch of keys from his pocket, he glanced up and down the street before unlocking a door set to the side of the shop window. 'Inside, quick.'

Sali found herself in a narrow corridor, lit only by a stained glass skylight above the door. Holding his finger to his lips Mansel led the way to a steep staircase. Sick, queasy and breathless, Sali counted the steps as they climbed. At fifty-two, she felt as though her lungs would burst. The steps ended abruptly in a door. Mansel pulled the keys from his pocket again and unlocked it. He stepped inside, waited until she joined him, then closed, locked and bolted the door. To her amazement they were in the small inner hall of the rooms above the shop.

'We walked up the fire exit,' Mansel clarified briefly. He went into the drawing room and threw the bolt across the door that connected to the corridor. 'Would you like me to make us some tea while you use the bathroom?'

Breathless, Sali nodded agreement.

'Don't worry about your clothes. I have sets of underclothes in the bedroom. Stockings too.'

'People will have seen us coming in . . .'

'There was no one close enough to say whether we went into the shop or the side door. It's never used and I'm sure no one was watching us that carefully. The shop shuts at seven tonight and by half past all the staff will have left. We'll burn my jacket and your ruined under-wear in the range, walk back down into Market Street, which is quieter than Taff Street at that time in the evening and, if anyone does ask, all we have to say is we went for a stroll by the river and on the way back you remembered that you had left your gloves here and we called in to pick them up.'

He went into the bedroom, opened the dressing-table drawer and removed several packages. Unwrapping a white silk robe from layers of tissue paper, he handed it to her. 'I asked the buyer to put together a trousseau as a surprise for you,' he explained in response to her quizzical look. 'There's everything you need and all in silk and lace. Drawers, petticoats, stockings, bust shapers, chemises . . .'

'I'll never explain silk and lace underwear to Uncle Morgan.'

'He looks at your underclothes?' His colour heightened in anger.

'Inspects the family wash.'

'Hide them, or tell him Aunt Edyth bought them for you. You can't go home in what you're wearing. Hand me some towels from the bathroom. I'll lay them on the bed and you can rest when you've washed. I'll make us some tea.'

Her ruined underclothes and stockings bundled together ready to go in the range, her skirt, blouse, corset, and unsoiled petticoats, brushed down and checked, Sali left the bathroom for the bedroom in the white silk robe. Still feeling nauseous, she slipped between the sheets.

'I'm sorry if I hurt you.' Mansel stood beside the bed.

'You didn't,' she lied, grateful for the gloom that shrouded the room in shadows.

'I've made tea but the maid took the milk.'

'It would have gone off.'

'You don't mind black tea?'

'No, you?'

'I've drunk worse.' He poured her a cup and set it on the bedside table. 'Are you in pain?'

'No, not really.' Mortified by his question, she looked away.

He poured his own tea, sat on the end of the bed and pulled at his tie. She stared at him in amazement as he began to undress.

'You want to . . . I mean again . . .'

'In comfort this time.' Kicking off his shoes, he unbuttoned his trousers. 'We should have sneaked back here in the first place instead of walking up the river.'

She tried not to watch, as unconcerned by her embarrassment, he stripped to his skin. 'You've never seen a naked man before?' he smiled, clearly amused by her blushes.

'No,' she whispered, disconcerted. He climbed into bed beside her.

'You'll soon get used to seeing me.' He slipped his hand between her thighs. 'Did it hurt very much, darling?'

'A little,' she confessed uneasily, shocked by the sensation of his bare legs brushing against hers.

'I am so sorry. Promise to tell me if I ever hurt you again.'

'Yes.'

'It shouldn't hurt this time, not after what we've already done, but you are so beautiful, I can't promise you that I won't get carried away again.' Untying the belt on her robe, he caressed her breasts. She steeled herself to receive his embraces. Whether it was the certainty of remaining undisturbed behind two locked and bolted doors, or because she knew what to expect, or was covered by a sheet and blankets, Mansel's lovemaking was neither as painful nor as traumatic as it had been on the river bank.

But neither was it pleasurable or beautiful. Aunt Edyth had been widowed for over fifteen years, however, and it was possible that her memory wasn't as clear as it had once been.

She thought of all the married women she knew and was confident that given time, she would overcome her shyness and become accustomed to Mansel touching her the way he was at that moment. She loved him, he was kind and thoughtful, and there were so many other, more enjoyable aspects to married life. She tried to think of them to take her mind off what he was doing to her.

Rides across the fields around Ynysangharad House . . . dancing in warm, perfumed ballrooms . . . long walks beside the river . . . dinner parties with friends . . .

'You have withdrawn enough money from the bank to pay your hotel bill and buy anything you and Sali will need?' Edyth placed her hand over her empty sherry glass as Mansel picked up the decanter.

'More than enough, Aunt Edyth.' Mansel refilled his own and Sali's glasses.

'And tonight, you won't drink too much . . .'

'In the New Inn? With Mr Richards watching over me?' He gave Sali an amused glance. 'I think not, Aunt Edyth.'

'I know what happens when young men get together in a hotel bar and just how hot-headed some of your friends can be.'

'You are talking to a sensible, almost married man.' He returned the sherry decanter to the sideboard.

'Well, as this will be the last time that you two will see one another until the ceremony tomorrow, I'll leave you to say your goodbyes in private. I promised Mr Richards I'd call on Mr Horton and his son at four o'clock to arrange payment of Mrs Horton's funeral expenses from Gwilym James's employees fund. I only hope that all the mourners will have left. The poor man looked absolutely dreadful in the chapel this morning.'

'Although Mrs Horton had been ill for years, from the few things Mr Horton said about her, I think they were close.' Mansel gave Sali a quick smile.

'I doubt that I'll be leaving Mr Horton's much before six o'clock, Sali. Would you like me to pick you up at your mother's house or here? On second thoughts, don't answer that question. I'll pick you up here and visit Gwyneth and Morgan with you. They have become excessively tiresome since you moved in with me and it's hardly fair to expect you to face them on your own. Goodbye, dear boy.' She left her chair and stood on tiptoe to kiss Mansel's cheek. 'The next time I kiss you, it won't be a boy I'll be kissing but a married man.' She poked him playfully with her lace mittened hand as he brought her cape. 'Don't be late at the chapel.'

'I'll be half an hour early. Just make sure my bride gets there on time.'

'I will. I'll see you downstairs in Mansel's office at six o'clock, Sali.'

Mansel closed the door behind Edyth and slipped the bolt home.

'Do you think she knows what we do when she leaves us alone?' Sali asked diffidently.

'Possibly, but given what is going to happen tomorrow it hardly matters, does it, darling?'

Sali returned his smile. In the six weeks that had elapsed since he had first made love to her on the riverbank, he had made love to her every time the opportunity arose, and there had been several opportunities since she had moved out of Danygraig House and into Ynysangharad House.

Aunt Edyth didn't watch her anything like as closely as her Uncle Morgan, and as Edyth had never suggested that Mansel relinquish his keys to her house, it had been the easiest thing in the world for him to dine in Ynysan-gharad House, leave at the end of the evening and slip in later through a side door and visit her bedroom after the maid had left for the night.

There had also been several lunches and teas like this one in his rooms above the store and, ever tactful, Edyth had made a habit of leaving early and picking up Sali later in her carriage. She never enquired what they did with the private time she engineered for them, but she had dropped a few heavy hints that she was looking forward to becoming a great-great-aunt on Sali's side and a great-aunt on Mansel's.

He opened the door. 'Shall I take the decanter?'

'Not for me.'

He held out his hand, she took it, and he led her into the bedroom.

If Mansel had noticed that Sali was uncharacteristically silent and submissive during their lovemaking, he never commented on it. The more he made love to her, the less she had come to hope for pleasure, let alone the beautiful experience Aunt Edyth had spoken of. To her it was an act of sacrifice, one she made willingly and gladly because she knew it pleased him. The lectures and sermons her Uncle Morgan had given them in her father's study to prepare them for marriage had detailed a wife's duty as much as the husband's responsibility to care for his family.

Much as Sali disliked her Uncle Morgan, she couldn't argue against his precepts. A wife's vow to love, honour and obey her husband was integral not only to marriage but the Christian faith. And, as she loved Mansel, so it had to follow that it was her duty to obey him, which was why she stood in the stuffy gloom of the bedroom, and allowed him to remove her clothes, prior to taking her to bed.

The best time for her was afterwards, when she lay in his arms, happy simply to be physically close to him, secure in the knowledge that he would make no further demands for a while, and if she were fortunate, not until the next opportunity arose for them to be in private.

'Mrs Mansel James.' He rolled back the sheet, baring her breasts as they lay side by side in the great bed. 'I forgot to tell you, I picked up your wedding ring today. And I have a surprise for you.'

'What?'

'You'll have to wait until tomorrow night to find out.' He glanced at the alarm clock on his bedside cabinet. 'Time to dress and go downstairs.' He left the bed and pulled on his drawers. 'Don't keep me waiting in the chapel tomorrow.'

'I won't.'

'Promise.'

'I promise,' she assured him seriously.

'Keep your word and there'll be a second surprise.' He smiled down at her. 'I'm going to enjoy having a wife to spoil.'

Edyth would not have admitted she was the slightest bit nervous but her hands shook as she checked that her hat, which had been firmly pinned on by her maid only a minute before, was securely in place. 'This is ridiculous, Geraint,' she complained. 'If your mother wanted to see Sali before she goes to the chapel, she should have stayed here last night.'

'Do you really expect Mother to leave Danygraig House when she hasn't even left her room since Father died?' he questioned mildly.

'Perhaps not,' she conceded.

They both looked up as Sali walked down the stairs, an ethereal vision in lace and silk.

'You look beautiful, Sali. The perfect bride.' Geraint picked up the bouquet of lilies from the hallstand and handed it to her. 'Father would have been very proud.'

'I see you've inherited Harry's silver tongue, Geraint.' Edyth deftly rearranged his tie. 'Llinos?'

'Here, Aunt Edyth.' Dressed in her bridesmaid's outfit of pale pink silk, and carrying a posy of pink rosebuds, Llinos left the morning room and ran dutifully to her aunt.

'Gareth?'

He walked in through the open front door. 'The carriages are waiting, Aunt Edyth.'

'Then we'll go on ahead. As you are the man of the family after Geraint, Gareth, you will have the pleasure of escorting two ladies. Well, Miss Watkin Jones?' Edyth blotted a tear with her white kid glove as she looked at Sali. 'Are you ready to become Mrs Mansel James?'

'Yes, Aunt Edyth.' Considering the solemnity of the occasion, Sali felt oddly calm and in control.

'See you in the chapel in ten minutes. You had better leave right behind us if you are intent on complying with your mother's ridiculous order to visit her. Don't let Gwyneth delay you,' she whispered to Geraint as he helped her into her carriage.

'Don't worry, Aunt Edyth, I'll get Sali to the chapel on time,' he assured her, glancing at Sali who was standing in the porch.

Despite her insistence that Sali visit her before the chapel ceremony, Gwyneth barely opened her eyes as the parlour maid ushered Sali and Geraint into her bedroom. Mari, Tomas and the rest of the staff had left the house half an hour before, having been given grudging permission by Morgan to attend their young mistress's wedding ceremony.

'Hello, Mother.' Sali leaned over and kissed her forehead.

Gwyneth waved her hand in the direction of the door. Taking the gesture as a dismissal, Sali backed out of the sick room.

'What does it feel like to be free?' Geraint offered Sali his arm.

'I'll tell you in an hour.'

'The four years ahead of me feel like a life sentence,' he grumbled.

'You've already served six months.'

'And I have eight times as much to go.'

'Is school that bad?'

'School, no.' He wrinkled his nose. 'But coming back here is. You wouldn't believe how awful this house is now that you aren't living here. Or Uncle Morgan.'

'You're forgetting I was here until a month ago. But things may improve. Mansel has promised to start working on Uncle Morgan today. He is going to ask him if you, Gareth and Llinos can spend your Christmas holidays with us in Ynysangharad House.'

'Good old Mansel.' Steering her through the crowd that had gathered at the gate to watch her leave the house, he handed her into the flower-decked carriage and arranged her train and veil away from the opposite seat so he could sit facing her without damaging her gown. They set off up Taff Street and Sali waved to the Saturday shoppers.

'What does it feel like to be almost royalty?' Geraint teased.

'I'll never be that.'

'Mansel is the town's youngest, most prominent, and wealthiest businessman.'

'You know I never think about money . . .' She broke off as a man ran alongside the carriage and tapped the door on the approach to Penuel Chapel.

'Mr Richards?' Geraint pushed down the window. 'Is anything wrong?'

Ignoring Geraint, the solicitor shouted at the driver, 'Drive through the town, turn up Mill Street into Catherine Street, then drive back here via Penuel Road – slowly.' He mopped his face with his handkerchief.

'Whatever's wrong, Mr Richards?' Sali asked in alarm.

'Nothing for you to concern yourself about, Miss Watkin Jones,' he said unconvincingly.

'Please, stop for a moment,' Sali ordered the driver. 'Mr Richards, is it my aunt?'

'It's Mr James; someone has gone to the rooms above the store. He's overslept. Slowly, driver,' Mr Richards ordered the coachman. 'I don't want to see you back here for ten minutes. Better Mr James wait than you, Miss Watkin Jones. And don't worry. You'll both be laughing about this tonight.' He stepped away from the carriage. Sali looked back but they were passing the burial ground behind the chapel. She caught a glimpse of her father's tombstone and Mrs Horton's flower-decked grave behind it. Then the driver whipped the horses and they moved on.

CHAPTER SEVEN

Sali raised her head and stared at the gilded French carriage clock set in the exact centre of her aunt's mantelpiece. The hands hadn't moved since the last time she had looked at them. She felt as though she was condemned to remain locked in this moment and place for ever. Half past ten in the evening in her Aunt Edyth's drawing room.

Jenkins routinely closed all the drapes in the house at nine o'clock in summer, but ignoring Morgan's, and even Geraint's protests, Edyth had ordered that all the curtains in the house be left open and all the lamps lit. Even Geraint's argument, that people curious about Mansel's disappearance on what should have been his wedding day, might gather outside the grounds to look in through the windows, could not dissuade her. Sali understood why. If – no, not if, *when* Mansel returned, he would walk up the sweeping carriage drive to the house and see them sitting, waiting for his return.

The clink of silver against china shattered the soul-crushing silence that had fallen over the room and Sali turned to see her Uncle Morgan pour himself a second cup of the tea he had requested Edyth send for, and only he had drunk. She looked anxiously at her aunt, who had remained slumped in her favourite chair next to the fire ever since they had returned from chapel at midday. Shell-shocked, grey and withdrawn, Edyth James had aged years in the space of a few hours.

Geraint shifted uneasily beside her on the sofa and Sali gazed down at her hands. She was acutely aware of her brother's presence, and she knew that every few seconds he gave her a surreptitious, worried look, but she couldn't bear to receive any more sympathetic glances or empty reassurances. She and her Aunt Edyth knew Mansel better than anyone and they had both realised from the moment his disappearance had sunk into their numbed minds, that the only possible explanation was that something, or someone, had prevented him from reaching the chapel. She feared that something dreadful had happened to him. An accident or perhaps even worse . . .

'Mrs James.'

Sali sat up instantly alert when Jenkins knocked and opened the double doors.

'Mr Richards, Mr Horton and Sergeant Davies are here, Mrs James. Mr Richards apologised for the late hour but—'

'Show them in, Jenkins,' Edyth cut in abruptly, the strain making her terse.

Sali knotted her fingers. Mr Richards, Mr Horton, Sergeant Davies . . . Not Mansel. But then news – any news – had to be better than the terrifying vacuum in which she and her aunt had been marooned since they had discovered Mansel had vanished.

'Please sit down, gentlemen. Can I offer you some refreshment?' Despite the circumstances, Edyth exercised the manners instilled into her by a lifetime spent in polite society.

'No, thank you, Mrs James,' the solicitor replied for all of them.

Looking distinctly ill-at-ease, Sergeant Davies and Mr Horton sat bolt upright on occasional chairs set back from the grouping of sofa and easy chairs around the sculpted marble fireplace, but Mr Richards moved his seat close to Edyth's.

'Both the town and the store have been thoroughly searched, Mrs James. As far as we have been able to ascertain, no one appears to have seen Mr James since I left him outside the New Inn Hotel last night.'

Logic dictated the answer to her question, but Edyth still had to ask. 'You remembered to look in his rooms above the store, Mr Richards?'

'Yes, I accompanied Sergeant Davies. Mr Horton gave us a set of keys that had been cut for the workmen who had recently decorated them. We found everything in order but there was no sign of Mr James.' Mr Richards shook his head. 'If only I'd insisted he accompany me home from the New Inn last night. I offered him a lift to the store in my cab but he declined . . .'

'The store is only a few yards from the New Inn,' Geraint interrupted, as if Mr Richards had criticised Mansel for refusing to ride in his hired cab.

'We are all aware of the geography of the town, Geraint,' Morgan observed cuttingly. 'Did you find anything of significance in Mr James's rooms or the store?' He directed his question at Sergeant Davies.

The sergeant looked to Mr Richards.

'A note, a message?' Edyth pressed urgently.

'I asked Mr Horton to check the safe in the store,' he divulged.

'Everything was in order,' Mr Horton assured her swiftly, 'apart from the banking. Mr James usually does it first thing in the morning.'

'He hadn't?'

'Not this morning, Mrs James. Of course, we balanced the store's daily takings as usual yesterday evening, and made up the floats—'

'The what?' Morgan questioned.

'The floats, Minister. We make them up at the end of the day and keep them in the safe. First thing every morning the cashiers in the store are supplied with a set amount of money with which to conduct their transactions. It used to be five pounds in copper, ten pounds in silver, and twenty in notes, the amount to be deducted from the takings at the end of the day. However trade has been so brisk lately . . .'

'Basically everything was order, Mrs James, apart from the fact that Mr James hadn't done the banking.'

For the first time in her life, Sali detected a note of impatience in Mr Richards's voice.

'As I was saying, Mrs James, Mr James usually banks the previous day's takings first thing in the morning.' Heeding the hard look Mr Richards sent his way Mr Horton made an effort to stick to the facts. 'When I saw that it hadn't been done, I naturally assumed that as it was Mr James's wedding day he had left that chore to me.'

'There is no sign that the store was broken into,' the sergeant assured Edyth. 'All the doors and windows were secure and Mr Horton noticed nothing out of the ordinary.'

'And Mansel's keys?' Edyth asked.

'No sign of them anywhere,' Mr Richards revealed edgily.

'His clothes?' Edyth sat on the edge of her seat.

'As I am not conversant with Mr James's wardrobe, all I can say is that there are gentlemen's clothes in the bedroom above the store.' Mr Richards had thought it extremely peculiar that two of the dressing table drawers in Mr James's bedroom held women's underwear, but he decided it wasn't the time or place to mention it. 'There was also a suitcase and hat box next to the door in the drawing room.'

'Mansel would have packed for his honeymoon.' Edyth remained on the edge of her seat.

'I hope you don't mind, Mrs James, but I opened both the suitcase and hatbox. Neither was locked and the keys were on the sofa table next to them. Judging by the contents, straw boaters, striped blazers, white flannels and so on, I agree. Mr James had packed for and fully intended to take his wedding trip to Swansea.' Mr Richards glanced at Sali. Although she hadn't joined in the conversation, he sensed she was listening carefully to every word that was being said.

'There is no doubt about that.' Edyth thought for a moment. 'What about personal money? Yesterday afternoon he mentioned he had withdrawn cash from the bank in preparation for his honeymoon, and knowing Mansel, it would have been a considerable sum.'

'Exactly how much would that "considerable sum" have been, Mrs James?' The sergeant removed a notebook and pencil from the breast pocket of his uniform.

'He didn't mention a specific amount, Sergeant Davies, but it would have been sufficient to pay his and . . .' Edyth looked at Sali and made the decision to say the word, '. . . his wife's hotel bill and buy any small luxuries they wanted.'

'We found no money in his rooms,' Mr Richards revealed, 'but Mr James's wallet was full when I met him in the New Inn yesterday evening. In fact I reprimanded him for carrying such a large amount on his person.'

'It was noticeable?' The sergeant poised his pencil over his notebook.

'Yes. I commented on it when I saw him open his wallet at the bar and warned him it was unwise to carry so much money around at that time of night in town. Afterwards, Mr James took a pound note from his wallet and placed it in his pocket before securing his wallet in the inside pocket of his jacket. He explained that he had forgotten about the money and had intended to lock it in the store's safe before meeting his friends in the New Inn but he had been so busy he had forgotten to do so.'

'Could you see exactly how much money was in the wallet, Mr Richards?' Sergeant Davies said.

'All I could see was there were several notes, but I couldn't tell you what denominations they were.'

'You wouldn't like to hazard a guess?'

'No, I wouldn't,' the solicitor replied shortly.

The sergeant scribbled in his notebook. 'I'll check with the bank tomorrow.'

'The Capital and Counties Bank hold Mansel's account,' Edyth revealed. 'If you have any problems getting information from them, refer the manager to me.'

'Miss Watkin Jones, I am afraid that I have to ask you this question and I would appreciate it if you could answer me honestly.' The sergeant turned clumsily to Sali. 'Have you and Mr James exchanged any cross words recently?'

'No!' Sali exclaimed indignantly.

'He was only twenty-four years old, a young man. Some might say, too young for marriage.'

'How dare you!' Edyth rose imperiously from her chair. 'Mansel was looking forward to marrying Sali . . .'

'Please, Mrs James, I am only doing my job,' the sergeant pleaded. 'No one has seen your nephew since eleven o'clock last night. All the witnesses I have spoken to agree that he spent the entire evening drinking with a group of his male friends in the New Inn. It is not for me to criticise my betters. I would be worried if any gentleman of his standing and importance in the town hadn't been seen for twenty-four hours, but his sudden disappearance on his wedding day, coupled with con-firmation from Mr Richards and yourself that he was carrying a great deal of money lends me to think . . .' He faltered under Edyth's glare.

'What exactly?'

'It is my job to consider every possibility,' the sergeant stated simply. 'I am not saying it was the actual case, but if Mr James did have second thoughts about marrying Miss Watkin Jones, it looks like he was carrying enough money to move on from Pontypridd and set himself up somewhere else until things calmed down here. And it is well known that no one thinks too clearly after a few drinks . . .'

'That is a preposterous suggestion,' Edyth dismissed. Mr Richards gripped her arm and lowered her gently back into her chair.

'Forgive me for saying this, Mrs James,' Morgan's soft,

oily voice filled the room, 'but I couldn't fail to notice how much you and my niece wanted this marriage to take place. Didn't you yourself, not Mansel, take over the planning of the wedding?'

'What are you suggesting, Morgan?' Edyth gave Morgan a frosty glare.

'Is it possible that as the day grew closer, Mansel, like many young men I have met in his situation, could have felt trapped?'

'Did Mansel say anything to you about feeling trapped, Morgan?'

'Not as such, no,' he conceded.

'Not as such or not at all? Be careful how you answer me, Morgan Davies,' Edyth warned. 'I brought Mansel up, we were close. He confided in me in exactly the same way that a son confides in a mother.'

'In my experience most young men keep secrets from their mothers. Especially when those secrets do not coincide with what their mothers want or expect of them,' Morgan pronounced authoritatively.

'If Mr James did change his mind about getting married, he would have left the town after eleven o'clock last night,' the sergeant mused. 'I'll send men out to check with the staff in the railway station and the cab drivers.'

'I thought you had already questioned everyone in the town,' Edyth commented irritably.

'His friends, everyone he was with last night, but not all the station staff and cab drivers, Mrs James. Those on last night's shift would have spent the day sleeping.'

'And if you still don't find anyone who has seen him?' Edyth questioned.

'We will have to consider other possibilities,' the sergeant answered evasively.

'Such as?'

'As I recall it was a fine night, he could have gone for a walk along the river bank and fallen in.'

'Are you suggesting that my nephew was so drunk, or

careless, as to go for a walk along the river bank late at night with a full wallet in his pocket, Sergeant Davies?'

'We have established that he had been drinking in the New Inn all evening, Mrs James. It was the night before his wedding. His last night of freedom as it were.'

'Mr Richards,' Edyth turned her attention to the solicitor. Tell me, truthfully, was my nephew drunk?'

'He had certainly had a few drinks,' the solicitor prevaricated.

'Was he, or was he not, drunk?' Edyth repeated. 'If he was . . . if . . .'

'Mrs James . . .' The sergeant leapt to his feet as Edyth fell back in her chair.

Mr Richards lifted Edyth's hand and felt her pulse. 'Would someone please send one of the servants to fetch the doctor? At once.'

Sali left her aunt's bedroom and returned to the drawing room to find her uncle standing alone in front of the fire.

'At last,' he greeted her impatiently. 'I have sent a maid upstairs to pack your overnight things. As soon as she brings them down, we will leave. I will send the coachman for your trunk tomorrow.'

'I can't leave now, Uncle. Aunt Edyth is ill. I only came to see if Mr Horton or Sergeant Davies needed anything.'

'I sent Geraint to fetch the carriage to take you home. And, as there was no point in Mr Horton and Sergeant Davies remaining, they decided to walk back to town with him.'

'Aunt Edyth needs me,' she protested.

'She has servants to care for her.'

'But no family except me. I can't desert her, Uncle Morgan, not after everything she has done for me since Father died. She may need nursing.'

'As does your mother,' he reminded heavily, 'and your first duty is to your immediate family, not a distant relative.'

'Aunt Edyth—'

'Is a distant relative,' he reiterated. 'Do I have to say it?' He moved from the fireplace and towered over her. 'I can see that I do. You have been jilted, Sali. I had serious doubts about allowing you to live with Mansel James's legal guardian, but both you and Mrs James were so insistent that I allowed myself to be overruled. Unwisely as it transpires, now that events have proved those doubts to be well founded—'

'Aunt Edyth was Father's aunt—'

'How dare you interrupt when I am speaking! I can see that Edyth James has allowed you to run wild. You have been jilted,' he repeated forcefully. 'And under the circumstances, it would be inappropriate for you to remain within these walls. Therefore, you will get your coat and hat, summon the maid, check that she has packed everything you need for tonight and leave this house with your brother and me as soon as he returns with the carriage.'

'And if Mansel returns?' Tears burned at the back of Sali's eyes as she mentioned her fiancé's name, but unwilling to give her uncle the pleasure of seeing her break down, she fought to control her emotions.

'As he has been living in the rooms above the store, why would he return here?' Morgan enquired coolly.

'Because this was, and soon would have become his home again. And he'd expect to find me here.'

'You are hysterical, Sali. Go and find the maid.'

'I am of age. I can live where I please.'

'At your own expense. And you have no money.'

'There is my dowry,' she countered defiantly.

'The dowry is payable on marriage.'

The impasse between them shattered as the door opened and the doctor entered with Mr Richards.

'How is Aunt Edyth?' Sali asked.

'That is difficult to say, Miss Watkin Jones. One side of her face and body appear to be paralysed and she has undoubtedly suffered a stroke. As to its severity, it is too early to make a prognosis. What I can tell you, however, is that any recovery Mrs James may make, is dependent on the care she receives. I prescribe total rest, peace and quiet. That means absolutely no noise or raised voices in the house.' He looked from Morgan to Sali.

'I am about to take Sali home,' Morgan informed him.

'I told Uncle Morgan that Aunt Edyth needs me.' Sali appealed to Mr Richards in the hope that he might persuade her uncle to allow her to remain.

'I have sent for a qualified and experienced nurse.' The doctor gripped Sali's hand sympathetically. 'I know how fond you are of your aunt, Miss Watkin Jones, but she needs very special care.'

'The arrangements the doctor has made for Mrs James are for the best, Miss Watkin Jones,' Mr Richards added earnestly.

'Sali?' Morgan looked to his niece.

Realising that there was no way she could fight all three of them, she went to the door. 'I will find the maid.'

Sali meandered through the days and nights that followed in a trance. The only time she showed any sign of animation was when she roused herself from her torpor to search feverishly for Mansel. Then, obsessed and preoccupied, she ignored her uncle's edicts that she remain in the house and walked the length and breadth of the town until exhausted, and mindful of the sergeant's theory, she ended her hunt at the riverbank.

Geraint spent every minute he could with her, leaving her only when she retired to her bedroom for the night, but she was oblivious even to his gentle attempts to draw her back into a semblance of what had been her normal life.

As she counted the days, then the weeks, Morgan tried to bully her into concentrating on her domestic duties. When his shouts failed, he increased her workload. But she ignored everything that he, and everyone else in the house said to her. If Morgan bellowed specific instructions at her long and loud enough, she carried out her chores mechanically, pacing the passages of Danygraig House, cutting flowers in the garden for her mother's room, unaware that Mari and Geraint were dogging her steps and setting her mistakes to rights before her uncle discovered them.

The nights when she was alone were the worst – and the best. On the rare occasions she managed to snatch a fitful sleep, she dreamed of Mansel. She knew it was Mansel, because she recognised his black coat, narrow grey trousers and high-crowned, grey hat, but he was always walking away with his back turned to her. No matter how desperately she struggled to call out to him, she could never make a sound and although she strained to lessen the distance between them, she never quite managed to draw alongside him. But occasionally, just before she woke, he turned his head and smiled; that warm, private, loving smile she knew he kept just for her, before vanishing into a thick grey mist that blotted everything, even her own body, from sight.

Mr Richards called every afternoon to give her progress reports on her aunt's condition, which remained unchanged. And every day she pressed him to repeat his and Sergeant Davies's theories on Mansel's disappearance. But he never had anything new to report. Worn down by her uncle's constant assertion that she had been jilted, she eventually began to believe that Mansel really had vanished into that thick, all-enveloping mist of her nightmare world.

At her uncle's insistence, she followed the routine of the house he had set after her father's death. Punctual to the minute, she joined him, Geraint, Gareth and Llinos for meals in the dining room. She poked at the food Mari set before her with her knife and fork, pretending to, but never actually eating. She replied in monosyllables to attempts to draw her into conversation. She visited her mother's room at the times appointed by her uncle, to plump her pillows, dispense her medicines and read to her, although the words she gleaned from the pages of her mother's favourite books were meaningless.

Even her uncle's reprimands and his vigilant imposition of petty rules and regulations, failed to break through the shell she had spun around herself. As she withdrew from the outside world, she became increasingly obsessed by thoughts of Mansel. She constantly picked over the events of the last hours and days she had spent with him. But even when she was certain that she could recall, word for word, everything Mansel had said to her, and every expression on his face when he had spoken those words, she was no nearer to unearthing a clue as to what might have happened to him.

I forgot to tell you, I picked up your wedding ring today. And I have a surprise for you.

What?

You'll have to wait until tomorrow night to find out. Time to dress and go downstairs. Don't keep me waiting in the chapel tomorrow.

I won't.

Promise.

I promise.

Keep your word and there'll be a second surprise. I'm going to enjoy having a wife to spoil.

It was the not knowing that was the worse. She read the obituaries in the *Pontypridd Observer* of young colliers killed in pit accidents and envied their widows because they had a body to bury. Mari, who was as devastated by Mansel's disappearance as the rest of the family, but who was also addicted to the lurid Gothic romances she borrowed from Pontypridd Lending Library, firmly believed that he had been kidnapped. When two months passed without anyone receiving a ransom note, she dropped her kidnapping theory in favour of Mansel losing his memory, and began to weave elaborate tales for Llinos and Gareth, of Mansel wandering Cardiff Docks in rags with no way of knowing who he was, or where he had come from.

At the end of the first month after Mansel's disappearance, Sali was depressed enough to believe Uncle Morgan's assertion that Mansel had run off to start a new life without her. But although Morgan constantly and cruelly reminded her that she had been jilted, by the end of the second month she no longer cared about her own pain. Only that Mansel was safe and alive somewhere – anywhere. She couldn't bear the thought that he no longer existed. That he lay as dead and beyond her reach as her father.

The doctor insisted that Edyth James remain in complete seclusion for the first month after her stroke and placed a ban on all visitors. As soon as he lifted it, Sali ignored her uncle's edict to stay away from Ynysangharad House and went to see her. But her stolen visits proved pointless when her aunt remained resolutely locked in the coma she had sunk into on the night of Mansel's disappearance.

Gradually, even her bouts of frenzied searching through the town ceased. She sunk deeper and deeper into a lethargic state where nothing registered, not Mari and Tomas's kindness, her brothers' and sister's concern, her uncle's spite, her mother's carping, food, sleep, drink – nothing mattered, until the morning two days after Geraint, Gareth and Llinos returned to school when she was too weak even to get out of bed.

'Leave us, Mrs Williams,' Morgan ordered the house-keeper as he and the doctor walked into Sali's bedroom.

Mari squeezed Sali's hand. The girl lying still and white in the bed was barely recognisable as the happy, vivacious bride-to-be, who had been making wedding preparations only two months before. Skeletally thin, Sali lay on pillows as blanched as her skin. The only colour was in her smoky grey-green eyes and the blue-black shadows beneath them.

'Miss Sali?' Mari whispered earnestly.

Sali continued to stare upwards at the ceiling, immobile, unblinking.

'Miss Sali,' Mari repeated.

'Mari,' Morgan reprimanded sternly.

'If the doctor is to examine Miss Sali, sir, shouldn't I remain?' she ventured, risking a reprimand for the sake of her young mistress.

The doctor muttered something to Morgan but spoke too low for Mari to hear. Morgan moved behind Sali's dressing screen, folded his arms across his chest and stood, staring straight ahead. Mari knew that anyone behind the screen could look through the gaps between the hinges into the room, but as her presence was dependent on Morgan's permission, she dared not make a protest.

She stepped back as the doctor approached the bed and watched anxiously as the doctor took Sali's pulse and laid his hand on her forehead. When the doctor folded back the sheets and unbuttoned Sali's nightdress she expected Morgan to leave, but the minister remained behind the screen, his eyes focused on the cracks between the hinges, as the doctor applied his stethoscope to Sali's chest. Mari blushed in indignation as the doctor opened Sali's nightdress and exposed her breasts but Morgan continued to observe the examination.

The doctor pinched Sali's nipples between his finger and thumb several times. Sali's eyes widened and she looked from the doctor to the screen seeing her uncle's silhouette outlined behind the Japanese paper. Colour flooded into her cheeks and she cried out as she tried to cover herself. Ignoring her embarrassment, the doctor folded the bedclothes to the foot of the bed and slid his hand beneath the hem of her muslin nightdress.

'Bend your knees and open your legs, Miss Watkin Jones.'

'Must I? I . . .'

'Do as the doctor says, Sali.'

Mari bristled when she saw a peculiar glint of excitement in Morgan's eyes.

'Uncle Morgan, I . . .' Sali bent over quickly, grabbed the sheet and pulled it to her chin.

'It might be as well if you leave, Minister,' the doctor suggested.

'I am behind a screen, I am Sali's guardian and given her mother's frail condition, her only active parent. As I am legally responsible for her moral well-being, I have a right to know the facts behind her ill-health.'

'Propriety—'

'The housekeeper is present,' Morgan reminded curtly.

'Mrs Williams.' The doctor glanced over his shoulder at Mari. 'Will you hold Miss Watkin Jones's hand while I carry out an intimate examination?'

Mari's first instinct was to scream at Morgan Davies to leave the room but she remained silent out of concern for Sali. Since her master had died, she and the remaining staff had discovered that Morgan never forgave any servant for answering back. He had no hesitation in dismissing anyone who had not obeyed one of his edicts to the letter, no matter how long they had worked in Danygraig House.

The doctor folded the sheet Sali had pulled over herself, from the bottom of the bed together with her nightdress, and bunched them over her chest. Sali whimpered as the doctor pushed her legs apart and inserted his fingers into her. Mari glanced sideways and saw Morgan's breathing quicken.

'Take a deep breath, Miss Watkin Jones,' the doctor ordered. She squirmed in discomfort and embarrassment. 'There is no doubt about it, Mr Davies, she is with child,' he informed Morgan baldly.

Mari turned back to Sali. She had closed her eyes tightly, but not tightly enough to prevent tears from squeezing out from beneath her eyelids. The doctor left the bed and went to the washstand. Mari immediately pulled down Sali's nightgown and the bedclothes. Morgan moved out from behind the screen and stood at the foot of the bed.

'My niece is carrying a bastard?'

The doctor remained silent.

'When will she deliver?' Morgan's face contorted in disgust and anger.

'Seven . . . perhaps six and a half months.' The doctor poured water from the jug into the bowl, immersed his hands, took soap from the dish and worked it into lather.

'I presume Mansel is the father?' Morgan said to Sali.

Curling into a ball, she turned on her side and sobbed.

'Was that why he disappeared?' Morgan demanded. 'Because you told him you were with child?'

'I doubt it,' the doctor rinsed his hands and shook them over the bowl. 'The wedding was to have taken place . . . seven . . . eight weeks ago?' He looked to Morgan for confirmation.

'Eight weeks.'

'Not even Miss Watkin Jones could have had a suspicion that she was carrying a child at that time.' He removed the towel hanging on a rail at the side of the washstand, dried his hands and dropped it to the floor. 'Needless to say, you can count on my discretion, Mr Davies.'

'Not for long.' Morgan snapped. 'The fruit of her sin will soon be evident for the world to see. I'll see you out, Doctor.'

Mari strained her ears as the two men left the room and walked down the stairs. She caught snatches of conversation and picked out individual words, among them the one that struck terror into every young girl and woman in the town – 'workhouse'. A bastard child brought shame and internment for a working-class woman. For a girl of Sali's class it meant ostracism, disgrace, and at the very least, exile from her family and friends.

Not for the first time since Mansel's disappearance Mari felt a murderous rage towards the young man of whom she had once been so fond, who had brought ruin and disgrace to her young mistress.

'You understand, Mari?' Morgan eyed the housekeeper over his reading glasses.

'Yes, sir.'

'And you are to do what exactly?'

'Not to say a word about the doctor's visit to anyone. If any person should enquire about Miss Sali's health, I am to tell them that Miss Sali has succumbed to brain fever as the result of Mr Mansel's disappearance. Miss Sali is to be kept in her room at all times and no one is to visit her except me. And I am to visit her only to take her meals and see to her needs.'

'Breathe a word of what the doctor said to anyone, Mari, and I will dismiss you, instantly and without a character.'

'Yes, sir.'

'You may go.'

'Sir,' she threw all caution to the wind, 'how long will Miss Sali be kept in her room?'

'Until I make arrangements for her to leave it, Mari.' He opened his Bible on the desk in front of him. 'You are dismissed.'

'Sir.' She bobbed a curtsy and left. Morgan Davies had made his threats but this was one situation where she needed help and there was one person she could trust. Not only with her own life, but that of her late master's family.

'There has to be something we can do, Tomas,' she begged, looking to the butler to solve the young mistress's problems as she sipped a glass of the forbidden sherry he hid in the depths of his butler's pantry.

'What, Mari?' He lowered his voice, although his pantry was at the end of a long flagstoned corridor and they would have heard anyone approach long before they reached the door.

'Miss Sali has friends . . .'

'Plenty,' he agreed, 'but can you see any of them helping her in this situation, particularly the parents of girls her own age? If Mrs James were well, I would visit her, but I met Mr Jenkins this morning at the Post Office when I sent off Mr Davies's mail and he told me that the doctor thinks it unlikely that Mrs James will make even a partial recovery. No one knows where Mr Mansel is . . .'

'There is Mr Richards,' Mari interrupted eagerly. 'He is Miss Sali's joint guardian.'

'And a solicitor, and for all his education and learning, employed by the family, which places him on the same footing as us. You go to Mr Richards with this, Mari, and you'll put him in an impossible situation. He can do nothing for Miss Sali without the consent of her other guardian.'

'She is of age. She can live where she likes. He can take her in and give her a roof over her head.'

'He could, and being a bachelor, he would set the entire town talking.' Tomas held up the sherry bottle. Mari shook her head, emptied the dregs from her glass and pulled a tiny bottle of essence of peppermint from her pocket. She poured water into her glass, added a few drops from the bottle, filled her mouth and swished the water around to remove all taint of the sherry.

Much as she hated to admit it, Tomas was right. With Mrs James ill and Mr Mansel God only knew where, there was no one in the town they could turn to for help. 'We'll just have to help her ourselves, Tomas.' She left her chair and went to the door.

'How?' he enquired bleakly.

'I don't know, yet,' she qualified, 'but there has to be something that we can do. There is no way that Miss Sali is going into the workhouse, that's all I can say. Not while I have breath in my body.'

CHAPTER EIGHT

'Miss Sali, if you don't start eating soon, you will make yourself seriously ill,' Mari reprimanded, deliberately and consciously breaking Morgan Davies's rule that she was to visit Sali only to take her meals and see to her needs. The supper tray she had carried upstairs an hour before remained untouched. The lentil soup, cold and congealing, the spoon she'd laid next to it spotless, and the slices of bread and butter, triangle of cheese and slices of tomato, exactly as she had arranged them on the plate.

'I am not hungry,' Sali murmured distantly, without turning her head from the window that overlooked the garden.

'You haven't eaten a thing in a week. And it's not just you. You have to think of your baby.' Mari braced herself as she broached a topic they had yet to discuss.

'The bastard.' Sali finally looked at Mari.

'It wouldn't have been anything of the kind if Mr Mansel hadn't gone and disappeared,' Mari stated briskly, in an attempt to break through the daze Sali had sunk into since her uncle had confined her to her room.

The door opened and Morgan strode in without knocking. 'Leave us,' he ordered Mari.

Mari picked up the tray and bobbed a curtsy. Morgan had hardly spoken to her or any of the servants during the last week and she was afraid that he might take it into his head to forbid her to talk to Sali, or even worse, ban her from Sali's room.

Morgan closed the door. 'You will be dressed and ready to leave this house first thing tomorrow morning.'

'Where am I going?' Sali asked tremulously.

'You have a choice. You can go to the workhouse, or,' his eyes glittered, 'you can marry Councillor Bull.'

The room spun around her and she grabbed the arms of her chair for support.

'He is aware of your condition and prepared to give you and your bastard a home and his name in return for your dowry.'

She shuddered at the thought of sharing a bed with Owen Bull, of undressing in front of him, of allowing him to touch her the way Mansel had.

'What is it to be?' Morgan demanded.

'I can't marry Councillor Bull, Uncle Morgan. Please . . .'

'A marriage to Councillor Bull would give you respectability and enable your mother, brothers and sister to hold their heads high again in this town. But I see that you are determined to be selfish to the last. There is no need to pack. No workhouse inmate is allowed to keep any personal possessions, not even clothes.'

The degradation of the workhouse was nothing in comparison to the thought of Geraint, Gareth and Llinos being tainted by her disgrace. 'Please . . .'

'You have reconsidered?' he said harshly, when her voice failed her.

'Yes.'

'Pack everything you want to take with you tonight. You will not be returning. I will clear the servants from the landing stairs and hall at five o'clock in the morning. You will not leave this room before then.'

'Mother—'

'Do you think I would allow you to say goodbye to your mother after the shame you have brought on this house?'

Mortified, Sali bowed her head.

He left and Sali heard the key turn in her lock. Even if there had been somewhere or someone she could go to, she was trapped. She rose from her chair and looked around. She didn't doubt for one minute that it would be her last night at home, at least until Geraint came of age and, even then, her brother would probably be too mindful of Llinos's reputation to allow her to return.

She lifted the valise her father had bought for her when she had been accepted into Swansea Training College out of her wardrobe. Made of sturdy leather, it seemed twice as heavy as she remembered. Opening it, she set it on the bed and began to transfer the contents of her wardrobe and chest of drawers. Leaving out one of her black suits and a black blouse for the morning, she packed as many clothes as she could fold into it, before taking a second case from the top of her wardrobe. Her carved wooden jewellery box, a birthday present from her father was empty, all her jewellery apart from a plain silver bracelet watch, still in the bank where her uncle had deposited it, but she packed the box anyway. She ran her fingers along the shelves of her bookcase. Every volume had been carefully chosen and she regarded them as old friends, but she had only two cases and she hadn't room for more than three or four books. She read the titles over and over again, choosing and discarding each in turn only to change her mind. Eventually she settled on an album of family photographs, a copy of *Children of the New Forest* because it was the first book she could recall her father reading to her, *Pride and Prejudice* and the collected works of Lord Byron, which Mansel had bought.

Holding out her hand she gazed at her engagement ring. She remembered the day Mansel had given it to her, the day they had made love for the first time, and tears blurred her vision. If only she had fought him off, asked him to wait until they were married, would he have still disappeared? Why had he left her?

Her mind buzzing with unanswerable questions, she tried to concentrate on practical matters. If she left the ring, she would never see it again and no man, let alone a chapel deacon like Owen Bull, would allow his wife to wear another man's ring.

She opened her manicure set and removed her nail scissors. Unpicking the waistband of her skirt, she cut the thread of the button. Slipping the ring into the band, she sewed the button in the centre of it and stitched back the waistband. She couldn't bear to be parted from the ring but she knew that from tomorrow, she would never be able to wear it openly again.

Sali woke to the unmistakeable sound of the key being turned in the lock outside her door. Panic stricken, she sat up. Her uncle had told her to be ready at five . . . she looked around confused. It was still dark and dawn broke at four o'clock in August. She couldn't have slept late . . .

'Who is there?' she cried out, fumbling with the candlestick and matches on her bedside cabinet. A floorboard creaked as someone walked into the room. Freezing in terror, she dropped the matches.

She held her breath listening intently as the door whispered shut and the key turned in her lock a second time.

The mattress sank as someone sat beside her and a hand closed over her mouth. She clenched her hands into fists and tried to thrust whoever it was from her. A sharp blow to the side of her head stunned her. She clutched the bedclothes to her chest but they were torn from her hands. A second punch to her bruised temple sent her reeling backwards. Red lights flared like sparks from mountain beacons across her eyes.

A hand, damp, fumbling, scrabbled at the neck of her nightgown. She dug her nails in, stripping skin from the fingers that pawed at her lace collar. The hand moved downwards, snapping the lace, wrenching open her bodice and sending pearl buttons flying. One landed on her neck, bruising her.

A cry strangled in her throat as she fought with every

127

ounce of strength she could muster to dislodge the hand from her mouth, but her jaws were prised apart and the hand plunged between her teeth. She gagged at the salt taste of sweat on her lips, reeled at the acrid stench of oily pomade as a face loomed over hers in the darkness.

A sharp crack rent the air and a cool draught blew across her naked body as her nightgown was torn from waist to hem. Slowly, inexorably, she was forced on to her back. Her assailant heaved himself on top of her and wedged his knees between hers. She gasped as he allowed his full weight to drop on her, expelling the breath from her lungs. He pinched her nipples before his fingers travelled downwards, prodding and poking at her tensed body. She made one last effort to push him from her, and received a third blow to the head. Then it was too late.

Desperately trying to divorce herself from what was happening, she closed her eyes and tried to conjure an image of Mansel . . . Mansel walking along the river, the sunlight glittering on his blond hair . . . Mansel asking her to marry him . . . Mansel kissing her . . . Mansel dancing with her in a warm, perfumed ballroom . . . Mansel lying beside her in his bed in the rooms above the store . . .

The images barely formed in her mind before they shattered in the sickening reality of what was being done to her.

She gagged again as he rolled off her and if there had been anything in her stomach she would have vomited. He'd finished using her. She could wash away the sweat, the smell . . . hands closed around her neck, encircling and tightening until she could no longer breathe. There was nothing she could do but grit her teeth and bear it. She could bear it! Bear it . . .

That was her last coherent thought before she sank deeper into the mattress and the bleak respite of nothingness.

When she wavered back to consciousness, she sensed she was alone. She tried to move. Her neck was sore and stiff. Her head and every part of her body ached but the pain was nothing in comparison to the shame and degradation she felt at allowing herself to be raped.

Sali was sitting, waiting, dressed in her plain black suit, her cases packed and set at the foot of her bed when her uncle unlocked her bedroom door. The clock in the hall struck the first chime of five o'clock. She rose as he entered.

He turned to the window, but not before she saw the scratches on his face and fingers, and an unmistakable bite mark on his left hand. Refusing to meet her gaze, he went to the wardrobe and opened it to check that she had emptied it. Carefully, methodically, he searched her dressing table, chest of drawers, washstand and bedside cabinet. She had stripped her bed and folded the linen into one pile, the blankets and bedspread into another and with all the cupboard and wardrobe doors open and drawers pulled out, the room already had a forlorn, abandoned air.

'Leave your cases and follow me.'

The familiar morning sounds of the house echoed from the kitchens and family rooms as she walked down the stairs behind him. The clatter of irons as fires were laid and hearths swept in the dining, morning and drawing rooms, Tomos's footsteps resounding over wooden floors as he opened drapes, the soft murmurs of conversation accompanied by the banging of pots and pans emanating from the kitchen as the cook and maid prepared breakfast.

'Put on your coat and hat.'

Sali took her coat from the hall cupboard, slipped it on and lifted her hat from the rack. She turned to the mirror and was shocked by the apparition that stared back at her. If Mansel were to walk through the door, she doubted he would recognise his fiancée in the old woman she had become in the space of a few weeks. She had lost so much weight, her clothes hung loose on her wraithlike frame. Her face was drawn, pale and so thin her bloodshot eyes glowed unnaturally large, like those of a terrified animal. And her throat and the left-side of her face were black with bruises.

Her uncle opened the front door. Standing behind him, she dropped a letter to the floor addressed to Mari that enclosed another for her brothers and sisters. She put her head down and stepped outside. He closed the door and walked so quickly towards the centre of town that she had to run at his heels to keep up with him. By the time they reached the gates of Penuel Chapel she was breathless.

Four people had gathered outside the chapel railings. Councillor Owen Bull, another deacon she knew by sight, Iestyn the gravedigger and a man formally attired in a bowler hat and an overcoat that was too heavy for the time of year. Morgan nodded to them before producing a key and unlocking the padlock that fastened the gates. Walking up the short flight of stone steps that led to the door, he unlocked the chapel and stood back to allow them to enter. When they were inside, he looked to where Sali stood waiting.

Faint and dizzy, she grabbed the stone pillar at the foot of the steps for support.

He looked away from her.

Forcing herself to put one foot in front of the other, she climbed the short flight of stone steps and walked into the chapel.

'I now pronounce you man and wife.'

There were no smiles or congratulations after Morgan had spoken the words that concluded the marriage ceremony. Owen Bull walked over to the table where the Registrar was sitting and signed the marriage certificate. The Registrar took the pen from Owen and held it out to Sali. 'Mrs Bull.'

Sali reeled as the enormity of what she'd done sank into her mind. Seeing her hesitate, Owen took the pen and handed it to her. She signed her name in the spot the Registrar indicated.

'Witnesses.'

Iestyn gave Sali a shy smile as he stumbled after the deacon to sign his name. The Registrar handed Owen a copy of the certificate, which he folded and placed in the inside pocket of his jacket.

'I will send your cases to your new home with the coachman this morning, Sali. Councillor Bull, Mr Phillips, we have a deacons' meeting at seven o'clock this evening.' Morgan strode into the vestry and closed the door behind him.

Owen looked to Iestyn, not Sali. 'Take Mrs Bull home, Iestyn. Tell Rhian I'll expect dinner on the table at one o'clock sharp as usual.'

'It's nice to get married in the morning. You have the whole day in front of you,' Iestyn chattered as he lurched down the aisle of the chapel alongside Sali. 'We had a night burial a few weeks ago. Owen says it makes for more free time in the day. And it will be nice to have you living with us. We have plenty of room above the shop in Mill Street. There's a parlour, three bedrooms and a kitchen. I sit in the kitchen when I've finished my work for the day. It's warm in there. Rhian sits with me and if she's in a good mood she reads to me. It's nicer when someone reads to you than when you read to yourself. Don't you think?'

Her senses deadened by the devastating events of the night and the surreal ones of the morning, it was as much as Sali could do to nod.

'Rhian was ever so pleased when Owen told us that he was getting married last week.'

'Last week,' she murmured, realising that a wedding, even a hole-in-the-corner one at half past five in the morning, would have taken a certain amount of planning, including an application for a special licence.

'I was pleased too,' Iestyn continued simply. 'It will be

nice for all of us to have someone else to talk to, but it will be especially nice for Rhian because she is the only girl. Me and Rhian are younger than Owen. Our dad was married twice, and Owen had a different mam to us. Dad made him promise to look after us when he died.'

Grateful to Iestyn for talking, so she didn't have to, Sali kept her head down in the hope that no one would recognise her as they walked past the turning to Market Street and Gwilym James.

'I help Owen in the shop, as well as look after the burial ground. I work the sausage and mincing machines and boil the heads to make brawn. Rhian serves in the shop, but Owen is the one in charge. Will you be serving in the shop?'

Sali cringed at the thought of having to face people. Her hasty marriage was bound to set the town talking and when the baby arrived, everyone in Pontypridd would know that it wasn't her husband's. Owen Bull – her husband! What kind of man would risk his reputation for three thousand pounds? She had no illusions that he had married her for any reason other than her dowry.

Sali smelled the river that ran behind Mill Street before they turned into it and her empty stomach heaved at the overpowering stench of rancid meat, rotting vegetation and excrement. She gazed with a sinking heart at the row of crumbling buildings her father had called a disgrace to the town. A sign, 'Owen Bull – Butcher' hung over the doorway of a dingy shop set in the centre of the dilapidated terrace. Above it were two billboards, one advertising 'Milkmaid – all-purpose milk,' the other 'Oakey's Berlin Black' for grates.

The façade was blotched with green mould, the doors and windows too blackened by wet rot to hold any trace of the colour they may have once been painted. The front door, which served as both shop and house entrance, was wedged open with a piece of broken brick, the shop window beside it, patched by a sheet of board. Inside, the shop was on the right and a dark passage ran straight ahead through the building to a back door, which was propped open. Sali glimpsed the grey light of an enclosed yard.

'The *ty bach*, coal house, dogs, pigs and pump are through there.' Iestyn pointed to the back. The shop was open and Sali looked in on a large square area floored with a layer of sawdust. A high wooden counter piled with tin plates of sweetbreads, tripe, sausages, brawn, pigs' trotters and minced offal, buzzed with flies. Behind it, breasts of lamb hung between pigs' and sheep heads, ox tails, and beef hearts. A young girl, about Llinos's age, stood behind the counter, wrapping a liver in newspaper for a woman carrying a baby.

'Rhian, we're here.'

She barely glanced at them. 'Go upstairs, Iestyn. I'll be with you when I can.' If she saw Sali she chose not to acknowledge her, and Sali wondered just how 'ever so pleased' Rhian had been, when Owen had broken the news that he was about to be married.

'Do you want to see the dogs and pigs before we go upstairs?'

'I'll see them later, Iestyn.' Sali trailed behind him up a steep flight of creaking wooden stairs and down a passage into a ramshackle kitchen. A black leaded stove filled the back wall; beside it were two full-size, battered, open metal milk churns that contained water. A peeling, green painted table holding a tin bowl stood below a small window on their left. To the right, an open-shelved Welsh dresser held an assortment of odd bits of china, pots and pans, crumpled pieces of stained paper covered in scribbles, pencils and rubber bands. A pine table, its surface pitted and grooved by years of scrubbing, stood in the centre of the room. Around it were four unmatched chairs, scuffed and blackened by age.

The room was dark and gloomy, and Sali instinctively headed for the window. It overlooked the yard and beyond that the River Rhondda, its waters and banks blackened with coal dust and thick with scum and floating clumps of excrement.

'I can show you the other rooms, if you like.'

The last thing Sali wanted to see was any more of this dirty, miserable hovel, but she followed Iestyn down the passage to the front of the house.

'This is the parlour.' Swollen by damp, the door grated over the floorboards as Iestyn pushed it open. Sali looked in on a cheerless room that contained four upright chairs upholstered in rusty green set around a table covered with a red woollen cloth. In the centre lay a leather-bound Bible. A rag rug had been thrown before the empty hearth, the bare floorboards around it spattered with the tell-tale pinholes of woodworm. There were two framed photographs on the mantelpiece, both of the same man but with different women. On the wall above the fireplace was an embroidered tract – 'Blessed are those that are undefiled in the way; and walk in the law of the Lord. Psalm 119'.

'My mother sewed that,' Iestyn informed Sali proudly.

Undefiled in the way. Sali didn't doubt that Owen Bull regarded her as defiled. She walked to the window and looked down on the street.

'Rhian's room is here.' Iestyn closed the parlour door, turned down another passage and opened the door on a tiny room, just big enough to hold a truckle bed, chair and chest of drawers that did double service as a washstand. 'Mine is here.' He opened another door and showed Sali an identical room and she realised that one room had been divided to make the two sleeping cubicles. 'You'll share with Owen,' he informed her artlessly, 'married people do, and Owen sleeps down here.' He ambled back down the passage, turned a corner just before the kitchen and walked along another shorter passage. He opened the door but remained outside.

An old-fashioned double brass bedstead covered with a patchwork quilt blocked a window that overlooked the yard.

'It was Mam and Dad's bedroom when they were alive. In those days, Owen and I shared a bed.' His face brightened as he closed the door. 'Would you like a cup of tea? Rhian showed me how to make it and now she says I make a better pot of tea than her.'

Exhausted by his incessant chatter, Sali said, 'Yes, please.'

'You sit next to the fire. It's warm there.' He pointed to the only easy chair in the kitchen as they returned to the room. 'That used to be my mother's chair.' He gave her another of his broad, childlike smiles as he lifted the kettle from the stove. 'It is good to have someone else to talk to.'

At one o'clock Rhian raced up the stairs and into the kitchen. Physically and emotionally drained, Sali was still sitting in the easy chair and Iestyn was standing in front of the green painted table. He had heated water from one of the milk churns on the stove, and poured it into the tin bowl so he could wash their cups.

'Have you put the stew on for Owen's dinner?' Rhian asked.

'I'm sorry, I didn't know I had to.' Sali sat up in the chair.

Rhian opened one of the hot plates with a pair of iron tongs and heaved a heavy pan from the back of the stove to the front, setting it to boil. 'I don't know what you're used to, but we've no maids here to wait on us and Owen expects everyone to pull their weight. He dismissed a woman who helped in the shop yesterday because he wants you to take over the housework so I can work in the shop full-time.'

'You have no help in the house?' Sali quailed at the thought of keeping house, not only without help, but also none of the conveniences she had taken for granted in Danygraig House, like running water and a sink in the kitchen.

'None.' Rhian took a wooden spoon from a jar on the

dresser, lifted the cover from the pan and stirred the contents. 'Haven't you run a house before?'

'We had a housekeeper.'

'So you're not used to housework.'

'No.'

'I could help you get organised,' Rhian offered, relenting at the stunned expression on Sali's face. 'It's not that hard once you get into a routine. Here, Iestyn, you lay the table the way I taught you, for four mind, and soup not dinner plates, while I talk to Sali. You don't mind me calling you Sali?' she asked. 'Mrs Bull sounds odd when you're my sister-in-law, even though you are years older than me.'

'How old are you?' Sali asked, disconcerted by hearing her new name a second time.

'Twelve, but I've been running the house and helping in the shop since Dad and Mam died of scarlet fever four years ago.'

'That must have been hard,' Sali sympathised.

'At first,' Rhian agreed, 'especially when Owen used to get cross when I forgot to do something important like clean his shoes or iron his Sunday shirt in time for chapel. But I got used to it. It helped when I wrote down everything that needed doing.' She opened a drawer in the dresser and pulled out a schoolbook and pencil. 'You can look at it, if you like. I hated having to leave school,' she confided when she saw Sali reading her name on the cover of the book, 'but Owen couldn't run everything by himself . . .'

'I helped,' Iestyn broke in from the table where he was setting out spoons.

'Yes, you did. If you've finished laying the table you can go down and feed the dogs, Iestyn. I've chopped up their scraps. They are all ready in their bowls.'

'Iestyn told me that you have dogs and pigs.'

'We have two guard dogs for the shop and fatten pigs on the waste from the carcasses. They are penned in the yard but Owen lets the dogs loose after he locks the meat away for the night.' Rhian opened a cupboard door set in the lower part of the dresser and lifted out a loaf of bread, a board and a bread knife. Setting them on the table, she cut thin, even slices. 'Iestyn tries to help but he can't always be trusted,' she warned. 'He is like a child.'

'He has been very kind to me this morning.'

'I think he was hoping you'd be a bit like Mam. He misses her a lot.' Her face fell as the front door opened and closed. 'That will be Owen. You'd better get up,' she hissed. 'He doesn't allow anyone to sit in his chair when he is at home.'

The stew was greasy, more gristle and bone than meat, and the vegetables mushy. It was eaten in silence. If anyone noticed that Sali barely tasted it and only nibbled at a corner of the coarse-grained bread Rhian had cut, they didn't say anything. When Owen's plate was empty, Rhian cleared the bowls and spoons to the green table and set them next to the tin bowl ready for washing.

Iestyn made tea and with a sly look at Sali, added an extra spoonful of sugar to her cup. As soon as it was drunk, Owen left the table, sat in his chair and ordered Rhian to open the shop and Iestyn to sweep the chapel steps and tidy the burial ground. Only when he and Sali were alone, did he finally acknowledge her presence.

'Rhian has told you that you will be running the house?'

'Yes, but I've never run a house without help before.'

'If you don't know how to do anything, ask Rhian. She's been doing it since she was eight years old.'

Feeling chastised and useless, Sali murmured, 'I'll do my best.'

'Your cases arrived, they are downstairs. When Iestyn comes back, ask him to carry them upstairs. Did he show you around?'

'Yes.'

'There are a few things that need to be said, and now is as good a time as any. Your uncle told me that you are

137

carrying a bastard,' he informed her coldly. 'In return for giving you and the bastard my name, I expect you to be a dutiful and obedient wife. Everyone in this house works for a living. I'll make no concession to your condition, which I consider normal for a woman. There are no maids, airs, graces or pampering here. I won't tolerate it. You won't leave this house or enter the shop until after the bastard is born. There'll be enough gossip without you adding to it by flaunting yourself in public. Iestyn is simple-minded but willing. He will fetch whatever you need from town; he knows the shops we deal with. All you have to do is write a note to the shopkeeper. Your uncle told me your father gave you a personal allowance. I believe personal allowances encourage profligacy and squandering. I am the only one to handle money in this house, and I warn you, I check the accounts. If you want anything besides the necessities you will have to clear it with me first, or you may find yourself in the embarrassing position of having to ask Iestyn to return whatever it is to the shop. Do you understand?'

'Yes.'

'Your uncle asked me to inform you that you will not be welcome in Danygraig House and should you try to visit anyone there you will find the door closed in your face. It has been decided that you will not be allowed to attend chapel. The Minister and deacons will discuss your case again after the bastard is born, and your return to the congregation will depend entirely on the sincerity of your repentance and the Minister and deacons' charity. No decent woman, or man will want to mix with you while you are in that condition. Until the birth you will restrict your conversation with my sister and brother to essential domestic matters. I will not have you corrupting their minds. Is that understood?'

'Yes.'

'I believe I detect a note of defiance.' He glared at her through small, brown eyes, sunk deep in the fleshy folds of his round face.

'It wasn't intentional.'

'Your uncle told me that you have a devil in you. But I warn you there's no point in trying to exercise your wiles here. We have been warned and are on the alert. Is there anything you want to ask me?'

'Yes.' She steeled herself to look at him. 'Why did you marry me?'

'Out of respect for your uncle and Christian charity. You have fallen, and are carrying the fruit of your sin, but our Lord Jesus Christ believed no one to be beyond redemption. However, I will not tolerate a second moral lapse. You have sinned once, should you sin again, I will turn you out naked into the street. Is there anything else you would like to say?'

'No,' she whispered.

'Not even gratitude for marrying you?'

'Thank you,' she repeated dismally, looking down at the worn wedding band he had placed on her hand in the chapel.

'That was my mother's. She was a good Christian woman and I'll expect you to honour it and my charity.' He left his chair. 'I'll be back at seven o'clock for my tea. After you have cleaned and tidied this room, you may familiarise yourself with the house. Do not open your cases or remove anything from them. I will inspect your things later.'

After Owen left, Sali looked around for a slop pail she could empty cold water into. She found one in the corner, then filled the kettle as Iestyn had done, from one of the milk churns with a soup ladle. As she set it on the hob to boil, she thought of the pump in the kitchen of Danygraig House and hoped she wouldn't be expected to carry the milk churns down to the yard to fill them.

When she had washed and put away the dishes and cutlery and tidied the kitchen to the best of her ability, she lifted the slop pail. It was heavy, but she struggled down the stairs, stopping three times on the way to rest and catch her breath.

The stink in the yard was even more overpowering than it had been in the street. Two huge black dogs started barking as soon as she stepped outside. She retreated into the passage until she was sure that they were securely penned into a corner behind high wooden railings. The pump was next to the back door; beside it were a coalbunker and woodshed. The pigpen and a small wooden hut, she presumed was the *ty bach* were at the bottom of the yard built over the riverbank. But she couldn't see a drain to dispose of the slops.

'We throw the slops down the *ty bach*.' Rhian stood behind her in the doorway. 'Everything from there goes straight into the river. Just watch out for the rats.'

'The rats,' Sali echoed faintly.

'They come up from the river. If you're not careful, they can give you a nasty bite.'

Sali brushed the back of her hand across her forehead and picked up the pail again.

'Have you emptied the chamber pots in the bedrooms?'

'No.' Sali's stomach heaved at the thought.

'It's a pity Iestyn is at the graveyard. He will help with the slops if you ask him. And if he hasn't too many other things to do, he'll carry up the wood and coal and top up the water in the milk churns first thing in the morning. There are a couple of big jugs in the pantry that we use to fill them.'

'Then you don't carry the churns?'

'I doubt even Iestyn could lift one of them if it was full.' Rhian glanced behind her. 'I have to go, there's someone in the shop.'

'Wait,' Sali shouted. 'Owen said he wants his tea on the table when he gets in. What should I do?'

'It's all in the book,' Rhian called over her shoulder as she returned to the shop.

EVERY DAY: Sweep and scrub the pavement outside the shop, the backyard and the passage to the shop. Clean the dog, pigpens, and *ty bach*. Check there is newspaper in the *ty bach* (after Owen uses it). Empty all slops from the bedrooms and kitchen, and top up milk churns with water. Fill coal bucket and wood cupboard. Make the beds. Clean the kitchen, rake out the ashes and blacklead the stove. Scrub the larder floor and wash down all the shelves with soda and water. Scrub the meat safe in the house and all the meat safes in the shop. Wash out all cloths used in shop and kitchen and boil in soda and water. Check supplies and shop for anything that is missing. Last thing at night check Owen's shoes are clean and he has a clean collar, handkerchief and white overall for the morning and there are no bloodstains on his clothes. Sprinkle chloride of lime into the soak away below pump. Soak all the cloths used in the shop overnight together with any stained aprons and overalls.

MONDAY: Strip and re-make the beds with clean sheets. Collect and do all the washing. Sweep and dust every room, scrub the kitchen and *ty bach* floors and walls with the leftover washing water.

TUESDAY: Ironing, bread and stew making. Baking. Jam to be made in season.

WEDNESDAY: Clean the entire house, sweep and wash down all the floors in the house.

THURSDAY: Beat all mats and rugs, bread and stew making, baking. Jam in season.

FRIDAY: Wash the windows, do the shopping, allow range to go out in kitchen, take apart, blacklead all parts (even those not seen) and relight.

SATURDAY: Bread making and baking, make rissoles, prepare vegetables for Sunday dinner. Heat water for baths. Scrub out bath after use and hang back on yard wall.

SUNDAY: The only work to be done is the Sunday dinner.

Breakfast every day is porridge, tea, toast, margarine and jam.

Monday: Dinner – leftover joint to be eaten cold with fried leftover vegetables and gravy; tea – boiled eggs for Owen, bread, jam and cheese.

Tuesday: Dinner – stew, bread and tea; tea – beefsteak for Owen, tripe and onions.

Wednesday: Dinner – stew, bread and tea; tea – pork cutlet for Owen, stewed calf brains.

Thursday: Dinner – stew, bread and tea. Tea – lamb chops for Owen, stuffed beef heart.

Friday: Dinner – stew, bread and tea; tea – fish fillet for Owen, fishcakes and bread.

Saturday: Dinner – fried liver for Owen, rissoles, bread and potatoes; tea – cold tongue for Owen, kidneys and bread.

Sunday: Dinner – roast dinner; tea – cold meat for Owen, bread and jam.

Sali closed the book. Just reading it made her feel tired and after Owen's speech she had the feeling that the notes had been made by a terrified eight-year-old girl who had displeased her brother more than once. What possible chance did she have of doing any better when the closest she had come to housework was to watch Mari and the maids carry out their chores? She would have to begin her married life by disobeying her husband, and going down to the shop to talk to Rhian. It was Tuesday, and she had absolutely no idea what tripe and onions looked like, let alone how to make it. Or how to cook a beefsteak.

CHAPTER NINE

'That's everything.' Rhian yawned and helped Sali push the last of the bloodstained butcher's aprons into a tub they had filled with cold water and half a dozen handfuls of soda crystals, and carried into the scullery behind the shop.

Sali glanced at her watch. It was past eleven and, the only time she had sat down since midday dinner was for ten minutes at the tea table.

Rhian massaged her back as she stood upright. 'Don't forget to clean Owen's boots when he comes in. He can't stand seeing his boots dirty in the morning.'

'What time do you get up?'

'Five. We breakfast at half past so Owen can be at the slaughterhouse by six. The best carcasses go first and he likes to get in early.'

'Thank you,' Sali said, as they climbed the stairs.

'For what?' Rhian asked.

'Helping me. I could never have made that tripe and onions.'

'Ssh,' Rhian lowered her voice, although Owen had yet to return from his chapel meeting. 'Just be grateful that Iestyn was around to keep an eye on the shop for ten minutes while I helped you. It's always slow on a Tuesday afternoon. You won't be so lucky on a Friday or Saturday.' She shuddered as the front door opened and closed. 'That's Owen. Be careful, he's usually in a mood when a chapel meeting finishes this late.'

They went into the kitchen where Iestyn was sitting at

the table looking at a picture book. He hid it under a pile of papers on the dresser before Owen joined them.

Owen swayed and gripped the back of his chair at the head of the table. Taking a prayer book from his pocket, he opened it and squinted at the page. Iestyn bowed his head and stood behind his chair next to him. Rhian moved behind her chair, but when Sali went to take her place, Owen stopped her.

'It is not fitting for one in your condition to ask for God's blessing in the company of the faithful. You may pray alone in the bedroom in the hope that God will hear and forgive you.'

Sali ran from the room.

Sali had washed and changed into a nightdress by the time Owen entered the bedroom. Closing the door he peered at her through half-closed eyes. Her father had drunk whisky and she recognised the smell on Owen's breath. He had obviously moved on to a public house after the chapel meeting and she wondered if her uncle knew his senior deacon drank spirits. As he stumbled to a halt in front of her, she realised that not only had he been drinking, he was as drunk as her brother Geraint had been when he had stolen a bottle of her father's whisky on his fourteenth birthday.

'Kneel, and lift out the chamber pot from beneath the bed.'

She did as he asked.

'Hold it.'

Her hands shook so much when he unbuttoned his trousers and used it that she was terrified she'd drop it.

'Put it back.'

She slid it beneath the bed.

'Have you prayed?'

'Yes.'

'On your knees?'

'Yes.' She didn't tell him that she had prayed for the

return of Mansel and a swift release from the nightmare of life in Mill Street.

'Take off your nightgown.'

Sali stared at him in horror.

'This morning you promised to love, honour and obey me. I told you not to open your cases or remove anything from them.'

'I needed a nightgown . . .'

'And I am your husband and you have disobeyed me. Take off your nightgown.'

Averting her eyes from his, Sali slowly unbuttoned her bodice, lowered the nightgown over her shoulders and allowed it to slip to her feet.

She stared at the floor as Owen walked around her, and although she didn't look at his face, she felt he was appraising her the way farmers did cattle at market. He reached out and fondled her breasts, squeezing them between his thumb and forefinger, pinching her nipples until tears formed in her eyes. 'Open your legs.'

When she hesitated, he thrust his face close to hers. 'You did it for him and you did it in sin.'

'I . . . It wasn't . . .'

'I don't want the details of your whorings,' he roared. 'I am your husband, and I am demanding my rights. Open your legs.'

Stretching her hands behind her, she steadied herself against the headboard of the bed and closed her eyes as his fingers probed inside her.

'Kneel on the bed.'

She bent to pick up her nightgown.

'Leave it! Kneel on the bed.'

Too terrified to protest, she did as he asked.

She sensed him moving behind her, heard the rustle of cloth as he removed his clothes, felt the warmth emanating from his body and smelled the sour stench of his unwashed skin as he moved close to her. Grasping her by the waist, he plunged himself into her. She cried out in pain and humiliation as he continued to hold her in a vice-like grip, using her until, what seemed like hours later, he eventually grunted and withdrew. But there was no respite. Knotting his fingers into her hair he forced her head down on to the worn patchwork quilt.

'Forgive me, God, for succumbing to the lures and sinfulness of this Jezebel. I am but a man.' He tugged painfully at her hair and stretched out to reach for something behind the bed.

She screamed as the buckle end of his leather belt whipped down on to her bare back. Seconds later it landed on her naked flesh again – and again and again . . .

'Owen, please stop,' she begged thickly.

'One day and already I have lost count of the number of times I have had to remind you of your duty. A wife must above else obey her husband. You have sinned and you have caused me to embrace the sin of lust.'

'For God's sake, we are married . . .'

'For God's sake, a dozen strokes, to drive the devil's wickedness from you. Another dozen to teach you not to use the Lord God's name in vain, and another dozen to teach you not to lead me into temptation.'

Her senses dulled by pain she barely heard the clatter after he delivered the final blow and dropped the belt to the floor.

'Leave the bed.'

She crawled upright.

He took a coarse grey blanket from the wardrobe and tossed it to her. 'A whore is unfit to share the bed of a decent, God-fearing man.'

'Where do I sleep?' she whispered hoarsely.

'At the foot of the bed.'

Hours later, curled into a tight foetal ball of agony, she was still crying for Mansel, her baby, but most of all herself.

Sali was on her hands and knees scrubbing the passage-way when Owen returned to the house the following afternoon.

'Join me in the bedroom.'

The cuts and bruises on her back, buttocks and thighs burned agonisingly to life as she rose to her feet and followed him. He had opened her case and valise and spread their contents over the bed she had made that morning.

'You will have no need for the extravagant luxuries of your past life here.' He handed her a brown parcel. 'Open it.'

She fumbled with the knots and unfolded the paper. She lifted out two shapeless grey flannel smocks of the kind Rhian wore. They were virtually identical to the workhouse uniform and she wondered where Owen had acquired them. Below the smocks were two brown canvas overalls, a couple of calico nightgowns and two sets of coarse woollen underclothes and stockings.

'I want to see you in those clothes and no others from now on. Understood?'

'Yes.'

'Yes, Owen, and thank you. I have seen precious little of your gratitude as yet.'

'Yes, Owen, and thank you,' she repeated mechanically.

'These,' he grabbed a handful of the silk and lace lingerie Mansel had given her, 'are degenerate and sinful.' He dropped them into the case. 'Give me everything else.'

One by one she handed him all the underclothes, dresses, suits, skirts, pullovers, cardigans, nightgowns and blouses she had packed the day before. They filled the case. He closed it, carried it to the door, set it down and returned to the bed.

'Your coat, mufflers, shawls, gloves and hats.' Seeing her reluctance, he barked, 'You will not be leaving this house, so you will have no need for outdoor clothes.'

She handed them to him and he dropped them into her valise. 'Your spare boots and the clothes you are wearing.'

She thought frantically of an excuse she could make to

keep the suit she had on, which had Mansel's ring sewn beneath the button. 'May I keep the clothes I am wearing, Owen?' she pleaded. 'My mother's health is delicate and I might need mourning clothes ... for the funeral,' she added, bracing herself for an outburst, or a blow.

'You may wash the clothes you are wearing and parcel them up and place them in the drawer. But you may not under any circumstances wear them without my approval.'

'Thank you, Owen,' she mumbled sincerely, elated at the thought of keeping the ring.

'Your watch and your spare boots.'

She passed him her boots and unclipped the silver bracelet watch her father had given her. She dropped it into Owen's palm, drawing comfort from the knowledge that her uncle had placed all the jewellery her father, brothers and Aunt Edyth had given her over the years in the family bank box.

She stood and watched Owen pack her empty jewellery box and perfume bottles. The only things left on the bed were her books and the photograph album. Slowly, deliberately, he took her leather-bound album and placed it in the valise.

'No! Please!'

'Obedience! Your family have disowned you. It would be inappropriate for you to keep any mementoes of your past life.' Grabbing the books, he threw them on to the album.

He picked up the valise, walked to the door and lifted the suitcase. 'When I return, I will expect to find you wearing clothes suitable to your station.' He left the room and a few seconds later she heard his footsteps on the stairs.

She grabbed the headboard so hard the brass rail dug into her fingers, leaving dents in her skin. Owen was right, she no longer needed finery, but it was hard to see him walk away with every single reminder of her past life. She slid her hand around the waistband of her skirt. Except one.

Four weeks after her wedding, Sali was kneeling on the kitchen floor attacking coal smears in front of the range with a scrubbing brush, bucket of water and washing soda. She was exhausted, sick to the pit of her stomach and every time she raised her head, the room spun around her, but she continued to scour as though her life depended on the removal of the stains. She didn't even pause as she checked the time on the grease-stained face of the clock. She had barely an hour to finish cleaning the kitchen before Owen came home for dinner and she was determined not to give him cause to find fault with her – again.

One month in Mill Street had transformed her life. She followed the routine of housework Rhian had set down without question or thought. She collected and emptied slop buckets, cleaned the dog and pig pens, used brushes to chase away the rats that occasionally left the yard for the upper storey of the house, scrubbed, cooked, laundered and mended until her hands were as sore and calloused as the kitchen maid's in Danygraig House. When she had time to consider her position, which wasn't often, she envied that maid. Bullied by Cook and Mari, she at least had her duty defined and a few hours off a week to call her own.

She had also become accustomed to refer to 'lunch' as 'dinner', regard the itchy, shapeless Welsh flannel smock, heavy cotton overalls and ugly woollen stockings as normal wear, and to check the time constantly, because every hour of her day and night was earmarked to run the house and service Owen Bull's demands.

Owen did not spend much time in the shop and the rooms above it, but his presence dominated the household. He was Master, King and God in one. Nothing was done or said between her, Rhian and Iestyn without them bearing Owen and his rulings in mind. Every minute they stole to read anything other than the Bible, or spent in conversation that wasn't related to him or the house, engendered a feeling of guilt.

Every weekday morning he jointed the carcasses he brought from the slaughterhouse in the yard, and supervised Iestyn's mincing and sausage making from the offal, tails, hooves and ears of the animals. He also oversaw Iestyn's boiling of the brawn, checked Rhian's entries in the ledgers after tea every evening, and collected his customers' payments on pay nights, but he left the actual running of the shop to Rhian. His life revolved around committee and council meetings, and organising town council and chapel affairs.

Sali had cause to be grateful to the council and chapel. Their business took Owen from home most evenings. The single evening he had spent at home since their marriage, he had ordered her to lay and light a fire in the parlour and sat in solitary splendour reading his Bible while she, Rhian and Iestyn remained in the kitchen. Rhian was furtively reading *Pride and Prejudice*, which Iestyn had borrowed from the lending library on Sali's recommendation, and which Rhian kept hidden beneath her mattress. And Iestyn, who was pathetically grateful for any attention shown to him, was happy if she could spare the time to read to him from the books he smuggled into the house from the library. And when she had no free time, he delighted in simply talking to her.

Already, she dreaded some nights more than others. Fridays and Saturdays were the worst. Owen didn't return until the small hours and she had discovered that the later he came home, the stronger the smell of whisky on his breath and tobacco smoke on his clothes. On the first Friday, tired of waiting for him, she had tried to go to the bedroom, but Rhian and Iestyn had warned her that Owen would be furious if they didn't wait up for him.

When he finally walked in, he was as drunk as he had been on their wedding night. He found fault with the house and when they were alone in the bedroom, reached for his belt, although he had never again given her as many strokes as he had on their first night together. The beatings were easier to bear than his demands for 'his rights'. She no longer even tried to protest that she was too ill or tired. Attempts to dissuade him inevitably culminated in a more vigorous and brutal attack than when she submitted without protest. Either way, the result was the same; she was left battered, bruised, degraded and resentful that the respectability her uncle had bought for her had come at the price of marriage to Owen Bull.

Hearing footsteps on the stairs a full hour before Owen's dinnertime, she jumped up, set the stew pan on the hob, and returned to her scrubbing. Owen had pointed out the marks to her that morning and complained the house was looking neglected under her care. He would be furious if he returned to find the floor still dirty, and his fury meant a beating with his belt . . .

'Sali,' Owen stood in front of her, his blood and mud-stained boots planted firmly on the boards she had just scrubbed, 'you have a visitor.'

She wiped her hands on her overall and rose. Mr Richards stood behind Owen, his opinion of his surroundings evident from his shocked expression, but he recovered sufficiently to remove his hat and offer her his hand.

'Mrs Bull, I had hoped to see you sooner to congratulate you, but your husband said you were too busy to receive visitors.'

She checked her hands. They were chapped, bleeding and grimy from constant immersion in water, soda and chloride of lime, her nails were cracked and split, and her arms to her elbows were covered in a film of dirt. 'My hands aren't clean, Mr Richards.' She went to the tin bowl on the stand and washed them. 'Would you like a cup of tea?'

'No, but thank you for asking, Mrs Bull.' He turned to Owen. 'May I speak to Mrs Bull alone?'

'Being a bachelor, you may not realise there is a sacred bond between husband and wife, Mr Richards.' Owen sat in the only easy chair. 'My wife has no secrets from me.'

'Please, won't you sit down?' Sali pulled two chairs out from the table. Mr Richards sat on one and looked expectantly at her. Steeling herself, she winced as the hard wooden seat pressed against her cuts and bruises.

He looked intently at her. 'As your solicitor as well as legal guardian, Mrs Bull, I have to ask you if this marriage was of your own volition.'

Acutely conscious of Owen monitoring every word being said, she murmured, 'Yes.'

'You are aware of the dowry your father left you?'

'Yes.'

'Mr Bull has applied for it to be paid to him. I suggested that it should be used to set up a trust fund for you and any children of this marriage.'

'A suggestion I am opposed to,' Owen interrupted. 'I am head of this household and I handle my family's financial affairs.'

'Are you happy with that arrangement, Mrs Bull?' Mr Richards probed gently.

Mr Richard's caring concern coming after a month of contempt, hostility and abuse from Owen was more than Sali could bear. She stifled a sob.

'As you see, Mr Richards, my wife is incapable of conducting a normal conversation, let alone making a considered decision about her financial affairs.'

'Your wife looks ill, Mr Bull,' Mr Richards commented tersely.

'I agree, but without a maid to fuss over her, she has let herself go. Most days, I or my sister have to remind her to wash herself and comb her hair.'

Ashamed and embarrassed of her filthy state and unkempt hair, Sali tried to brush it away from her face with her fingers. 'I am all right, really, Mr Richards,' she protested unconvincingly, terrified of what Owen might do to her after Mr Richards left, if she said anything else.

'Are you?' Mr Richards gazed at their miserable surroundings.

She wondered if her Uncle Morgan had told Mr Richards why he'd married her off so suddenly. Surely it had to be blatantly apparent to everyone in Pontypridd by now. Bitterly ashamed of her state and her condition, unable to lie to a man she had known and respected all her life, she gazed down at her lap.

'You assured me that once you had seen and talked to my wife, you would release her dowry. Well, you have seen her.' Owen left his chair, effectively putting an end to the visit.

'You are determined to ignore my advice about setting up a trust fund, Mr Bull?' Mr Richards made one last attempt to persuade Owen to change his mind.

'From my understanding, my wife's late father attached no conditions to the payment of the dowry.' Owen towered over the elderly man seated at his table.

Refusing to be intimidated, Mr Richards left the chair and faced Owen. 'You may pick up the cheque from my office next week.'

'I have already waited one month. It would suit me to receive it sooner.'

'The late Mr Watkin Morgan invested the money in a high-interest fund that requires notice.'

'There is interest to be paid?' Owen puckered his lips and his small, mean features disappeared into folds of fat.

'None,' Mr Richards replied flatly. 'The money in the investment account has been set aside to cover family trusts and dowries besides Mrs Bull's. The three thousand pounds is a single, once only payment, which is why I consider it vital you set up a trust fund.'

'I will decide how best to support my wife, Mr Richards.'

'None of us knows what lies ahead, Mr Bull.'

'How is my aunt?' Sali enquired, desperate for news but even more concerned that Mr Richards didn't provoke Owen any more than he already had.

'Of course, you wouldn't know, Mrs Bull.' He smiled at her. 'She is out of her coma. Her speech is affected and she has limited movement in her right arm, but the doctor is cautiously optimistic that she will make progress. She will never be quite the same as before, but he is confident of a partial recovery. She would be delighted to receive a visit from you.'

'My wife does not go out into society, Mr Richards.'

'Surely a visit by your wife to her aunt cannot be classed as going out into society, Mr Bull?'

'Given my wife's circumstances, it is out of the question,' Owen snapped.

'Please, Mr Richards,' Sali begged, 'tell Aunt Edyth that I was asking after her and give my love.'

'I will.' Mr Richards took his hat from the table and placed it on his head. 'As Mrs Bull's guardian, may I call on her, again, Mr Bull?'

'My wife is of age, and no longer requires a guardian to oversee her affairs, so any visit would be inappropriate, Mr Richards. As you see, her circumstances have changed. We live very quietly and simply.'

'If you ever need anything, anything at all, Mrs Bull, you know where to find me.' Mr Richards took her hand into both of his and shook it warmly.

'Goodbye, Mr Richards, and thank you for bringing me news of my aunt.' Sali sank to her knees as Owen closed the door behind him and Mr Richards. Picking up the scrubbing brush, she set about the stain again, in the hope that Owen wouldn't return for another hour, by which time she might have lifted the smears from the unvarnished wood.

'Sali?'

She turned to see Owen standing behind her.

'Whose house is this?'

154

'Yours, Owen.' Her hands shook and her heart beat faster.

'Then why did you offer Mr Richards tea?'

'I didn't think . . .' She fell silent.

'You didn't think! You never think!' He slammed his fist on the kitchen table, sending the cutlery rattling in the drawer. 'I take you into my home. I give you and the bastard you are carrying a roof over your heads. I feed and clothe you. I give you my name and hold myself up to ridicule by conferring respectability where there should be only scorn and disgust. I allow you to live with my brother and my sister, exposing them to your corrupt and sinful ways and how do you repay me?' Red-faced, livid, he glared at her. She knew he expected an answer but all she could do was hang her head. 'Into the bedroom.'

Tears rolled down her cheeks and she hung back.

'Even now, when I am trying to teach you the error of your ways, you dare to disobey me. Into the bedroom,' he repeated.

She led the way; he walked in behind her and closed the door. 'You know what to do.'

Eyes downcast she removed her drawers and knelt on the bed. He threw back her smock and petticoats, exposing her buttocks. Then he unbuckled his belt.

Afterwards, when he was buttoning his trousers, he asked, 'What is a wife's first duty?'

'Obedience,' she muttered, choking back her sobs.

'May God forgive you for your denial of his ways and lead you back to the paths of righteousness. Tonight you will pray, naked and on your knees for one hour. Perhaps that will teach you the humility you so sorely need.'

'Thank you for coming to see me, Mrs Williams. I appreciate it couldn't have been easy for you to get away. Please sit down.' Edyth James indicated the easy chair set across the hearth from her own in her drawing room.

'Will you ask the maid to bring us some tea please, Jenkins?'

Ill-at-ease at being treated as a visitor by one of the gentry, Mari sat awkwardly and looked shyly across at Edyth. The old woman's skin was so pale it was translucent and every vein could be seen beneath its parchment surface. Thin to the point of skeletal, she half sat, half lay, against the pillows propped against the backrest of her chair. Her feet were propped on a stool, her legs covered by a plaid travelling rug, but despite her fragility, there was strength and resolution in the way she held herself and a determined sparkle in her deep blue eyes. Mari suddenly understood why Sali loved her so much. A woman who had the courage to fight a stroke wouldn't baulk at defending someone she loved, even if it meant crossing Morgan Davies.

'How are you, Mrs James?' Mari enquired, as a parlour maid wheeled a tea trolley on to the hearthrug between them.

'Fighting,' Edyth answered dryly. 'Not fighting fit yet, but battling to get there. Leave us please, Davies,' Edyth ordered the girl. 'Mrs Williams will serve me.'

The girl curtsied and closed the door behind her.

'Have you seen Sali?' Edyth asked, as soon as they were alone.

'I have tried, but Mr Bull keeps her in the house. Tomas and I have called in the shop several times, but if Mr Bull sees us he asks us to leave, and he has instructed his brother and sister not to allow anyone upstairs. Unfortunately, we have no excuse to go to Mill Street other than to visit Sali, since Mr Morgan has taken on the responsibility of dealing with the tradesmen and ordering in the household goods.'

'Hasn't Morgan Davies anything better to do than play housekeeper to Danygraig House?' Edyth enquired acidly.

Mari would have loved to have commented, but remembering her position, refrained. 'I tried to give Mr

Bull's sister a letter for Miss Sali but she wouldn't take it.'

'Has anyone seen Sali?' Edyth looked impatiently at Mari. 'I know it's not done for a housekeeper to criticise those regarded by some as her betters, but you have my word that nothing you say within these walls will go any further. This is Sali we are talking about, Mrs Williams. And I know that you are as fond of her as I am.'

'She couldn't be more precious to me if she was my own flesh and blood,' Mari burst out fervently. 'And when I think of the way Mr Morgan spirited her out of the house and married her off to that butcher, I could strangle him with my bare hands.'

'If only Sali had come here,' Edyth murmured disconsolately.

'None of us thought you were going to recover,' Mari observed bluntly.

'Has anyone seen Sali since Mr Richards visited her last October?' Edyth pressed.

'Master Geraint, Master Gareth and Miss Llinos wanted to see her when they came home at Christmas. Mr Morgan wouldn't hear of it and forbid them to go near Mill Street, but Miss Sali did send them a letter on Christmas Day. No presents, just a letter. Master Geraint knew how worried I was about her so he showed it to me. It was her writing all right, I'd recognise it anywhere, but it didn't sound a bit like her and at the bottom of the page there was just one line – "Remember me to the servants." Not a word about Tomas or me, just that.'

'What is the gossip in the town?' Edyth looked Mari in the eye. 'Come on, Mrs Williams, I know Pontypridd, there is bound to be some and if you don't tell me, no one else will. Mr Richards was dreadfully upset when he saw Sali, but he has had no success in trying to see her since. Morgan refuses to visit me and won't allow Sali's brothers or sister here either. That only leaves you and Tomas.' Edyth sank back on to her pillows. 'Forgive me if I'm asking too much, I know you risked your job to come here. It couldn't have been easy for you to get away this evening and I am grateful.'

'Even I am entitled to a night off every fortnight, Mrs James, although to be honest I wouldn't have risked it if Mr Morgan was in town.'

'He's away?' Edyth enquired.

'In Cardiff at a Methodist conference.' Mari poured two cups of tea. 'You take milk and sugar, don't you, Mrs James?'

'Two sugars, please.'

Mari handed her a cup of tea, took one of the crumpets and set it on a plate.

'My appetite isn't what it used to be, but don't let that stop you from eating,' Edyth demurred.

'It doesn't seem right to eat in front of you, Mrs James.'

'Please, you do me an honour by being my guest, Mrs Williams. I am not short of visitors but I have no one, apart from Mr Richards, with whom I can discuss Sali.'

'I've heard that Miss Sali and Mr Bull's sister live in fear of him and it's common knowledge that he bullies his half-witted brother unmercifully because everyone who goes to Penuel Chapel has seen him doing it.'

'Who told you that Mr Bull's sister and Sali are afraid of him, Mrs Williams?'

Mari hesitated before blurting, 'Mrs Hughes, the tanner's wife who lives next door to Mr Bull's shop.'

'She has seen Sali?'

'In the yard, but not to talk to. She told me she looks very poor in all ways and Mr Bull works her half to death. He makes no allowances for her . . .' Mari paused, 'condition.'

'Could she talk to Sali?'

'Mr Bull doesn't allow anyone to go near Sali except his brother and sister. But Mrs Hughes does talk to Mr Bull's sister, Rhian, sometimes. I tried giving Mrs Hughes a letter and money to pass on to Miss Sali but she wouldn't take it, no more than Mr Bull's sister would.

She said Owen Bull watches every single thing that goes in and out of that house like a cat at a mouse hole and if he suspected someone was passing on any extras to his sister or Sali, it would ... it would ...'

'What, Mrs Williams?'

'It wouldn't go well with them,' Mari answered evasively.

'He beats them?'

Mari bit her lip. 'Mrs Hughes said that sometimes late at night and especially at weekends they hear cries coming from the Bulls' house. They even wake the children.'

Edyth clenched her fists. 'And she's never thought to call the police?'

'They wouldn't interfere, Mrs James. Not between husband and wife or a man and his family. And everyone suspects that the baby Sali is carrying is Mr Mansel's.'

'If she is with child, then of course the child is Mansel's,' Edyth said warmly.

'Mrs Hughes said there's no doubt about it. The last time she saw Miss Sali ... Mrs Bull, she was big in the way.'

'If only Mansel were here,' Edyth cried impotently. 'I can't understand where he could possibly be ...' She looked keenly at Mari. 'There is something else, isn't there?'

Mari set down her teacup.

'It's about Mansel isn't it?' Edyth asked perceptively.

'You know what people are. They love to gossip. I for one don't believe it for a minute.'

'What is it, Mrs Williams?' Edyth interrupted. 'Whatever it is, it can't be worse than lying here day after day wondering if he's alive or dead. And if he is alive, what could possibly have driven him away, leaving Sali to face Morgan Davies alone?'

'There's a girl, Mary Jones. She's just come back to Pontypridd after spending two years in London. She used to work in the store. She's not married and she has a three-year old son . . . and . . .'

'And she says the boy is Mansel's.' Edyth's eyes clouded in misery.

'You know?'

Edyth stared into the fire and watched the flames lick around the coals. Mr Richards had tried to shield her, but after her husband's death she had learned to read account books and seen the payments marked in the store's ledgers. Pensions of five shillings a week paid to young women who had worked there for no more than a year or two, when men who had given over twenty years' service to the business left with nothing. Girls she had seen in her husband's office. Girls he had smiled at in her presence and later sworn meant nothing to him.

Her husband had loved her, she never doubted that, but she had been forced to accept that she had never been quite enough for him. And when she had checked the store's accounts eighteen months after Mansel had taken over, there had been two new pension payments carefully detailed and marked 'miscellaneous' by Mr Richards in the hope that she wouldn't pry. But she had pried, and confronted Mansel with the evidence of his philandering. Telling him in no uncertain terms that the example his uncle had set him was wrong and he couldn't expect any decent woman to marry him while he continued to seduce young girls.

He had sworn he would change his ways and shortly afterwards had begun to pay attention to Sali. And there had been no more payments, not in the two years before his disappearance. Years during which he had been totally and completely in love with Sali to the exclusion of all others, she was sure of it.

'I know about Mary Jones,' Edyth confessed wearily. 'But Mansel swore to me when he began to court Sali that he had given up other women. And I believed him. They were happy together and he was looking forward to settling down. But with hindsight, perhaps I should have said something to Sali to warn her in case she heard something about this woman and her child . . .'

'What could you have said?' Mari asked practically. 'And even if she heard the rumours, I doubt that Miss Sali would have thought any the less of Mr Mansel for something he did before they became engaged. Young men make mistakes and the ones with money in their pockets will always turn the heads of pretty young girls with none. It's human nature. And with a young man as good-looking as Mr Mansel . . .' Mari only just stopped herself from saying 'was', 'who is to say who did the chasing? By all accounts this Mary Jones is a right baggage, out for whatever she can get.'

'Do people really think Mansel left town because she came back?'

'Only the ones who don't think. As Tomas said, why would Mr Mansel leave town when he had more than enough money to pay the girl to keep quiet?'

'Mary Jones has been and is being well paid.' Edyth moved restlessly in her chair. 'But this doesn't help Sali. There has to be something I can do. I could visit her . . .'

'You are not well enough to go out, Mrs James, and even if you were, Mr Bull would only turn you away the same he has everyone else.'

'There has to be a way to get in touch with Sali.'

'None that I can see, Mrs James. She never leaves the house. Not even to go to chapel.'

'The doctor,' Edyth said eagerly. 'He must visit her.'

'I doubt anyone down that end of Mill Street can afford to call him out and certainly not for a baby. They make do with a midwife and there are several of those in town. One or two drink more than is good for them and all of them like a good gossip. You give a letter to a midwife to pass on to Miss Sali and everyone in Pontypridd will know about it in a week.'

'If Owen Bull won't allow his wife to receive a letter, perhaps he'll read one from me,' Edyth persisted earnestly.

'Be careful, Mrs James,' Mari warned. 'From what Mrs Hughes told me, an act of kindness to Sali could result in her being treated worse by Mr Bull than she already is.'

'You can't expect me to simply stand back and do nothing while Owen Bull works the girl half to death, while doing God only knows what else to her.'

'No, Mrs James. All I'm saying is you have to tread very cautiously. For Sali's sake.'

CHAPTER TEN

'You have a fine boy, Mrs Bull.' The midwife cut the cord, bundled the squalling baby in a towel and set him on the pillow next to Sali.

Worn out by a thirty-six-hour labour, Sali barely had the strength to hold the child. She cried out softly as she moved the towel from his face. The baby was a miniature replica of Mansel. His soft, downy hair the exact same shade of wheat-blond, the eyes that squinted into hers a deep cerulean blue she sensed wouldn't change, and even his tiny hands had the same long, elegant, tapering fingers.

The midwife took her time over washing her hands in the iron bowl on the cheap, metal-framed washstand. She had believed herself immune to the squalid conditions her poorer patients lived in, but she had been shocked by the state of the rooms above Owen Bull's shop. Considering he was a councillor and deacon as well as a businessman, she had expected better.

The bedroom she had delivered Mrs Bull's baby in was so narrow there hadn't been room for her to move around the truckle bed. The linen was old and darned, there was only one blanket and no provision had been made for the baby beyond a towel. No cot, baby carriage or baby clothes, not even napkins.

Given Councillor Bull's reputation as a God-fearing, Christian man, she had also been taken aback by the scars, cuts and bruises on Mrs Bull's body, but she had seen worse on the wife of another councillor, and she hadn't been carrying a bastard on her wedding day. She reflected that Mrs Bull was more fortunate than some. Her bastard hadn't been born in the workhouse and wouldn't be taken away from her when it was six weeks old.

'I'll tell your husband it's over. I expect a cup of tea wouldn't go amiss. Do you want something to eat?' She dried her hands and went to the door.

'No, thank you.' Sali clutched her baby closer as the midwife's footsteps echoed down the passage. She was engulfed by a sudden, overwhelming wave of love that encompassed every fibre of her being. But she couldn't suppress her tears, not when she thought how different his birth would have been if she had married Mansel and the child had arrived at Ynysangharad House instead of Mill Street.

Owen looked up from his tea when the midwife opened the kitchen door.

'I heard a baby crying.' Rhian left her seat at the table.

'Mrs Bull has had a baby boy,' the midwife revealed flatly.

'A boy!' Iestyn grinned.

'Can I see him and Sali?' Excited, Rhian ran to the door, then looked back at Owen. He gave a curt nod and she opened it and left.

'It's been a long labour. Your wife is worn out. She'd like a cup of tea.' The midwife walked to the stove and warmed her hands. It had been a cold April and the bedroom at the front of the house was freezing.

'I'll make it.' Iestyn jumped up from the table and picked up the kettle.

'How soon before my wife can resume her household duties?' Owen enquired.

'Ten days or so, although as I said, she is worn out and quite weak. But if I know your neighbours they'll be willing to help.'

'I'll have no meddling women in my house outside of

family,' Owen said sternly. 'I'll get help in the shop and my sister can run the house for a week.'

'I couldn't find any baby things,' the midwife said pointedly.

'My wife is in my brother's room. We thought it best she go in there so she wouldn't disturb the rest of us.'

'Then the cot, napkins and baby clothes are in your bedroom, Mr Bull?'

'No. The baby came early,' he muttered. Sali had been begging him to allow her to prepare for the birth for weeks but he had refused. Now the baby was here – a boy ... He left his chair and walked to the kitchen window so the midwife couldn't see his face. It would be unChristian of him to wish the bastard dead. But he was here, in his house ...

The midwife glanced at the clock. 'The shops will all be shut now, Mr Bull.'

'My wife can make do until morning.'

'Only if you have plenty of towels and sheets.'

'I've made the tea, Owen,' Iestyn said proudly.

'You'll want to see your wife, Mr Bull,' the midwife prompted.

Owen took the cup. 'Stay and have your tea here,' he ordered the midwife. 'I'll send Rhian back. You can tell her what we need.'

Owen set the tea Iestyn had made on the floor beside the bed, straightened his back and looked down on Sali and the baby.

'Your bastard is here.'

'Yes, Owen.' There was a peculiar expression in Owen's eyes Sali couldn't decipher and she was terrified he'd hurt her baby.

'It is not easy for a man to accept another's leavings. No other man in Pontypridd would take you and the bastard, and I wasn't the first your uncle asked.'

'I didn't know,' she whispered, wanting to, but not

daring to move her baby out of his reach, lest she provoke him.

'And what with your keep and his, your dowry won't go far. In fact, most of it has gone.'

'So soon?' Her father had told her that she was unworldly when it came to money but three thousand pounds had seemed a vast sum.

'My father left debts, the shop was mortgaged, I have heavy expenses and responsibilities. There are Iestyn and Rhian's mouths to feed as well as yours and now this bastard.'

Unnerved by his strange mood, she shrank back in the bed.

He looked down at the child and moved the towel away from his face. 'He looks like Mansel James,' he pronounced in disgust.

'All babies are born with blue eyes and most with fair hair. Both will darken as he grows older.' She thought of her own and her father's colouring and hoped for her son's sake that he would follow her side of the family, and not his father's.

'I'll not give the bastard any of my family names.'

'I'd like to call him Harry Glyndwr after my father. If that is all right with you,' she added, afraid he would reject the name simply because she had suggested it.

'It is just as well your father is dead. If he weren't, he'd hardly think it a compliment that you want to name your bastard after him.'

Wanting to appease Owen for the child's sake, she almost suggested he name the baby, then realised as he would be the one to register the birth he could put whatever he wanted on the certificate, including 'unknown' next to father if he chose to.

'Before I married you I promised your uncle I would give you a roof over your heads. I am not a man to go back on my word.'

'Thank you, Owen,' she cried in relief.

He stared at the child and again she trembled at the strange expression in his eyes.

'I think something biblical to remind the child of his Christian duty and obedience to his elders.' He thought for a moment. 'Isaac would be suitable. The sacrifice Abraham was prepared to make and would have if it were not for God's intervention and mercy.' When she said nothing, he barked, 'You disapprove?'

'No,' she acquiesced, realising that her son was even more vulnerable than her.

'Then I will register him as Isaac Bull.' He went to the door. 'Everyone in Pontypridd will know that my wife has given birth to a bastard. That is hard enough to bear, but God will give me strength to cope. However, I warn you, I'll kill you and this boy before I'll allow you to drag my name any further into the dirt.'

'I won't bring any more shame on you, Owen, I swear it.' He was threatening her with the life of her baby and there was nothing she could do except obey him, in the hope that he would treat the child more kindly than he treated her.

'You were a spoiled, useless creature when I married you. A good for nothing. You couldn't even comb your own hair let alone run a house.' He bent over the bed and she moved the baby protectively closer as he folded the towel away from his face. 'Keep the child quiet and away from me. I'll expect you to resume your duties in a week.'

'Owen,' she braced herself for an outburst, 'the baby will need clothes and a cot.'

'You think he deserves them from me?' he said venomously. He turned his back and walked through the door.

Rhian carried a bowl of stew and a spoon into Iestyn's room. She stood holding it when she saw Sali sitting up in the bed feeding the baby.

'Your uncle came this morning. He brought things for the baby.'

'My uncle?' Sali trembled at the mention of his name. 'Are you sure it was him?'

'I see him in chapel every week.'

Since Sali had been excluded from the congregation, she had ceased to think of chapel as a place to worship and more as a respite from the treadmill of life. She had to cook the dinner when Owen, Iestyn and Rhian went to morning service, but she didn't mind because as soon as they left the house she was guaranteed two hours to herself. And because of Owen's edict that no work other than the cooking of Sunday dinner be done in the house on the Lord's Day, Evensong meant another two uninterrupted hours, the only two in the week she was free from domestic drudgery.

Knowing she wouldn't be disturbed, she defied Owen's command that she spend the time praying, and read one of the library books Iestyn smuggled into the house.

There were times when she would have gone mad without those solitary hours. But the week since the baby's birth had been a good one. Owen hadn't been near her since his visit just after the baby was born and, as he had forbidden Iestyn to go into his old room, that only left Rhian, who was run off her feet, but never too busy to bring her food, cups of tea, and help her with the baby at intervals throughout the day.

'I made tea for your uncle and Owen. They drank it in the parlour.' That in itself was an event for Rhian. She couldn't remember Owen inviting anyone into the house, let alone the parlour before. 'There's a load of things. I helped carry them upstairs. A cot, baby carriage, clothes and a lovely shawl. I'll get the clothes now if you like.' She slipped the spoon into the bowl, set it on the floor and returned a few minutes later with a pile of baby nightgowns, knitted cardigans, bonnets, shawls and bedding. Sali recognised them. Under Mari's supervision she had even stitched and embroidered some of the nightgowns for Llinos.

Rhian pushed the door shut with her foot and

whispered, 'The coachman tried to give me a letter for you but I couldn't take it, not with Owen around. He asked after you and the baby. I said you were fine.'

'Did he say anything else?'

'There wasn't time, because Owen came with Iestyn to unload the carriage.'

Sali flicked through the stack of neatly folded, newly laundered blankets, napkins and clothes, and suspected the gifts had been Mari's idea. The housekeeper would have known how to get round her uncle. By giving her Llinos's cast-offs, her Uncle Morgan could appear generous without paying out a penny.

It was just as well. Rhian and the midwife had compiled a list of things she'd need for the baby but all Owen had allowed Rhian to get was a dozen napkins and three nightgowns. At night the baby slept in one of Iestyn's drawers padded with a pillow from Rhian's bed.

'Owen said that as they are from your family you may accept them.'

'I will have to thank him.' Terrified for her child, Sali spoke without irony. She lifted the baby from her breast. His head lolled sleepily, his mouth still full of milk.

Rhian sat at the foot of the bed. 'I'll take him while you eat your stew,' she offered, as Sali blotted the surplus milk from his mouth with her handkerchief. 'Make the most of today.' Rhian lifted the baby on to her shoulder and rubbed his back gently to wind him. 'Owen has given notice to the woman in the shop. Today is her last day, but as tomorrow's Tuesday, it should be fairly quiet and Iestyn can keep an eye out for customers when Owen isn't around, so I can help you.'

'I wouldn't want you to get into trouble on my account.'

'I won't.' Rhian looked at the baby clothes on the bed. 'Some of these things are really beautiful,' she said wistfully, fingering a finely crocheted woollen shawl.

'They were my sister's when she was a baby.'

'Don't you miss having nice things?'

'Do you?' Sali asked softly, lowering her voice. Without a watch or clock she had lost track of time and had no idea whether Owen was home or not.

'I've never had any, but when I see girls wearing lovely clothes and shoes I wish I could buy ones like them. Owen says fancy clothes are a waste of money.' She plucked at her flannel smock and canvas overall. 'You can hardly call these pretty.'

Footsteps resounded in the passage and Sali froze. 'Thank you, Rhian,' she said loudly. 'You may take the bowl.'

Rhian deposited the baby in the bed next to Sali and took the bowl. Owen entered and stood silently until Rhian left.

'From tomorrow you will run the house again.'

'Rhian told me, Owen.' Sali wrapped the baby in the shawl Rhian had admired.

'You can sleep in here with the baby for six weeks. When you return to our room, the child will sleep in the kitchen. You may set the cot your uncle sent you in the corner behind the door.'

'Yes, Owen. Thank you for allowing me to keep the things Uncle Morgan brought.' Sali knew there was no point in arguing, or asking for an explanation as to why the baby was to sleep in the kitchen. Owen didn't want her bastard in his bedroom. It was as simple as that. She only wished she had the courage to ask if she could sleep in the kitchen alongside her son; the boards were no harder there than the bedroom.

'Why are you shaking?'

'A sudden chill, that is all, Owen.'

'It is not cold in here.' He looked at her through narrowed eyes. 'The last thing I need is a sickly wife.'

'I will be fine tomorrow.'

'Just see that you are.'

When Owen left, Sali cuddled her baby and concentrated on the good things in her life. Her baby was beautiful and healthy, and she would be allowed to keep him. Thanks to Mari, she had everything she needed for him. And once she was busy again she wouldn't have time to brood over the loss of Mansel, her past life, or might-have-beens.

Any faint hopes Sali had that the birth of her baby might change her life for the better were soon dashed. Much as she longed to leave the confines of Mill Street for an hour or two, she knew better than to ask Owen for permission to visit her Aunt Edyth. And she accepted that her uncle would not allow her to visit even the servants' quarters of Danygraig House. But a walk on one of the hills that surrounded the town where she could breathe in air free from the rancid taint of Mill Street would have been glorious. She even dreamed of green fields and woods, and began to wonder if the only way she would leave the house was in her coffin.

The endless routine of housework kept her chained to the rooms above the shop and the yard that bordered the filthy river. Iestyn continued to place the orders for the household goods, which were delivered by tradesmen and taken in by Rhian, so she never saw anyone to speak to other than Owen, Iestyn and Rhian. When the baby was a month old, she summoned the courage to ask Owen if she could take him for a walk on a Sunday morning or evening when he was in chapel. He flew into a rage, told her there was no way he'd allow her to flaunt her bastard around the town, especially on the Lord's Day, and warned her not to ask again. She didn't need the warning. No matter how little, or what time of the day she angered him, he always vented his rage on her back with his belt at night.

The hardest part of her life was keeping the baby away from Owen. Iestyn and Rhian adored the child and helped as much as they could, because Owen couldn't bear the sight of him. She returned to Owen's room to sleep on the floor when the child was six weeks old. After that, if he cried in the night, it was Rhian or Iestyn who tended him, because no matter how distressed he became, Owen would not allow her to leave his bedroom. If the baby was hungry, Rhian fed him scalded cow's milk, which he sucked from a boiled rag. At first he refused it, within a week he became accustomed to it, and by the time he was three months old, he was sleeping through the night.

When the baby was six months old, Owen insisted Sali wean him, and finally allowed her to sleep alongside him in his bed, but she slept no easier than she had done on the floor. She dreaded the nights he demanded 'his rights'. And the baby's birth made no difference; he always took her the same way, with her kneeling, naked, facing away from him. She learned to endure his intimate assaults on her body, just as she endured his beatings, and, as the months passed, even began to believe his assertion, that considering the magnitude of her sin, he treated her more leniently than she deserved.

Owen never mentioned her return to chapel and after his reaction to her request that she be allowed to take the baby for a walk, she limited her conversation with him to domestic matters. No criminal had ever been incarcerated closer than she was in Mill Street and her son's imprisonment was as complete as her own. The only outlet she had for her emotions was Harry, as she privately called her son. And she lavished all the time and energy she could steal on him. He was not only her pride and her joy, but Rhian and Iestyn's too.

When the child was ten months old he began to walk and they could hold conversations with him. He recognised the pictures she drew on odd scraps of paper Iestyn scavenged. He played with wooden spoons and saucepans, the only toys she could give him, and he learned never to make a sound when Owen was around.

Until the Saturday night when he was two and half years old and Owen came home earlier and drunker than usual.

*

Worn out by the busiest day in the shop, Rhian had fallen asleep. She was sitting at the table, her head slumped forward, buried in her arms. The baby was feverish, hot and exhausted from a chill Sali had blamed the rats for bringing into the house. August had been insufferably hot and they had multiplied and grown bold, frequently invading the upstairs rooms in their search for food. The child had been fretful the whole day and even when Sali finally managed to lay him down in his cot, he whimpered and thrashed around in his sleep.

At nine o'clock Iestyn pleaded with her to read a passage from his latest library book. She had just opened it, when the front door slammed downstairs.

She shook Rhian awake and handed the book to Iestyn who hid it beneath a mound of papers on the dresser. They all looked anxiously to the child as Owen stumbled noisily up the stairs. The last time he had cried when Owen had come home drunk, Owen had threatened to put the cot in the dog kennel.

The door burst open and Owen stood, red-faced and red-eyed in the doorway. 'Get them.'

'What, Owen?' Sali asked nervously. Never logical when drunk, Owen expected her to understand him instantly.

'The clothes I allowed you to keep. And I'll take this.' Grabbing her wrist he wrenched the wedding ring from her finger. She cried out as he sliced her skin and Iestyn was on his feet in an instant.

'Don't hurt Sali, Owen.' He stepped between her and his brother.

'Don't hurt Sali, Owen,' Owen taunted.

The baby's whimper escalated to a cry and Sali backed towards the cot.

'I told you to get those clothes.'

All Sali could think about was the ring hidden in the waistband of the skirt. Her last link to Mansel and the old life that had begun to seem like a dream. But she dared not disobey Owen. She looked to Iestyn. He understood her and moved protectively closer to the cot. When she returned with the brown paper parcel that held her suit, Iestyn was still standing between Owen and the cot. Rhian had retreated to the corner next to the window in the hope of remaining unnoticed.

Sali folded her arms across the parcel, clutching it to her chest. 'It's my last good suit, Owen.' She knew she shouldn't have said the words as soon as they were out of her mouth, but all she could think of was the ring, and the loving expression on Mansel's face when he had slipped it on to her finger. She hadn't even seen it since she had sewn it into the skirt, but losing it was like losing Mansel a second time.

'Hand it over.' The baby whimpered and Owen turned to the cot.

'Take it.' She thrust the parcel at Owen.

'Take it? It's not yours to give, whore! All you ever do is defy me.'

Sali watched mesmerised as Owen drew his arm back, but drunk as he was, she didn't believe he'd hit her. Not in the kitchen. Not in front of Rhian and Iestyn. He had always beaten her in private in their bedroom . . .

A burst of crimson exploded in her head as Owen slammed his fist into the side of her face. Disorientated, she fell against the cot, striking her head on the iron bars. Dimly, as if the sound were travelling over a great distance, she was aware of her son crying. She had to reach him . . . had to . . . She struggled to her feet but another explosion sent her catapulting backwards away from the cot into the range. A deafening crack rent the air as the back of her head connected with the oven door. She could smell the acrid stench of her hair burning. Rhian screamed, Iestyn shouted and the baby's cries escalated.

She struggled to open her eyes but a thick curtain had fallen over her face, blinding her. She tried to wipe it away but her left hand refused to move. She lifted her right and clawed at whatever was obscuring her sight.

Through a dense, red-black haze she glimpsed Owen leaning over the cot.

Iestyn grabbed his brother's waist and wrenched him away. She threw herself over the cot, shielding the child from Owen. The baby's sobs filled her ears and to her horror she saw blood dripping on to his blanket.

A pain shot through her neck as Owen's hands closed around her throat. He lifted her off her feet. She tried to beg for her baby's life, her lips moved, but the sound remained strangled in her larynx.

As Iestyn fought to prise Owen's hands from her neck, Owen tightened them. Dense waves of grey mist washed over her, blurring shapes and sounds. Weak, nauseous, she was aware of the kitchen floor hurtling towards her. Rhian shrieked and threw something at Owen. There was a splintered crash of a chair breaking and the sound of something heavy tumbling down the stairs.

Someone lifted the baby from the cot, as she lay on the floor unable to summon the strength to raise her head. Owen bellowed. Quick, light steps ran down the stairs. Rhian shouted from somewhere far away. She looked up. Owen was standing over her, his fists raised. It was the last thing she saw before she tumbled into absolute darkness.

'We'll not interfere in a domestic,' Sergeant Davies declared unequivocally, looking from Rhian Bull, who was trying to soothe a hysterical child, to Mrs Hughes. The oldest Hughes boy, who'd been sent to fetch the police when Rhian had emerged screaming into the street with the child, peered around the open door of Owen Bull's shop. A constable left the group of officers gathered around a dark heap at the foot of the stairs, pushed the boy aside and joined the sergeant in the street.

'One of them's dead, Sarge.'

'You sure?'

'I'm sure. Want me to fetch the doctor?'

The sergeant made a wry, lemon-sucking face as he

nodded. Domestics could be ignored; dead bodies meant filling in forms, taking and writing statements, and coroner's inquests. Every officer on the Pontypridd force could recite a list of the men in the town who knocked their wives about. Some women, like Sali Bull who'd married carrying another man's bastard, deserved everything they got. Others developed slovenly ways that a tap or two occasionally sorted. He'd never thought any less of a man for trying to keep a difficult wife in order the old-fashioned way. Not that he'd ever had to resort to beating his own. She'd learned to toe his line after he'd given her a warning on their honeymoon.

Rhian blocked the constable's path. 'Is it Sali?' She clasped the baby so hard he stopped crying, swallowed hard and let out a harsh sob.

'It's your brother, Miss Bull. The half-wit.'

She thrust the baby at Mrs Hughes and ran into the house. One of the constables had lit his lantern and was holding it above Iestyn, who lay sprawled on his back behind the door, staring up at the ceiling, exactly as he had been when she had run past him and out of the house. She knelt beside him and tried to lift his head.

'Don't touch him, Miss Bull.' The sergeant moved in behind her.

'Are you sure he's dead?' she pleaded. 'He looks as if he's been knocked out . . .'

The sergeant closed Iestyn's eyes. 'I am sure, Miss Bull. There is nothing you can do for him now.'

'Sali is still upstairs with Owen.' She looked up the staircase. Dark even in daylight, the top of the stairs was shrouded in shadows as black as coal.

The sergeant listened for a moment. He could hear a faint noise, like a man grunting – or crying. 'Griffiths, you stay here. Gurner, I'll be right behind you.'

Owen Bull was slumped in the easy chair in the kitchen, snoring in the profoundly deep sleep of the drunkard. His wife lay, sprawled unconscious on the floor beside a cot, her left arm twisted beneath her at an unnatural angle, her face a bloodied, jellied mass, her singed hair matted with clots of congealing blood.

'Get downstairs and tell the doctor to come up here first. Iestyn Bull can wait, she can't,' the sergeant ordered.

'And the girl?' Constable Gurner noted the blood smeared over Owen Bull's knuckles.

'Bring her, so she can tell us what went on here. And send up another two officers. The biggest on duty.' He jerked his head towards the chair where Owen snored. 'Looking at the mess in this place, chapel deacon or not, I'm not giving the order to wake him until he's hand-cuffed and outnumbered.'

Rhian stood in the kitchen while two of the largest officers stationed in Pontypridd, half dragged, half carried Owen, who was ranting and raving at the top of his voice, out through the door and down the stairs.

'I'm a patient man, Miss Bull,' the sergeant said in a tone that suggested he was anything but. He waited until Owen's shouts faded as he and his escort turned the corner of Mill Street and headed for Catherine Street and the police station. 'Not only am I patient, I like to get things right. Tell me again, what went on in this house tonight?'

'My brothers started arguing,' she clutched the baby and choked back her tears.

'Over what?'

She shrugged.

'Was it Mrs Bull?' the sergeant suggested archly.

'No!' she exclaimed angrily. 'Owen came home early. He was in one of his bad moods.'

'He was drunk,' the sergeant suggested.

'I don't know. Sali and I just call it Owen's bad mood. The baby was crying . . . Owen went to the cot . . .'

'So, Iestyn thought your brother was going to hurt the baby?' he interrupted.

'Yes . . . no . . .' She contradicted herself. 'I don't know what Iestyn thought.'

'Has Owen Bull ever hurt the child?'

'No, but Owen doesn't like him and, as I said, he was in one of his moods. Iestyn tried to pull him away from the cot, they struggled and Iestyn fell downstairs.'

'You are quite sure Iestyn fell? That Owen didn't push him?' The sergeant questioned carefully.

'I didn't see. I can't be sure. I don't know,' she cried out in confusion, shifting the weight of the baby who had finally fallen asleep, in her arms. 'It happened so quickly . . .'

'Stay still, Mrs Bull.'

As the doctor's order cut through Rhian's protestations, Rhian and the sergeant turned to the corner of the room where the doctor was crouching beside Sali.

Sali could hear the soft murmur of voices and was conscious of people around her. She struggled to open her eyes but her eyelids were heavy and unresponsive.

'Don't move, Mrs Bull.'

She recognised the calm, authoritative voice of the doctor. His face blurred above her, unfocused and unrecognisable.

'My baby . . .'

'Your baby is fine, your sister-in-law is here with him.'

'He's fine, Sali. He is sleeping.' Rhian's voice was clotted with tears. 'Don't worry, I'll look after him. I promise.'

'I want to hold him.'

'I wouldn't advise that, Mrs Bull.'

The sergeant squatted beside Sali. 'Can you remember what happened, Mrs Bull?'

'Mrs Bull isn't in a fit state to answer any questions, Sergeant Davies,' the doctor said firmly. 'If you check with me in a day or two, you might be able to send someone to the Graig Infirmary to question her.'

'The workhouse . . . you can't send me to the workhouse,' Sali pleaded. 'Who will look after my baby?'

'I will, Sali,' Rhian reassured. 'Don't worry, I will take care of him.'

'Owen . . .'

'Owen is not here, Sali. The baby is safe.'

The sergeant gave Rhian a hard look. In his book, there was a world of difference between a man hitting his wife to keep her in order and a man venting his drunken rage on a defenceless child. But he couldn't see a mark on the boy.

'Please, let me stay with my baby,' Sali begged. 'Don't send me to the workhouse.'

'You are going to the infirmary, not the workhouse,' the doctor said calmly.

'The infirmary costs money.'

'That is nothing for you to worry about.' He grimaced as he studied the extensive injuries to her face. When the police had woken him in the early hours, he had been furious, but as the constable had outlined the events in Mill Street, he recalled Edyth James asking him to do whatever he could to help her niece if he was ever given the opportunity.

He would never have recognised Sali Watkin Jones if the police hadn't told him who she was. Her face was battered beyond recognition, her eyes sunk into black bruises, her eyelids and lips split, bleeding, and the whites of her eyes crimson with burst blood vessels. She was so painfully thin he could count her ribs. Her hair, which had always been immaculately styled, had burned away on the back and crown of her head, leaving singed, broken stubble, the rest was matted, unkempt and clotted with blood. She looked like an old woman of sixty. Whatever the girl had done, she had undoubtedly suffered for it, and he felt sorry for her and her child.

'Don't worry, Mrs Bull, a few weeks of rest and care, and you will be fine. And you'll be in a private room,' he promised, knowing Edyth James would pay any amount of money to ensure Sali's comfort.

'What's the damage to Mrs Bull?' the sergeant enquired, holding his notebook.

'She has a dislocated arm, severe bruising and cuts to the head and face, a cracked cheekbone, and a fractured skull. She'll need at least six weeks rest and I don't want her interviewed until I give you permission to do so.'

'I have a dead man out there and another man in custody. A girl,' he gave Rhian a scathing look, 'who doesn't seem to be at all sure what happened, other than her brothers were fighting, possibly over the baby. Mrs Bull's evidence could be crucial.'

'She is in no condition to give it.'

'Could you examine the child to see if he has any marks or bruising?'

'As soon as Mrs Bull is on her way to the infirmary.'

As if on cue, a constable entered the kitchen and announced, 'The ambulance is here, Sarge.'

'Send the driver and his mate up with a stretcher, Constable.' The doctor stretched his legs as he rose to his feet. 'Would you order your officers to clear the street so we can put Mrs Bull in the ambulance, Sergeant Davies?'

'You promise to look after the baby?' Sali reached out to Rhian as they loaded her on to the stretcher, but all she could see was her shadow.

'I promise.' Rhian stooped to the floor and picked up the parcel Sali had thrust at Owen. She laid it on the stretcher beside Sali. 'You'll need your best clothes.'

The doctor took time to examine Isaac after the ambulance left. The child looked up solemnly and silently from his cot as he was poked and prodded.

'He has a temperature.'

'Sali thought it was a summer chill,' Rhian murmured.

'It could be.' The doctor folded his stethoscope and placed it in his bag. 'The child is malnourished, but there's no sign of violence.'

'So, your brother Owen never touched the child, Miss Bull?'

'I never said he did,' she remonstrated.

'No? You weren't sure, were you?'

Constable Griffiths tapped the door. 'The second ambulance is here, Sergeant Davies. The men want to know if they can move the body.'

'Not until the doctor has seen it.'

The doctor picked up his jacket from the back of one of the kitchen chairs and followed the sergeant out of the room. Rhian crept on to the landing but not down the stairs. She watched from above while the doctor examined Iestyn.

'No doubt about it,' he declared flatly after a few minutes. 'His neck is broken.'

'What I want to know is, was he pushed or did he fall?'

'Could have been either from the way he is lying,' the doctor answered.

'There's no way of knowing?' the sergeant pressed.

'Not for certain. All I can say is he fell backwards down the stairs, landed on his head and broke his neck. How he came to fall is for you to decide.'

'There was blood on his brother's knuckles.'

'There's none on him.'

'The men are anxious to get on, Sarge. Can we move it,' the constable glanced up at Rhian, 'Mr Bull to the mortuary in the Graig Hospital?' he amended.

'Yes, Griffiths. And while you're at it, clear the street of nosy parkers. Tell them there's nothing more for them to see tonight.'

'If you don't want me for anything else, I'll be on my way.' The doctor snapped his bag shut.

'Nothing else. Thank you for coming out, Doctor.' The sergeant closed his notebook and walked up the stairs. 'You'd best lock the door behind us, Miss Bull.'

'What about Owen?'

'The way things stand, once he's sober, we'll let your brother out first thing in the morning. If as you say, Iestyn fell downstairs, the only charge we can make against him is drunk and disorderly. I don't know what the chapel or the town council are going to say about it, but that is their problem, not mine. You sure you want to take care of the nipper? I could arrange to have him taken to the workhouse.'

'I'll take care of him,' Rhian said firmly.

'Are you sure you can't tell me any more, Miss Bull?' Sergeant Davies looked Rhian in the eye.

'I am sure.' She watched him walk back downstairs.

'Miss Bull?'

'Yes, Sergeant?'

'Lock the door,' he said again as he closed it behind him.

CHAPTER ELEVEN

Thoughts whirled without reason or coherence in Rhian's mind when she returned to the kitchen. The sergeant had said he'd release Owen when he was sober. That meant he'd return, and there was only her and the baby. She couldn't face living with him alone. She simply couldn't! Not without Iestyn to help and protect her.

What if Owen attacked her the way he had Sali? And he hated the baby. She was no match for Owen but she had no money, nowhere to go, no friends . . . She looked at the clock. It was half past five. How long would it take Owen to sober up?

She took a sheet from the baby's cot and spread it on the floor. Removing the child's clothes and blankets from the outgrown baby carriage where Sali kept them, she bundled as many as she could on to the centre of the sheet. Tying it in a knot, she left Isaac in his cot and went to her room. Setting a sheet from her bed on the floor, she wrapped her spare clothes in it. Taking both bundles she lifted the baby from his cot, wrapped both of them in his shawl, Welsh fashion, crept down the stairs and slipped out of the house.

A misty dawn had broken, portending a fine day. Trying not to think about the enormity of what she was doing, she turned right towards Taff Street.

'Rhian, where you off to at this time in the morning?' Mrs Hughes shook an eiderdown out of an upstairs window.

'Nowhere, Mrs Hughes.'

'Funny nowhere, carrying the baby and two bundles that size. Wait.'

Uneasy, lest Mrs Hughes try to persuade her to stay, Rhian reached the corner of the street before her neighbour caught up with her. Heaving for breath, Mrs Hughes pressed something into Rhian's hand.

'It's not much, but it may help.'

Rhian didn't opened her hand until she reached Taff Street, then she saw that Mrs Hughes had given her three shillings.

Bless me, child, what are you doing here at this hour with the baby?' Mari glanced anxiously around the yard of Danygraig House before opening the back door wider. 'Quick.' She took one of Rhian's bundles and ushered her into the passage that linked the pantries with the preparation kitchens. 'Down here.' She led the way to the butler's pantry and knocked on the door. 'It's me, Tomas, let us in.'

'Good God!' Tomas opened the door and stepped back when he saw Rhian and the baby.

'I can't allow her in the kitchen, you know how Mr Morgan prowls round every inch of the house as soon as he gets up.' Mari dropped the bundle she was carrying inside the door and took the child from Rhian. 'Sit down, girl, you must be worn out after carrying those through town. Has Sali sent you here?'

'Sali couldn't send me anywhere.' Fighting tears and sheer weariness, Rhian proceeded to tell them about the traumatic events of the night. They listened in an attentive tight-lipped silence that Sali would have recognised as the beginning of slow anger, but it unnerved Rhian. 'I know I shouldn't have come here,' she apologised. 'But I didn't know where else to go with the baby and he's not well, you only have to look at him to see that. If it was just me I'd try to get a place somewhere, but I couldn't leave the baby. My brother hates him and without Sali and Iestyn . . .' She finally shed tears for the simple-minded brother she had loved.

'It's right you came here.' Mari glanced at the clock. 'Tomas and I have to go, but you'll be safe here and I'll bring you food and milk for the baby as soon as I can. The beautiful little lamb.' Mari dropped a kiss on the top of his head. 'Considering what he's been through, he's ever so good.'

'He's wonderful. But where am I to go?'

'You leave that to me. I have to see to the breakfasts but I'll be back.'

'Why don't you and the baby curl up in my bed?' Tomas offered. 'You both look as though you could do with some sleep.'

'I have to change him first.'

'There's clean water in the jug on the washstand. Everything else is where you'd expect to find it.'

'Thank you.' Rhian took the boy from Mari.

Tomas reached for the bottle he kept hidden under his mattress and poured her a small glass of sherry. 'Drink this.'

'Don't make a sound,' Mari warned. 'Mr Morgan has never come down here but that's not to say that he won't take it into his head to do so.'

'We'll lock you in. Don't answer to anyone, no matter what they say. We have the only key to the room. So long as you remain quiet, no one will know that you are here.' Tomas patted her arm, stroked the child, checked his tie was straight and followed Mari into the corridor.

'If Morgan Davies sees her or that child in this house, we'll both be on the streets,' he cautioned as they scurried towards the kitchens.

'I know.'

'Have you any idea where they can go?'

'My sister is housekeeper to a big house in the Rhondda. Her master's a bit of a soft touch.'

'Unlike ours,' he commented dryly.

'Ours is in his grave,' she countered sharply. 'And my sister could probably use another kitchen maid.'

'The girl's not trained. She has no character.'

'The girl's been keeping house for Owen Bull since she was eight years old. She's trained and I'll give her character enough for my sister.'

'And the boy?'

Mari pursed her lips. 'There are always women willing to look after a child for a few shillings a week.'

'What kind of women?' he enquired warily.

'Hopefully, good-hearted ones,' she replied unconvincingly. 'While Mr Morgan eats his breakfast, send the stable boy to the station yard. If a cab comes into the back yard from Crossbrook Street at ten past eight Mr Morgan won't see it. The cab can take her . . .'

'Not to the station, she'll be seen. And if Owen Bull is released this morning he'll be looking for them.'

'Not at Trehafod station he won't.'

'And who is going to pay for a cab to take her and the child to Trehafod and their train tickets to the Rhondda? And she'll need more if your sister can't find a place for her, or a woman to look after the child. It's not often I disagree with you, Mrs Williams,' he lowered his voice as they approached the kitchens, 'but I think we should send her and the child to Mrs James.'

'Mr Bull knows Mr Mansel is the father of Miss Sali's baby and that Mrs James is fond of Miss Sali. It's the first place he'll look for them.'

'Let him look.'

'The girl is his under-age sister. He is the legal father of that baby. If he wanted them back, the law would be on his side. And once they are under his roof, who knows what he'll do to them?' Red-faced with suppressed anger at the thought of Sali's injuries, Mari heaved for breath. 'I have some money in my box.' She wished she hadn't put quite so much of her savings in the bank. The last time she had looked she had only two pounds and no one would look after a child for less than five shillings a week.

'I have five pounds.' Tomas held up his hand as if to ward off Mari's thanks. 'Let's just hope that your sister can find the girl a job and knows someone who can care for the child. If she can't, we'll all be in trouble.'

As Sali awoke to a painful consciousness she sensed she was in a strange place. She could hear the soft squeak of rubber-soled shoes moving over hard floors. The distant rattle of enamelware banging and the clink of cutlery and china provided a musical accompaniment to whispers delivered in the muted tones of a sick room. She struggled to open her eyelids. They felt heavy and gritty as if sand were trapped beneath them. She attempted to focus, looked and looked again, wondering if she were dreaming.

Her Aunt Edyth was sitting in a chair next to her bed, thinner and older than she remembered.

'How are you feeling, darling?' Edyth reached out and took her hand.

Before Sali could answer, a nurse appeared. Taking her wrist, she lifted it and checked her pulse rate against the watch pinned to the top corner of her apron.

Edyth tried to smile. Sali didn't attempt to because her face felt as though it were on fire. She remembered a doctor telling her that he was going to send her to the Graig Infirmary. She remembered waking afterwards, but she had lost count of the number of times and she could recall being given injections whenever she opened her eyes, numbing, sleep-inducing injections that deadened the sharp throbbing in her head.

'My son . . .' Her voice was hoarse, rusty from disuse.

'Is well, happy and being looked after, Sali,' Aunt Edyth murmured.

'Owen . . .'

'He is not with Owen and neither is Rhian.'

'Iestyn . . . he tried to help me . . .'

'Iestyn fell down the stairs and broke his neck, Sali. He is dead.' Edyth said the words as gently as she knew how, but she could not cushion their devastating effect.

The nurse nodded to someone standing behind her. A second nurse stepped into view carrying an enamel tray that held a glass phial and a syringe. The first nurse helped her aunt from the chair as the second turned back her bedclothes.

'I have to leave now, Sali, but I will be back to see you soon.' Edyth dropped a kiss that didn't quite reach Sali's bruised forehead, picked up her cane and tottered unsteadily from the room.

'The man deserves to be horsewhipped,' Edyth declared to the doctor when he joined her in the corridor.

'I don't disagree with you, Mrs James, but his punishment is for the police and the law to decide.' He opened the door for her and offered her his arm.

'I can't understand how they could let him walk free from the police station the morning after he did this to my niece.'

'Without any witnesses or evidence . . .'

'Evidence!' Putting her full weight on his arm, she turned and shook her stick in the direction of the ward. 'Isn't that evidence enough?'

'Mr Bull said his wife tripped, fell and hit her face on the range,' he reminded her.

'As well as the back of her head?' Edyth enquired sceptically. 'And his brother fell downstairs? Isn't that rather too much falling in one house in one night?'

'Put yourself in the position of the police, Mrs James,' he remonstrated. 'The only witness was his sister who has vanished. Mrs Bull was too ill to give a statement—'

'And the police will not interfere between a man and his wife,' she broke in acidly, quoting the sergeant she had summoned to visit her.

'I'll grant you Mrs Bull looks dreadful now, but she will make a full recovery.'

'And the scars?'

'Will fade in time.'

'I can see her next week?'

'Visiting is every Sunday, two until three o'clock.' The doctor escorted her to the front door of the infirmary where her carriage was waiting. 'Goodbye, Mrs James, and don't worry about your niece. We will take good care of her.' The doctor handed her over to Jenkins who opened the door of the carriage. The butler settled her on one of the seats, spread a travelling rug over her legs, closed the door and joined the coachman on the box.

Edyth stared blindly through the window, as they passed through the gates set in the high walls that surrounded the workhouse, infirmary and fever hospital complex. They reached the bottom of High Street and drove under the railway bridge into Tumble Square. She rapped her cane on the roof in Taff Street and shouted, 'Drive home via Mill Street, Catherine Street, Gelliwastad Road and Bridge Street, and drive slowly in Mill Street.'

'Yes, Mrs James,' came the coachman's muffled reply.

Edyth removed a lavender-scented handkerchief from her handbag and held it over her nose and mouth as she studied the dilapidated terrace that backed on to the river. The heat of August had abated, the evenings were growing shorter, and people were taking their coats out of mothballs to prepare for the winter, but the stench of sewage, rot and decay was still overwhelming. She saw the sign over Owen Bull's shop and imagined Sali and her child living within those mouldering walls, breathing in the foul air day after day.

'No more!' she promised herself fervently. No matter what the police said, or what 'rights' Owen Bull claimed as Sali's husband, there was no way that she was going to allow her niece, or Mansel's son to return to that slum to live in those foul conditions with a man she regarded as a murderer, even if the police didn't. Not while she still drew breath.

*

'He was banging the front door and shouting, Mr Jenkins. He wouldn't listen to anything we tried to tell him, so I sent for the police. Did I do right?' Robert, the footman who had once worked for Harry Watkin Jones, looked apprehensively at the elderly butler who was busy opening the door of the carriage and folding down the iron steps.

'You did right, Robert,' Jenkins replied gravely. He helped Edyth alight from the carriage and they watched two burly policemen and Sergeant Davies bundle Owen Bull from the porch of Ynysangharad House into the back of a Black Maria.

'I came for my sister!' Owen Bull shouted, struggling to free himself.

'Your sister isn't here, Mr Bull,' Edyth said calmly.

'The child.'

'The child isn't here either, Mr Bull.'

Her cool assertions only served to infuriate Owen all the more. 'They are my family, and they should be living with me . . .' He kicked out, losing his temper as the sergeant closed and fastened the back doors of the van in his face.

'We'll charge him with disorderly behaviour and breaching the peace, Mrs James.' The sergeant signalled to the driver to move off. 'The magistrates will most probably sentence him to be bound over to be of good behaviour. Then, if he comes back here or tries to bother you again, we can re-arrest him and he'll lose his bond or be sent to prison. I think it's safe to say that a man of previously good character like Owen Bull won't risk that, or forfeiting his bond, which should be set at quite a considerable sum. I doubt you'll be seeing him again.'

'I sincerely hope so, Sergeant Davies.' She laid a hand on his arm to delay him. 'I have just come from visiting Mrs Bull in the infirmary.'

The sergeant ran his finger inside his collar as if he were suddenly too warm. 'How is Mrs Bull?'

'As well as anyone can be two weeks after she has been beaten half to death.'

'We've no proof that she was beaten, Mrs James,' he retorted defensively. 'Her husband says she fell.'

'Forgive my cynicism, Sergeant,' she interrupted, 'but how many other people have you known to cut and bruise every inch of their face, as well as fracture the crown of their skull and burn the hair from the back of their head from a single fall? My niece is also right-handed. Don't you think it more likely that she would have dislocated her right, not left arm, if she were trying to save herself from a fall?'

He shifted uncomfortably from one foot to the other. 'That is not for me to say, Mrs James. And we've no evidence that contradicts Mr Bull's side of the story.'

'So when you charge him with breaching the peace, you couldn't also charge him with assault?'

'Not on his own wife, Mrs James.' The sergeant evinced a sudden interest in the geraniums that filled the flowerbeds either side of the front door. 'In my experience, wives will never give evidence in open court against their husbands.'

'And if I guarantee that Mrs Bull will?'

'Mr Bull could plead provocation or any number of things in his defence. There are bound to be things that have happened in private between Mr and Mrs Bull that Mrs Bull wouldn't want aired in public court. You do know that the *Pontypridd Observer* sends representatives to the courts?'

'I read the local paper, Sergeant.'

'In my book, whatever goes on between husband and wife behind closed doors shouldn't become the subject of gossip.' He gave her a tight smile.

'I think everyone in Pontypridd is aware of what went on behind Mr Bull's doors two weeks ago, Sergeant.' She nodded to the coachman who dismounted and led the horses around the house to the stables at the back.

'Let's say for argument's sake that the court does find

Mr Bull guilty of assaulting Mrs Bull, not that they will because there's no evidence,' the sergeant amended hastily, 'Mr Bull wouldn't get a long sentence, not for a domestic altercation. A few months, a year at the most and he'd be free again. And then where would Mrs Bull be? I dare say homeless and penniless without a man to run Mr Bull's business.'

'Mrs Bull would be safe with me.'

'Every minute of every day?' The sergeant lifted his eyebrows.

'Are you saying that Owen Bull is free to murder his wife when she leaves hospital, Sergeant?' she enquired with a detachment that belied her rage.

'Not murder, Mrs James. If he does that, we'll arrest him.'

'And apologise to Mrs Bull at her funeral?' Edyth didn't wait for the sergeant to answer. She leaned on her cane and hobbled in through her front door.

Sali washed her face and patted it gently dry with a towel marked 'Property of Pontypridd Union'. She felt weak, faint and her left arm, newly freed from the restricting bandages that had been wound in place to help her torn muscles and tendons heal, ached dreadfully, but she was elated. She had been allowed to walk unaided from her cubicle to the bathroom, and after four weeks spent in bed and another week of being escorted to the bathroom by a nurse, the independence felt wonderful. Soon, very soon, she would be reunited with her son.

She set the towel aside and studied her face in the blotched mirror above the washbasin. It didn't even look like hers. Misshapen and swollen over her left cheekbone, it was pockmarked by scabs and discoloured by bruises that had lightened during the past six weeks from black, through purple to a dark then lighter yellow which lent the impression she was suffering from jaundice.

She lifted her right hand and felt her head. The paralysing, nauseous headaches of the past few weeks had lessened until they were just about tolerable. Her hair was half an inch long, soft, silky and, to her amazement, curly. She had been upset when the sister had said that they'd had to shave her head in order to stitch three deep wounds on her scalp. But she had also told her that it had been just as well, as the hair on the back of her head had burned away when she had fallen against the stove.

She pulled out a tiny curl and watched it spring back into a corkscrew. Mari had described her hair as 'poker straight' when she had been a child, and said it was a sin that Geraint should have curls and she none, because boys didn't need them. But then it had been Mari's job to wind her hair in rags every night so it could be curled into ringlets the following day. She wondered if it would remain curly, then reflected it didn't matter how her hair, or indeed she looked any longer because with Mansel gone there was no one left to notice, let alone admire her.

She left the bathroom and walked slowly down the corridor. Nurses were moving swiftly between the twin lines of beds in the general ward, straightening bed-clothes, removing cups from lockers and stacking them on a trolley. The staff nurse looked up from the duty desk where she was making entries in a ledger, set aside her pen and went to her. 'Are you all right, Mrs Bull?'

'Yes, thank you.'

'It is good to see you up and about, Mrs Bull.' The nurse walked alongside her as she returned to her room.

'It feels good,' Sali tried a smile. Whether it was her imagination or not, it seemed to hurt less than it had done the day before.

'Is Mrs James visiting you today?'

'She promised she would.'

'We'll miss her fruit baskets, fresh eggs and cakes, when you are discharged next week.'

'Knowing my aunt she'll keep sending them.' Sali sat on the bed. 'Do I have to get into bed for visiting? My aunt said she might bring . . . a friend and I'd like both of them to think that I'm better.'

'Your aunt and your friend will see that you are making a good recovery. And regulations are regulations.' The sister waited until Sali lifted her feet up on the bed before tucking the sheets around her and under the mattress. 'That's the first bell. They'll be coming in any minute. Don't tire yourself out by talking too much. You may feel better but that's only because you've done nothing but rest for five weeks. It will be different when you go home.' Seeing Sali's eyes round in horror, the nurse turned around.

'I'm Councillor Bull.' Owen strode into the cubicle. 'Sali's husband.' He pulled a wooden stool up to the bed.

Sali trembled as Owen sat next to her, as self-possessed and unconcerned as if nothing had happened between them.

'I've not visited you before, Sali, because I've been busy arranging Iestyn's funeral and trying to keep the shop going.'

Sali heard her aunt's voice, high-pitched and anxious, further down the ward.

Owen smirked. 'I told your aunt to wait. As your husband and nearest relation I take precedence.' He looked at the nurse. 'I have private matters to discuss with my wife. Close the door behind you when you leave.'

'Regulations state that all doors in the ward have to be left open during visiting, Mr Bull.'

The sister walked briskly into the room. 'Mrs Edwards needs urgent attention, Nurse.' After the girl left, she went to the foot of Sali's bed and picked up her chart. She flicked through it before addressing Owen. 'I am sure that I don't need to warn you not to upset Mrs Bull, Mr Bull. She has been extremely ill.'

'How can a visit from me possibly upset my wife, Sister?'

'Mrs Bull is in an extremely fragile state.'

'But she is recovering after her fall.' It wasn't a question.

'Yes, she is making a recovery,' the sister conceded.

'Then, if you don't mind, I think we have wasted enough of the visiting hour. I'd like a word with my wife in private.'

'If you feel worse, Mrs Bull, or you are in any pain, ring the bell.' The sister removed it from the locker and pressed it into Sali's right hand, on the opposite side of the bed to where Owen was sitting. 'We'll look in on you at regular intervals.' The sister gave Sali a sympathetic look as she retreated.

Owen rose from the stool, hitched up the trouser creases on his best suit, and sat back down. 'Not that you've asked, but Iestyn's funeral went well. Over sixty people turned out to bury him.'

'Everyone liked Iestyn.' She moved as far away from him as the bed would allow.

'Where are Rhian and the baby, Sali?' he asked, his voice ominously soft.

She plucked nervously as the bedcover. 'I don't know.' All Aunt Edyth had said was that they were together and safe, away from Pontypridd. And now she understood why her Aunt had refused to disclose their exact whereabouts.

'Before I repeat the question, you will remind me of a wife's first duty to her husband.'

'Obedience.' She chanted the reply he had beaten into her.

'Where are Rhian and the baby?'

'I honestly don't know, Owen.' An ice-cold trickle of fear oozed down her spine, chilling her blood and raising goose pimples on her skin.

'I don't believe you.' He leaned forward, locking his fingers together as if he were about to pray. 'Are they with your aunt?'

'No.'

'For someone who doesn't know where they are, you seem very certain of that fact.'

'She would have told me if they were with her.'

'Since Rhian left, the shop has been costing me money. The woman I have employed says there are no customers.' His round piggy eyes appeared to have sunk deeper into the rolls of fat that wreathed his face since she had last seen him. 'Will they return when you come home?'

'Home?'

'You are coming home.'

Although they had never discussed it, she knew her aunt expected her to move into Ynysangharad House when she was discharged. But wherever she went, the one thing she did know was that she couldn't bear the thought of living with Owen Bull. Not ever again. She bit her lip and turned away from him to the high window. The square of sky was grey, overcast . . .

'When are you leaving here?'

'I don't know.'

'Look at me when I speak to you.' He gripped her hand and squeezed her fingers painfully, until she faced him. 'You do intend to come home?'

'I haven't thought about leaving here yet . . . I've been very ill, Owen . . .'

He smiled at her, a smile crueller than his scowl. 'You wouldn't listen if any of your friends tried to persuade you to go and live with them, would you?'

'No one's asked me to go and live with them, Owen.'

'Not even your aunt?' There was malice in his voice.

'I have nowhere to go, you know that. My uncle—'

'Your uncle is a God-fearing man who knows a wife's place is with her husband.'

As a nurse in starched long skirts and apron swished past the door, he relaxed back on the stool but did not relinquish his grip on her hand. 'I warn you, Sali, a wife who leaves her husband is nothing. She may as well cease to exist. She has no place in society. The only profession open to her is that of whore. But then you've already been a whore, haven't you, Sali?' His fingers compressed hers until she thought he would crush her bones. 'Mansel James's whore.'

'If you think I'm a whore, Owen, why stay married to me? Divorce me.'

'That is the sort of thing only a whore would say. There is no divorce in the eyes of our Lord,' he pronounced sternly. 'I warn you, and it is a solemn warning, leave me and you, and whoever you run to, will suffer. I have a husband's rights under God's law "and those whom God has joined together let no man break asunder".' He watched the tears roll down her cheeks. 'You are overwrought, which is understandable after five weeks in this place. I will find out when you will be discharged and when you are, I will be outside, waiting to take you home. Once you are busy again with your household duties, you won't have time to gossip with your aunt or pine for the luxuries of your past life.' He fingered the silk and lace nightgown and lace bed jacket her aunt had given her. Releasing her hand, he stroked it. 'Whatever I've done, I've done for your own good, Sali. You know that. You needed to be taught obedience and you are still learning. But I have hope that one day you will become a dutiful, God-fearing wife. When you come home I will ask your uncle to consider re-admitting you to the congregation of the chapel. You would like that, wouldn't you? Acceptance that might ultimately lead to forgiveness for your sin.'

Worn down by his bullying, she whispered, 'Yes', in the hope that by agreeing with him, he'd leave her in peace.

The sister looked in. 'Mr Bull, you have taken up more than half of the hour. Your wife does have other visitors.'

'I am sorry. It is selfish of me to monopolise her. Send them in and I'll leave. After all, I'll soon have Mrs Bull to myself when she comes home. When exactly will that be, Sister?' he enquired artfully.

'I am afraid I can't tell you, Mr Bull. It is for the doctor, not me, to decide.'

'You must have some idea from similar cases.'

'No, because I have never seen such severe injuries as those sustained by your wife before.'

Owen looked back at Sali as he went to the door. 'I will be up to see you next Sunday, Sali. In the meantime I will make daily enquiries as to when you will be discharged. If Rhian should write to you, tell her to bring the boy home so she can prepare for your return.'

Trembling and fighting tears, Sali curled into a tight ball as Mari helped Edyth through the door. Mari settled Edyth into a chair before sitting next to Sali on the bed. Opening her arms, she hugged her as she had when she'd been a child.

'Don't cry, lamb,' she reverted to a pet name she hadn't used since Sali was six years old. She made a face at the empty doorway. 'I don't know how that man has the nerve to come here after what he did to you.'

'He is looking for Rhian and the baby,' Sali murmured.

'He won't find them,' Mari declared confidently.

'You've heard from them?' Sali lifted her head from Mari's shoulder. 'Are they well? Are they—'

'They are fine, and they can do what they like to me, I'll not tell Owen Bull or anyone else where they are.' She looked to the door. Seeing no nurses in the corridor, she closed it. 'Rhian is working as a kitchen maid and she has found a woman, a good kind woman who has a boy of her own, to look after your son.'

'Where are they?'

'Not too far away,' Mari hedged.

'Please, I must see them . . .'

'And you will, as soon as you leave here,' Edyth consoled.

'Owen says he is going to take me home.'

'So he can beat you again? That is out of the question.' Edyth dismissed.

Mari opened her handbag and pulled out an envelope. She removed a letter and a photograph. 'Doesn't he look fine? Quite the young boy.' She handed the photograph to Sali.

'Exactly like his father,' Edyth said wistfully.

Her son stood in front of a canvas backdrop painted to resemble an ornate eighteenth-century garden, complete with Grecian urns and broken columns. He was wearing one of Llinos's white linen, drawn-work aprons, and holding a teddy bear that looked so new, Sali suspected it was the photographer's prop.

'When was this taken?' Sali drank in every detail. The wary, confused expression on the child's face, the sturdy chubbiness of his legs, the way his mouth almost turned up at the corners but didn't.

'My sister had it taken—'

'Your sister,' Sali broke in eagerly. 'The one who is a housekeeper in Tonypandy?'

Mari put her finger to her lips. 'She found Rhian a position and someone to look after the child.'

'What if Owen finds out where they are?'

'We must take care that he doesn't.' Edyth pursed her lips as the bell rang. 'We seem to have been here less than five minutes. Damn that man for coming here.'

It was the strongest language Sali had ever heard her aunt use.

Mari proceeded to empty her bag on to the bed. 'I brought you some preserves, a fruitcake, an apple tart and a bottle of my raspberry syrup. The sweets and this bottle of cordial are from Tomas, who sends you his very best. And you know what that means.'

'You shouldn't have.' Sali stared at the pile of gifts.

'Don't worry, there is nothing there that your uncle knows about and what he doesn't know about, he can't miss. He is just the same as he was the day he moved into Danygraig House and so is your mother. When I next write to Masters Geraint and Gareth and Miss Llinos, shall I send them your love?'

'I thought I heard voices.' The sister opened the door. 'Mrs James, Mrs Williams, I am sorry, but I will have to ask you to leave.'

'We are just going, Sister. If you would be so kind.' Edyth took the sister's hand to steady herself as she left the chair.

'Geraint, Gareth and Llinos don't know I'm here, do they?' Sali asked.

Mari shook her head.

'Mother?'

'Your mother doesn't know what day of the week it is, bless her, let alone what is happening in the town. Your Uncle Morgan knows you are here and who put you here, as does everyone in Pontypridd. Take care of yourself. Another week or so and you will be safe with Mrs James. She'll take care of you.'

CHAPTER TWELVE

'Can't you sleep, Mrs Bull?' The duty night nurse walked into Sali's room to find her staring blankly at the ceiling.

'No.'

'Are you in pain? If you are, I could give you some tablets or a sleeping draught.'

'No, thank you.' Sali tried to smile and discovered it wasn't her imagination. The pain in her face was lessening. 'With all the sleeping I've done for the past five weeks I'm just slept out.'

'It is strictly against regulations, but as you are in here on your own and wouldn't disturb anyone, I could put the light on so you could read.'

'I'd like that, thank you.'

'There's a copy of last week's *Observer* in the sister's office. You could find out what has been happening in the town.'

'Please.'

The nurse brought Sali a cup of heavily sugared tea along with the paper. She sat up and opened the paper. It was such a simple thing to do, drink tea and read in bed, but it had been a long time since she'd had the leisure to read a newspaper.

The Christmas before her father died, she reflected. Since then her life had deviated drastically from the plans she had made with her father and Mansel. Plans that had seemed cast in iron at the time. Since then, she had witnessed her Uncle Morgan's transformation of Danygraig House from a happy family home into a mausoleum where everyone went about 'their duty' in fear. She smiled as she recalled the weeks of happiness she had enjoyed with Mansel when they had planned their wedding. And . . .

Refusing to think about her life since the day Mansel had vanished, she smoothed the first page of the paper, which was covered in advertisements, turned it, and scanned the first article that caught her attention.

She sipped tea and read about Miners' Federation Meetings, Licensing Offences, and a diatribe by someone who signed himself 'Onlooker' on the sad state of social life in Pontypridd, which he attributed to the high pay 'given to' colliers; the drunkenness, crime, lunacy and lustful practices indulged in by the overpaid miners and the inability of the churches and chapels to deal with the situation and channel young men's energies into more useful occupations.

It was the type of article her father had loved to read aloud to her and Geraint and discuss with them afterwards. The remembrance of those conversations made her realise just how drastically her horizons had narrowed since her marriage. Until she had been admitted to hospital she hadn't talked to anyone other than Owen, Rhian, Iestyn and her baby for over three years and what was worse, she hadn't thought of anything other than housework and pleasing Owen so he wouldn't find cause to beat her.

She had ceased to think, to read, to attend concerts, visit the theatre or do any of the things that had meant so much to her when she had been growing up. The knowledge was painful. She had become one of the women her father had despised, who couldn't see further than the walls of their own houses and never voiced an opinion other than that of their husbands.

She turned over the page and looked at the list of misdemeanours at the Police Court. When she reached halfway down the column she sat bolt upright and re-read the paragraph.

Following an incident at the home of Mrs Edyth James, Ynysangharad House, Pontypridd, Mr Owen Bull, butcher, of Mill Street, Pontypridd, was bound over in the sum of £20 for six months to be of good behaviour. The defendant apologised to the court and stated that at the time of the offence he was of the opinion that members of his immediate family were inside Ynysangharad House. The solicitor for the defence undertook to see that the fine was paid within a fortnight.

Owen had gone to her Aunt Edyth's house and made a scene. She imagined him shouting on the doorstep, demanding Rhian return to Mill Street with the baby. Her aunt hadn't told her, because she knew if she did, she would never persuade her to move into Ynysangharad House. There was no way that she'd put her aunt's life or the lives of her aunt's servants at risk. Knowing Owen as she did, she realised he was quite capable of turning up there drunk, and ready to attack anyone who stood in his way. She recalled the thinly veiled threat he had made that afternoon.

Leave me and you, and who ever you run to, will suffer.

He hadn't said what he would do to make them suffer, but then, there was no need. She fingered her swollen, cracked cheekbone. He didn't have to tell her what he was capable of doing to her, her son, Rhian, or her aunt, because he had already shown her.

After the ward maids had cleaned Sali's room the following morning, her Uncle Morgan walked into her cubicle.

'Don't disturb yourself,' he said, as she instinctively clutched the edges of her lace bed jacket together. He pushed aside the stool and sat on the chair, staring at her, making her feel as though he could see right through her jacket and nightgown. 'I regularly visit the infirmary to offer spiritual comfort to those unable to attend chapel through ill health and I decided to call on you. Is there anything you want to tell me?'

'No.' She began to tremble. First Owen, now her uncle. Owen had made her life a hell. Her uncle had raped her. And both visited and sat with her as if they had never treated her anything other than benevolently.

'Ask me then?'

She shook her head.

'I thought you'd at least want to enquire after your mother's and siblings' health.'

'How are they?' She looked through the open doorway for a nurse she could call.

'Your siblings are in rude health. Your mother is failing. But then perhaps you heard how they are from the housekeeper yesterday. Mari did come to see you?'

Sali pulled the bedclothes to her neck and huddled beneath them. If she answered 'no' and her uncle knew for certain that Mari had visited her, she would be damned in his eyes. But if he wasn't sure whether Mari had visited her, and she told him Mari had, he'd dismiss the housekeeper.

'You refuse to answer?'

'I was ill yesterday,' she muttered.

'Too ill to recognise your visitors?' He paused. 'No matter. I was told by a reliable witness that she was here.'

She realised that if Owen were still on speaking terms with her uncle after his arrest, he wouldn't have wasted any time in informing him that he had seen Mari with her aunt.

'I have dismissed her, and engaged a more suitable housekeeper for Danygraig House.'

'Mari has been with us since before I was born.'

'*Us*, Sali?' he said. 'You forget yourself. I spoke to Owen after Evensong yesterday. He told me he had visited you. You are truly fortunate to have such a forgiving, Christian man for a husband. All he could talk about was your return to his house and the fold.

Admirable sentiments from a man driven to drink by your behaviour.'

Driven! Sali could not believe that she had heard her uncle correctly.

'We had a full deacons' meeting. Owen testified before God that he had visited a public house for the first time in his life and it was your recalcitrance that drove him there. You sinned and he paid for it. Yet, although that night cost him his brother's life, he is prepared to forgive you and take you and the child back into his home.' He leaned very close to her. 'I was sorry to hear that his sister has taken the child and left. You do know where they are?'

Tight-lipped, Sali shook her head.

'You are not only defying your husband, Sali, but me, your senior male relative.'

'I don't know where they are.'

'And I don't believe you. But, I will leave you to your thoughts and conscience for twenty-four hours. Perhaps you will have an answer for me tomorrow morning.'

'I cannot tell you what I don't know.'

'One more thing, Sali.' He left his chair, glanced into the corridor and closed the door. 'You are not thinking of leaving your husband, are you?'

She curled into a ball and opened her mouth, preparing to scream if he touched her.

'You have brought enough grief to your family without courting more dishonour and disgrace. Your mother and I would rather see you dead and in your coffin than living apart from your husband.'

'You would prefer me to die than live?'

'If you should leave your husband, yes. I now see and understand that Owen Bull has cause to be disturbed by your sinful arrogance and pride. Pray, Sali, pray to the Lord for guidance and humility. A wife's happiness is only to be found in unquestioning obedience to her husband. I am sorry to see that you are taking so long to learn that simple lesson.' He opened the door, placed his hat on his head and walked away.

'I hear you couldn't sleep last night, Mrs Bull.' The sister bustled into Sali's cubicle and ran her fingers over the window sill and locker, to check the ward maid's work. She frowned disapprovingly when she saw the *Pontypridd Observer* folded on a stool next to the bed. 'Where did you get this? It's against regulations for patients to read newspapers.'

'I hardly looked at it.' Not wanting to get the night nurse into trouble, Sali avoided answering the question.

'Do you think you will sleep tonight?'

'Yes,' Sali lied.

'Good. Sit up and I'll put down your pillows for the night.' She adjusted the metal support frame in the bed head, lowered Sali's pillows, retrieved the newspaper and switched off the light. 'Sleep well. See you in the morning, Mrs Bull.'

'Goodnight, Sister, and thank you.' Sali stared blankly into the darkness. Soon, she would have to leave the infirmary and then what? She ached to be with her son. But, after Owen's veiled threats she couldn't go to Ynysangharad House. Her uncle, on his own admittance, would rather see her dead than living in Danygraig House and she couldn't, wouldn't, return to Owen Bull.

She thought of Mansel and how he had disappeared without a word. It would take courage and money to build a new life for herself and her son. Much as she hated the thought of parting with it, she could pawn the engagement ring Mansel had given her. It might raise enough money to keep both of them until she could find work. As what? Even if she had completed her teaching certificate, no authority employed married women as teachers. And no respectable household would employ a woman who had left her husband, even as a skivvy. If she left Pontypridd she might be able to pass herself off as a widow ... But there was still Harry. How could she work and take care of him? She couldn't abide the thought of him living with another woman now; if the arrangement were to become permanent she thought she would go mad.

After tossing and turning on the hard narrow bed for hours she crept out of her cubicle and went to the bathroom. The duty nurse was slumped over the desk in the middle of the ward, her head resting on a book, sleeping. Sali read the clock on the wall. Four o'clock and she hadn't closed her eyes. She was exhausted but she might never have another or better opportunity. She went to the bathroom and washed. Returning to her cubicle, she pulled the door until it was almost closed, then moving stealthily and silently, opened her locker.

The shops opened early on a Monday morning and none earlier than the pawnbroker. She had seen the queues of women, waiting to pawn their wedding rings so they could buy food for the week after their husbands had drunk away their wages on Saturday night. All she had to do was dress, leave the hospital, get the money, catch the train to Tonypandy and look for her son – and make sure that no one followed her who would carry news of her movements back to Owen, her uncle, or, the one person in the world who would be most hurt by her disappearance, Aunt Edyth.

She lifted out the underclothes, woollen smock and canvas overall that had been stripped from her when she had been admitted and the ward maids had since washed and ironed. Below them was the brown paper parcel that Rhian had put on the stretcher when they had carried her from Mill Street. She struggled to untie the string and the paper crackled alarmingly as she unfolded it. She lifted out her skirt and probed the waistband beneath the button. It was still there, securely sewn into the band. She looked around for something she could use to unpick the stitches. Settling on a hook from her corset, she ripped at the thread until the ring Mansel had given her tumbled into her hand.

The gold and diamonds shone, even in the muted light that came through the crack in the door. She lifted the half circle of diamonds to her lips, kissed it, and closed her fingers tightly around it. If . . . if only . . .

No! She couldn't afford to think about Mansel, not now. She had to move forward, not dwell on the past, for her son's sake. If only she knew how he was coping, living with strangers. Mari had said the woman her sister had found was kind and had a boy of her own, but she was bound to be kinder to her own child than Harry. And what if he didn't like living with them, or preferred living with them to living with her? Given the miserable life they'd had with Owen, she couldn't imagine a worse home than Mill Street.

She opened her hand. She had clutched the ring so hard, it left an impression in the palm of her hand. It was the last link to her past and it was going to be difficult to let it go, but pawning it was the only option left to her if she was going to forge a future away from Owen Bull. Setting the ring on her locker, she stripped off the bed jacket and nightdress her aunt had given her and dressed in her underclothes. This was no time to daydream. She had to escape from the infirmary, find a job, make a home and get her son back.

She dressed hurriedly in her underclothes, corset, stockings and the black suit that was now far too big for her. After lacing on the boots that had been parcelled up with the suit, she looked down on the sum total of her worldly possessions. One Welsh flannel smock, one pair of heavily repaired, rough working boots that Owen had given her and a canvas khaki overall. Her aunt had brought in what she regarded as the absolute essentials for a lady: three silk and lace nightdresses, two bed jackets, three sets of fine lace and silk underclothes, a dozen lace and muslin handkerchiefs, a toothbrush, soap and bottle of lavender water. She didn't have a hat, coat, gloves, towel or even a hairbrush, but then, she reflected philosophically, she had so little hair it didn't need brushing.

Discarding the clothes Owen had given her, she wrapped her aunt's gifts in the brown paper, picked up the parcel and holding her breath, tentatively opened the door. The ward was in silence, the nurse still asleep. Walking on tiptoe and sticking close to the side of the corridor, she crept to the door that connected the ward to the rest of the hospital. Opening it just wide enough to slip out, she found herself on a landing. Gripping a wooden rail for support, she began the descent to ground level.

The sky was just beginning to lighten but not enough to dispel the shadows that shrouded the grim, grey stone buildings. After the overheated atmosphere of the ward the fresh autumn morning seemed bitter. Moving in the coal-black gloom that shrouded the foot of the high walls surrounding the infirmary, she stole to the side gate and found it locked. She continued to walk around, close to the wall, until she reached the Porter's Lodge at the front entrance. A light shone from the window and she heard voices. Two men were standing in the doorway engrossed in conversation, but a small gate set beside the main gates was open.

Her heart played a staccato drumbeat as she made a dash, but she didn't dare start breathing again until she left Courthouse Street and reached the white-tiled tunnel beneath the railway bridge. A train thundered overhead and she instinctively clapped her hands over her ears. A man stopped and stared at her. Acutely aware of her shorn head and lack of hat, coat and gloves, she put her head down and made her way into Taff Street. People were already walking around the town and, just as she remembered, there was a queue of women outside the pawnbroker's. A fat, middle-aged woman eyed her curiously as she joined them, and she tried to cover her bruised and scabbed face with her fingers.

'You look cold, love.'

'I am,' Sali acknowledged cautiously, too afraid not to answer lest she draw even more attention to herself.

'Take this, I'm popping it anyway and you may as well make use of it before I do.' The woman handed her a shawl.

'Thank you.' Sali took it, and draped it over her head, hiding most of her face.

'Beat you about, did he?' The woman didn't wait for Sali to answer. 'Brutes, that's what men are. All men,' she added. 'Damned brutes. You take my Alf. He can't have a pint without knocking me about afterwards. Not that he ever sticks to a pint, mind.'

Sali crept between the woman and the shop window. The woman carried on talking regardless and Sali was grateful. By holding the interest of the others in the queue, she drew attention away from her.

The shop opened and the queue shuffled forward. She deliberately hung back, waiting until the shop was empty. It was going to be difficult enough to face Mr Goodman, who had been a friend of her father, without having an audience watching her pawn the only valuable she owned.

'Can I help you, Miss . . . Miss Watkin Jones . . . Mrs Bull, is it you?' Mr Goodman peered uncertainly at her. When she nodded, he ran around the counter and pulled up a chair for her. 'Please, sit down.'

'I am fine, thank you, Mr Goodman.' Sali felt tears forming in her eyes. It was hateful to think that she was incapable of controlling her own emotions, especially when someone was showing her kindness

'You don't look fine, Mrs Bull. I heard you were in the infirmary. When did you get out? Does—'

She cut him short. 'Could you advance me some money on this, please?' She handed him the ring she had clutched in her hand since she had left the hospital.

He held it to the light, before reaching for his jeweller's eyeglass. 'This is a very valuable ring, but I couldn't give you anywhere near its worth. There is no call in Pontypridd for anything like this. If you didn't redeem it, I'd never sell it.'

'I will redeem it the moment I can afford to. And I wouldn't want its full value. Could you advance me . . .' She thought rapidly. She didn't even know what Rhian was paying the family who were looking after her son but she guessed it couldn't be less than five shillings a week and she'd have to reimburse her for what she had already paid out. And she might not find work straight away and she'd have to pay for respectable lodgings because she couldn't possibly take the child to a slum, and there was food and train fare and she'd have to buy a hat, coat, and clothes for Harry . . . 'Ten pounds?' she asked breathlessly.

'That is a lot of money.'

'I know, but you said yourself that the ring is worth more. And could you please hold it for me for six months?'

'I think I could manage that. You know I charge two shillings in the pound a week interest?'

'Two shillings . . . but that would be a pound a week, Mr Goodman. I could never earn that much money to repay you.'

'I'll tell you what, Mrs Bull, out of respect for your father, I will advance you ten pounds and charge you two pounds interest for the six months. If you redeem it before, it will still be two pounds, but I think that is fair, don't you?'

'More than fair, Mr Goodman, I'll take it, and thank you.'

He opened the safe, removed a velvet-lined box and laid the ring inside. After locking the safe he went to a clothes rack. 'As a bonus I can let you have a coat and,' he lifted down a valise, 'this.' He handed her the case and a black coat. A broad-brimmed black hat was pinned to the front of it, and a black muffler and gloves hung from the pockets. He added a black shawl that was folded on a shelf. She recognised them. They were all her possessions. 'Mr Bull brought them in a few years ago. It was a straight sale. A bad investment on my part.' He shrugged. 'My customers prefer more showy clothes.'

'I can't possible take all this,' she protested.

Ignoring her assertion, he lifted a tray of wedding rings on the counter. 'You'll also need one of these.'

She glanced down at her bare hand. Owen hadn't returned her ring, which he had torn from her finger the night Iestyn died. 'How much are they, Mr Goodman?'

'Call it an extra bonus for the business I have transacted with your husband over the years.'

'I couldn't possibly—'

'I don't offer all my customers a bonus.' He wrote out a ticket, counted ten, one-pound notes and laid the wedding ring on top of the pile. He pushed it towards her, walked around the counter and held out the coat. She slipped her arms into the sleeves, took the ring, ticket and money and secreted the notes in one of her gloves.

'There's a mirror behind you,' he said, as she picked up the hat.

Sali pulled the brim low over her face, wound the muffler around her mouth and pushed the shawl into the valise. It was then that she realised there were clothes already in the case.

'I couldn't sell those either,' he lied.

'Thank you very much, Mr Goodman. You have been very kind.'

'Good luck, Mrs Bull.' He opened the door for her.

Sali hesitated. 'If Mr Bull or anyone else should come in asking for me . . .'

'I never saw you. And if you want to redeem your ring by post, just send me the ticket and I'll forward it to wherever you are, by registered post.'

'Thank you again, Mr Goodman.' She held out her hand and he shook it.

He stood back watching her as she crossed the road. When she disappeared from sight he opened the safe again. Taking an envelope he pushed the ring box into it and wrote the ticket number he had given Sali on the outside followed by '*Property of Sali Watkin Jones – to be returned to claimant without charge.*'

Sali Watkin Jones, as was, might be too proud to take charity but if anything should happen to him he didn't want his heirs profiting from the daughter of the only man in Pontypridd who had extended a hand of friendship and offered help to a penniless Russian Jewish refugee when he had come to the town in search of work and a new life.

Sali left the pawnbroker's and walked towards the imposing red-brick façade of Pontypridd Railway Station. Keeping her head down, she entered the ticket office. There was a short queue in front of the circular counter and as she waited her turn she saw two of her uncle's chapel congregation. Turning her back, she pretended she hadn't seen them.

'Where to?' Tomas's brother asked through the cubbyhole window without recognising her.

'Cardiff, please.'

'Return?'

'One way.' She opened her purse. 'Third class, please.'

Taking her ticket and her change, she thrust both into her pocket and ran up the steps to the platform. After showing her ticket to the official manning the gate at the top, she walked through. The Cardiff train was standing alongside the platform. She walked to the end of the train, deliberately holding back until the guard moved forward with his flag. As he lifted his whistle to his lips, she stepped into the last carriage. It was empty. Heart pounding, she sat in a corner seat opposite the window and next to the corridor clutching her valise. Pulling the brim of her hat down low, she glanced towards the window when they drew into the first station after Pontypridd, Treforest. She shrank back as bowler-hatted men in suits walked past her carriage towards the first-class cars. Two workmen joined her and she stared down at her bag, not daring to raise her eyes again until they drew into Cardiff.

She left the train, walked into St Mary's Street and stopped at the first draper's she came to. She bought two pairs of stockings and almost bought an identical khaki canvas overall to the one Owen had given her. Then she realised she didn't have to wear Owen's choice of clothes – not any more. Feeling defiant and immoral, she bought a pretty navy-blue cotton overall patterned with white daisies. Before she left the shop, she removed her hat and draped her shawl over her head, covering as much of her face as she could.

She found a stationer's and bought a packet of envelopes, a cheap writing pad, a bottle of ink and a pen. She picked up a stamp at the Post Office, and went into a temperance café. After ordering a cup of tea and a plain bun, she opened the writing pad, unscrewed the ink bottle, dipped the nib of the pen into it and began to write quickly, without allow herself time to think about what she was saying.

Dear, dear Aunt Edyth,
I can't thank you enough for all your kindnesses. I hope you understand why I can't live with you and why I had to leave without saying goodbye. I will try to write to you to let you know how I am. Please don't look for me and please try to do something for Mari. Uncle Morgan told me that he sacked her for visiting me in hospital.
I am so sorry to hurt you in the same way that Mansel did.
Your own Sali

She folded the paper into the envelope, sealed it, stuck on the stamp, and addressed it to her aunt. She posted it as she walked back to the station. When the ticket office was empty, she bought a third-class, one-way ticket to

Tonypandy. All she could think about was her son. And before the end of the day she might be with him, if she could find the house where Mari's sister worked.

Sali left the train at the newly built Tonypandy and Trealaw Station and followed her fellow passengers into Dunraven Street. She had never visited Tonypandy and had expected to find a village with a few small shops, not a busy, bustling, small town. Wares from a furniture shop and ironmonger's spilled out on to the pavement. A haberdasher had hung coats from hooks suspended above his window. The appetising smell of roasting coffee beans vied with the pungent odours of cheese and the acidic tangs of fruit in the entrance to a provision shop as large as anything that Pontypridd had to offer. Hungry, she was tempted to go in and see if they sold bread rolls. As she stepped up to the door she saw a notice in the window.

Housekeeper wanted. Keep plus fifteen shillings a week. Apply within.

The paper was yellow from exposure to sunlight. The post might be already filled, but if it wasn't? The one thing she did know about after running Owen Bull's house for over three years was housekeeping. She opened the shop door and with the bell clanging overhead walked inside.

'Can I help you, madam?'

The woman who addressed Sali in a lilting Irish brogue could have been anything between thirty and forty-five years of age. Tall, thin, angular, she had green eyes and red hair. No one could have called her beautiful, or even pretty, but she was striking.

'I'd like to apply for the housekeeper's position, please, if it's not taken.'

'It's not taken,' the woman answered, 'and even when it is, it's not for long. Look after things here for me, Dewi.'

A young boy with a spotty face took her place at the counter and gazed curiously at Sali while the assistant disappeared through a door set in the back wall of the shop. She returned a few minutes later.

'Mrs Rodney will see you now.' She lifted the counter and opened a half-door set beneath it. 'If you'd come this way, Miss . . .'

'Mrs Jones, Mrs Sali Jones.' Sali crossed her fingers in her coat pocket in the hope that Mrs Rodney wouldn't object to employing a housekeeper with a child.

'I'm Annie O'Leary.'

'Pleased to meet you, Miss O'Leary.' Encouraged by the woman's smile, Sali ventured, 'What did you mean just now, Miss O'Leary, when you said the job is never taken for long?'

'Mrs Rodney is best placed to answer that.' She led Sali down a short corridor and opened a door marked 'Office'. 'This is the applicant for the position of housekeeper, Mrs Rodney.' She showed Sali into a large, square room lit by a high window and carpeted with a red and blue Persian rug. A functional desk, fitted with drawers both sides, stood in front of the window. On it were arranged a typewriter, an enamel tray of four ink bottles with blue, black, green and red labels, a pen set with a rack of spare nibs of various sizes, a large blotter, and a wooden rack containing sheets of paper, billheads, pencils, rulers and rubbers. The iron grate was stoked with a blazing fire, the tiled hearth held a set of fire irons and brass coal and wood buckets. A bureau bookcase was shelved with neat rows of ledgers. Two comfortable armchairs and an enormous sofa that could have easily doubled as a bed completed the furniture.

It was warm and welcoming, as much living room as office. Silver-framed photographs of an elderly couple and a beautiful young girl were arranged either side of a silver carriage clock on the mantelpiece. A landscape of sea fringed by palm trees hung on the wall and Berlin wool-work cushions and colourfully crocheted blankets littered the chairs and sofa.

A handsome, well-dressed, middle-aged woman, with strong, classically beautiful features and dark eyes, looked up from the desk. 'Please, sit down.' She turned her chair to face Sali. If she was shocked by the scars and bruises on Sali's face she didn't show it. 'My assistant tells me that you want to apply for the position of housekeeper.'

'Yes.' Sali felt positively shabby in her old-fashioned, ill-fitting black suit. Mrs Rodney's thick, glossy, blue-black hair was swept up in a style she had never seen before, but guessed was highly fashionable. Her bottle-green, fine wool dress was close-fitting, the neck, sleeves and hem trimmed with froths of hand-worked ecru lace. Even her jewellery was understated and elegant. Her ears were pierced by small gold hoops and a dark blue cameo was pinned into the lace at her throat.

Sali breathed in Mrs Rodney's exotic, floral perfume and dropped her valise next to her chair. She realised that she'd look even shabbier if she removed the hat she had put on when she had left the train and revealed her cropped hair. 'I am a hard worker,' she began eagerly, too eagerly, she realised when she saw the expression on Mrs Rodney's face harden.

'I am not the one looking for a housekeeper, Miss—'

'Mrs . . . Mrs Sali Jones,' Sali removed her gloves and offered her calloused right hand deliberately exposing the wedding ring she had been given by the pawnbroker on her left.

'You are married?'

'Widowed.' Sali's conscience pricked as one lie followed another.

'You appear to have been in an accident.'

'I was knocked down by a cart in Cardiff. I was in the infirmary for so long I lost my home.' That at least wasn't a complete lie.

'When did you leave the infirmary?'

'This morning.'

'Cardiff Infirmary?'

Sali hesitated for the barest fraction of a second before answering, 'Yes.'

Mrs Rodney sat back in her chair and pressed the top of her pen thoughtfully to her lips. 'Mrs Jones, the position is housekeeper to four miners. It will be hard work—'

'I am not afraid of hard work.'

'But you are not in the best of health.'

'I soon will be,' Sali crossed her fingers again. She had to get this job. She *had* to.

'Have you a character?'

Sali's face fell. She had no references and in her present position she could hardly ask anyone for them, not without revealing her whereabouts. 'No, but I studied for two and half years at Swansea Training College.'

'You didn't complete your training?'

'My father died and I was needed at home. Shortly afterwards I married.'

'You are not needed at home any longer?'

'There is no one left to need me.'

'You look like a decent woman, Mrs Jones, but without a character it would be remiss of me to employ you on behalf of my relatives. With all due respect, you could have come from anywhere. Even prison.' Mrs Rodney turned her chair back to her desk.

'I give you my solemn word that I have done nothing . . .' Sali almost said 'wrong', then substituted, 'illegal', at the last moment.

'But all you can give me is your word that you are a respectable woman. I am afraid that is not enough, Mrs Jones.'

'I need to build a life for myself, Mrs Rodney. If you give me a chance, I will work without pay for two weeks. If, at the end of that time your relatives do not want me, I will leave.'

Mrs Rodney turned back to Sali. 'You are so desperate that you will work for nothing?'

'Yes,' Sali answered in a small voice.

'I will write to the Training College.'

'If you do, could you please ask them not to let anyone know where I am?' Sali sensed she'd ruined what little chance she had of getting the position as soon as she'd voiced her request.

'Has anything you've told me been the truth, Mrs Jones?' Mrs Rodney enquired caustically.

'My maiden name was Jones. My husband isn't dead. But I do desperately need to find work.'

'Your husband won't support you?' When Sali didn't answer, Mrs Rodney said, 'He put you in the infirmary.' It wasn't a question.

Sick to the pit of her stomach, Sali whispered, 'Yes.'

'You are not from Tonypandy?'

'No.'

'Does anyone know where you are?'

'No. I posted a letter to the one relative I have who does care for me from Cardiff. I hope that if she does look for me, she'll look there. Please, I really need . . .'

Mrs Rodney left her seat and reached for a dark blue cape that hung on a hook at the back of the door. 'I will be honest with you, Mrs Jones, you may not suit but I am inclined to give you a week's trial.'

'You'll give me the job?' Sali stared incredulously at the woman.

'Please listen attentively. I am inclined to give you a trial for one week, a paid trial,' she added so there would not be any mistake. 'However, it will not be me, but Mr William Evans who will be your employer and he will have no compunction in asking you to pack your bags if you don't suit him. I take it from the valise that you are able to start right away?'

'Yes.'

'Follow me. I'll show you the house.'

CHAPTER THIRTEEN

Sali walked behind Mrs Rodney up Dunraven Street. At the end of the street they turned left up a steep hill. After a few minutes they turned left again into a narrow street of eleven houses, six one side, five the other. Mrs Rodney stopped at the door of a house that bordered an open patch of mountainside. A large key protruded from the lock; she turned it and stepped inside.

'Mr Evans and his three sons work the day shift in the colliery. Six until two.' She glanced at her bracelet watch. 'They will be in at half past two, you have four hours, so perhaps you could start by cooking their dinner. Like most men, none of them have the faintest idea how to prepare food and the meals in the public house aren't exactly what you'd call good home cooking. Leave your bag there,' she pointed to a spot at the foot of the stairs, 'and I'll show you around.'

Mrs Rodney opened a door on their left. 'This was the parlour.' Sali looked in and saw a brass-framed double bed, chest of drawers, washstand and chaise longue. A thick layer of dust greyed the slate mantelpiece and dulled the bright colours of a pair of Staffordshire china dogs. 'Mr Evans's wife died of cancer six weeks ago. He can't bring himself to return to the bedroom upstairs and, as this is the room she died in, he has been sleeping here since. He is a broken man, Mrs Jones, although you wouldn't think it to look at him. Grief has made him short-tempered and difficult to live with. Do you understand what I am saying?'

'Yes.'

'This middle room now contains the parlour furniture.' Sali saw an even dustier room crammed with a horsehair sofa, two high-backed chairs and a full-sized dining table, sideboard and six upright chairs. Bookshelves lined the walls, every shelf filled to capacity with the overflow piled on top of the cases. The mantelpiece and sideboard held good quality china and porcelain ornaments. Photographs covered the walls, mostly of young boys and men, although there were a few of a beautiful young woman who closely resembled Mrs Rodney. A copy of Bellini's *Madonna of the Meadow* hung over the fireplace. When Mrs Rodney saw Sali looking at it, she explained, 'The late Mrs Evans was my father's sister and like him born a Spaniard. We are Catholic. Is that going to be a problem for you?'

Sali shook her head. 'Not at all.'

'And you are?'

'I was chapel, but I haven't been to a service in over three years.'

'Then you may fit in here after all,' Mrs Rodney said wryly. 'The sixth housekeeper I engaged for my uncle left ten days ago. She only lasted two days and point blank refused to work for heathens a moment longer. When I said we were Catholic, Mrs Jones, I may have given you the wrong impression. Mr Evans's two younger sons are Catholic. Mr Evans and his eldest son are Marxists and atheists. Do you object to Marxists or atheists, Mrs Jones?'

'No. My father was interested in Marxism,' Sali replied cautiously. Her father had read Marx, but as an ardent Capitalist, only for the purpose of finding flaws in his arguments.

'Another right answer, Mrs Jones. As long as your idea of Marxism coincides with my uncle's. This,' she opened a door directly in front of them, 'is the upstairs kitchen. There are two,' she clarified in response to Sali's bemused expression. 'One in the basement and one here. Both have ranges. The one in the basement is larger and used for washing clothes and bathing.'

'A pump and sink,' Sali went to a large Belfast sink set below a window that looked out over the town to the valley, the collieries and the mountain beyond.

'There is a tap in the basement as well.'

'What is this?' Sali indicated a wide copper pipe topped with a funnel that rose from the floor to waist height in the corner next to the range.

'One of Victor's inventions. He is the colliery black-smith and the most practical of my three cousins. He was constantly searching for ways to lessen his mother's workload. The pipe leads directly down into the base-ment. Before they came home from the colliery, my aunt would heat water for their baths on the range here and downstairs in the basement. Unlike most families, my uncle and his sons don't share a bath, and given their combined coal ration they don't have to, which is why they keep the two ranges going every day except Sunday. My aunt would drag one of the baths below the pipe, pour the water down it and fill the bath. It saved carrying buckets of boiling water up and downstairs.'

'That sounds wonderful,' Sali smiled.

'You've obviously carried water.' She turned to the dresser, which was fronted by wooden doors a shade lighter than the frame, opened a door and revealed shelves of blue Delphware. 'My aunt liked good china and used it every day. Victor made the doors and put them on last winter to save her from dusting the shelves. Cutlery,' she indicated a drawer in the table, 'cooking utensils and saucepans in the cupboard next to the range. And here is the larder,' She opened a door and walked into a long, narrow room that held marble slabs for cheese, butter, eggs, lard and milk. A wooden rack was filled with potatoes and a meat safe, set on a shelf apart, held a large piece of beef.

'I intended to put that in the oven earlier but forgot. Cook it any way you want. I have been sending up one of the assistants from the shop at two o'clock to start the meal and set water on to boil for the baths. You'll need to boil eight buckets and put two buckets of boiling water in each. The men will put in their own cold when they are ready. My uncle has an account in the shop and since my aunt's death I have been sending the errand boy up every day with bread and whatever meat I've chosen. But from tomorrow you can take over. You can either bring your order to the shop or send it down with the boy. He will deliver it. As you see, my aunt was meticulous.' Mrs Rodney pointed to enamelware bins of various sizes, marked *flour, sugar, rice, oatmeal, tea and coffee*. 'The biscuit and cake tins are all empty,' Mrs Rodney said, as Sali lifted the lid of one.

'This pantry is well stocked,' Sali commented. Owen would have expected the store in the larder to have kept the four of them in Mill Street for a month.

'Never sit on either of my aunt's chairs.' Mrs Rodney pointed to the easy chair set to the left of the hearth, and the chair at the end of the table closest to the range. 'Housekeeper number two was sacked for that. Also, you may clean my uncle's bedroom but you may not touch any of my aunt's things except to dust them. House-keeper number one went when he caught her trying on one of my aunt's shawls.'

'Thank you for the warning.'

'That,' she pointed to a door set in the back right-hand corner of the kitchen, 'leads to the stairs to the basement. These,' she opened the cupboards built in either side of the range, 'hold more books. This house is overrun with them. There are four bedrooms.' She returned to the front of the house, walked up the stairs ahead of Sali and opened the door that faced them on the landing. 'This was my uncle and aunt's room.' A brass bedstead had been dismantled and leaned together with a blanket-shrouded mattress against the wall. The wardrobe door was closed, but Sali detected the scent of rose water in the air. The dressing table held tortoiseshell backed hair-brushes and mirrors and a carved jewellery box. The washstand was furnished with a Royal Doulton toilet-ware set.

Mrs Rodney opened yet another cupboard. 'This is the household linen. Given the number of housekeepers who have been in and out of here, and the short duration of their stays, I think you will find all the beds need changing. 'And this is your bedroom. For as long as you last,' she added deprecatingly.

It was a box room, no more than five by six feet, but it held a single, iron-framed bedstead, the mattress folded double on top of iron springs, and a travelling wash-stand, with a tin jug set below a tin washbasin, and a chamber pot, discreetly hidden in a box at the base. 'There's a chest of drawers and hooks and hangers on the back of the door.'

'It will be fine,' Sali said earnestly.

'Really, Mrs Jones?' Mrs Rodney answered sceptically. 'Well, you are not easily daunted; I'll give you that. The *ty bach*, coalhouse and vegetable garden are out the back; the easiest way to get to them is through the basement. You'll find a wash tub, mangle and dolly there.'

Sali sensed a hesitation and realised Mrs Rodney was loathe to leave a stranger in charge of a fully and comfortably furnished house.

'If you are worried about leaving me on my own, Mrs Rodney, I could pay you a five pound-bond,' she offered, holding the rest of her money back for her son, when she found him.

'Five pounds! But you said you were desperate.'

'I am. I pawned the only thing I owned of any value to get here and I intend to redeem it.' Sali pulled off her glove and began to count off five pounds.

'None of the other housekeepers paid a bond,' Mrs Rodney said doubtfully.

'But they all had references.'

'Yes. I tell you what I'll do, Mrs Jones, you last the

month and I'll return this with an extra pound. It will be worth that in saved wages from my staff in the shop. But, should my uncle throw you out sooner, I'll return it in full. Just come to me at the shop and ask for it.'

'You told me why your uncle sacked three of his housekeepers. Why did he ask the others to leave, Mrs Rodney?' Sali asked diffidently.

'He didn't like their cooking. Oh, and by the way,' she turned back at the head of the stairs, 'I'll tell my uncle the first version you gave me of your life story. In my experience, men are unsympathetic to women who leave their husbands. Goodbye.'

Only four hours! Sali considered what she should do first to create a good impression. Baths, miners needed to wash as soon as they came home, and food. She unfolded the mattress, laid it flat on the iron bedstead in the box room and opened her valise. Taking off her hat and coat, she hung them on the back of the door, slipped the overall she had bought over her suit and went to the kitchen.

The range was stoked to burn for hours. It was dusty, but that could wait. She found tin buckets in the pantry, filled four at the pump and lined them up in front of the range ready to be put on the hobs at two o'clock. She ran down the staircase to the basement. The range was burning and the room warm, but she was daunted by a mammoth pile of washing that reached halfway up the wall and filled a quarter of the room. The dirty clothes would have spread even further if a makeshift wall, cobbled together from a wooden tub, dolly, mangle and row of buckets hadn't contained them.

Deciding that the washing too could wait, she filled another four buckets with water from a tap in the corner that didn't have a sink, only a drain set in the floor beneath it. She lined them up next to the range, which was in even more need of a clean than the one upstairs. A second walk-in pantry contained dozens of empty preserving jars, earthenware containers filled with salt that she guessed had been used to preserve eggs, and empty jam jars.

Recalling that there hadn't been any vegetables other than potatoes in the pantry, she went outside. The first door she opened was the *ty bach*. The lavatory and seat were cleaner than she expected them to be after the dust and dirt of the house and there was a pile of newspapers on a stand behind the door. It was conveniently close to the back door, which seemed a luxury after the long trek down the yard in Mill Street. She opened the two brick-built sheds alongside it. One had coal heaped almost to the ceiling. She recalled her father telling her that miners received a coal allowance as part of their wages and with four colliery workers in one house that either amounted to more than they could use, or they had just had a recent delivery. The wood shed was filled with split logs.

Rows of leeks, runner beans, onions, cabbages, turnips, peas and raspberry canes stretched from the shed down to a chicken coop and dog run at the bottom of the garden. The coop held a black cockerel and several white-feathered hens; the run housed two dogs that started barking as soon as they spotted her. When she looked at them, the Jack Russell and black Labrador stopped barking and gazed curiously at her. She approached the wooden palings and the Labrador stuck his head out and wagged his tail.

'Some guard dog you are.' She fondled the dog's ears in a way she would never have dared do with Owen's dogs.

There were no weeds in the vegetable plot and both chicken run and dog pen were clean with freshly filled bowls of water. She reflected that someone in the house spent more time tending to the yard than the living quarters.

She retrieved a bucket from the basement, filled it with beans, leeks, onions, turnips and carrots and scavenged enough late raspberries for a summer pudding. The garden clearly produced more vegetables than one family could use, and she understood why there were so many preserving jars. She was beginning to feel that there was enough work in this terraced house to occupy the time of the entire complement of servants who had worked in Danygraig House in her father's time.

As she wasn't used to the oven, she decided against roasting the beef. After her father had died she had persuaded Mari and the cook to give her occasional cookery lessons, as much to give her an excuse to stay in the kitchen away from her uncle and mother as from any desire to learn. And Owen had never found fault with her pastry, or at least hadn't said he had, so she thought she would make a pie. Seeing a small herb bed, she recalled some of the things her father's cook had done to make meals more interesting and spent a few precious minutes picking sprigs of rosemary to mix in the pastry, mint for the peas, and enough horseradish to make a sauce. Tempted by a clump of heavily scented stock that suddenly and painfully reminded her of her childhood home, she picked a small bunch and arranged them in a vase she found in the basement kitchen.

The next hour was spent cubing and braising the meat, cleaning the vegetables, and mixing the pastry from flour, lard, rosemary and water. She decanted cream from the top of the milk in the jug in the pantry, added a few spoonfuls of sugar, whipped it and returned it to the slab to cool. She made the pie in the largest dish she could find and the summer pudding in the largest bowl.

When the pie was in the oven, the peas podded and mixed with mint in a saucepan waiting to go on the hob, and the raspberries encased in a bread crust ready for baking, she cleaned the gas lamps, washed every surface in the kitchen, scrubbed the table and lino-covered floor and polished the dresser and window. She did her best with the range but it was obvious that it hadn't been taken apart and given a thorough cleaning for weeks. If

Mr Evans allowed her to stay, she would clean it in the morning.

She found clean bed linen, towels and tablecloths in the linen cupboard, made her bed and changed the others. She only stopped work to set the buckets on the hobs to boil and set out towels on the rail on the basement range to warm. The soiled linen, she tossed on top of the mountainous pile in the basement.

She laid the table with crockery, cutlery and water glasses, filled a jug with water and set it and the vase of stock in the centre. The bread she used for the summer pudding and cut for the meal wasn't as soft as the ones she had learned to bake under Rhian's guidance. Seeing no yeast in the larder she resolved to order some from the shop tomorrow, if she still had a job.

The buckets started bubbling at twenty-five minutes past two on the kitchen clock. Using a jug she tipped the contents of two buckets down the tube. She ran down to the basement, dragged the full bath away from the pipe and replaced it with another. She found it harder, heavier work to carry buckets from the basement range to fill the baths than to tip water down the tube.

She left three baths steaming, and returned upstairs to tip down the last two buckets of water. She was returning the buckets to the pantry when she heard the door slam in the basement accompanied by the sound of masculine voices.

She opened the oven door. She hoped her employers wouldn't take too long over their baths. Another ten minutes and the pie would be browned to perfection. She was making extra gravy in the pan she had used to braise the meat, when footsteps sounded on the stone steps and the door opened.

'You're the housekeeper Mrs Rodney has hired for us.'

The man in front of her was massive and she instinctively dropped a curtsy. Her father had been six foot but this man was taller and broader, with wiry, grey curly hair and a stern expression in his grey eyes. He was also turned out in a white shirt, collar, black tie and suit, more suited to a tradesman than a collier. He glanced around the kitchen, then at the table. 'Have you made a meal for us, Mrs Jones?'

'Yes, sir.'

'Mr Evans will do, I'm not used to being called sir. Mrs Rodney stopped us on the way home and told us about you. I take it she has also told you what we expect from you?'

'Yes, Mr Evans.'

'The boys will be up in a minute.' He sat at the head of the table.

She picked up a pair of thick crocheted oven cloths, unlatched the oven door and, straining to hold the weight, heaved the pie on to a wooden board she had placed on the table to receive it. Straining the peas she had boiled with the mint into a bowl, she set them besides the pie, filled the gravy boat, put it on its saucer next to the peas, stood back and waited.

A man opened the door and smiled at her. She retreated, terrified. She had thought Mr Evans enormous but he stood half a head taller. He had to stoop to negotiate the doorway and his shoulders were wider than the door. He was young, with light brown hair and grey eyes like his father, but when she dared to look into them, she saw that they were softer and kinder. He was dressed in moleskin trousers, a dark shirt without a collar, and had a red handkerchief tied around his neck like a farmer.

'This is the new housekeeper Connie has engaged for us,' his father informed him abruptly.

'Hello, I'm Victor Evans.' He offered her his hand. 'Connie said she'd told you all about us.'

'Connie?' Sali repeated in confusion.

'Mrs Rodney.' Mr Evans looked suspiciously at the pie. 'I thought we had a joint of best sirloin in the meat safe.'

'You did, Mr Evans,' Sali answered nervously, 'but as

I'm unused to the oven, I hoped you wouldn't mind if I turned it into a pie.'

'When did you arrive?' He looked around the kitchen.

'Four hours ago, Mr Evans. I am afraid I haven't had time to do very much, but if I stay on, I will do better tomorrow.'

'Waste of good sirloin if you ask me.' Mr Evans cut into the pie and spooned a generous helping on to the top plate of the four Sali had stacked in front of him.

'That looks good, Mrs Jones,' Victor complimented, and Sali realised he was compensating for his father's rudeness. 'It is Mrs Jones, isn't it?'

'Yes.' Sali stepped back as a young man rushed headlong into the room.

'Where have you been?' Mr Evans demanded.

The breath caught in Sali's throat. She had thought Mansel and her brother Geraint handsome, but the boy standing in front of her was the most beautiful she had ever seen. No other word could possibly describe him. His hair was as thick and curly as his father's but blue-black like Mrs Rodney's, and his enormous eyes so dark, the irises appeared to be as black as his hair. His features, smooth, perfect, reminded her of a print she had once seen of a portrait of the young Lord Byron.

Like his father he was dressed in a white shirt, collar, tie and suit as if he were going to a social, or the theatre for the evening.

'You must be the new housekeeper.' He walked over to Sali, took her hand into his, shook it and to her embarrassment continued to hold it. 'It was so kind of you to get the baths ready and warm the towels. And this,' he looked at the pie, 'smells wonderful . . .'

'Stop flirting, Joey, and sit down and eat,' his father ordered brusquely. He eyed Sali. 'How old are you, Mrs Jones?'

'Almost twenty-four,' she answered, hoping he wouldn't regard her as too young for the post.

'And already a widow.'

'Yes, Mr Evans.' She found it even more difficult to lie to him than to Mrs Rodney.

Mr Evans filled another plate and handed it to his youngest son. 'I'll need a ladle for the gravy in this pie.'

'Yes, Mr Evans.' She lifted it from an overhead rack as his eldest son walked through the door. He was dressed, like his younger brother and father, for an evening out, in a dark suit, white shirt, collar and tie.

'Damn you, Joey. You have absolutely no sense of responsibility—'

Sali dropped the ladle and it went crashing to the flagstones.

'I'm sorry. I was so busy having words with my brother that I forgot Connie had engaged a housekeeper for us.'

Sali gripped the Belfast sink for support.

The man standing in front of her had been her father's deputy manager and had inherited five per cent of the Watkin Jones Colliery's stock on her father's death. Lloyd Evans. He obviously hadn't recognised her. Or had he? She wavered indecisively for a moment.

'Mrs Jones.' Lloyd nodded to her and took his place at the table.

'Mrs Jones, are you all right?' Mr Evans enquired frostily.

'Yes, Mr Evans. Would you like more gravy?'

'I'd like you to get another plate for yourself and sit at the table so we can start eating.'

'That wouldn't be proper, Mr Evans.'

'Proper! Where do you think you are, girl? Living with the crache with their upstairs, downstairs, kitchen and parlour maids? I'll have no class distinctions in this house. You sit at this table. Now!' He banged his knife on the table.

Too terrified not to, and mindful of Mrs Rodney's instructions not to sit on either of the late Mrs Evans's chairs, she took another plate from the dresser, gave it to Mr Evans and took the empty seat next to Lloyd, opposite Joey, who flashed her a dazzling smile. Even in her present panic-stricken state, she sensed it was one that he had practised many times in the mirror.

Mr Evans handed Lloyd her plate, which held the same sized portion of pie that he had given his sons.

'Please, Mr Evans, I can never eat all that,' she demurred.

'I suggest you try, Mrs Jones. If you intend to carry on working at the rate you have begun, you are going to need it. And don't stand on ceremony. Victor and Joey might follow the Popish doctrine but I'll have no grace said in this house. This food doesn't come courtesy of any God, but from our sweat and labour.'

After the summer pudding had been eaten and she'd made the tea, Sali cleared their dessert dishes to the sink.

'Mrs Rodney showed you where you are to sleep?' Mr Evans sugared his second cup of tea.

'Yes, Mr Evans.'

'She warned you that you are on a month's trial? If you don't suit, you will have to go.'

'Yes, Mr Evans.' A month, a whole month before she could start looking for her son, because she would never find the courage to ask this man if she could bring her child into his house. But a month's employment would give her time and money to look for another position, hopefully one where she could keep her son with her. And there was always the possibility that she might find something before the month was up.

Mr Evans patted his pockets and pulled out his pipe and tobacco pouch. He took his time over filling it, eyeing his sons as he did so. 'I am going to the County Club. If any of you need me I will be in the library there. I will be back before ten o'clock. I take it you will be going down to Connie's to do her accounts, Lloyd?'

'Yes. I'll walk part of the way with you.' Lloyd pushed his empty teacup into the centre of the table. 'Thank you, Mrs Jones, that was a good meal.'

'Victor?' Mr Evans addressed his middle son.

'I'm meeting the boys and taking the dogs rabbiting over the mountain. Do you know how to cook rabbits, Mrs Jones?'

'Yes, Mr Evans, and joint and skin them.' Sali found it strange to think that she had found the task so distasteful when she had first moved to Mill Street.

'No one calls me Mr Evans, Mrs Jones. I'm Victor.' He gave her another of his shy smiles. 'So, if I'm lucky, we could have rabbit pie before the end of the week.'

'After the pie tonight, perhaps you'd prefer stew?' she suggested tentatively.

He looked at the pie dish that had been scraped clean by him and his brothers in search of second helpings. 'Pie will be fine, Mrs Jones, but you'll need at least half a dozen rabbits to fill a dish that size.'

'Where are you off to, Joey?' his father enquired, as Joey left his chair, picked up a bottle of cologne from the window sill and splashed it liberally over his cheeks and neck.

'Out and about,' Joey replied airily.

'Out and about where?' Mr Evans questioned sternly.

Joey bent his knees to study himself in a mirror that had been hung low on the wall at the side of the range. 'Some of the boys are going to catch the show at the Theatre Royal. I thought I'd go with them.'

'Just make sure that you stay with the boys and leave the variety acts to the professionals. I don't want to hear any more complaints about you or your antics,' his father warned. 'There is no need to wait up for us, Mrs Jones. We are on the six to two shift. I would appreciate it if you have breakfast on the table at half past four sharp in the morning. You will find bacon, eggs, lava bread and sausages in the pantry. And don't forget to cut the snap boxes and fill the water bottles.' He pointed to four square tins and four tin bottles stacked on the cupboard next to the sink.

Lloyd angled his trilby on his head, his father picked

up his cap and they went out through the front door. Joey lifted his cap from a row of hooks on the wall, gave Victor, who was finishing his third cup of tea, and Sali a broad wink, and left by the basement stairs.

Sali opened one of the boxes and gazed at the small tin bottle and crumbs it contained. 'Victor, please tell me, what I should put in your snap boxes?' she asked, as he rose from the table.

'You've never cut a snap box before?' he asked incredulously.

'No,' Sali admitted sheepishly.

He picked up the small tin bottle. 'After you've washed these out, you fill them with strongly brewed tea, four sugars and a dash of milk to a bottle. The larger ones you wash out and fill with water.'

'Won't the tea be cold?'

'All colliers drink cold tea. It's the one thing that gets the dust out of your mouth. In the boxes we like two rounds of sandwiches, meat, omelette or cheese. Nothing soft like tomato or cucumber that makes the bread soggy. My mother used to put in a slice of fruit cake or some of her cinnamon biscuits . . . but we haven't had anything like that for a while.' He reached for his cap.

'Thank you, Victor. Good luck with your rabbiting.'

'It might help if you made the boxes tonight, Mrs Jones. My mother used to do that. We're always in a rush in the morning.'

Lloyd made a cross in pencil against the last entry in the ledger, leaned back in his chair and stretched his hands above his head.

'Tired?' Connie Rodney's question was casual, but her eyes glittered as she gazed at him.

'No more than usual.' He closed the book. 'Your shop is doing remarkably well.'

'Your shop,' she corrected.

'Some day the government of this country is going to

wake up and give women equal property rights alongside men.'

'Is that going to be the same day they change the law so husbands can't get their thieving hands on their wives' assets?' she enquired sceptically. 'You're forgetting that it's men who run the country, Lloyd.'

'Please don't hold me personally responsible for the tyranny of my sex.'

'You know as well as I do, that if my father had left the shop to me, Albert George would have gambled away every single penny I own by now,' she reminded acidly.

'I'm on your side, remember. Any time you want to organise a suffragette march I'll walk every step of the way with you. And you know my thoughts on this ridiculous situation. The shop may be registered in my name but I have absolutely no moral right to own it. I still think I should change my will and leave it to Antonia.' He referred to Connie's fifteen-year-old daughter by the husband she had left after two years of troubled and disastrous marriage.

'So Tonia can make the same mistake as me and marry a worthless idiot who will gamble away everything we own?'

'Not all men are like Albert George, Connie.' Lloyd laid his hand over hers, as she leaned on his shoulder.

'And not all men are principled and honourable like you, your father, and Victor.'

He looked quizzically at her. 'You've heard about Joey's latest escapade?'

'I should think everyone in Rhondda Fach, Fawr and South Wales has heard of it by now. Even Tonia came home with a mercifully censored version from the Grammar School. She told me that one of the teachers from the infant school caught Joey climbing out of his wife's bedroom window at eight o'clock in the evening. Fortunately she didn't know that the poor man had come home unexpectedly from a Boys' Brigade meeting because he was feeling ill, and walked in on your brother doing a whole lot more than climbing out of a window. Apparently neither Joey nor his wife had a stitch on, and now the poor woman has been sent back to her family in disgrace and the husband has given notice and is looking for another school – in England. Tonypandy will lose a good teacher and according to the vicar of St Andrew's, the young wives group in his church will never be the same. Mrs Perkins is the fourth young wife Joey has been caught with since he turned sixteen and that's only the Anglicans. Doesn't he realise he is wrecking lives? It would serve him right if one of the husbands beats him to a pulp.'

'All Joey realises is that his hormones are rampaging. Like mine were at his age.'

'I don't believe I heard that. You, making excuses for Joey?'

'I'm not,' Lloyd protested. 'I told him exactly what I thought of him.'

'As if that will stop him from seducing every young girl and married woman he takes a fancy to in the Rhondda,' she said angrily. 'Why is it that when men sleep with women outside marriage, they're regarded as a man's man, a bit of a ram and attract envious sniggers, while women are labelled sluts and whores and thrown on to the street or into the workhouse by their families?'

'I surrender,' Lloyd shouted, hoping to get a word in edgewise. 'Do anything you want with me, woman, but spare me the suffragette talk. Just for tonight.'

'Thank you for the invitation.' Connie left him and locked the door.

'Connie,' he remonstrated. 'You know how I feel about this. It's not going anywhere.'

'Why does it have to go somewhere?' she enquired innocently. 'What's wrong with lovemaking as a hobby? It's good exercise and nowhere near as corrupting as the music hall.'

'Says who?' Lloyd watched as she went to the sofa and unbuttoned her dress.

'Me, darling. How many years have we been doing this now?'

'Thirteen, as if you didn't know.'

'And I still have a guilty conscience for leading astray a fifteen-year-old boy half my age.'

'The fifteen-year-old boy was grateful, at the time,' he added sardonically as her dress fell to the floor. She stepped out of it and hung it on the back of a chair.

'But the twenty-eight-year-old man isn't?' she challenged.

'We talked about this after I left Tonypandy for Pontypridd. And again when I came back. I don't regret what happened between us—'

'That's big of you.'

'I like you . . .'

'And I like you.'

'But every time we do this, all I can think about for days afterwards is you.'

'And that's so bad?'

'Connie . . .'

'Yes.' She dropped her petticoats and walked towards him in her corset, chemise, drawers and stockings. Kneeling before his chair she unbuttoned his trousers and slid her hand inside his fly, teasing his erection.

'Not yet.' He pushed her hand aside, left the chair and helped her unlace her corset. 'This has to be the absolute last—'

She laid a finger over his mouth to prevent him from speaking as she removed her drawers. 'No lectures on morality, Lloyd.'

He tugged at his tie. Loosening it, he unfastened his collar studs. There had been a time when he had pleaded with Connie to marry him. Fearing his parents' opposition he had waited until his twenty-first birthday to ask her. She had reminded him that they were first cousins. When he had replied that it wasn't illegal for first cousins to marry, she had cited her marriage as an insurmountable obstacle. When he suggested she divorce Albert

George, she had told him that the Church didn't recognise divorce and she couldn't bear the ignominy of excommunication.

He had been so in love with her at the time, he had taken whatever crumbs she had thrown his way and been grateful for them. But when he had begun to work for the Watkin Jones Colliery in Pontypridd, his life had changed. He had mixed in, if not the top echelons of society, the middle ranks, where an up-and-coming engineer had been considered a desirable match and courted by the parents of eligible daughters. Although he met no one he could bear to spend more than a couple of evenings with, let alone the rest of his life, it was then that he realised he wanted what his parents had, a loving happy marriage and children.

Later, when he met girls he had wanted to see more of, and brought them home to meet his parents, Connie wormed invitations to the teas his mother laid on in hope of acquiring a daughter-in-law. And somehow, Connie always managed to draw him back to her. Like a drunk who couldn't stay away from pubs, he found himself returning to the sofa in her office, time after time, no matter how often he tried to break off their relationship. He simply couldn't help himself. Just like now.

Connie stripped off her chemise and stood before him naked except for stockings and garters.

'I suppose you are going to confess this on Sunday?'

'Of course,' she answered smoothly, refusing to be riled.

'You and your damned Church . . .'

'In the eyes of the Church, it is you who are damned, my dear Lloyd.' She spread one of the crocheted blankets over the sofa and lay down, folding her arms above her head. 'Besides, as I keep telling you, it is not done for a boy to love an old woman twice his age.'

'You are not twice my age any more,' he growled.

'There will always be fifteen years between us. You are a young virile man of twenty-eight and I am an old woman of forty-three who should spend her evenings knitting by the fireside.'

'You will never be old.'

'There will come a time when you will think so.'

Lloyd recognised the attempt to make him feel guilty and was even more irritated with himself for succumbing to her. 'I've been trying to think so ever since you refused to marry me. But just like a bad penny, I keep coming back.' He hung his jacket on the back of a chair, removed his collar, untied his tie and pulled his shirt over his head.

'To do the accounts.'

'The wonderful, blessed accounts. I often wonder what would have happened if we hadn't been able to use them as an excuse for our meetings.' Slipping his braces over his shoulders, he unbuttoned his trousers, took them off and folded them along the creases before laying them on top of his jacket. He stripped off his socks and sock suspenders, unbuttoned his vest and drawers and dropped them on to the desk.

'Slowly, Lloyd.'

'How slowly?' He kissed her breasts, the flat of her stomach and the sensitive skin between her thighs.

'Very slowly and very gently,' she moaned, as his tongue played over her. 'Make my pleasure last for ever.'

CHAPTER FOURTEEN

Connie had been christened Consuela Rodriguez. Like many other young Spaniards of their generation, her father and his younger sister had left their native country in search of work in the newly opened pits in the Welsh Valleys. When a collier's life had taken a toll on his health, he borrowed money from his mother-in-law and leased a small shop in Dunraven Street. Shortly afterwards he changed the family name to Rodney because he thought it sounded more British and he hoped, acceptable to his customers.

Disregarding her parents' opposition, Connie married Albert George on her twenty-first birthday. Albert was handsome and kind, and she had been absolutely and besottedly in love. Charmed by his manners, open-handed nature but most of all, his expertise as a lover, she would have defied anyone who had tried to stop her from following him to the ends of the earth. As it happened, Albert only asked her to move into the rooms above the barber's shop that he had inherited from his late, thrifty and hard-working father.

What Connie didn't know was that Albert's prowess between the sheets had been acquired and honed by making love to every professional and amateur prostitute in the Rhondda. It was an occupation he did not give up after their marriage. At first she loved him so much she pretended she hadn't heard the whispers that circulated about his women. When he returned home late, she didn't question him because she wanted to believe the stories he told her about visiting sick customers in their own homes. She buried her suspicions and didn't challenge him until the day the bailiffs knocked on their door and Albert was forced to tell her not only about his first weakness but also his second – gambling.

Her father already knew all about Albert's faults and the money he had won, staked, and lost again at cards. The discovery that he had spent hundreds of pounds on prostitutes came later, after the bailiffs came for more than their furniture and evicted them because Albert had mortgaged and lost the shop. Connie returned to her father's house on her second wedding anniversary alone and deeply disillusioned.

Although she told Albert that she would never live with him again as his wife, he continued to pursue her. Every time he won at cards, he turned up in the shop with extravagant bunches of flowers, boxes of chocolates and expensive, impractical lingerie. Sometimes, her Latin temper roused, she would fling the gifts back into his face, to her father's customers' entertainment and delight. But there had been one thing that she had been unable to resist.

Albert had aroused Connie's passionate nature, and his lovemaking was like a drug. Desperate, lonely and devastated by her father's death, she allowed him back into her life and bed, but the second honeymoon had ended when she discovered money missing from the till. Without her knowledge, Albert had tried to raise a mortgage on the shop and had been furious when he had been told by the family solicitor that Manuel Rodney had left his entire state to his eldest nephew, Lloyd, then only twelve years old, who was to hold it in trust for his daughter.

Connie threw Albert out and despite his pleadings, refused to take him back even when she gave birth to his daughter nine months later. Instead, she hired Annie O'Leary. For three years they worked hard and long hours, sharing the care of the baby Connie had named Antonia after her dead mother, building and enlarging the customer base of the shop and taking on the leases of four adjoining shops until Rodney's finally became the store her father had dreamed of. Then one day, shortly after his fifteenth birthday, Lloyd had offered to take over the accounts for Connie. He was a bright boy and her aunt and uncle hoped he'd go far. Connie agreed, and two months later they became lovers.

And now ... now, Connie simply couldn't imagine living without Lloyd's visits. They knew one another's bodies as well as they knew their own. She had taken the time and trouble to teach him everything that Albert had taught her; that there could no shame, no embarrassment between lovers, that there were only two rules. First, whatever they did had to bring pleasure to them both, and second, a woman's pleasure was more important than a man's because a woman who did not find fulfilment and delight in lovemaking was unlikely to want to repeat the experience.

William Evans walked into his house at a quarter to ten and smelled baking. The rich, Christmassy smell he associated with fruitcake, underlined by the warm, exotic tang of cinnamon. He walked into the kitchen to find the new housekeeper standing next to the table, closing the lids on the snap boxes.

'What on earth do you think you're doing, girl?' He lifted his hand intending to hang his cap on the hook on the wall and the girl cowered, clearly terrified.

Shocked by the sight of her waiting for a blow, he softened his voice. 'Miners have campaigned and won the right to work an eight-hour day, Mrs Jones. I don't expect my housekeeper to work longer hours. It's high time you were in bed.'

'Yes, Mr Evans. I'll just put these tins in the larder.' Sali left them on the marble slab alongside the cheese and closed the door. Wary of Mr Evan's gruff, off-hand manner, she was glad to leave the kitchen.

'Goodnight, Mrs Jones, I hope you sleep well.' It was

the first thoughtful comment William Evans had made in the six weeks since his wife had died but Sali wasn't to know that.

'Goodnight,' she echoed diffidently, closing the door behind her.

'Happy?' Connie asked Lloyd, as she lay naked in his arms on the sofa in front of the fire.

'No. Just satisfied, momentarily,' he growled, refusing to be placated.

'Momentarily?' She smiled in amusement. 'Sometimes, I think you are insatiable.'

'That's rich coming from you.'

'Me?' she repeated innocently.

'You use me, exhaust me and refuse to listen to a word I say.'

'How can you be so unkind?' She moved her head downwards, kissing his chest, his navel.

'Because you know I won't find happiness with anyone else until I break free from you.' He locked his fingers in her hair and pulled back her head, forcing her to look at him.

'So, what do you think of your new housekeeper?' she asked, deliberately changing the subject.

'She's a timid little thing, and ugly. I know you warned us that she'd had her head shaved and was covered in scars, but she's too afraid to answer a simple question. However,' he cupped her breasts and thumbed her nipples as she slid back up alongside him, 'she can cook.'

'Then it's true, the way to a man's heart really is through his stomach,' she laughed.

'Victor is pleased.'

'And you, of course, are not.' She ran her nails over his shoulders.

'Judging by the way my father cleared his plate he was impressed by the meal she made, although he would probably die rather than admit it. She is the first housekeeper we've had, who has had our baths and meal ready when we came in after work. And she cleaned the kitchen. It hasn't looked the way it did tonight since my mother died.'

'Then she stands a chance of lasting more than two days.'

'Victor and I will do our best. My father's already slapped Joey down for flirting with her.'

'Joey made a play for her?' she asked incredulously as he lifted her on top of him.

'Joey will make a play for anything in a skirt. He calls it practice.' He slipped his hands between her thighs, as she moved over him. 'You'll be the death of me.'

'I hope not, I do enough penance for my sins now, darling.'

He kissed her breasts. 'Damn you.'

'You mean that?'

'As soon as I have my clothes back on I will. Can I pick up the books and do the accounts at home from now on?'

'I hate to let them out of my sight.'

He slid inside her. 'Right now, I couldn't agree more.'

Lloyd left Connie's shop by the back door at a quarter to ten and walked towards the Theatre Royal. The street was crowded with people who had left the second house, and he cursed himself for not leaving Connie's sooner. If Joey had charmed a woman out on her own for the night, there was no saying whose bed he'd be in by now.

He walked around to the stage door and saw his brother sitting on a step alongside a girl dressed in a bright pink outfit, with a neck so low and a skirt so high it would have given a chapel minister an apoplexy.

'Hello, Lloyd, meet Binnie.' Joey introduced the girl as if they were at a church social.

'Hello, Binnie.' Lloyd shook the girl's hand before clamping Joey's shoulder. 'We have to go.'

'Binnie's just going to show me around backstage. I'll catch up with you.'

'I think not, little brother. We're expected at home.'

Joey knew there was no point in arguing with Lloyd when he was one of his intractable moods, so he kissed Binnie's hand. 'How about we take that tour tomorrow, between the houses?'

She giggled throatily, ran her fingers through his hair, kissed his cheek and whispered something in his ear before disappearing up the steps.

'I take it she likes your idea,' Lloyd suggested cuttingly, as Joey fell into step alongside him.

'Jealous, big brother?'

'Of that little tart? When are you going to find yourself a decent girl and stop playing around with loose girls and married woman?'

'Never,' Joey replied. 'Because a hour's fun with a decent girl leads to irate fathers, her growing a big belly and a forced march to the altar. If I slip up with a tart or a married woman I can always stand before the bench and truthfully say, I wasn't the only one, Milord.'

'You're disgusting.'

'Because unlike you and Victor I don't live like a monk,' Joey bit back. 'At least Victor has his dogs and Megan next door to moon over. Sometimes I wonder if you have ice water in your veins instead of blood.'

Lloyd fell silent. He and Connie had been careful to keep their relationship secret. He had loved her once, but now he had the uncomfortable feeling that he was using her and she him in exactly the same way that Joey was using the bored wives and Binnies of this world. And every time he thought of his parents' loving marriage, he knew there had to be more. Much, much more if only he could break free from Connie long enough to look for it.

When Lloyd and Joey walked into the house through the basement door, they paused, mesmerised by the sight that greeted them. The mountain of washing had been sorted into piles and all four baths and the washtub were full of clothes, bedding and linen, soaking in water and soda. The floor had been washed and the range cleaned.

'Someone's been busy.' Joey stripped off his shirt and pushed it into a tub of whites.

'There's no need to make extra work,' Lloyd admonished. 'You've only had that on for a couple of hours.'

'It stinks of cheap scent and lipstick, and I need to wash before the old man gets a whiff. You know what his nose is like.' Joey picked up a bar of soap, went to the tap, turned it on and stood, legs on either side of the drain, so the water wouldn't splash his trousers.

Lloyd climbed the steps into the kitchen. His father was sitting, reading Dostoevsky's *Crime and Punishment* in his chair by the fire.

'Have you seen downstairs?' Lloyd asked.

'Yes. Where's Joey?'

'In the *ty bach*, he'll be up now.'

'Has he been behaving himself?'

'So far as I know. I met him outside the Theatre Royal,' Lloyd replied vaguely.

'Tea's brewed and there are cheese sandwiches under the plate on the table for both of you, and fruitcake, scones and cinnamon biscuits in the tins. She's also cut the snap boxes and Victor came down after he went to bed to tell me that all the beds have been changed.'

'She couldn't have stopped except to eat her meal after she walked through the door.'

'No, she couldn't have.' Billy Evans knocked his pipe against the range, scattering ashes over the newly cleaned hearth.

'Connie asked if I thought she'd do.'

'It's early days,' Billy commented evasively as he rose to his feet. 'Let's see how she is at the end of the month.'

Sali left her bed the minute she heard the alarm clock ring in Mr Evans's downstairs bedroom at four the next morning, and assumed she was the first up. But after she had laid the table and was turning bacon, black pudding, sausages and lava bread in the frying pans, Joey walked up the basement steps with two buckets.

'It's my job to see to the coal and wood for the fires,' he said, as he filled the brass scuttles next to the range.

'I could do that.' She chipped salt from a block and sprinkled it over the eggs she'd beaten.

'My father wouldn't hear of it. In this house the men do the heavy work. I also fill the water jugs and empty the slop pails in our bedrooms before we go on shift, but I won't be doing yours. My father won't allow me to go into the housekeeper's bedroom.' He gave her a charming smile full of innuendo.

Sali was relieved at only having to carry one pail and jug of water up and down two flights of stairs as opposed to the ten or twelve buckets she had hauled up and down the stairs in Mill Street every day. She poured the eggs she'd beaten into a pan and stirred them.

Joey piled the empty buckets one inside the other and went to the sink to wash his hands. 'Victor and my father see to the garden, and Victor cleans the hen and dog runs and collects the eggs every morning. He's down there now. Lloyd empties and cleans the baths every night, chops the sticks and carries in the coal when it's delivered, so don't you dare do it. My father would be angry.'

'I'll remember.' Sali trembled at the thought of igniting Mr Evans senior's anger.

'My father does the household accounts, paints and papers the house when it needs it, with our help, and we clean our own boots.'

She glanced at the clock. It was almost half past four. 'Breakfast is ready, shall I put yours on the table?'

'Please.'

She filled his plate and set it in front of him. 'You're not wearing your working clothes,' she commented.

'We keep them in the basement and dress and undress for the pit down there. My mother said it helped to keep the house clean.'

'Nine eggs this morning.' Victor walked in, set an enamel bowl on the cupboard next to the stone sink and picked up a bar of soap. 'They're laying well for the time of year. That looks good.' He eyed Joey's plate.

Sali felt ridiculously pleased by Victor's praise. She had fried the bacon and lava bread together, the way her father had liked it, scrambled the eggs and fried the sausages with a couple of soft tomatoes she had found in the pantry that morning.

'You'd like the same, Victor?'

'I'd like four sausages not three, please. I'm glad you found a use for the tomatoes; they seem to go from green to overripe overnight at this time of year. And before I forget, the dogs caught three rabbits last night. I put them in the basement larder. They taste better after they've been hung for a couple of days. When they're ready, I'll skin them for you.'

'I could—'

'That's my job,' he said firmly.

Lloyd and his father came downstairs together. She managed to avoid looking directly at Lloyd while she served them breakfast and by five o'clock they were in the basement changing into their working clothes. She watched them leave by the garden gate as she washed the dishes at the sink. Fortunately for the clothes soaking in the baths, it looked as though it was going to be a fine day. By seven o'clock she had filled both washing lines in the garden with men's shirts and small clothes and was looking round for somewhere to dry the sheets when a remarkably pretty girl with red-gold hair called to her from over the garden wall.

'As it's Tuesday I won't be using our washing lines, so if you want to hand over those sheets I'll peg them out for you here.'

'That's kind of you.'

'No it isn't,' the girl contradicted. 'Because if the pile had grown any higher, Victor would have asked me to do some of it, and I've enough to do with my own wash. And in case they haven't told you, I'm Megan.'

'I'm Mrs Jones, the Evans's new housekeeper.' The girl

looked so friendly Sali was tempted to ask her to call her by her name, but she was still unsure whether Lloyd had recognised her and if he hadn't she didn't want to risk jogging his memory by using her Christian name.

'I hope you last longer than the others, for my sake as well as your own. Victor and Joey have been calling round our house twice as often as usual to forage in our cake and biscuit tins. I've doubled my usual baking quantities and still can't keep up with them.' Megan took the basket of sheets Sali heaved over the wall. 'When you've finished your washing, come round and have a cup of tea.'

'I'd like to but I have too much to do. The house is in a bit of a state.'

'You can't work all the time. I make myself a sandwich and a cup of tea about ten o'clock, join me then. You have to eat,' she pressed when she saw Sali hesitate. 'Besides, Victor ordered me to ask you.'

'He did?'

'Last night, when he came back from rabbiting with my uncle and his brothers.' Megan filled one line and started on the second. 'He said you're a great cook but obviously not used to miners, as you didn't know how to cut a snap box. He wants me to help you as much as I can, because he doesn't want his father to send you packing the way he did the others. Not that they didn't deserve it. Well, some of them,' she qualified, pushing a dolly peg into the centre of a sheet.

Taken aback by Megan's candour, Sali murmured, 'In that case, thank you.'

'Don't kill yourself with that washing,' Megan advised as she gave Sali back the basket.

By nine o'clock Sali had finished the laundry, although more than half of it was in baskets and the tub waiting for space on the line. She was standing in the larder staring at the empty meat safe when a sharp rap at the door was followed by a shout of, 'Rodney's delivery.'

A young boy on a bicycle handed her a parcel when she

opened the door. 'Mrs Rodney sent up pork chops, Missus, and said I was to wait for you to give me tomorrow's order.'

'Thank you.' Sali took the parcel. She went into the kitchen and picked up the list she had begun to make. Yeast was written at the top; below it she scribbled, four pounds of beef mince, two blocks of salt, and two dozen rubber preserving jar rings. If she bottled some of the surplus vegetables in the garden for winter, the way Mari had done, it would save money. Then she remembered she was only the hired housekeeper. It wasn't her place to make plans. And even if Mr Evans kept her on, how many preserves could she make before she found her son and moved on?

'I've been here five years.' Megan sliced tomatoes and laid the rings on the two rounds of bread and cheese she had cut. 'My father has a farm in the Swansea Valley. The land's not up to much, it's forty acres of rough hillside grazing, but he keeps sheep, a couple of cows and a herd of goats. I have two sisters and two brothers younger than me, and the farm isn't big enough to support us all. So when my mother's sister died having her youngest, and my uncle asked if I could help out, she sent me here.'

'So you're a sort of housekeeper too.' Without thinking what she was doing, Sali cut the cheese and tomato sandwich Megan had set in front of her into four neat triangles, then she saw that Megan had cut hers into squares and realised she was betraying her middle-class origins.

'It feels more than "sort of". My uncle's three brothers lodge here, they're miners as well, and there's the children. Five of them, John's twelve, Alun's eleven, and they've just gone down the pit. Dai is ten and due to go down next year. Daisy is six and Sam five.'

'A houseful.'

'It is, even for a farm girl, but my uncle's brothers help

with the heavy work and although I'm family, my uncle pays me the going rate for a housekeeper. Fifteen shillings a week plus keep, which is more than some would in his place.' Megan poured two cups of tea and pushed one together with the sugar bowl and milk jug towards Sali. 'What do you think of the Evanses?'

'I haven't had time to get to know them,' Sali answered cautiously.

'I'm biased, but I think Victor is the nicest.'

'He seems kind.'

'He is. Mrs Evans's death hit them hard. They were – are, a close family and it was awful for the boys to see her go the way she did. Wasting away until she was just skin and bones. Mr Evans hasn't been the same since they buried her. He was such a happy-go-lucky man.'

'Was he really?' Sali had a problem imagining Mr Evans anything other than gruff.

'Except when Joey did something he shouldn't have, which has been more often than not, since he turned sixteen. My uncle's a chapel deacon and he's always telling me that gossiping is the eighth deadly sin, but it would take a saint not to gossip about Joey Evans.'

'He is very good-looking.' Sali bit into her sandwich.

'And doesn't he just know how to use those looks? We're the same age. When I first came here I spent all my time mooning after him. He didn't even go through the spotty, gangly phase most boys go through. But when I became better acquainted with the Evanses, I decided there was only one for me and, as you've probably guessed from what I've said, that's Victor.'

'You're engaged?'

Megan's face fell. 'Victor has asked me to marry him and I'd like nothing better, but my family and not just my uncle, my father and mother as well, are dead set against it. Not against Victor, everyone likes him. And my uncle and my father agree he will make a good husband, but he's a Catholic and they regard that as one short step removed from Satan.'

'But if you love one another . . .'

'I am only eighteen.' Megan collected their empty plates and took them to the sink. 'So, at best, we have another three years to wait before I can marry without my father's permission. And in three years, Daisy will be only nine. You can hardly expect a nine-year-old girl to keep house for four grown men and four boys. 'And my uncle says he doesn't want a strange woman in his house.'

Sali thought of a sad and lonely eight-year-old girl who had been taken out of school to keep house for her two older brothers. 'You have problems.'

'So, do you think you'll be happy housekeeping for the Evanses?'

'I think it's more a question of whether they'll be happy to have me housekeeping for them.' Sali finished her tea. 'Thank you for the sandwich.'

'You must come again.'

Encouraged by Megan's smile, Sali blurted, 'What do you think of Lloyd Evans?'

'I don't know him as well as Victor and Joey. He was working away when I first came here and he only returned about two years ago. Victor adores him, but he's quieter and more serious than the other two, more of thinker like his father. My uncle says he is the only management lackey he has any faith in.'

'He is a management lackey?' Sali questioned, unsure what Megan meant by the term.

'Lloyd's in charge of the repairmen in the pit and one of the few men trusted by both workers and management, even though he is a Marxist.'

'You don't like Marxists?'

'To be honest I don't know much about them, other than they think the pits should be owned by the men who work them. And even my uncle who hasn't any time for Marxists, because they don't believe in God, says that is a good idea. 'Don't misunderstand me,' Megan walked ahead of Sali into the passage, 'Lloyd's polite and nice enough, but difficult to get to know. Victor says most of the time he's at home his head is buried in a book. Why do you ask about him?'

'No reason,' Sali lied. 'Thank you for the sandwich. If Mr Evans keeps me on, I'll ask him if you can have tea with me next time.'

'Do want me to check if your sheets are dry?' Megan asked.

'Please, if you wouldn't mind.'

'I'll see you in the garden in a few minutes.'

Sali sensed she'd aroused Megan's curiosity by asking about Lloyd. She only wished she could be certain that he hadn't recognised her, or if he had, that he would continue to keep her identity a secret.

It was dinnertime on Saturday afternoon before Sali had cleaned the house to her satisfaction. She had caught up with the washing and ironing and had also managed to preserve two dozen jars of green beans and two dozen jars of carrots as well as make fifteen pots of jam from the raspberries, blackberries and gooseberries Victor had brought in from his allotment. She was working as hard as she had ever done in Mill Street, but she felt safe for the first time since she had left Danygraig House.

At the sound of footsteps on the basement stairs she lifted the leg of lamb she had roasted from the oven and set it before Mr Evans's chair.

'Pandy Parade tonight, Mrs Jones. You looking forward to going?' Joey followed his father into the kitchen and lifted the lids on the pans on the stove. 'Mashed and roast potatoes, Yorkshire pudding, sage and onion stuffing balls, and boiled peas and carrots. You really do know how to please a man, Mrs Jones.'

'No picking at the meat.' His father slapped Joey's hand away as he broke off a piece of crisply roasted skin.

Victor smiled at the bemused expression on Sali's face as he joined them. 'Mrs Jones has probably never heard of the Pandy Parade, Joey.'

'I haven't.' Sali set the last of the vegetable dishes and the gravy boat on the table and took her place next to Lloyd, taking care to avert her face from his.

'It's pay night in the pits and the big shopping night in Tonypandy,' Joey explained. 'The whole town turns out and the shops stay open until eleven o'clock.'

'I don't need anything.' Sali took the plate of lamb Lloyd handed her.

'Whether you do or you don't, you should see it,' Victor coaxed. 'As Joey said, everyone turns out.'

'Everyone?' she repeated, thinking that if she went, she might see Rhian, Mari's sister or even, her heartbeat escalated to twice its normal rate, her son.

'Come with Megan and me,' Victor offered.

'I couldn't possibly,' Sali protested, appalled at the prospect of playing gooseberry.

'If you keep Megan company when she looks around the shops, I'll be able to sneak off and have a pint with Joey and Lloyd.' The suggestion was that she would be doing him a favour.

'Only if you are sure that Megan won't mind,' she qualified.

'She won't, so that's settled.'

'Tomorrow is your day off, Mrs Jones,' Mr Evans announced flatly.

'There is a chicken in the meat safe. I was going to cook it for Sunday dinner.'

'The chicken can keep. I told you on Monday that I don't expect you to work any more hours or days than we do in the pit. And this week you have put in a month's hours.'

'I really don't mind making the breakfast.'

'Lloyd and I sleep late on a Sunday. Victor and Joey will be up early for mass but as they can't eat before church and Joey will probably take all day to make his confession,' he gave his youngest son a stern look, 'it's anyone's guess what time they will be back. There's enough bread, cheese and cold meat in the larder for everyone to fend for themselves. All I ask is that you return before ten o'clock.'

'I won't be that late, Mr Evans, thank you.' If she didn't see Rhian, Mrs Williams or her son that evening, there was a chance that she might find one of them tomorrow. There couldn't be many big houses in Tonypandy and with luck, Megan would know them all. But she had to be more careful in phrasing her questions than she had been when she had asked about Lloyd, so Megan wouldn't get suspicious.

'I am glad you could come with us.' Megan forged a path for herself and Sali through the crowds and into the haberdasher's where she was hoping to buy a length of dress material. 'Victor never says he's bored when he comes shopping with me, but I know he'd rather have a pint in the Pandy with his brothers, and to be honest I'd prefer to shop with a woman. Sometimes it feels as though I spend my entire life surrounded by men.'

'It's nice of you to say so,' Sali murmured absently, scanning the crowds for a glimpse of Rhian's or her son's fair hair or a short stout woman who might be Mari's sister.

Megan headed for the back of the shop. 'The dress lengths are behind the counter.'

The shop was packed with women of all shapes and sizes, but the only blonde head wasn't Rhian's and although there were numerous short, stout ladies, none bore the slightest resemblance to Mari. Sali continued to search the crowds pouring in and out of the shop as Megan wavered between blue woollen cloth and brown for her new winter dress.

'You don't think the blue is too showy for chapel, do you?' she asked Sali.

'Are you Methodist?' Sali asked.

'Baptist.'

'Of course!' Rhian went to chapel every Sunday, but was that because Owen had forced her to go? Mari was

Methodist and so was her sister. Would she go to the Methodist chapel with Rhian?

'Pardon?' Megan said bewildered.

'Is there a Methodist chapel in Tonypandy?' Sali enquired urgently.

'Yes.'

'Would you show me where?'

'On the way home. So what do you think, the blue or the brown wool for a winter dress?' Megan said impatiently.

Sali looked at both and knew which she'd prefer. 'Blue,' she said, making the first decision, albeit for someone else, since she had left Danygraig House. But she couldn't help hoping that the Tonypandy Baptists had a kinder and more tolerant minister than her Uncle Morgan, who would have thought blue far too gaudy for the Lord's Day.

Sali went to bed disappointed on Saturday night. She slept fitfully, her dreams filled with images of her son screaming as Owen lunged over his cot, that terrible last night in Mill Street. Her son chattering happily and silently creeping into a corner the moment Owen opened the door, sitting on her lap learning his first words, banging a saucepan with a wooden spoon only to have the spoon snatched from his hand and brought sharply across his leg by Owen. And, worse of all, a new dream, of him dirty and neglected, being beaten by a strange woman and crying for her.

She rose early, dressed in her black suit, blouse, hat and coat, and walked down to the Methodist Church. She didn't dare join the congregation lest she recognise the Minister as an acquaintance of her uncle's. Instead, she stood across the road, watching people dressed in their Sunday finery file in before the service, and although she was certain that neither Rhian nor Mari's sister was among them, she waited until they filed out.

She mingled with the crowds and spent the day

walking from one end of Tonypandy to the other. Seeing people on the mountain, she walked up there and with her hat pulled low, covering her face, studied everyone she met, but she saw no one she knew. When darkness began to fall, she made her way back to the house, too tired and dejected to register anything except the aching void engendered by her son's absence.

Monday morning she immersed herself in housework again and the week passed busily and quickly. When she wasn't washing, cleaning, scrubbing, dusting, ironing or sweeping, she studied the recipes in Mrs Evans's hand-written notebooks and tried to follow them, cooking meals the way she imagined Mrs Evans had. When the men went out for the evening she preserved vegetables and fruit, and made jams and pies from the produce Victor brought up from the garden and allotment. And all the while she waited for Saturday night and Sunday, the free time she could use to look for her son. When the third Sunday came and went, she gave herself one more week. If she didn't find Rhian, Mrs Williams or her son the following Sunday, she resolved to risk writing to her aunt to ask for the address.

CHAPTER FIFTEEN

'I enjoyed that meal, Mrs Jones, thank you.' Mr Evans gave her his first and unexpected compliment on Saturday afternoon, as she cleared the remains of the vegetables and the chicken carcass from the kitchen table.

'Victor's chicken was good.'

'My wife used to say that the quality of the bird was as much down to the cooking as the way it had been reared and killed.'

'Thank you.' She cleared the plates and set down an apple pie she had made from a bag of windfalls Victor had brought home.

'No cream?' Joey asked plaintively.

'I made custard sauce.' She lifted an enamel jug from the warming plate on the range. She had blended milk, eggs, sugar and almond essence using one of Mrs Evans's recipes.

'You joining Megan and me this evening, Mrs Jones?' Victor asked.

'If I may?'

'We'd be glad to have you.'

'What do you mean "we"?' Joey poured a lavish helping of sauce over the slice of pie his father had served him. 'You will be spending most of the time in the Pandy with Lloyd.'

'And where will you be, Joey?' his father enquired pointedly.

'With them, of course.'

'There's no "of course" about it,' his father muttered.

'I've turned over a new leaf,' Joey protested, his face a study in innocence.

'That's another lie you'll have to tell the priest about.' Mr Evans spooned the last of his pie into his mouth and left the table. 'I am going into the middle room to read. Would you bring me my tea in there, Mrs Jones?'

'Yes, Mr Evans.' Sali's heart lurched. Her month's trial was up in two days. What if Mr Evans were going to ask her leave? She looked to Victor and Joey. Both refused to meet her gaze and she couldn't look at Lloyd. She had avoided him since she had entered the house and all the more since her bruises had begun to fade.

While she warmed the teapot and waited for the water to boil she decided to ask Mr Evans if she could stay until Monday morning. That would give her one last opportunity to search through the crowds of the Pandy Parade and one more Sunday. After that she would have to find herself another position and begin looking all over again . . .

'If you take my father his tea, Mrs Jones, I'll pour ours,' Victor offered, as she spooned three sugars in to Mr Evans's tea and added milk.

'Thank you.' She picked up the cup.

'Aren't you going to pour one for yourself?' Joey asked, as she went to the door.

'I'll have mine later.' She opened the door, closed it behind her and knocked on the door of the middle room.

'Come in.' Mr Evans was reading in one of the easy chairs. 'Thank you.' He took the tea. 'Would you sit down for a moment, please, Mrs Jones?' He looked around. 'This used to be a comfortable room, but it's too small for all this furniture. Perhaps we should move the table and chairs into the kitchen, relegate the kitchen table and chairs to the basement, and turn it into a small parlour. What do you think? Will this table and chairs stand kitchen use if we cover the table with oilcloth?'

'It is not my place to say what you should do with your house, Mr Evans.'

'You have been here a month.'

'Not quite a month, Mr Evans,' she corrected. 'I am still on trial.'

'I thought it blatantly obvious after twenty-four hours that you were here to stay, girl.' He set his tea in the hearth next to him. 'Or have you changed your mind about working for us?'

She stared at him in amazement. 'Are you asking me to stay, Mr Evans?'

'I am trying to, but you seem determined to misunderstand me.'

She imagined her son as she had in her nightmares. Dirty, unkempt, crying for her. 'I am sorry, Mr Evans, but I can't stay with you.'

The clock ticked loudly into the silence.

'Do you mind telling me why?' he enquired.

'Because I lied to you, Mr Evans.' She forced herself to look directly into his eyes. 'I am not a widow. I am married and I have a child.'

'Oh hell,' Joey swore, as he heard his father shout. 'I really thought he'd let this one stay.'

'He will.' Victor set his mouth into a grim line and pushed his chair back from the table.

'Wait.' Lloyd gripped his brother's arm to prevent him from leaving, although given Victor's extra height, build and strength, it was little more than a gesture.

'I am not going to sit here doing nothing while our father sends the best housekeeper we can possibly hope to get packing from this house.'

'He's calling for Joey.' Lloyd glared at his younger brother. 'If you—'

'I swear by all that's holy, I haven't touched her,' Joey interrupted earnestly. 'Come on,' he looked from Lloyd to Victor. 'The woman's bald and ugly.'

'See what Dad wants,' Victor snapped. 'Now, before I shave your head and reshape your face into something even a horse wouldn't look at.'

Once Sali had told Mr Evans she was married, it was as if she had opened a floodgate. It all poured out, her father's death, Mansel's disappearance, her pregnancy and forced marriage to Owen Bull, the birth of her son, the beating that had ended with her being admitted to the infirmary, Owen's visit and his attempt to intimidate her by threatening not only her and her son, but also her aunt, her subsequent escape and her search in Tonypandy for her child. She told Mr Evans everything, except her name, the name of her husband and her most shameful secret, that her uncle had raped her. He listened in silence. When she finished speaking, she gripped the arms of her chair and levered herself to her feet.

'I'll pack my things.'

'Where will you go?'

'I don't know.'

'Joey?' He had to shout three times before his youngest son opened the door.

'You called,' Joey asked warily.

'We're looking for a maid in one of the big houses around here. Name of . . .' Mr Evans looked to Sali.

'Rhian,' Sali said, doubting that Rhian would have used her own surname.

'There's one up at Llan House. The housekeeper, Mrs Williams, sent me packing when she saw me talking to her,' he added defensively. 'She's a pretty little blonde, only fifteen, but I swear I haven't touched her.'

'That has to be her,' Sali broke in excitedly.

'Mrs Williams obviously knows you, Joey,' Mr Evans stated caustically. He looked at Sali. 'I suggest you go up there now with Joey and Victor. When you've found your son, bring him back here.'

'Here?'

'Knowing you, I think I can safely say that your son will be reasonably well behaved, which is more than can be said for Joey. And I'd rather a housekeeper who knows how to cook and keep house with a son, than a childless one who doesn't. Joey, take Mrs Jones and Victor up to Llan House and find this pretty little blonde and when you do, keep your distance and let Mrs Jones do the talking.'

'It's Sali, Mr Evans.' Sali looked up and saw Lloyd and Victor standing in the passage behind Joey. 'I was Sali Watkin Jones.'

'You really didn't recognise her?' Billy Evans asked Lloyd when they were assembling the brass bed in the master bedroom.

'I would never have taken Sali Watkin Jones and Mrs Jones to be the same woman.' Lloyd pushed a brass bolt through the headboard.

'What was she like when you knew her?'

Lloyd pushed a washer over the bolt and screwed on a nut. 'I didn't know her. I knew her father because he was the hands-on manager of his own pit, but Miss Sali Watkin Jones didn't move in the same social circle as her father's deputy. Although I remember I did ask her to dance once, and she looked right through me as if I didn't exist.'

'You said Harry Watkin Jones was a decent man.'

'He was, but his decency didn't extend to allowing his daughter to hobnob with his employees. She was rich,' he said derisively, 'pretty and rich with the kind of gloss that comes from having money and an indulgent father. But I'll give her this much, she wasn't brought up to be useless like most of her class. Before her father died, she was studying at Swansea Training College. The first thing her uncle did before selling the Watkin Jones Colliery was remove her from college to run her mother's house. No one felt too sorry for her then, because she was set to marry Gwilym James's heir, Mansel. They were distantly related in some way. Then, as you know from the newspaper reports, he disappeared on their wedding day.' Lloyd tightened the nut with a spanner. 'But before that happened, I returned here and it's amazing how moving a few miles can give you a entirely different perspective on life. Pontypridd and its concerns could be on the other side of the moon for all that anyone in Tonypandy cares.'

'From what she told me, she's had a rough time.'

'I'd like to hear about it.'

'Why?'

'Because her father was good to me,' Lloyd said frankly. 'And because by the look of her, I got more of his money after he died than she did.'

'You again?' Mrs Williams gave Joey a disdainful glare as he stood on the doorstep of the back entrance to Llan House. 'I told you to stop hanging round my maids.'

'He brought me here, Mrs Williams.' Sali stepped out from behind him.

'Miss Sali? My God, what have they done to you? Your hair! Your look half starved. Come in.' Mrs Williams opened the door. 'If you can put up with the mess of the cook and the maids preparing dinner you can sit in the kitchen.' She eyed Joey. 'You, wait here, and if any maid walks past, you will not say a word to them. You will not even look at them. You will do absolutely nothing. And if you even try, you'll have your backside warmed by my carpet beater.'

'I'll see that he behaves, Mrs Williams.'

'You do that.' Mrs Williams looked Victor up and down. 'You're not like him, are you?'

'No, Mrs Williams.'

'I don't know why I believe you, but I do. Come on, Miss Sali, we've got a bit to catch up on.'

Rhian dropped the knife she was using to peel potatoes and looked at Sali with terrified eyes. 'Owen . . .'

'Doesn't know where we are. I'm hiding from him too, Rhian,' Sali assured her swiftly.

Rhian gripped the back of a chair to steady herself. 'He really doesn't know where I am?'

'No, Rhian. I've come for Harry, I mean Isaac.'

'Sit down, Miss Sali.' Mrs Williams pushed a chair beneath her. 'Your boy is with a girl who used to work here before courting ruin in Pontypridd.'

'Is he in Tonypandy?' Sali asked impatiently.

'Clydach.' Mrs Williams opened a drawer in a dresser and removed a notebook and pencil. 'I'll write down the address for you.'

'I owe you money.'

'If you owe anything, you owe it to my sister not me. Rhian came with enough to pay for the boy's keep.'

'Have you heard how my aunt and Mari are?'

'Your aunt is not so bad, considering what she's been through. Do you know your uncle sacked Mari?'

'He told me he intended to.'

'There's no need to look so tragic. It turned out to be the best thing that ever happened to her. She landed right on her feet. She's companion and nurse to Mrs Gwilym James, now. Will you write to them?'

'Perhaps,' Sali replied guardedly. 'Will you tell them that I was here and I am well and thinking of them?'

'You don't want to give me your address?'

Sali shook her head. 'I'd rather not.'

'Might be as well, not that I'd tell anyone any more than I'll tell a soul where this one is.' She pointed to Rhian. 'No girl should live in fear as she does.'

Sali embraced Rhian and she sensed that her sister-in-law was having as much trouble holding back her tears as she was. 'I looked for you on the Pandy Parade and on Sundays around the chapels.'

'I've been too afraid to go out.'

'There's a provision shop, in Tonypandy, Rodney's, you can't miss it. If you ever need me, go there, tell them who you are and they'll give you my address. Take care of yourself.' She squeezed Rhian's hand.

'Reunions are all very well, Mrs Williams, but I've a dinner to get on the table.'

'Sorry, Cook.' Rhian picked up the knife from the floor. 'Give Isaac my love. See you, Sali?'

Sali went to the door wondering if she would ever see Rhian again.

After they had finished assembling the bed and making it, Billy Evans laid a fire in the master bedroom.

'To air it, because the room's not been used for so long,' he explained defensively to Lloyd, who was stunned by his father's decision to make over his mother's bedroom to the housekeeper. 'The boy's two and a half. He should be sleeping in his own space, not with his mother.'

'You think he should sleep in the box room?'

'Perhaps not his first night here, but soon.' Billy ignited the paper he'd set beneath the wood and coal, and watched the flames curl upwards. 'Give me a hand to clear the dressing table and wardrobe of your mother's things.'

'Where do you want to put them?' Lloyd asked, dreading the thought of handling his mother's personal possessions.

'There are two trunks in the attic, I'll get them.' His father went out on the landing and opened the hatch in the ceiling.

'They'll get damp in the attic,' Lloyd warned.

'They are not going in the attic.' Billy stood on a chair and lifted down the first trunk. 'We'll put them in a corner of my bedroom in the old parlour.'

Dusk was falling when Joey, Victor and Sali reached 'Bush Houses', two rows of small terraces set in the middle of a sea of colliery waste in Clydach Vale. A gang of children of varying ages and sizes were playing in the thick black dust between them. Two of the smallest had gleaming blond hair, but one was taller and heavier than the other. As Sali watched, the bigger of the two pushed the other one over, face down into the dirt. The child didn't cry, simply sat up, and with his bottom lips trembling, stared defiantly at his attacker.

'That wasn't very nice,' Victor addressed the older boy.

'He deserved it,' the boy chanted.

'Why?' Victor enquired.

'Because he did.'

Disregarding her clothes, Sali knelt in the dust beside the child on the ground. 'Harry,' she whispered, using her private name for the boy Owen had registered as Isaac and refused to have baptised.

The child looked back at her.

'Harry,' she repeated softly. 'Don't you remember me?'

He flung his thin arms around her neck and hugged her so tight, she never thought he'd let go.

Victor crouched on his haunches beside the boy who had knocked Harry down. 'Where does he live?' he pointed to Harry who'd buried his face in Sali's shoulder and locked his arms around her neck.

'With me, my mam and the lodger.'

'And where's that?' Victor persevered.

'By there.' The boy pointed to a door in the terrace behind them.

'Can you take us to see your mam?'

'For a penny.' Unabashed, the boy opened his hand and waited. Against his better judgement, Victor dropped two halfpennies into his palm.

The boy ran ahead of them. 'Mam,' he wailed. He opened the front door and charged down a passage into a kitchen.

'You little swine, you don't give me a bloody minute's peace.' The woman reached for a greasy frying pan as Joey, Victor and Sali filed in behind the boy. 'Who the hell are you? And what do you think you're doing with that boy?' she demanded of Sali.

'He's my son.' The woman looked vaguely familiar and Sali was sure she had seen her before, but couldn't recall where. Grimy, slovenly, she could have been any age between twenty and forty, and she might have once been pretty. But her black hair was dull and matted, tied back from her bloated, red-veined face with a piece of string. Her grey overalls were stretched to seam-bursting point over a bulging pregnancy, her coarse black stockings rolled down around her ankles and her feet encased in a tattered pair of men's boots. She stank of tobacco, stale beer and sweat, and when she scratched her forearms, Sali saw the red welts of fleabites.

'So that's why he's wrapped around you. Little bugger never touches me, even when I try to kiss him goodnight.' She glanced from Sali to Joey and Victor who had stationed themselves in front of the door. 'And I suppose now, after all I've done for him, you bloody well want him back.'

Appalled by the woman's language, her dirty, dishevelled state, and the filthy kitchen, Sali nodded.

'I didn't take him in just for the five bob a week Mrs Williams promised me and I haven't had for the last two weeks. I took one look at him and I had to take him. Well, didn't I?' she challenged when Sali didn't comment. 'Look at them. My Aled might be three years older and bigger, but they are two peas in a pod. It's obvious the same bastard fathered both.' Sali was only aware of her son's arms tightening around her neck as Victor guided her to a wooden chair.

'You must have worked in Gwilym bloody James's as well.' Oblivious to the effect she was having on Sali, the woman continued in a strained attempt at a 'posh' accent. '"I'd appreciate it if you would give me some help with the orders." Orders be damned,' she swore, reverting to her Valleys accent. 'Less than a month after I started working in the store, Mr butter wouldn't melt in his mouth, Mansel James, had me flat on my back and my knickers off. And I was untouched before he had me. Untouched and stupid. Some girls from round here have had fifty guineas from toffs in Cardiff for what he took from me. All he gave me was ten quid and a few small presents.' She sank down on a chair next to Sali and leaned her elbows on the table, which was covered with sheets of newspaper and potato peelings. 'There's no need to look so bloody shocked,' she said to Victor and Joey. 'By the look of you, and especially you,' she jabbed a grimy finger in the direction of Joey's chest, 'you both know bloody well what I'm talking about.'

'Mr James raped you?' Sali didn't want to believe it, but she couldn't stop looking at the woman's child. Just like her own son, he resembled Mansel in every way. Blond hair, blue eyes, slim hands with tapering fingers . . .'

'A man like Mansel James doesn't have to force himself on a girl. We're dull enough to queue up for his favours. And from that stupid look on your face I bet you did it willingly and for nothing. That makes you a bigger bloody fool than me. But I don't doubt you got some expensive clothes out of him. I'll give him that much, he never stinted on anything I wanted from the store.'

Sali blanched as she remembered Mansel's drawer. His explanation for the clothes it contained.

I asked the buyer to put together a trousseau as a surprise for you. There's everything you need and all in silk and lace. Drawers, petticoats, stockings, bust shapers, chemises . . .

'Little wonder he disappeared.' The woman rummaged in her overall pocket and pulled out a clay pipe. 'That aunt of his must have got tired of coughing up. One of the supervisors told me that his solicitor was paying out child maintenance payments to another girl before he had me. When he dropped me because he wanted to start courting some rich girl who'd taken his fancy, I threatened to go to a magistrate unless he gave me ten quid to keep quiet. Bloody fool that I was, I would have gone for a lot more if I'd known I was having him.' She clipped her son around the ear.

'We need the boy's things,' Victor said forcefully, as Sali paled.

'What bloody things?' the woman challenged. 'He's wearing my Aled's clothes because nothing he came with fits him any more. He's put on that much weight since I've been feeding him. And I'm owed a month's money and another instead of notice. He's cost me—'

'Give her two pounds.' Easing her son's legs away from her pocket, Sali extricated her purse and handed it to Victor.

Victor took the purse. 'I think a pound—'

'Please, just give it to her.' Needing to get out of the house, and quickly, Sali braced herself to bear Harry's weight.

'Give the boy to me.' Joey opened his arms.

Sali shook her head.

'Then I'll go and find a brake to take us home.'

'He's filthy, there are nits crawling in his hair and he probably has fleas as well. The rags he's wearing aren't fit to use as floor cloths, he's barefoot and his legs and feet have been cut to ribbons.'

Sali bit her lips as she opened her coat and cushioned the child against her to protect him from the jolting of the carriage that had been especially designed to cope with the Rhondda's steep hills. He snuggled in closer and she wrapped her coat around his frozen, shivering body.

'We've a fine comb at home that gets rid of nits and their eggs, a bath will drown the fleas and we'll buy him clothes and boots.' Victor patted her arm awkwardly. He was accustomed to seeing half starved, barefoot urchins in rags, but he sensed that it wasn't only her son's bedraggled and filthy appearance that had upset Sali. The two boys had borne an uncanny resemblance, and the knowledge that she hadn't been the only woman seduced by Mansel James had clearly come as a shock.

'We can't take him into Pandy. Not the way he is.'

'First things first,' Victor said calmly. 'We'll get him home so you can bath him, get rid of those nits and fleas, give him a good meal and pack him off to bed. Joey and me will see to everything else. Now what's this little fellow's name?' he asked as the boy finally lifted his head from Sali's shoulder and stared at him through enormous blue eyes.

'Harry,' Sali said decisively. 'Harry Glyndwr Jones. I named him after my father.'

'I am very pleased to meet you, Harry Glyndwr.' Victor shook the boy's filthy hand as if he were an adult and an equal. 'Do you think you will like living with us?'

'I live with Victor and Joey too, Harry,' Sali murmured, as the boy buried his head in her shoulder again.

'So, as well as getting your mam back you will acquire four uncles.' Joey sounded more cheerful than he felt.

'Uncle Iestyn?' Harry looked up at his mother.

'He's gone, Harry,' Sali said gently.

'I'm your Uncle Joey, and if you are a good boy for your mam tonight, I'll buy you a bag of sweets. Do you like gobstoppers?'

Ignoring Joey's question, Harry burrowed under Sali's coat. But then Sali reflected, he'd never heard the words 'sweets' or 'gobstoppers' in Mill Street, and if there had been money for treats in Bush Houses, she doubted any had come Harry's way.

They entered the house through the basement. As soon as Joey lit the gas lamp, Sali stood Harry next to the bath, filled buckets with water and put them on the range to boil. Victor ran upstairs and returned with a tape measure, nit comb, towel and Joey's smallest shirt, which was twice as long as Harry.

'It will do until Joey and I get back.' He folded it over the bar in front of the range to air. 'If you hold Harry, Mrs Jones, Joey and I can measure him.' Victor spread a sheet of newspaper on the floor. 'Can you stand on this, Harry?'

Harry stepped on to the sheet of newspaper without once looking away from his mother. Victor drew around his feet and carefully cut out his footprints while Joey combed his hair, cleaning the comb in between combings with newspaper that he tossed into the fire.

When the bath water was ready, Sali mixed in cold and stripped Harry. She cried out softly when she saw the cuts and bruises on his thin body.

'They'll soon heal,' Joey said.

'How do you know?'

'Because you looked a damned sight worse when you turned up here.'

'Language,' Victor reprimanded sharply, nodding to Harry. 'He's probably heard enough foul words in Bush Houses to last him a lifetime.' He picked up the tape measure, the notes he had made of the boy's measurements and Harry's paper footprints. 'We won't be long, Mrs Jones. Hang your coat and jacket close to the range and have a piece of soft soap ready to pick up any fleas you've caught from the boy. They'll be easy enough to see. They always jump towards heat.'

'Thank you, Victor. I couldn't have managed without your and Joey's help. And my name is Sali.'

'We won't be long, Sali,' Joey smiled.

'She didn't say that *you* could call her Sali,' Victor chafed as he opened the back door.

'Can I call you Sali, Mrs Jones?' Joey gave her his most charming smile.

'Of course, Joey, and thank you. I wouldn't have known how to get rid of those nits.'

'I've had a lot of practice on Victor's head over the years,' he joked before Victor pulled him out of the door.

Sali wrapped Harry in the shirt and a clean dry towel and sat him next to the range while she scrubbed out the bath. She opened the oven door and burnt the newspaper they hadn't used. After feeling in the pockets of Harry's rags and finding only sticks and stones, she added them to the flames. Then she checked her clothes and herself carefully, combing through her short hair with the fine comb to check that she hadn't picked up any nits. Only when she was absolutely certain that both of them were clean and free from vermin, did she lift Harry into her arms.

'I expect you are hungry.'

The child nodded. Clean, dressed in the white shirt, his blond hair shining under the gas lamp, he bore little resemblance to the ragged urchin she had brought into the basement barely an hour before. She carried him up into the kitchen. Lloyd and Mr Evans were sitting at the table reading, and she had the uneasy feeling that they had been waiting for her.

'So this is your boy.' Billy Evans closed his book and eyed Harry, who shrank back against Sali.

'Harry Glyndwr Jones.' She set him down on a chair at the table. 'Say hello, Harry.'

Harry said a quiet 'hello'.

'As you're going to live in this house, I'm Uncle Billy and this is Uncle Lloyd,' Mr Evans informed him gruffly.

'I'd like to make Harry something to eat if that is all right with you, Mr Evans? And I have to pay for his keep, so could you please reduce my wages to ten shillings a week?'

'We'll talk about it, Mrs Jones.' Billy read the tell-tale signs of early malnutrition in the boy's swollen stomach, pasty face and thin cheeks. 'You can give the boy whatever he wants, but as it doesn't look like he's seen too many square meals lately, I'd stick to plain food for a couple of days, if I were you. Just until his stomach gets used to eating again and then he can have the same as us. My wife used to swear by watered milk, porridge with plenty of brown sugar, soups, custards and bread and butter to tempt the boys' appetites when they were ill as children.'

'Then I'll make him porridge, Mr Evans.'

'I've sorted the master bedroom upstairs and lit a fire for you. I don't doubt the boy will want to cling to you for a few days but if I were you, I'd put him the box room as soon as he'll go there. He's already a bit big to sleep with his mother.'

'Thank—'

'I'm off to the County Club now.' Red-faced, Billy reached over Sali and Harry to lift his cap and coat from the hook on the back of the door. Harry dived under the table, clearly terrified.

'It's all right, Harry.' Sali crawled after him. 'It is all right. No one is going to hurt you here.'

'Tomorrow, you move that coat rack into the hall, Lloyd.' Setting his mouth into a grim line, Billy tossed Lloyd his coat and trilby before leaving.

'I am sorry.' Sali emerged from under the table with Harry and set him back on the chair.

'Harry,' Lloyd looked into the child's eyes, 'your mother is right. No one will hurt you here.'

'I am sorry,' Sali repeated.

'There is nothing to be sorry for, Mrs Jones.'

'I didn't even thank your father properly for giving me the master bedroom and lighting a fire.'

'You have just discovered my father's Achilles heel, Mrs Jones.' Lloyd closed his book and took his hat and coat from the table. 'He cannot bear to be thought of as kind or thanked for anything. Sleep well, Harry, I'll see you in the morning.' He handed the boy a picture book he'd hidden under his own book and gently ruffled his hair. After he closed the door behind him, Sali reflected that Billy Evans wasn't the only one in the house who couldn't bear to be thought of as kind.

'Auntie Rhian's gone like Uncle Iestyn?'

'We may see her, darling, but she won't be living with us,' Sali explained.

'The man?' As Owen had never allowed the boy to talk to him or call him by any name he had become 'the man'.

'We won't be seeing him again,' Sali said shortly.

'And we are going to live here, together?'

'Yes.' Sali gazed at the porridge bowl in dismay. She had made a child's portion, but Harry had declared himself full after eating only a quarter of it. 'Would you like to go to bed now?'

'Are you going?'

Sali looked at the clock. It was only eight o'clock but she had no idea when Victor and Joey would be back with clothes for Harry. And, as he had a shirt for tonight, he didn't need them until morning. 'As soon as I've made some sandwiches for your . . . uncles.' The word sounded strange.

'Can I wait for you?'

'Yes, darling.' She dropped a kiss on the crown of his head. 'You can wait for me.'

He watched solemnly over the rim of his cup as she brought out bread, cheese and butter, and made a pile of sandwiches that she wrapped in a scalded linen teacloth and set between two plates on the table.

She put the food away, banked down the fire with small coal for the night, tidied the kitchen and turned down the gas. Lighting an oil lamp, she lifted Harry from the chair and carried him up the stairs.

'A fire, in our bedroom.' He tried to jump on the bed when she set him on it and fell over, bouncing on to his back as he became hopelessly tangled in Joey's oversized shirt. 'I didn't hurt myself,' he declared manfully, as she rushed to him.

'You sure?' She turned back the bedclothes and tucked him between the sheets.

'I'm sure. I like this room, Mam.'

She looked around. Her clothes had been carried in and hung in the wardrobe. Billy Evans had left his wife's beautiful china toilet set decorated with daisies on the washstand for her. There was fresh water, soap and towels, and the bed had been made with thick blankets and a quilted patchwork bedspread. 'It's sheer luxury, Harry.'

'What's sheer luxury?' Harry asked after she had undressed, washed, changed into her nightdress and crept into bed beside him.

She laid her hand over his small fragile body and hugged him. 'This,' she whispered, holding him close as she kissed him goodnight.

'You and me together? That's sheer luxury?'

'The best kind there is, Harry.'

CHAPTER SIXTEEN

'You knew she wasn't a widow?' Lloyd asked Connie.

'Yes.'

'And you didn't think to mention it?' Saturday wasn't one of the evenings Lloyd worked on the accounts because Connie kept the shop open until eleven. But preoccupied by Sali's revelations, and hoping to find out more than his father had told him, Lloyd had waited in the Pandy until midnight. When the streets were clear of stragglers he made his way to the alleyway behind Rodney's. Seeing a light burning in Connie's office he had taken a chance that she was working late and thrown stones at the window until she let him in. What he hadn't bargained for was that she'd only be wearing a silk robe, chemise, corset and stockings.

'Would it have made any difference if I had told you that her husband was alive?' She kicked off her shoes, unbuckled her garters and rolled her stockings from her legs.

'It might have.'

'I can't see why. Aren't you going to undress?'

Slowly, almost reluctantly, he removed his jacket. 'I don't see why you thought it necessary to lie to us.'

'She was obviously too frightened to tell me her real name in case her husband tracked her down. And, after seeing her bruises, I could understand why she didn't want to see him again.'

'Did she tell you that her husband had beaten her and put her in the infirmary?' He sat on a chair and tugged off his boots.

'Sort of.' She turned her back to him. 'Unlace my corset.'

'I can't understand why you women strap yourself into these contraptions,' he grumbled as he tugged at the laces. 'And what do you mean by "sort of"? She told you her tale of woe because she wanted you to feel sorry for her?'

'No, she didn't,' Connie mused thoughtfully. 'Come to think of it, she didn't tell me at all. I guessed. When I said I couldn't give her the job because she didn't have a character, she told me I could write to Swansea Training College, but she also asked me not reveal her whereabouts, so I assumed she was hiding from someone. I suggested it was her husband and she didn't contradict me.'

'She didn't tell you that she had a child.'

'No. If she had, I would never have engaged her as your housekeeper.'

'Why?'

'Because you four are soft touches. Before you know it, he'll be calling you Uncle Lloyd, Uncle Joey and Uncle Victor.'

Lloyd had trouble keeping a straight face. 'Not to mention Uncle Billy.'

'Your father is worse than any of you and I should know. He's been my uncle for long enough.' Stripping off her corset and chemise, she lay on the sofa and watched him as he peeled off his socks and drawers. 'I had no idea she was a colliery owner's daughter. It must be tough coming down in the world.'

'As opposed to never being up in the first place.' Reaching into the pocket of the jacket he'd hung on the back of a chair, he removed a tobacco tin, opened it, and took out a French letter.

'You ever offered anyone one of those instead of a pipeful of tobacco?' she asked playfully, as he lay beside her.

'Not yet.'

'I like it when you turn up unexpectedly.' She closed her hands around his erection.

'You know just how to get me going, don't you?'

'And don't you ever forget it. Now!' she whispered urgently, moving closer to him. 'Right now, but slowly ... Much more slowly, Lloyd,' she moaned, as he penetrated her.

'You always want this to last for ever.' He rolled on his back and shifted her on top of him as he moved inside her.

'And what's wrong with that?' She kissed him, thrusting her tongue into his mouth.

As always, he held back until she'd climaxed, only then did he allow himself to indulge his own pleasure.

'Be careful with the French letter,' she warned, as he finally withdrew from her.

'I always am.' He left the sofa and went to the cupboard at the side of the fireplace, opening it to reveal a built-in washstand.

He washed and dried himself and the letter before returning it to the tin. 'I hate using those damned things,' he swore.

'A little bastard would kill my reputation and my business. Not to mention your plans for a happy family life with some sweet young thing half my age,' she added cuttingly.

'Which is why we have to stop doing this.'

'Who came to whose door tonight?'

'I came to find out what you knew about our housekeeper.'

'You are in danger of becoming a bore, my darling. We have a warm, comfortable room, a fire to bask in front of, and,' she reached for a packet of cigarettes and a box of matches, 'a cigarette to share. Let's just enjoy it and each other.' She tickled his groin, as he lay beside her again.

'Repeat that, and it's not a cigarette I'll be lighting.' He took the cigarettes from her.

'Promise?' She rested her head on his chest. He struck a match, lit a cigarette and passed it to her. She inhaled and handed it back to him. 'You are going to find a difference with a small child in the house.'

'We all are.' He blew a smoke ring at the ceiling.

'Is that why you want to get married? To have children?'

'I wouldn't say no to a couple.'

'You mean that, don't you?'

'I've never made any secret of wanting a family.' He knew he was hurting her, but he refused to demean her or himself by telling her a lie.

'Then I'm not enough for you?' There was anger and something else in her voice that he couldn't quite decipher.

'When we are like this, you've always been enough for me, but we're not always like this, and it was you who refused to marry me, remember?' The scent of her perfume suddenly caught at the back of his throat, and he moved away from her. 'You should have seen Joey and Victor tonight in the Pandy.' Weary of discussing their complicated relationship, he changed the subject. 'They went shopping for clothes for Sali's son and bought all kind of other rubbish as well. Sweets, comics, toys. The poor kid's been pushed from pillar to post for the last couple of months. By the look of him he's never seen a square meal in his life and Joey wants to give him a bag of gobstoppers.'

'While you, of course, are totally indifferent to him?'

'Not entirely.' He reached for his drawers. 'He looks a quiet enough child and his grandfather was good to me.'

'And his mother?' She snatched the drawers from his hands.

'Creeps round the house like a frightened mouse waiting for a cat to pounce.'

'You aren't attracted to her?'

'For pity's sake, Connie, have you seen her?'

279

'Not since her bruises have faded. The delivery boy says they have. Is he right?'

'Yes,' he snapped in exasperation. 'She also has a figure like a twig with the bark scraped off, a convict hairstyle and about as much personality as a hat stand.'

'Then I can expect you to carry on visiting me for a while yet.' She slipped her hand between his naked thighs.

'I'd rather we switched to a platonic relationship.'

'So you keep saying, but you never start doing.'

'Because you always end up seducing me. But I warn you, someday I'll develop willpower.'

'Not for a long while yet, I hope. I enjoy sinning with you too much to forgo the pleasure.' She removed the cigarette from between his lips and tossed it into the fire. 'Besides, it gives me something to confess.'

'Do you tell the priest everything about us?' he asked, horrified.

'Absolutely everything.' She slipped her hand higher. 'The poor man is supposed to live a celibate life so he's entitled to a little excitement now and then, even if it does come second-hand. Our friend is stirring. Shall I pass you the tobacco tin?'

'Can't we give them to him as a present?' Joey pleaded.

'No,' Sali countered sternly. 'Harry is my son and I will buy his clothes and pay for his keep. Now, can I please have the bill for everything you bought?'

'You can have the bill for the clothes and boots.' Joey smiled at Harry.

Harry glanced timidly back at Joey. He was sitting at the table struggling to eat all his porridge because his mother had asked him to. Dressed in his new Sunday best – a sailor suit with breeches that buttoned at the knee over long, thick woollen stockings – he felt warmer, more comfortable and more dressed up than he ever had in his life before. The only problem was, his boots hurt and he wasn't sure he should tell his mother in case it upset her and made her shout even louder at his new Uncle Joey.

'Joey.' Sali held out her hand, and Joey produced the bill from his shirt pocket. She read it carefully.

One sailor suit, two pairs of cord breeches, one waistcoat, two woollen jerseys, three flannel shirts, three sets of underclothes, two nightshirts, three pairs of stockings, a pair of boots, a woollen coat and a cap.

All essential, but the total was two pounds, nineteen shillings and seven pence. Nearly three pounds! She took her purse from her pocket opened it and counted out the exact money. 'Now I want the bill for the comics, toys and sweets.'

'No!' Joey said emphatically.

'Yes,' she contradicted, holding out her hand.

'You won't let him eat the sweets,' Joey protested.

'Not yet, no—'

'No, Mam! No shouting! No shouting!' Harry left the table and ran to her. Wrapping his arms around her legs, he burst into tears.

'It's all right, Harry.' She tried to crouch down to his level, but he was holding on so tightly it was impossible for her to move without hurting him.

'Harry.' Kneeling, Victor gently unwound the boy's arms from around Sali's legs. 'Mam and Joey will stop shouting, right now,' he murmured, giving them both a stern look. 'They were only arguing because your mam wanted to pay for the comics that Joey bought for himself.'

'And I suppose you never looked at them?' Joey retorted.

'Ssh, no shouting, Joey.' To Sali's amazement, Harry clung to Victor as he rose to his feet.

'Come on, Sali,' Joey coaxed in a softer voice. 'We only bought him a ball and a teddy bear. He can accept presents, can't he?'

'This once,' Sali relented, seeing Harry stroke the bear that Victor picked up from the table and handed to him.

'But he's my son, not yours, and he's not used to being given things. I don't want him spoiled.'

'We'll ask your permission before we give him anything else,' Victor conceded.

'Thank you.'

'And now we're late for mass.' Forewarned by his father and Lloyd, who hadn't had time to move the coat rack, Joey looked at Harry. 'Is it all right if I lift the coats and caps down, Harry?' He waited for the boy to nod before grabbing them. 'Look after Mr Bear, Harry. See you later, Sali.'

'I'll be making dinner.'

'It's your day off,' Victor reminded.

'I don't feel like going anywhere. It will be on the table at one o'clock.'

'What's all the noise?' Lloyd brushed past Joey in the passage.

'Sali being bossy.' Joey slammed the front door behind him.

'What have you been doing to my brothers?' Lloyd asked Sali in amusement as he sat at the kitchen table.

'Ordering them not to spoil Harry. There's tea in the pot.' She set a cup, saucer plate, knife and fork in front of him. 'What would you like for breakfast?'

'It's your day off.'

'I really don't mind.'

'In that case, bacon and eggs, please.'

She watched her son struggle with a spoonful of porridge and decided it was better he eat a little than make himself ill forcing down food he would have trouble digesting. 'You can leave the table if you can't eat any more, Harry.'

Holding his teddy by the arm, Harry picked up the comics Joey had given him and walked to Mrs Evans's chair.

'Not there, Harry,' Sali warned.

'If you come here, I'll read you those comics while your

mother cooks my breakfast, Harry.' Lloyd pushed out the chair next to his.

Harry waited for Sali to give her approval before climbing on to the chair.

'Now, what have we here?' Lloyd opened the comic. 'Coloured comics with Frog Faced Ferdinand, Watty Wool Whiskers, the Monkey and the Bathers. I'll read it to you if you like, then later on, I'll get something I think you'll enjoy a whole lot more. Do you like reading?'

'I . . . we didn't have books,' Sali explained as she laid strips of bacon in the frying pan. 'But I taught Harry his letters.'

'F', Harry pointed to the 'F' in Ferdinand.

'Clever boy,' Lloyd said approvingly. 'We'll have you reading *Das Kapital* next week.'

'I think Harry might prefer fairy stories,' Sali said.

It was the first time Lloyd had heard Sali express an opinion on something since she'd moved into the house and he decided to push her to see how far she would go to defend her viewpoint. 'Fairy stories are for girls.'

'They are suitable for small children,' she persevered.

'I cut my reading teeth on the children's version of the *Iliad* and the *Odyssey*. I still have the copies. How about we start Harry on those?'

'I think I'd prefer them to Frog Faced Ferdinand and Watty Wool Whiskers,' she agreed. 'Would you like one egg or two?'

'Three, fried with soft yolks, and bread and butter soldiers for Harry to dip.'

After Lloyd and his father left the house to go to the County Club, Sali cleared the breakfast things, prepared the vegetables, put a chicken in the oven, tidied the kitchen and made the beds. Tempted by the cold, clear autumn day, she dressed Harry in his coat and cap, slipped on her own coat and hat, gave him the ball Joey and Victor had bought for him and took him into the garden. Harry dragged his steps as she led him past the vegetable plot, which Victor had stripped of plants. The dogs wagged their tails in their pen.

'These are Victor's dogs, Harry. They are friendly; you can pat them.'

The child did as she suggested, but Sali sensed only because she had told him to and she wondered how long it would take for the shadow of the monstrous regime Owen Bull had imposed on them to lift from their lives.

'You can't play football in the garden, Harry.' Lloyd opened the gate and joined them.

'I wouldn't have allowed him to,' Sali protested defensively.

'I didn't mean it that way.' Lloyd held his hand out to the boy. 'Come into the street. There's a patch of ground next door that the council keep threatening to build a school on. It will be a pity if they do; it makes a great football pitch.'

Harry tightened his grip on her hand. 'You come too, Mam.'

Sali followed Lloyd into the street. To her surprise it was deserted, then she realised it was Sunday. 'You can't play football.'

'You don't want Harry to play football?' Lloyd asked in surprise.

'It's Sunday.'

'And God will rain down a pestilence if you allow your son to play football on the Sabbath?'

'No . . . I . . .'

'We'll play quietly so no one will hear us, not even God.'

'That's blasphemous.'

'As Marxists are atheists, they can't commit blasphemy.'

She hesitated. Was Harry playing football on a Sunday so different to her reading library books instead of the Bible when Owen was in chapel? Or her father smoking and enjoying a glass of whisky with Mr Goodman in his study?

'I didn't mean to mock your religion,' Lloyd apologised, wondering if he had offended her. 'I didn't even realise you had one.'

'I don't, not really.'

'Do Harry and I play football, or not?'

'Do you mind if I watch?'

'No, Mrs Jones, I don't mind.'

'Call me Sali.'

'It is good to see that you can make a decision when you want to, Sali. We'll make a Marxist of you yet.'

'My father always said Marx's views were too extreme.'

'Your father owned a colliery among many other things. A workers' revolt would have cost him a great deal. But how about you, Sali? Do you think Marx's views too extreme?'

'I don't know enough about him to have an opinion one way or the other.'

'And you were doing so well at making decisions until now,' he derided. 'You'll find his collected works on the bookshelves in the middle room. If you get tired of reading romances, you could give him a try.'

'I do not read romances.'

'I've seen you read Charles Dickens, Charlotte Brontë and Jane Austen.'

'They are great writers,' she remonstrated.

'I beg to differ. But if you'd like to convince me otherwise, we'll discuss the subject again, after you've read *Das Kapital*. And while you debate whether or not to read it, why don't you come down the library with me a couple of evenings a week? The miners' union are running evening classes and we are desperate for teachers.'

'I never qualified.'

'The colliers and their wives who didn't have a chance to go to school are so keen to learn to read and write, they won't care whether you qualified or not.'

'I have to look after Harry.'

'Bring him. You can teach him at the same time. Run out of excuses?' he taunted when she didn't answer.

'How long are the lessons?'

'One hour. You can spare a couple of hours a week, can't you? Starting at six o'clock on Tuesday.'

'I've never actually taught an adult to read but I'll try.'

'Excellent. Now, Harry, I am going to teach you to kick a ball. I'll kick it to you first, then you kick it back.' Lloyd set the ball on the ground and gently nudged it towards the child. When the boy kicked it back, he shouted, 'Well done, you are a born footballer.'

Harry flushed with pride. 'Did you see me, Mam?'

'I saw you, darling.'

'This goes even better with three, Harry. Shall we let your mother play, even if she is a girl?'

Harry slipped into life in the Evanses house more easily than Sali had expected him to after their separation. Within days they had established a routine and by the end of the month he was sleeping on his own in the box room. He played happily by himself while she worked during the day and after a few days, even allowed her to go down to the basement and the garden without him, although every time she did so, she saw him watching her anxiously from the window.

All her plans to do her work, bring up Harry and live a quiet life dissipated as the Evanses and their neighbours roped her into Tonypandy life. Megan called on her most days and Megan's youngest cousin, Sam, introduced Harry to his 'gang' of boys who ranged from two to seven years old. To her surprise, she enjoyed teaching the colliers and their wives to read, and began to pick up the rudiments of Spanish and Italian from her students. Harry liked the library and sat quietly deciphering words in picture books while she tried to concentrate on teaching, as opposed to listening to Lloyd who lectured on philosophy, history, Marx and Engels at the opposite end of the library.

Victor and Joey insisted on looking after Harry while she went to the Pandy Parade, although she and Megan always made a point of returning by eight o'clock so they could go out for a drink with Lloyd. As winter set in, Sunday dinners became a tradition in the house and even Mr Evans stopped lecturing her about taking her one day off a week. Sunday afternoons she reserved for reading to Harry, who soon began to repeat word for word the stories in the children's books Joey, Victor and Lloyd 'lent' him. When he turned the pages in the correct place, even she began to wonder how much he remembered and how much he could actually read.

Her life was very different from what she had once planned, but apart from concern for her brothers and sister, and her Aunt Edyth, she was content. She and Harry had a comfortable home with good people. She could keep both of them in necessities, and although she insisted that Mr Evans drop her wages to ten shillings a week to pay for Harry's food, she calculated that by Christmas she would have earned enough to redeem Mansel's ring.

She had truly believed herself in love with Mansel, and felt as though she had lost him twice. On what should have been their wedding day and a second time when she had listened to the revelations of Harry's foster mother in the filthy kitchen in Clydach Vale. But Harry was bright and she had aspirations for him beyond their present life. The ring was valuable and if sold in the right place, it might pay for him to go to university some day.

He was her greatest joy. He grew stronger and healthier every day and learned to laugh and play for the first time in his life with Sam and his newfound friends. Using kindness and a patience she hadn't suspected them of possessing, Joey, Victor, Lloyd and Mr Evans taught him that not all men were to be feared. And the very first time Harry left the house without her, he went to play football on the mountain with Joey and Victor.

There were times when she might have believed herself

almost happy if it hadn't been for the nights when both she and Harry woke from the nightmare world of Mill Street crying and screaming. And then the spectre of Owen Bull and the pain and misery he had inflicted on them rose and returned in full force, and she wondered if they would ever feel truly safe.

'What a cake! I've never seen anything like it in my life,' Joey gushed as he walked into the kitchen the Monday evening before Christmas, to find Sali standing at the table, struggling to mix icing in a bowl.

'You, Joey Evans, are a flatterer and a liar,' Sali countered irritably. 'And get your hands off that marzipan,' she ordered, as he broke a piece from the side of the cake. 'It took me over an hour to cover that cake and there's a hole there now.'

'I'll smooth it over.' He pinched the pieces either side until they met and popped the piece he'd stolen into his mouth.

'Well?' She watched him anxiously.

He frowned. 'I'm not quite sure. I think I should try a piece with cake.'

'Oh no, you don't.' She picked up a wooden spoon and knocked his hand away. 'If you want to taste the cake, I made a small one. It's in the blue tin in the pantry. I was going to put slices in your snap tins tomorrow.'

Joey went to the pantry and opened the tin. 'There's no marzipan on it,' he complained mournfully.

'And there won't be, given the price of ground almonds.'

He sniffed the tin theatrically. 'It smells all right. Have you been feeding it with whisky?'

'Brandy. Should I have used whisky?' she asked anxiously.

'Brandy's better. It's what my mother used.'

'I know. I followed a recipe I found in her notebook, but don't expect too much. This is the first Christmas cake I've ever made.'

'How long ago did you make it?' He opened the drawer and took out a knife.

'In October along with the puddings. Connie sent up the ingredients with a note telling me it was time to make them. She also warned me that if I didn't hide them from you and Victor I'd have only crumbs left by Christmas Day, and looking at the size of the slice you've just cut from that taster cake, you greedy boy, she was right.'

'This is for Victor and me.' Stung by her criticism, he halved the slice. 'So where did you hide the cakes?' he enquired innocently.

'If I told you, I wouldn't be able to use the same place again. Oh . . . sugar!' she cried in exasperation as the icing she had been trying to beat stuck in an unwieldy lumpy mass around the spoon.

Joey took a teaspoon from the drawer, scooped up a blob of icing and dropped it on to his slice of cake. 'I take it you've never made icing before either?'

'Does it taste that bad?' she asked apprehensively.

He made a face. 'It's not mixed properly. I just tasted something sour and it's dry and powdery.'

'The ingredients cost the earth. There's fresh lemon juice and egg whites in that bowl as well as sugar.'

'Have you been sitting here filling your face instead of going to the meeting?' Lloyd demanded of Joey as he walked in from the passage.

'I've only just got in,' Joey protested.

'From where?' Victor closed the door, rubbed his hands together and held them out to the stove.

'The Bridgend. I called in for a quick drink.'

'You promised you'd go to the meeting. Management are trying to cut our wages by seven and half per cent.'

'And they'll do it with or without our agreement,' Joey interrupted testily, raising his voice to the level of Lloyd's.

'If we don't show a united front—'

'I am united. Right behind the rest of you,' Joey retorted.

'Wrapped around the new barmaid in the Bridgend?' Lloyd enquired caustically.

'She's right behind us as well.'

'This isn't one of your crazy jokes, Joey. The way management are eating away at our wages, we won't be able to afford bread and scrape soon, let alone beer, meat and cake. And we're better-off than most families. When you go down in that cage tomorrow, take a long, hard look at the men who are trying to keep a wife and children on less than you earn.'

'You know you can count on me.'

'No, I don't,' Lloyd snapped. 'And neither do the other men. All you ever think about is chasing skirt and boozing down the pub.'

'I do more than my fair share when I'm in work.'

'Only because there's no beer or women underground.' Lloyd glowered at Joey, who retreated into sullen silence.

Sali still found the arguments between the brothers disquieting, but she had come to realise that they never bore a grudge. Summoning her courage, she broke the silence. 'Would anyone like tea and cake?'

'Tea would be great,' Victor said, as Joey handed him half of the slice of cake he'd cut.

'Please,' Lloyd relented.

Joey winked at Sali and muttered, 'Thank you,' behind Lloyd's back. Pretending she hadn't seen him, she cut another slice of the 'taster' cake and handed it to Lloyd before setting the kettle on the hob.

'Was anything decided at the meeting?' Joey ventured.

'The union is going to offer the Coal Owners' Association a five per cent cut in wages. We have to be realistic,' Lloyd protested defensively, in reply to the angry look on Joey's face. 'And frankly, I think we'll be lucky to get away with five per cent. The owners were complaining about the soaring costs of production before the new

Coal Mine Regulations were introduced this year to improve safety.'

'Why the hell should we pay to improve safety?'

'Language! There's a lady present,' Victor reprimanded through a mouthful of cake.

'You want a repeat of what happened four years ago?' Lloyd enquired tartly.

Sali recalled her father's devastation in March 1905 when thirty-three miners had been killed in an explosion in the Cambrian Colliery in Clydach Vale. And the death of another 119 men in a similar explosion in the National Colliery in Wattstown four months later had driven him to install every safety measure designed to improve conditions in the pits in the Watkin Jones Colliery.

Silence again fell over the kitchen. She poured out four cups of tea and handed them around. While Lloyd was sugaring his, he peered into the bowl in which she had been trying to mix the icing.

'You trying to put this on the cake?' He lifted his eyebrows.

'Sali was thinking of serving it separately as a sauce,' Joey joked.

'Do that, and we'll be chipping it out of the bowl with pickaxes on Christmas Day. Royal icing sets as solid as cement. It is Royal Icing?' Lloyd said

'I tried to follow the recipe in your mother's book, but I made a real mess of it,' she confessed. 'It's such a waste of expensive ingredients.'

Lloyd poked at the icing with the end of his teaspoon. 'It's not past salvaging. If you boil some water, I'll see what I can do.'

'You can ice a cake?' she asked in astonishment.

'Lloyd is a man of many talents. You should see his knitting and embroidery.'

'Keep it up, Joey, and I'll be knitting socks from your intestines,' Lloyd threatened.

'That's Dad coming in, I'm off to bed.' Joey rushed up

the stairs as Billy Evans opened the door from the basement.

'Joey?' Mr Evans asked, hearing a door slam upstairs.

'Just gone to bed.' Victor finished his tea and stretched his arms above his head. 'That meeting went on for ever. I think I'll go on up, too.'

'I'll be right behind you.' His father looked at Lloyd and gave the first smile Sali had seen on his face. 'You're icing a cake?'

'An engineer can do many things,' Lloyd informed him gravely, pounding a wooden spoon in the bowl.

'I'll take your word for it. I'm surprised to see you still up, Sali.'

'I wouldn't be if the cake had gone right, Mr Evans. Would you like a piece of the "taster" I made?'

'Keep it for my snap tin tomorrow. I wasn't expecting a Christmas cake this year,' he said. 'But seeing as how you've gone to the trouble of making one, you may as well have the crib. You know where it is, Lloyd. See you in the morning.'

'Why should I need a crib for the cake?' Sali whispered, as Mr Evans climbed the stairs.

'It's a china one. My mother always put in the middle of the cake. Do me a favour,' Lloyd lifted an enamel jug from the cupboard, 'fill this to the top with boiling water and make sure that it is boiling.'

Sali sat at the table, watching while Lloyd softened the icing with drops of boiling water and beat it to a fine paste. When he was finally happy with the mix and consistency, he dipped the longest, thickest carving knife he could find into the jug of hot water and after leaving it for a full minute, used it to spread the icing in a deep, smooth layer over the cake.

'You make it look easy.'

'It is easier and less messy than greasing some of the machinery we have underground.' He slipped the knife back into the jug. 'You looking forward to Christmas Day?'

'Apart from making the puddings and cakes, I haven't thought about it.'

'Your father organised some memorable parties for the workers of the Watkin Jones Colliery in the Horse and Groom on the Graig Hill.' He mentioned her past life for the first time.

'My father loved Christmas. We used to have wonderful parties at home when I was growing up.' She brushed aside a mist that clouded her eyes.

'You're talking like a woman of ninety and you can't be much over twenty-five.'

'Twenty-four,' she amended, 'and sometimes I feel like a woman of ninety.'

'I take it your husband didn't celebrate Christmas.'

'Not outside the chapel,' she concurred abruptly, hoping to dissuade him from further probing.

'You didn't enjoy the services?' he pressed.

'As a fallen woman I wasn't allowed to attend services and as a bastard, Harry wasn't either.'

'Then we'll have to make it up to both of you this year.'

'Do atheists celebrate Christmas?' she questioned suspiciously.

'No.' He stepped back and studied the cake as he put the finishing touches to the icing on the sides. 'But as the Christians purloined the ancient heathen festival of Winter Solstice, which atheists are allowed to celebrate, I feel perfectly justified in enjoying Christmas Day. Have you bought Harry a present?'

'Every time I take him into Pandy Square, he drags me over to the fancy goods shop to look at a toy horse and cart, so I bought one for him last week. I've also had our photograph taken and ordered enough copies to send to my brothers, sister and friends. Mrs Williams said she'd put them into her Christmas parcel to Mari, but I'm afraid they'll get bent.'

'I'll take them to Pontypridd for you,' he offered.

'I couldn't put you to any trouble.'

'You wouldn't be. I've arranged to meet Mr Richards in his office on Wednesday afternoon to discuss the shares your father left me. And, as I have to go anyway, I thought I might as well make the trip on market day. You could come with me and pick up any last-minute bits and pieces we need for Christmas.'

She shook her head as she cleared away the bowl she'd used to mix the icing in.

'You don't want to see your family?'

'I'd give a great deal to see my brothers, sister and mother, but my uncle wouldn't allow me in the house, or them to talk to me. And much as I love and miss my Aunt Edyth, I'm too afraid of what my husband might do to her if he sees me in Pontypridd.' She filled the bowl with cold water and set it beside the sink ready for washing with the breakfast things in the morning.

'You're living in a house full of men who can protect you, Sali.'

'Not against my husband.' She shuddered involuntarily.

'He can't make you go back to him.'

'You have no idea what he's capable of.'

Whether or not she had reason to be terrified, he sensed that she was, and didn't repeat his offer to take her to Pontypridd. 'Do you want me to take your letters and presents and give them to Mr Richards to pass on to your sister and brothers?'

'And my Aunt Edyth and Mari,' she added. 'Yes please, Lloyd. But could you just leave them in his office and not tell him where they came from. And there is something else.' She pulled her purse from her skirt pocket. 'If I give you the money, would you redeem something from Mr Goodman the pawnbroker for me?' She handed him the pawn ticket and twelve pounds.

'You have twelve pounds when we're paying you ten shillings a week?'

'Mr Goodman advanced me ten pounds when I pledged the engagement ring Mansel gave me. I thought

I'd need that much to buy essentials and keep Harry and myself until I found a job, but as I was lucky enough to start working here the day I left the infirmary, I soon saved enough to replace what I spent.'

Lloyd recalled what Victor and Joey had said about the woman who had looked after Harry and her claim that Harry wasn't the only bastard fathered by Mansel James. 'You want the ring back.'

'Mr Goodman told me it was worth a great deal more than he advanced me.'

'Then why not sell it?'

'Mr Goodman said there is no call for expensive rings in Pontypridd and he couldn't make me a realistic offer. I know it probably sounds ridiculous but I have ambitions, not for me, but for Harry. And I hope that if I take the ring somewhere like Cardiff or even London, I might be able to raise enough to send him to a good school and possibly university when he is older.'

'Harry's a bright boy and your ambitions for him aren't ridiculous, but aren't you afraid Mr Goodman will tell people that you have redeemed the ring.'

'No. He was a friend of my father and he promised he wouldn't tell anyone he'd seen me. He even gave me my coat and valise, which my husband had pawned, and wouldn't take any money for them. He said he had made enough profit from my husband selling my things as it was. Will you get the ring for me?'

'Yes.' He pocketed the notes. 'We'd better find that crib before the icing sets rock hard on the cake.'

CHAPTER SEVENTEEN

'Are you absolutely certain that you want me to liquidise your shares in the Collieries Company, Mr Evans?' Mr Richards enquired tactfully. 'The shares have accrued in value and are likely to go on doing so. A young man in your position—'

'A young man in my position, Mr Richards, cannot continue to take dividends from a Collieries Company that is hellbent on forcing men to work in filthy and dangerous conditions for less wages than they earned a year ago.'

Mr Richards coughed discreetly. 'Mr Watkin Jones told me more than once that your political beliefs will be the death of you.'

'If they are, Mr Richards, at least I'll die with my integrity intact.'

'If you intend to invest the money elsewhere, I may be able to help you.'

'It's already earmarked, Mr Richards.'

'In that case, I will forward you a cheque as soon as I have sold your shares.'

'No hurry, Mr Richards, sell any time you see fit, so long as it is within the next couple of months.' Lloyd left his chair. 'If you'll excuse me, I have errands to run.'

'Christmas shopping, Mr Evans?' Mr Richards walked out from behind his desk and shook Lloyd's hand. 'May I extend the compliments of the season to you and your family.'

'And I to you, Mr Richards,' Lloyd replied, aware that the solicitor was a bachelor with no living relatives.

'Mr Evans?' Mr Richards's clerk called him back into the outer office, as Lloyd was leaving the building. 'You have left a parcel.'

'It isn't mine.' Lloyd shrugged on his overcoat and placed his hat on his head.

'Are you sure? I thought you were carrying it when you came in.'

Lloyd looked at Mr Richards who was still standing in the doorway of his office. 'I assure you I was not. Goodbye, Mr Richards.'

Lloyd left the solicitor's office and walked down the hill to Market Square. Every inch of space between the tarpaulin-covered stalls was crammed with shoppers, most of them hauling bags and baskets. As he forced his way through, he had difficulty standing his ground. Women jostled, pushed and pressed from all sides, fearful lest he grab a bargain before they had an opportunity to reject it; small children crawled beneath his feet and under the stalls looking for 'pickings'. Older boys hung around, waiting for the stallholders to be distracted long enough for them to filch goods worth the risk of a few strokes of the birch. Vendors' cries filled the air, along with the rich, meaty odour of faggots and peas, and the sharp, vinegary tang of cockles. Only the men seemed to slouch aimlessly along, hands in pockets as they searched the stalls for gifts for their wives and sweethearts.

Buttoning his overcoat over his jacket, Lloyd kept a firm grip on the wallet in his pocket as he brushed past a quack selling 'cure-all' powders from a basket slung around his neck. The story of a man having his cigarette case lifted by a pickpocket at one end of the market and sold back to him at the other might be apocryphal, but like all tales about Pontypridd market, it held a grain of truth and, he didn't want to lose Sali's money – or his own.

He fought his way through to the toy shop at the end of the arcade. Turning his back on the girls' side of the window with its rag, wooden and porcelain dolls, and dolls' houses and carriages, he looked to the boys' side. He had promised his father and brothers that he would buy a present for Harry, but the last thing he wanted to do was present him with a toy that would upstage the horse and cart Sali had bought.

As he gazed at the display of tin mechanical toys, spinning tops, iron-banded hoops, balls, stuffed toys, and lead soldiers and animals, he recalled the toys that had been consigned to the attic by his mother after Joey had finished playing with them. When Christmas was over he would go up, take stock and bring down one or two. Sali couldn't object to them 'loaning' second-hand toys to her son, but that didn't solve his immediate dilemma. Then he saw the perfect gift for Harry. The child was always scribbling and drawing in the margins of old newspapers and odd bits of paper that were left in the kitchen. He would buy him a book of plain sheets of paper, wax crayons and pencils.

Carrying his parcel, he left the market, went to the pawnshop and joined the queue of women waiting to pledge their winter coats and wedding rings to buy extras for Christmas. When it was his turn, he handed a young boy the slip Sali had given him.

'Redeeming?' the boy asked.

'Yes.'

The boy passed the slip to a middle-aged man sitting at a desk. He looked up from the slip at Lloyd, then back to the slip. Leaving his chair, he signalled Lloyd to move along the counter. Opening a gate set at the end of the run, he beckoned him into a back room. Windowless, with three walls shelved from floor to ceiling and every one groaning with the weight of ticketed items, it was an Aladdin's cave of everyday and bizarre goods.

China ornaments, from cheap Staffordshire dogs to elegantly painted Royal Doulton lords and ladies, were ranged on the topmost shelves. Below them were layers of flat cutlery boxes stacked alongside piles of neatly folded damask and chenille tablecloths. Oil lamps, brass and wooden coal scuttles, sets of fire irons, brass, gilded and silver candlesticks, embroidered fire screens, framed oil paintings and prints of every description, stacks of wooden boxes that might have held anything, telescopes, books and expensive toys were heaped in separate compartments on the lower shelves. And on the floor were bins of umbrellas and walking sticks.

The old man pushed the door until it was almost closed. The dim light that filtered in from the passage lent the room an eerie, mausoleum-like atmosphere and Lloyd wondered how many people had pawned goods and died before they could redeem them. Hundreds, judging by the dust that lay thick and undisturbed over some of the items.

'You are?'

'I take it you are Mr Goodman?' Lloyd replied without revealing his name.

'Who gave you this?' Mr Goodman held up the slip.

'A lady.' Lloyd opened his wallet and extracted the roll of banknotes Sali had given him.

'Did she give you any means of identification?'

'Other than that receipt, no.'

'Then how do I know you haven't stolen the slip?' Mr Goodman crossed his arms across his chest, leaned against the shelves and studied Lloyd.

'She trusted me to come here and redeem her ring; she also trusted me enough to tell me that Mr Goodman was a friend of her father's and that he returned her coat and valise without charge when she pawned the ring. She also said that he understood her situation enough not to tell anyone she had been in his shop.' He held out the roll of banknotes but the pawnbroker made no attempt to take them.

'I know you. I met you once in Danygraig House. Didn't you work for her father?'

'If I did, you'd know why I don't want to answer that question.'

Opening the door, Mr Goodman ushered Lloyd along a short passageway into an office set behind the storeroom. He unhooked an enormous bunch of keys from his belt and opened a safe. After poking through the boxes it contained, he found the envelope he wanted, removed the ring box and handed it to Lloyd.

'Is that the ring?'

'There's no point in me opening the box, because I've never seen it,' Lloyd answered. 'And I will return it to her unopened; you have my word on it.'

'Half hoop of matching diamonds.' Mr Goodman took it from Lloyd, opened it and nodded. 'Expensive ring that. Tell her it's worth two thousand pounds to the right person and if she ever sells it, not to take a penny less than eighteen hundred.'

'I'll tell her.'

'Is she well?'

Lloyd saw concern in the man's face. 'She is well and so is her son.'

'I have an album of hers. I couldn't bring myself to strip the photographs from it.' He opened a cupboard, brought out a leather-bound photograph album and set it on a table. Lloyd ran his fingers over the ornately embossed cover.

'That's real quality.' Mr Goodman turned the page to reveal a painted garland of ivy and pansies encircling the title *Our Poets*. Above it, in a firm upright hand Lloyd recognised as Harry Watkin Jones's, was an inscription:

'*To darling Sali on her sixteenth birthday from her father, that this book may "List the legends of our happy home. Linked as they come with every tender tie. Memorials dear of youth and infancy."*'

'The decorated pages have poetry written on them as well as portraits of poets and paintings of their birthplaces and flowers. There's Byron, Dickens and Shakespeare as well as Walter Scott. That quote is one of his. It's full of family portraits.' Mr Goodman closed the book and kept his hand on the cover as if it would be sacrilege for either of them to look at the photographs.

Lloyd realised that the old man must have studied the book in detail. 'May I redeem it?'

'No, but you can give it to her from me.'

'Then it will be your Christmas present to her, Mr Goodman, not my family's.'

'There is something else.' The pawnbroker turned back to the safe and lifted out a wooden box. 'It was empty when it was brought in. But her initials are on it and when her silver bracelet watch came in, I put it inside.'

Lloyd ran his fingers over the mahogany box inlaid with gold letters, *SWJ*.

Like the album, it was beautifully crafted. He opened the box and looked at the watch. 'May I buy the two please?'

'That will be two pounds for the box and another two for the watch. Will you tell her the album is from me?'

'I will, Mr Goodman.'

'And there's no charge for the ring. I forgot that I owed her father twelve pounds when she came in to pawn it. As I can't pay him, it's only fair she collects his debt.'

'She hates taking charity, Mr Goodman.'

'You calling me a liar?'

'No, Mr Goodman.'

'She really is all right?'

'Yes.'

'And her boy?'

'They are both fine,' Lloyd reassured him for the second time. 'In good health, content and safe with people who care for them.'

'Glad to hear it.' He took the four pound notes Lloyd handed him. 'I'll wrap these for you. And you don't have to worry, I won't tell anyone about her or that you came and took these things away.'

'You have nothing else of hers?'

The old pawnbroker shook his head. 'But if anything I

recognise does come in, I'll set it aside, you can count on that. I owed her father a great deal.'

'So did I, Mr Goodman. And thank you.'

Lloyd went from the pawnshop to the best goldsmith Pontypridd had to offer. Even if he hadn't arranged to visit Mr Richards he would have found another pretext to travel to the town. It had become an annual pre-Christmas pilgrimage for him since the year he had first made love to Connie. If he had bought an expensive gift for a woman in a Tonypandy shop, it would have set the entire valley gossiping and speculating about the identity of the object of his affections. As he was a comparative stranger in Pontypridd, his personal life excited little interest.

He spent a few moments looking at the goods on display in the wire-caged window. There was a pretty art nouveau gold brooch that she might like, or a collection of thin, silver bracelets, a pair of earrings set with moon-stones ... Every year he bought Connie a piece of jewellery and every year she assiduously wore whatever it was until he replaced it with another. Then presumably she set the original aside in her jewellery box. It all seemed rather wasteful and pointless, just like the collection of gold and silver cufflinks and tiepins she had given him over the years.

Then he saw it. There was no mistaking the message it carried, if he had the courage to give it to her. Deciding he did, he reached for his wallet and walked through the door.

Lloyd checked his parcels and mentally ran through a list of his purchases as he left the jewellers. He had gifts for Connie, Harry and Sali. He had ordered three best quality linen shirts for his father and brothers in the haberdasher's in Tonypandy. He had asked Connie to deliver extra tobacco, a luxury box of chocolates and an assortment of sugar mice and other novelties for the family, and to bill it to his private account. He had left her to choose the novelties because she knew better than him what his mother had ordered to make their Christmases so perfect and this year was going to be a hard one for all of them, but especially his father.

Heading for the station, he made his way back through the town. He was just stepping through the entrance to the booking hall when someone called his name. He looked around and seeing no one he walked on.

'Mr Evans.' Mr Richards pulled down the window of a carriage. 'If you wouldn't mind catching a later train, there is someone who would like to talk to you.'

'There is no use in you denying it, Mr Evans.' Mr Richards gazed steadily at Lloyd, who was sitting opposite him in Mrs James's carriage. 'You were the only visitor to my office today. That is how I know it was you who left the parcel and letters from Mrs Bull.'

'You know Mrs Bull's present situation?'

'I know she is afraid of her husband.'

'Then you understand why she asked me to leave the parcel anonymously and not tell anyone in Pontypridd where she is.' Lloyd off-loaded his purchases on to the leather-upholstered seat beside him.

'Mrs James and I both understand why she does not wish to tell us where she is. But you have seen her. You must have,' he continued when Lloyd didn't answer, 'for her to have given you the parcel.'

'I have seen her,' Lloyd conceded.

'And if you have seen her, you must have also formed an impression as to how she is.'

'She and her son are well, content, safe and looked after.'

'All I am asking, Mr Evans, is that you ease an old lady's mind. Mrs James worries constantly about Mrs Bull and the boy.' He glanced out of the window as the driver negotiated the gates to the drive of Ynysangharad House. 'Will you meet with her?'

'I am on early shift tomorrow.'

'I'll ask the driver to wait. The next train leaves in half an hour, that will give you ten minutes with Mrs James, enough time to set her mind at rest.' Mr Richards played his trump card. 'Mrs Bull is very fond of her aunt. She would not wish to see her worried.'

Lloyd hadn't needed Mr Richards to tell him that. The look on Sali's face whenever she spoke about her aunt was enough.

'May I help you with these parcels?' Mr Richards picked up the jewellery casket and carried it into the house, where Jenkins relieved him and Lloyd of the shopping.

'Mrs James is in the drawing room, Mr Richards. Tea has already been served.' Jenkins opened the door and Mr Richards waited for Lloyd to precede him.

Lloyd knew Mrs James by sight, and of her charitable deeds by reputation, as did everyone who had lived or worked in Pontypridd. Sali had told him about her stroke and he had expected her to be frailer. She sat up and smiled as he walked through the door.

'It is good of you to visit me, Mr Evans. I appreciate that you young men have many calls on your time. Would you like tea?'

'No, thank you, Mrs James, I cannot stay long.'

'Won't you at least sit down?' She indicated the sofa and he sat close to her chair. 'When Mr Richards brought me this earlier,' she held up the photograph of Sali and Harry she had been studying when he had entered the room, 'and said that you had left it in his office, I had to see you. How is she?'

'Mrs Bull wrote to you, Mrs James,' he answered guardedly.

'A letter full of reassuring platitudes designed to set the mind of an old lady at rest. She says she is working, has a good job and earns enough to support her and Harry.'

'She does.'

'Are they both happy?'

'I will tell you what I told Mr Richards, Mrs James. Both she and her son are well, content, safe and looked after.'

'Not happy?'

'She was badly injured and very nervous when she entered her present home.'

'I wanted to help her.' Edyth looked to Mr Richards. 'We all did, we tried but perhaps not hard enough . . .'

'Sali blames no one for what happened to her, Mrs James.'

'She has told you about her marriage?'

'Enough for me to realise that she is afraid of her husband, not only because of what he might do to her and the boy, but also to you and her brothers and sister.'

'Are you and she—'

'I am her friend, Mrs James,' he stated firmly. 'And that is all I am.'

Edyth lifted an envelope from a table beside her chair. 'I have written her a cheque. It is enough for her to begin a new life well away from Pontypridd and Owen Bull. You look an upright, honest young man and Mr Richards tells me that my nephew, Sali's father, thought well of you. You will see that she gets it.'

'I promise, but I can't promise you that Sali will take it. She—'

'She?' Edyth looked expectantly at him as he hesitated.

'She is very independent and I think she feels safe where she is for the present.'

'You only *think* she feels safe, Mr Evans?' Edyth said apprehensively.

'She is safe. You have my word on that.'

'And her son?'

'Is learning to play and be happy.' He left his seat and took the letter she handed him. 'If you'll excuse me, I must leave.'

'If I want to get in touch with my niece urgently, could I write to her through you and Mr Richards?' Edyth asked.

'You could, Mrs James, but I'll be honest with you. Sali ... Mrs Bull doesn't confide in me, but when I suggested she accompany me to Pontypridd to visit her family, she was too frightened to take me up on my offer. If in trying to contact her, you compromise her present position, I believe she will take Harry and move on. Now that she has made a new life for herself once, she will have no qualms about doing so again.'

'I understand what you are saying, Mr Evans.' Edyth held out her hand. 'But if I can help Sali in any way, or if she needs anything, anything at all . . .'

'If I am ever in a position to advise her in such a situation, Mrs James, I will suggest that she turns to you.'

'There is one more thing. I have a trunk full of her clothes. I won't ask you where you are going but could you deliver it to her?'

'I could, Mrs James.'

'It was supposed to be her trousseau. It is such a pity to waste it.'

'I believe Mr Evans is only obeying Mrs Bull's wishes, Mrs James,' Mr Richards advised when he returned to her drawing room after seeing Lloyd, his parcels and the trunk into her carriage.

'Of course he is.' Edyth stared down at the photograph of Sali and Harry. Both stood, smiling in front of a painted backdrop of a mountain. But she could see the scars on Sali's face. Faint, but still there, along her cheekbone and jaw line. Her hair had grown just long enough to pin up. Harry was holding her hand and looking up at her with an expression so like Mansel's she felt that her heart would break. 'And I can understand why Sali is frightened. If Owen Bull ever got hold of her and the boy again . . .' She fell silent for a moment. 'It is hard to live without them. My children, my husband, Mansel, and now . . .'

Mr Richards sat on the sofa and held Mrs James's hand. He felt useless and ineffective, but whenever he doubted Mrs Bull's need to conceal herself, he recalled his visit to Mill Street and Mrs James's description of Mrs Bull's injuries when she had visited her in the infirmary. 'Times and circumstances change, Mrs James,' he consoled clumsily. 'Who knows what the future holds? Mrs Bull may be able to return to Pontypridd with the boy one day and perhaps even live here, in this house with you.'

'Thank you, Mr Richards.' Edyth made a valiant effort to control herself. 'Now, we can't allow the tea and crumpets go to waste. If you wouldn't mind pouring it.'

'It will be my pleasure, Mrs James.' But even as Mr Richards poured the tea and used the silver tongs to place a buttered crumpet on a porcelain plate for her, he knew they were both thinking the same thing. Time was the one thing Edyth James might not have. Would circumstances change for Sali Bull before Edyth's frail health gave way and she joined her husband in the burial ground behind Penuel Chapel?

The first thing Lloyd did when he reached home at nine o'clock was to ask the brake driver to help him put the trunk in Sali's bedroom. He hid his parcels in his wardrobe, walked downstairs, hung his overcoat in the hall and removed the letter Mrs James had given him together with the ring from the pocket. He found Sali in the kitchen dipping nuts and small pieces of marzipan into melted chocolate.

'I thought you'd stop off for a drink,' she said, flustered at being caught out.

'It looks as though you're determined to have us eating like kings on Christmas Day,' he commented, when he saw the layers of sweets she had placed between sheets of greaseproof paper in eight separate tins.

'They were meant to be a surprise. I bought the ingredients in Connie's this morning.' She didn't want him to think that she'd put the chocolate, nuts and other expensive ingredients on his father's household account.

'I promise to look astonished when I open my tin on Christmas morning. There is one for me, I take it?'

'And your father, brothers and Harry. The other three are for Connie and Megan's families and my sister-in-law Rhian. Homemade presents are all right, aren't they?'

'Very acceptable.'

'And you won't tell Joey and Victor? I'd hate them to think that they have to get Harry or me anything.' She scoured a nut in the bowl, picking up the last vestiges of chocolate before putting it on a tray to set.

'I won't if you allow me to taste one.'

'That's bribery.' She set three of the sweets she'd made on a plate, handed it to him, then carried the tray into the pantry where she slid it out of sight on the top shelf.

'These are very good,' he complimented, as she replaced the lids on the tins and cleared the table.

'Thank you.'

He waited until she had wiped down the oilcloth on the table before setting the ring, the twelve pounds she had given him, and the letter in front of her chair. She paled as she recognised the writing.

'You told my aunt where I was?' she charged accusingly.

'I left the things you gave me in Mr Richards's office, but unfortunately, as I was the only client he saw today, he guessed it was me who had abandoned them there. He asked if I'd meet your aunt—'

'And you went!'

'I didn't tell her where you were, Sali. She is worried about you and Harry.' He pushed aside the plate she'd given him. 'Why don't you sit down and check that it is the right ring and read your letter while I make us some tea.'

She opened the box.

'Is it the right one?'

'Yes. But you've given me back the money . . .'

'Mr Goodman insisted that he owed your father twelve pounds.'

'And I'm sure he didn't. This is charity.'

'When I tried arguing with Mr Goodman, he accused me of calling him a liar. As it was, I practically had to prise the ring away from him. He asked me all kinds of questions.'

'What questions?' Her voice was shrill with alarm.

'Where I got the pawn ticket, and how you and your boy were. Like your aunt, he's concerned about you, Sali. And if you hadn't told me about him giving you your coat and valise, I doubt he would have given me the ring. He also told me to tell you that it is worth two thousand pounds and if you ever sell it, not to take a penny less than eighteen hundred.'

'He said that?'

'Yes. Now read your letter.'

'I'll read it later.' She pushed the ring and the letter into her overall pocket. 'You're not just saying that Mr Goodman wouldn't take the money?'

'No, Sali,' he said seriously. 'I wouldn't lie to you about something like that.'

She finally pocketed the roll of banknotes.

'Mrs James told me that she enclosed a cheque for you. Enough for you and Harry to start a new life.'

'That was foolish of her. If Owen Bull ever discovers that I have money he'll come after me and take it away, just as he did my dowry.'

'How would he find out about it, Sali?' he enquired logically as he warmed the teapot with hot water. 'It is obvious that Mr Goodman hasn't said a word about you pawning your ring to anyone and I can't see your aunt or Mr Richards rushing to your husband to tell him you have money. So why won't you tell them where you are?'

'Because Owen might follow them if they tried to visit me, or break into my aunt's house to look for letters if he suspects we're in contact with one another.'

'You are paranoid.'

She went to the window and fiddled with the perfectly draped curtains. 'You don't know Owen, or what he is capable of doing, not just to me, but Harry, my aunt, even Mr Richards.'

'What I do know is that you have an irrational fear of him.' He picked up the kettle and poured boiling water into the teapot. 'You do feel safe, here in my father's house, don't you?'

'I did, when no one knew where I was,' she qualified.

'I didn't tell them, Sali.'

'They might have guessed and Mr Richards has your address. Don't try to tell me he hasn't. He writes to you here. I've seen his letters.'

'I didn't tell him you were in living in the same house as me, Sali.'

She turned away from the window. 'I'm going to bed. Please,' she indicated the sweets she'd given him, 'either eat those or put them away. I don't want the others to see them.'

'There's one more thing, Sali.'

'What?'

'Your aunt gave me a trunk full of clothes for you. She said it's your trousseau. I left it in your room.' The door in the basement banged shut. 'Do you want to carry on quarrelling with me in front of my brothers?'

'No.'

'I promise you, I didn't drop so much as a hint as to where you are living to anyone in Pontypridd.'

She left the room. Lloyd ate the last sweet and lifted down four cups and saucers from the dresser. He simply couldn't understand Sali. She was living in a house full of men well able to protect her, Harry and her aunt, should Mrs James chose to visit her, yet she was still terrified that Owen Bull would track her down. Why couldn't she understand that no one could force her to do anything she didn't want to do?

And there was the cheque that Mrs James had told him she'd enclosed in her letter. She hadn't mentioned an amount but he didn't doubt it was a substantial sum. Together with the money she could raise on the ring, Sali could buy herself a small business far away from Pontypridd, Tonypandy and Wales, and keep herself and Harry in comfort. He knew it was selfish of him, but he hoped she wouldn't use the money to start a new life elsewhere. During the last few months he had become accustomed to having her around.

My Darling Sali,

I am writing this in the hope that you will read it. I love and miss you and Mansel more than I can ever express in a letter and I wish that I had been able to say goodbye to you, Sali. I understand why you had to leave, and I am sorry that I couldn't protect you and the boy from Owen Bull.

I feel myself getting older by the hour. I do not say this to worry you or gain your sympathy, I have enjoyed a long life and for the most part it has been a good one. I was blessed with a loving, caring husband, two children I was privileged to bear and of course you and Mansel. It was hard to lose all of you, but Mari is looking after me better than anyone of my age has the right to demand of a companion and, if I am lonely, it is only for the people I love.

As I have grown older, I have found it easier to face unpleasant facts, especially the imminence of death. Should you discover that I have passed on, please, do not shed any tears for me. I have more to die for than to live for now, and my faith and trust in God tells me that Gwilym, my children, my parents and your father are waiting for me to join them. The only problem I have is how to ensure that you and Mansel, wherever he is, inherit the businesses and my estate.

Mr Richards, wise man that he is, has convinced me not to leave my estate to you directly, as that will give Owen Bull cause to track you down and take your inheritance just as he took your dowry, so on his advice, I have left everything to your son,

naming you and Mr Richards among others as
trustees until he comes of age. I have inserted a
clause precluding Owen Bull and Morgan Davies
from becoming trustees.

I have no idea how you are supporting yourself
and your son. I enclose a cheque for five thousand
pounds, made out to I. Bull, your son's name. I hope
that you are in a position to cash it and invest it,
although Mr Richards tells me that I am putting the
money at risk, as legally, Owen Bull is the father of
your son and can commandeer his assets.

I do understand why you cannot visit me, but
please remember that you and your boy have friends
who will do everything in their power to help and
protect you.

God Bless both of you,
Your loving Aunt Edyth.

Sali stared at the trunk Lloyd had set at the foot of her
bed. She could just imagine the reaction if she walked
into a bank in Tonypandy dressed in the finery she used
to wear and used the cheque to open an account for
Harry. It would be all over the Rhondda in five minutes
that the mother of a child who had thousands of pounds
was keeping house for the Evanses. And should the
gossip reach Owen's ears it would only serve to give him
an added incentive to hunt them down and imprison
them in squalor in Mill Street a second time.

She folded the cheque into the letter, replaced both in
the envelope and stowed it in the dressing table drawer
below her underclothes. It would be easier to tear the
cheque up and forget about it, than decide what to do
with it. And if she had only herself to consider she would
have destroyed it. But she had Harry to think about and
five thousand pounds was more than enough to set any
young man up for life.

She allowed herself a small congratulatory smile, she
hadn't done too badly on her own. As Lloyd had said,

she was safe in the Evanses' house – so long as Owen remained in ignorance of her whereabouts. If only she could be sure that he would never find her.

In the meantime she had a Christmas to look forward to. Wholesome food to cook and the look on a small boy's face when he came downstairs on Christmas morning to find the horse and cart he wanted under the Christmas tree.

CHAPTER EIGHTEEN

'You are spending Christmas Day with us, Sali?' Billy Evans asked at the tea table on Thursday.

'If that's all right with you, Mr Evans?' She placed a liver and bacon casserole in front of him and returned to the hob to fetch a pot of mashed potatoes.

'I was hoping you would. So, what are we eating?' He ladled a small portion of the casserole on to a plate for Harry.

'I have two chickens ready to be killed and Iorwerth up at the farm has promised me a goose as well as a leg of pork,' Victor announced.

'For how much?' his father enquired shortly.

'The price of shoeing his horses last summer.'

'So, it looks as though we'll have plenty of food. Do you mind cooking it, Sali?'

'If you say no, I'm going next door for Christmas dinner,' Joey chipped in before she could answer.

'Megan would have enough sense to throw you out.' Victor poured Harry a cup of milk.

'I ordered a few extras from Connie. On my personal account,' Lloyd added, when his father gave him a penetrating look. 'They'll be delivered tomorrow morning, Sali.'

'Are Connie, Antonia and Annie coming up for dinner on Christmas Day?' Mr Evans asked Lloyd.

'If they are, they haven't mentioned it to me.'

'They have every other year.'

'Three extra people for dinner will mean additional work for Sali,' Lloyd warned.

'I don't mind.' Sali set a bowl of mashed swede in front of Mr Evans and took her place at the table.

'In that case, tell Connie that we're expecting them when you do her accounts tonight, Lloyd.'

'You coming up to the farm with your Uncle Joey and me to get holly and a Christmas tree for the parlour, Harry?' Victor leaned towards Harry and cut his liver into bite-size chunks.

'Can I, Mam?' Harry looked to Sali.

'We won't be late,' Victor promised.

'And I promise to be a good boy, Mam,' Joey grinned.

'You don't know the meaning of the word, Joey,' Lloyd chafed.

'No one's complained to you about me lately, have they?' Joey enquired, an injured expression on his handsome face.

'If they haven't, it's only because you haven't been caught out,' Lloyd retorted.

'You can go, Harry, but only if you wrap up warm,' Sali qualified. 'And no climbing in the cow pens or pig sties. Your boots were filthy the last time you went up there.'

'Goody.' Harry set down his spoon and clapped his hands.

'As soon as we've finished eating, you boys can give me a hand to get the Christmas box down from the attic. As Sali's made a cake and puddings we may as well make it a proper celebration,' Billy glanced at Harry who was manfully working his way through his dinner, 'for Harry's sake.'

'Look what we found when we were looking for the Christmas box, Harry.' Joey dropped a cardboard box on the hearth rug, knelt down, opened it and pulled out a homemade fort, complete with a regiment of lead soldiers, half of which had black crosses painted on their backs.

'The ones with crosses are the enemy,' Joey explained. Harry picked one up. 'Soldiers need someone to fight.'

'I'm not sure I want my son playing war games,' Sali said doubtfully.

'Looks like he already knows all about them.' Victor commented, as Harry lined up soldiers on the ramparts. He went to the cupboard and took out a duster. 'This is to clean them with when we come back from the farm.'

As Harry was so delighted with the fort, Sali relented and told him he could have it 'on loan', but it would always belong to Joey and Victor. Five minutes later, she felt as though she had three children playing at her feet because Joey and Victor seemed to be enjoying themselves as much as Harry, especially when they found a couple of miniature cannons that fired matchsticks with sufficient force to knock over the soldiers. They finally left when she reminded them that they had to go to the farm. A few minutes later, Lloyd walked in with another box.

'If that's more toys for Harry, I won't let him accept them,' she informed him tartly.

'You'd rather Joey's old fort rotted in the attic than be played with?'

'No,' she conceded, realising how ungracious she had sounded. 'But I don't want him—'

'Spoiled, we know. This is the Christmas box and don't go expecting too much in the way of fancy decorations.' He dumped it on the table. 'There's nothing in there up to Danygraig or Ynysangharad House standards. Just a motley collection of homemade bits and pieces.'

'I wasn't expecting anything.' Sali was stung by the inference that her upbringing would lead her to expect better than the Evanses could provide.

Realising she'd taken his casual remark as criticism, he murmured, 'I shouldn't be long down at Connie's. I'll give you a hand to decorate the tree when I get back.' He waited for her to reply. When she didn't, he picked up his hat and left.

Sali washed and dried the dishes, and restored the kitchen to order before opening the box. Lloyd was right about the motley collection. Beautifully woven straw stars were packed between meticulously carved and painted wooden animals and tiny, crocheted angels in silver and white wool, but below them was a layer of crudely drawn and cut-out paper lanterns, moons and cribs.

Names were printed in pencil in childish scrawls at the bottom of the lanterns and she tried to picture the men as small boys running home from school, proudly clutching their 'makings' and eager to offer them to their mother. She found it easy to conjure images of Victor and Joey as children, but not Lloyd. There was an air of authority about him that defied her imagination.

'Sali?' Megan was in the doorway, a pile of parcels in her hand. 'Are you all right? You looked as though you were miles away.'

'I was.' Sali pointed to the clutter on the table. 'It's odd to unpack another family's Christmas decorations. They are so personal, I feel as though I'm snooping.'

'Mrs Evans wouldn't have thought of it like that.' Megan dropped her parcels on to the easy chair. 'I wish you could have met her. I know she would have liked you.'

'And I know from the way she organised this house, she would have hated another woman running it and looking after her family.'

'Maybe it wouldn't have worked if you had tried to run the house together,' Megan agreed, 'but I'm sure that she is smiling down at you now, because you keep her house as clean and welcoming as she did.'

Sali's faith had been so badly shaken by her uncle and Owen Bull that she wasn't at all certain there *was* an afterlife, but she was loathe to offend Megan by questioning her faith. 'Like a cup of tea?'

'I'd love one.' Megan picked up one of the parcels and Sali saw a label with 'Joey' printed on it tied to the string. 'Mrs Evans gave me these a month before she died and asked if I'd keep them for her until she felt well enough to finish them. I put them at the back of my wardrobe and forgot about them until this afternoon when I went to hide some sweets I bought for the children's stockings. They are pullovers that Mrs Evans knitted for Mr Evans and the boys. She always started making her Christmas presents early in the year.'

She unpicked the string and showed Sali a pair of knitted sleeves and the back and front of a pullover. 'They need pressing and making up. Perhaps you could show them to the boys and ask what they want done with them.'

'Or I could make them up and leave them under the tree.' Sali suggested. She looked at the blue pullover Mrs Evans had made for her youngest son. The stitches were neat and beautifully even, and she imagined the Mrs Evans she had seen in the photographs on the parlour wall, only smaller, darker and frailer, sitting up in bed in the front room, knitting.

'That will be a nice surprise for them. I'm only sorry I didn't bring them round before now.'

'I'll put them in my room.' Sali picked up the parcels and ran upstairs with them. By the time she returned, Megan had made the tea.

'You looking forward to Christmas?' Megan asked.

'To be honest, I've been so busy the last couple of months making Christmas cakes, puddings and biscuits that I haven't had much time to think about it. But Joey and Victor have managed to get Harry excited, and I am looking forward to seeing his reaction when he sees the horse and cart I bought him under the Christmas tree.'

'I've invited Victor to supper on Christmas Day,' Megan confided.

'Then I'll see that he doesn't eat too much for dinner and tea.'

'Victor!' Megan laughed. 'I don't think anyone could curb his appetite.' Her face fell. 'He wanted to give me an engagement ring for Christmas.'

'You wouldn't accept it?'

'It would only create more arguments with my uncle and then he'd write to my father who would threaten to take me back to the farm. It's hard enough for me to answer my uncle's questions about Victor's courtship as it is. And even without my family's opposition, I can hardly leave my uncle and the children to fend for themselves while I go off and get married.'

'You two are so much in love, things simply have to work out for you,' Sali sympathised.

'I wish I could believe that. Do you miss your husband?'

Sali's heart pounded erratically. Had rumours reached Tonypandy?

'I am sorry, that was tactless of me. It must have been terrible for you to have been widowed so young.'

Sali suddenly remembered that Megan only knew the story she had told the Evanses when she had first arrived. She sat at the table, pushed the Christmas decorations to one side, sugared her tea and thought of Mansel, of how much she had loved him and persisted in thinking of him as her husband, even after she had married Owen. How the whole time she had lived in Mill Street, she had woven dreams about Mansel and what their life would have been like if he hadn't disappeared. And what it would be like if he returned and took her away from Owen . . .

Sometime since she had moved to Tonypandy she had ceased to think of Mansel. Was that because of what Harry's foster mother had told her? Or because she no longer loved him? She found both questions impossible to answer.

'When . . . when it happened,' she concentrated on the weeks after Mansel's disappearance, 'I didn't want to go on living. But what people say is right, it does get easier as time goes on, and,' she beamed, when she heard Harry's high-pitched, excited chatter in the basement, 'I have a wonderful son, a good job working for kind people and a lot to be grateful for.'

'Are you sure that your father asked you to invite Annie, Tonia and me to dinner on Christmas Day?' Connie asked Lloyd, as he totalled a column of figures in her ledger.

'Yes,' he murmured absently.

'Do you want us to come?'

'You always have before.' He marked a figure with his forefinger. She leaned over the desk and dropped a kiss on his forehead, but he didn't look up from the page.

'We came because your mother invited us.'

'I think that is why my father wants you to come this year. So that the arrangements my mother made when she was alive will continue. Because while they do, she won't be entirely dead. Not to him.'

'There is life after death, Lloyd.'

'Spare me your religion and I'll spare you my Marxism.' He closed the ledger and turned around to face her.

'And my suffrage?' she asked. 'This liberal government of yours is force-feeding helpless women.'

'This liberal government is most certainly not mine.' He lifted his jacket from the back of the chair.

'You are not going?'

'I promised I'd be back early to help decorate the tree.'

'Promised Sali?'

'We've had all the conversations about my father's housekeeper that we are going to have, Connie,' he stated flatly.

'I'm in agreement on that one, darling.' Her fingers strayed to his flies as she kissed his lips.

'No, Connie.' He removed her hand and moved away from her.

'My, you are a grumps. You'll be here tomorrow evening?'

'I don't know.'

'The accounts will need totalling.'

'So long as it is just the accounts,' he said seriously.

'Nine o'clock, which will give us two hours before I have to get ready for midnight mass.' She absolutely refused to accept that he wanted to put their relationship on a platonic footing. He was in a bad mood, that was all. Tomorrow would be different. It had to be. 'If you walk us home after we have dinner with you on Christmas Day, you can give me my present, in private,' she murmured suggestively.

'You are very sure I have something for you.'

'Very.' She grasped his arm. 'Just don't wrap up too well. A woman can get impatient when there are too many layers to tear off.'

He pushed her away. 'Do you mind if I take some of that mistletoe you have in the storeroom in case Victor and Joey didn't find any up at the farm?'

'I'll put it on your bill,' she replied sulkily.

'I'll expect you to.' He took his hat from the stand, jammed it on his head, checked his reflection in the mirror and left.

Connie sat on the sofa in front of the fire and stared into the flames. Lloyd had told her that he loved her several times during the thirteen years they had been lovers, but only in the early years and never since he'd returned from Pontypridd. She had put his reticence down to the uncertainty and clandestine nature of their relationship. But could it really be possible that he no longer loved her?

As Billy Evans had prophesied, without the dining suite, which he and the boys had carried into the kitchen, the middle room made a reasonably comfortable parlour. Acting on Sali's suggestion, they had left the bookcases and sideboard and rearranged the chairs and sofa closer to the fireplace. Victor experimented with the Christmas tree, setting it in several different spots before Sali, Joey and Harry unanimously agreed the best place for it was in front of the window. While Sali, Harry and Joey hung their old decorations and some of the sweets and biscuits Sali had made on the branches, Victor laid a fire, ready to be lit on Christmas morning.

As a final touch, Sali arranged sprigs of holly over the picture frames, filled a vase with more and set it in the centre of the mantelpiece.

'Tomorrow night, we'll hang our stockings in a row along here,' Victor informed Harry, running his fingers over the brass rail below the mantelpiece. 'And, provided we are all good and go to bed early, Father Christmas will park his sleigh on the roof, climb down the chimney and fill them full of nice things.'

Harry looked to his mother for confirmation.

'Victor is right, darling.'

'I'll have presents?'

'If you are a good boy.' She picked him up and swung him on to her back. 'But now it's bedtime.'

'Can I have a story?' he begged.

'Two, as soon as you are curled up in bed, because you have been such a help in decorating the tree and fetching it and the holly from the farm.'

'Not to mention the mistletoe.' Joey pinned a sprig over the door just as Sali was about to walk through it. 'Kiss?'

'That only works on Christmas Day.' Ducking under his arm, she ran into the passage.

'Can Uncle Victor and Uncle Joey listen to the story?' Harry asked.

'It's their playtime,' Sali answered, loud enough for Victor and Joey to hear.

'Will I have playtime in the dark when I'm grown up like them?'

Joey and Victor's laughter followed them as they climbed the stairs.

'Not if I can help it, Harry,' she replied, stifling her own mirth.

'The minute you are old enough, Harry, we'll take you out to play in the dark, no matter what your mam says,' Joey shouted up the stairs.

Sali checked the clock when she returned to the kitchen. Although it felt later, it was only eight o'clock. Victor and Joey wouldn't be home before ten and Mr Evans never returned from the County Club before a quarter to. For all of Lloyd's assertions that he would be early, she knew that once he went down to Connie's to do the accounts he was gone for the evening. She presumed he went on to one of the pubs or the County Club to drink with his father.

It would only take half an hour to heat up two buckets of water on the range. She could have a bath. A luxurious, hot bath, which she hadn't enjoyed since she had left Danygraig House.

She ran downstairs, set the water on to boil, then went upstairs to fetch a clean nightgown, robe and the expensive soap and perfume her aunt had given her when she had been in the infirmary. Harry was fast asleep, his arm around Mr Bear. She tucked him and the bear beneath the flannel sheets and returned to the basement. After a moment's hesitation she slid the bolt home on the door connected to the front of the house. There was little likelihood of her being disturbed, and no one would come round the back of the house at this time of night, but just in case . . .

Lloyd met a miner who had lost his arm in a pit accident outside the Cross Keys pub. He was selling 'Yule' logs from a old baby carriage and despite their well-stocked wood shed, Lloyd bought half a dozen for the parlour fire and insisted on standing the man a Christmas drink, which became three when they met another two colliers who had once worked shifts with them.

Reflecting on his lack of willpower and broken promise to return early, Lloyd carried the logs and the mistletoe round to the back of the house. He burst in through the basement door just as Sali rose, naked from the bath.

They stared at one another for a single, blindingly awkward moment. Blushing, Sali turned and reached for a towel.

'Sali, your back!' Appalled at the sight of her scars, he loosened his hold on the logs and they plummeted, crashing on to the flagstones. He retreated outside and stood for a moment in the cold night air staring up at a sliver of moon surrounded by stars. He had assumed the injuries to Sali's face had been inflicted in a bout of drunken anger. But the scars on her back weren't the result of a single beating. She had been thrashed systematically and often, and for the first time, he understood her fear of Owen Bull and why she wouldn't take her son to live with her aunt in the comfort of Ynysangharad House.

A man capable of stripping the skin from the back of a helpless woman wouldn't hesitate to attack a frail, elderly woman – or child. He recalled Harry's reaction when his father had reached over his head for his cap when the boy had first come to live with them and burned to destroy the man who had blighted Harry's babyhood and transformed Sali Watkin Jones from the happy carefree student with whom he had been slightly acquainted, into the terrified, scarred and browbeaten woman who had applied for the job of their housekeeper.

He never knew what prompted him to act as he did and he never attempted to analyse his reasons. He only knew that the moment he thought of opening the door and stepping inside, nothing could have stopped him.

Sali was still standing in the bath clutching the towel around her and fumbling for her nightgown when Lloyd returned. Terrified, frozen, she watched him move towards her and she felt as though time had slowed. It seemed to take hours for him to reach her, and when he did, he cupped her face in his hands and kissed her so tenderly and gently she couldn't be sure that his lips had touched hers.

She pulled the towel closer and shivered as he released her. Lifting her from the bath, he carried her to the table, set her on the edge and brushed the towel aside. She thought of her uncle and Owen. The assaults they had made on her body. Crying out in distress she grabbed the towel.

'I'm sorry. I didn't understand.' Lloyd ran his fingertips lightly over the scars on her back.

'It wasn't just Owen.' Tears trickled, cold and wet down her cheeks. 'After Mansel . . . after he . . . my uncle . . .' The shame and degradation of her uncle's assault engulfed her in an crushing wave of self-loathing that had lost none of its intensity with the passage of time. She fought for breath, as once again she smelled the sour stench of his pomade, heard his quick panting gasps as he raped her, felt his damp sweating hands around her neck, suffocating, squeezing . . .'

'Sali!'

She opened her eyes and saw Lloyd looking intently at her. He murmured something, but gripped in the trauma of the most devastating night of her life, she didn't hear a word he said.

'I tried to fight him . . . I really tried . . .' Her voice rose hysterically as she pleaded for understanding. 'He was so strong I couldn't stop him . . . And afterwards . . . after what he did to me . . . I had to marry Owen or my sister and brothers would suffer because of my shame and Owen . . . Owen . . . he . . .' She dissolved into tears and Lloyd gathered her close to him.

'Owen said I was a whore,' she sobbed. 'That he did horrible things to me because I was full of sin and made him do them . . . That I wasn't fit to be with decent people . . .'

'And you believed him?' Lloyd slipped his fingers beneath her chin lifting her head until she met his steady gaze. 'Decent men don't rape women or flay the skin from their back, Sali.'

'I'm sorry . . .'

'You have nothing to be sorry for. If there is such a thing as sin, you were the innocent sinned against.' He kissed her again, lightly on the forehead intending to release her, but she clung to him, burying her head in his chest in the hope that he wouldn't see her tears.

He stroked her face gently with the back of his hand, smoothing the damp hair away from her forehead with his fingertips. His touch was light, loving, so chaste and gentle she could almost believe that she was a child again. She wished with all her heart that she was an innocent and precious child cosseted and cared for in the safety of the nursery of Danygraig House.

'Put the past behind you, Sali. None of it was your fault.' He turned her head and kissed away her tears. She gazed at him in wonder, realising for the first time that a grown man could be capable of tenderness.

His lips sought hers, and slowly, tentatively she returned his embrace. Almost before she realised what was happening they were kissing again, a heady, intense kiss that percolated through her lips to her entire body, setting her skin and nerve endings tingling and the blood scorching through her veins.

Weak, dizzy, she gazed into his eyes as softly and delicately he continued to explore her body, first with his fingertips, then later, after he had lowered her back on to the table, with his lips and tongue, evoking strange new sensations and desires she had never suspected herself of possessing.

He reached for something in his pocket and stripped off his clothes. Moments later, they were both lost. Immersed and absorbed in an intense new world where nothing existed outside of the fierce hunger they had aroused within one another. But even then, his movements were unhurried and leisurely as he controlled his ardour and taught her to subsume hers, until the shattering instant they climaxed in a sweeping wave of emotion that left her spent, exhausted and yet, calm, fulfilled and more alive than she had ever felt in her entire life.

Sali felt cold and bereft when Lloyd withdrew from her, and went to the tap. She fled to the other side of the basement. Turning her back to him she returned to the bath, washed and slipped her nightgown over her head, put on her robe and picked up her soap and perfume.

'I didn't mean for that to happen.'

She looked up and saw him watching her. She was devastated by his confession. He had used her, just like Mansel, her uncle, Owen . . . no, not like her uncle and Owen, nothing at all like them!

'We have to talk, but not now. My father and brothers will be in any minute. Leave that,' he ordered, as she went to lift the bath by the handles. 'I'll clean up here. You go to bed. I'll see you tomorrow after work. We can take Harry for a walk around the town.'

She pushed her feet into her slippers.

'Goodnight, Sali,' he called after her, as she ran up the stairs.

She snapped two fingernails to the quick in her impatience to pull back the bolt. She heard water running downstairs as he rinsed out the bath followed by the scrape of zinc against stone as he hung it back on the wall.

Terrified of meeting Victor, Joey or Mr Evans lest they see her and guess something had happened, she ran up the stairs, dived into her room and closed the door.

How could she have been so foolish as to risk her and Harry's home? Was it simply as Owen and her uncle had said? Was she was a whore, a woman who liked to do sinful things?

And she was married! She had stood in chapel and sworn before God to take Owen Bull and forsake all others.

She sat on the bed in the freezing cold room, hating herself for what she had done and wishing she still believed in God so she could get down on her knees and pray for forgiveness.

'Who is it?'

'Me, Connie.'

'Lloyd?' Connie opened her private door set beside the shop entrance and peered outside to see Lloyd's tall figure framed in the light of the gas lamp behind him.

'There's something wrong with the figures I added up this evening,' he fabricated, seeing Annie O'Leary's tall thin figure, and Antonia's more curvaceous form move behind Connie in the hallway.

'And you came round at this hour?'

'It's serious, Connie. I didn't want you to start trading tomorrow until I sorted it.'

She opened the door. 'Go into the office. I'll be down as soon as I've put some clothes on.'

Lloyd sat in the chair behind the desk, flicked through the ledger he had left there, rose and went to the fireplace. Leaning on the mantelpiece, he stared down at the dying embers of the fire. Unable to stay still, he paced uneasily from the hearthrug to the window and back.

'There isn't really an error in the accounts, is there?' Connie was in the doorway, her long dark hair hanging loose, framing her face, a navy blue woollen robe belted tightly at her waist.

'No,' he answered quietly.

She closed the door and stepped into the room. 'Something's happened to you and, by that look on your face, I'd say it's happened with another woman.'

'How do you know?'

'I've been waiting for you to say something ever since the bruises faded on that pretty face of hers, Lloyd.'

'It was that obvious?'

'I've never seen you together, but from the way you have been talking about her, or rather refusing to talk about her, I guessed.' She was unable to keep the bitterness from her voice.

'I didn't know until tonight.'

'You made love to her?' She sat on the sofa and linked her hands around her knees, holding herself rigidly upright so he wouldn't see her trembling. From the fixed expression on his face she realised that no amount of angry raving on her part would have the slightest impact on his resolution. The fact that he was visiting her openly, and at this hour of the night spoke volumes for his state of mind. Steeling herself, she muttered, 'I wish you well, Lloyd.'

'You mean that?' He stared at her.

'I do,' she replied insincerely, forcing a smile. 'We've been good friends. Good, loving friends. Please, let it remain that way.'

'Without the loving, Connie,' he warned. 'There can never be any more of that.'

'Pity. That, I'm going to miss. You were exceptionally good at it, and believe me, I'm an expert judge.'

'You never told me.'

'You were so considerate and anxious to please I didn't want you to get overconfident. She's a lucky girl, Lloyd, and I'll tell her so the next time I meet her.'

'Please don't.'

'You haven't told her that you love her?'

He went to the door. 'If you want me to carry on doing your books, I'll do them at home.'

'I'd prefer to hire a bookkeeper.'

'It might be for the best.'

'Go.' Hysteria welled within her and she rose to her feet, pushing him away from her. 'Go, before you have me crying. You know how I hate sentimentality.'

After he left, she heard someone lock and bolt the front door. A draught set the fire flickering again, and she looked to the door. Annie was standing behind her, her hair in rags, her red flannel robe wound tightly around her thin frame.

'It's finally over between you then.'

'It would appear so.'

'I'm sorry.'

'So am I, Annie.'

'What are you going to do?' Annie wrapped her arm around Connie and helped her up the stairs.

'Do? Run the shop as I have always done, look after Tonia—'

'I didn't mean that and you know it.' Annie smoothed the rumpled bedclothes and helped Connie into bed. 'You're a warm-blooded, passionate woman.'

'There's always old Mr Jones across the street.' Connie's attempt at a joke fell flat.

'He's ninety if he's a day. One minute with you and he'll be in his coffin.' Annie removed her robe and climbed into bed beside her. 'Do you want me to rub you down with lavender oil?'

'Please.' Connie sat up, pulled off her nightdress and lay flat on her stomach.

As Annie's hands caressed the soft skin on her back and shoulders, Connie allowed her first tears to fall. In her heart she had always known that one day Lloyd would walk away from her and never come back. But she hadn't anticipated just how much it would hurt.

'You looked tired this morning, Sali,' Joey commented, as she set his breakfast in front of him. 'What's the matter, couldn't you sleep?'

'I slept well.' She evinced a sudden interest in the bacon she was frying to avoid looking at Lloyd who walked into the kitchen as if the morning were no different from any other.

'Christmas Eve, Harry.' Victor cut his bread and butter into soldiers, dunked one in egg yolk and handed it to the boy. 'Tonight we hang up our stockings and hope that Father Christmas will bring us what we want.'

Joey cut into the sausages Sali had piled on his plate. 'What do you want, Harry?'

'Sweets,' Harry suggested hopefully.

'And a toy?' Joey asked.

'Will I get a toy, Mam?' Harry's eyes widened.

'You'll have to wait and see,' she murmured.

'Joey and I ran into Father Kelly last night, and guess what?' Victor addressed his father. 'Joey offered to man the sweet stall at the Christmas bazaar tonight.'

'Who's the girl manning it with him?' Billy Evans asked.

'Katie Kavanagh.' Joey grinned triumphantly.

'Gorgeous Katie with the brown curly hair,' Victor elaborated.

'Remind me to call in and warn Mrs Kavanagh about our Joey on the way home from work,' Mr Evans remarked.

'Why don't you and Harry come to the bazaar with us, Sali?' Victor asked. 'There'll be lots of stalls and a bran tub for the children. Rumour has it that Father Christmas may even call in before he does his rounds.'

'Father Christmas!'

Sali was certain that the only Father Christmas Harry had ever seen was in picture books, but that didn't stop him from getting excited every time his name was mentioned.

'That's a good idea, we'll all go to the Christmas Bazaar,' Lloyd said quietly.

Sali knew Lloyd was looking at her, but she kept her eyes averted.

'You boys can go if you like.' Billy sat back in his chair and Sali poured his tea. 'But you can count me out. I've sworn never to set foot in a church again.'

'It's in the church hall, Dad,' Victor protested.

'Same difference.'

'Harry and I aren't Catholic.' It was as much as Sali could do to remain in the same room as Lloyd. She couldn't bear the thought of going out in public with him.

'That won't bother Father Kelly any more than Dad and Lloyd's Marxism,' Victor said cheerfully. 'You'll like Father Kelly, Sali; he has a wonderful sense of Irish humour. Thank you, that breakfast was just what I needed to set me up for the last shift before a two-day holiday. It's very considerate of Christmas to fall on a Saturday this year.'

'Don't wear yourself out, girl.' Billy eyed Sali as he handed her his empty plate. 'Christmas is only one day. You want to be in a fit state to enjoy it. Most of the work is done, isn't it?'

'Yes, Mr Evans.'

'So, you've only the usual housework to do today.'

'Apart from preparing the goose for tomorrow, Mr Evans, and that won't take me long.'

'Leave it to Victor. He's a dab hand at plucking geese.'

'I really don't mind doing it.'

'If you must.' She saw him glance back at her as he opened the door to the basement stairs. Joey and Victor followed, but Lloyd hung back. He touched her hand as he handed her his plate and she jumped as if she'd been scalded. The plate fell and shattered on the flagstone floor.

'Are you all right?' he said solicitously.

She bent down to pick up the pieces. 'Yes.' She shrugged off his hand as he tried to help her to her feet.

'You look exhausted. My father's right; you should take it easy today.'

'Lloyd, we're going,' Mr Evans shouted impatiently from the basement.

'I'm coming. Bye, Sali.' He waited a few seconds. She turned her back to him and he walked away.

CHAPTER NINETEEN

Ignoring Mr Evans and Lloyd's advice to rest, Sali threw herself into the housework, working at an even faster pace than usual. While Harry played, engrossed with the fort and toy soldiers, she peeled enough potatoes and vegetables to last until Monday and made apple stuffing for the goose, sage and onion for the leg of pork, and chestnut for the chicken. She plucked, stuffed and trussed the goose ready for the pan, scored the rind of the leg of pork, and stuffed the knuckle before putting it in the oven. She made a saucepan full of apple sauce that would accompany both the pork and the goose, and cleaned the kitchen thoroughly.

Her mind a turmoil of guilt, shame and mortification, she ran up and down the stairs, making the beds and cleaning every corner of the house, but despite all the energy she expended scrubbing, sweeping and polishing, she could not erase the memory of what she had done with Lloyd the evening before. She knew that what had happened was as much her fault as his, if not more so. She had not been passive as she had been when Mansel had made love to her, or an unwilling victim as she had been with her uncle and Owen. She had not only accepted Lloyd's caresses, but returned them with a passion he had aroused, and she had not made the slightest attempt to control.

When she finished in the house, she scoured the front doorstep and polished it with a stone, scrubbed the pavement outside and the path in the back garden. An hour before the men were expected home, she remembered the pullovers that Megan had brought in the day before. The sections were so beautifully knitted it didn't take her long to sew them up. Warning Harry to stay well away from her and the fire, she opened the hob, set two irons on to heat and brought out the thick ironing cloth to cover the table. Wringing a towel in cold water she laid the pullovers out carefully, covered them with the damp towel, and pressed them into shape.

Mrs Evans had chosen the colours well. A mid-blue that stopped just short of being too bright for Joey, a deep rust for Victor, which would go well with his moleskin trousers, a rich green for Lloyd to complement both his dark good looks and subdued taste in clothes, and a serviceable brown for Mr Evans.

When she finished, she set the water buckets on the hobs to boil, the irons on the back of the stove to cool and wrapped the finished pullovers in the paper and string Mrs Evans had used, leaving the original labels. Harry followed her into the parlour and watched as she placed the parcels under the tree.

'I thought Father Christmas brought the presents.'

'His sleigh isn't big enough to bring them for grown-ups as well as children, darling.' She ruffled his hair. 'Everyone will be home soon. Will you set the table for me?'

'And then I can go with Joey and Victor to see Father Christmas?'

'Yes, you can.' Her heart sank. Harry had grown so fond of Joey and Victor she only hoped that they could continue to live with the Evanses after Lloyd had carried out his threat to talk to her.

'That's a fine piece of pork, Victor. Iorwerth did you proud,' Billy Evans said, as Sali wrapped the remains of the leg in a scalded cloth and placed it in the pantry.

'It was good,' Victor agreed, 'and there's plenty left for

sandwiches tonight. Let's hope the goose is the same quality.'

Billy finished his blackberry jam roly-poly and custard. 'That parlour will be freezing tomorrow if the fire isn't lit tonight to warm the room.'

'I'll do it, Dad,' Victor offered.

'You finish your meal. I'll see to it.' Billy left the kitchen and closed the door to keep the heat in the room. Seconds later he yelled, 'Sali.'

'That sounds ominous.' Joey divided the last of the jam roly-poly between himself and Victor.

Lloyd looked at Sali. 'Is something wrong?'

She opened the door without answering him and went into the parlour. Mr Evans was sitting on the sofa, an unopened parcel on his lap. He was holding the label that his wife had written between his fingers. 'Where did these come from?'

'Megan brought them around yesterday, Mr Evans.' Realising he was not only shocked, but angry, she explained how Megan had forgotten about them and she had made the pullovers up that day.

'And you thought you'd give them to us as Christmas presents?'

'Not me, Mr Evans.' She was horrified he should even think such a thing. 'Mrs Evans put a great deal of work into those pullovers. It seemed a pity to waste the effort she made.'

'You should have told me about them last night.'

'Yes, Mr Evans, I should have. I'm sorry. I realise that now ... it's just ...'

'What, girl?' he broke in impatiently.

'If my father had put that much work into making something for me before he died, I would have liked to have had it as a last present from him. I really am sorry if I offended you, I didn't think ...'

He cut her apology short by gathering all four parcels and leaving the room. Moments later she heard him walk

335

in and out of his downstairs bedroom. The front door banged shut behind him and she returned to the kitchen.

'I take it Dad's gone to the County Club?' Joey asked.

'He didn't say.' She began to clear the table.

'Time I was off.' Joey left the table and picked up the bottle of cologne from the window sill.

'Put any more of that stuff on and Katie Kavanagh will be fainting over the sweets,' Victor joked.

'You ready to come, Sali, Lloyd?' Joey asked, ignoring Victor.

'I have to wash the dishes.'

'I'll give you a hand,' Victor offered.

'I've no doubt Sali has a couple of other things to do for tomorrow and I have to write a letter to Mr Richards,' Lloyd interrupted. 'Why don't the two of you take Harry and go on ahead and we'll join you in half an hour or so.'

'That's a good idea.' Joey lifted Harry down from his chair. 'Let's get your cap and coat from the hall.'

'Just can't wait to be with Katie, can you?' Victor teased.

'Here's sixpence for Harry in case he sees anything he wants.' Sali pushed it into Victor's pocket before he could protest. 'And don't forget to take Harry to the *ty bach* before you go.'

'We won't.' Victor suspected that his father had said something to upset Sali, but decided that if she had wanted to tell them about it, she would have. 'See you later,' he said, as Joey handed him his coat and cap and Harry ran ahead of them down to the basement.

Silence closed over the kitchen, dense and suffocating. Acutely aware of Lloyd's presence, Sali began to rinse the dishes under the pump and stack them in readiness for washing. She took her time over cleaning each one, dreading the moment when she would have to turn to the stove and pick up the bucket of water she had set to boil because it would mean moving closer to the table where Lloyd was sitting.

As she rinsed the last dinner plate on the pile, it was taken from her. She knew that Lloyd was standing behind her, but she didn't turn her head.

'We have to talk.' He laid the plate on top of the others.

'I'm sorry—'

'What for, Sali?'

'For what happened yesterday, for behaving like a . . .' She couldn't bring herself to say 'whore' because it was what Owen had constantly called her. 'For behaving so badly.'

He took her hands into his and led her to the easy chair. Pushing her gently into it, he pulled a kitchen chair from the table and sat facing her. 'If anyone behaved badly it was me. I . . .' he gave her a wry smile, 'was somewhat carried away. Hardly surprising after walking in on you the way I did, and seeing you standing there looking very beautiful and desirable.'

'Now I know you're making fun of me.' She tried to leave the chair but he blocked her path, forcing her to sit back down.

'I won't allow you to leave until we have talked this out. And you are extremely beautiful and desirable. So beautiful, you even make short hair look good.'

'I am ugly . . . I have scars . . .'

'You had a husband who was a brute and after seeing what he did to your back, if I ever have the displeasure of meeting him I won't be responsible for my actions.'

'You knew he beat me.'

'I knew he beat you once, from the state of your face when you first came here. But I also heard that you had married him without telling him you were carrying another man's child.'

'Owen knew about Harry before he married me; my uncle told him. They struck a bargain; my dowry in exchange for Owen Bull's name.'

'The three thousand pounds your father left you?'

She forced herself to meet his steadfast, probing gaze. 'Didn't your father tell you what I told him the day he allowed me to bring Harry here?'

'When you get to know my father better, you'll realise that he never tells anyone anything that isn't their business. And he would regard anything you told him about your past as your business and no one else's.'

Haltingly, hesitantly, she told Lloyd everything she had told his father and more. How she had allowed Mansel to make love to her before their wedding and her despair and bewilderment at his disappearance. Her horror at finding herself pregnant, and the choice her uncle had forced on her between the workhouse and marriage to Owen Bull. How Morgan Davies had raped her the night before she left Danygraig House. The beatings and sexual humiliation Owen had inflicted on her. The tyrannical regime her husband had imposed and how he beat and abused not only her, but also his brother and sister. And finally how Iestyn had died during that last terrible night in Mill Street.

'Why didn't you leave Owen Bull earlier?' Lloyd questioned, when she finally fell silent.

'Because I had no money and nowhere to go.'

'You had your aunt. From what she said when I met her, she would have done anything to help you.'

'Owen threatened to harm her if I went to her, and he warned his brother and sister that he'd punish them if they allowed me to leave the house or speak to anyone.' She met his gaze and saw that his eyes were as dark as Joey's, only softer, more tender. 'And he would have, Lloyd. I can't prove it but I am convinced that Owen pushed his brother down the stairs because he was trying to protect Harry and me. And Owen went to my aunt's when I was in the infirmary to look for Harry and his sister. The footman was so afraid of what he'd do, he called the police.'

'But you are safe from him now.'

'Only so long as he doesn't find out where I am.'

'And that brings us back to what happened last night.'

'Can't we just forget it?' she pleaded. 'It won't happen again.'

'That's where we might have a problem. I want it to happen again and I hoped you would too.' He gripped her hands in his and looked deep into her eyes. 'I love you, Sali . . .'

'*Love me?*' She sank back in the chair and stared at him in disbelief.

'Why look so surprised? If what we did last night wasn't love, then what was it?'

'I don't know,' she stammered, unable to think of anything other than his shattering announcement.

He ran his fingers through his hair. 'Do you still love Mansel James? Is that it?'

'No. I hardly ever think of Mansel now except to wonder what happened to him,' she said truthfully. 'And although I made love to him, he never, ever made me feel the way you did last night.'

'Never?' He smiled.

'I had no idea that it could be like that. My aunt once told me that the physical act between a man and a woman could be the most beautiful expression of love but I never believed her. Until now,' she whispered.

'Then you do love me?'

'I've spent all day petrified that I'd have to leave here because you were disgusted with me.'

'You have that low an opinion of yourself?'

She summoned her courage. 'I'm a whore who gave birth to a bastard—'

He laid his finger over her lips. 'You're the woman I love.'

'My uncle told me that I was unfit for decent society, including my own brothers, sister and mother. Owen married me for my money and kept me hidden in his house in Mill Street for the same reason. Then I come here and you accept me. I told your father what I'd done

339

and he even allowed me to bring Harry into the house knowing he was illegitimate. I've met nothing but kindness from all of you—'

'Are you trying to tell me that you only feel gratitude towards me and my family?'

She looked him in the eye. 'I am grateful to all of you but even after last night I dare not love you. I'm a married woman, Lloyd. I promised Owen in chapel before God that I'd forsake all others . . .' A fragment of her father's voice echoed from other, happier days in Danygraig House.

A benevolent God would never frown on a man who allowed himself a few harmless indulgences after a hard day's work, only warped and twisted ministers who misinterpreted his Gospels.

In a single moment of revelation she realised she hadn't lost her belief in God, only in her Uncle Morgan and Owen Bull's brand of Methodism.

'You want to remain married to a man who degraded you, beat you to a pulp and threatened to harm your son and your aunt?'

'That's the last thing I want to do!'

'Then divorce Owen Bull and marry me.'

'I can't divorce Owen. If I even try, he'll find out where we are and come after us.'

'I can protect you.'

'Twenty-four hours a day for the rest of our lives? And if I make love to you again, I could have another child . . .'

'Like last night, I'll make sure that you don't. Not until we're ready.'

'I won't bring another bastard into the world, Lloyd.'

He sank his face into his hands before looking at her again. 'Everyone in Tonypandy thinks that you are a widow.'

'Yes,' she agreed, mystified by his train of thought.

'After Christmas I'll take a day off work. We'll dress in our best clothes, catch an early train to Cardiff and buy a wedding ring. When we return, we'll tell everyone that we married there by special licence.'

'Lie to everyone?'

'It won't entirely be a lie. We'll see a solicitor, change your name to Evans by deed poll and I'll make a will leaving everything I own to you. There'll be enough to keep you and Harry if anything happens to me.'

'If anyone from Pontypridd heard that I was married to you they'd think I'd comitted bigamy. Besides your father knows I'm married. We'd be living in sin . . .'

'My father has even less respect for organised religion and preaching designed to keep the working classes in their place than I do. And, would us living without the blessing of a parson and a meaningless piece of paper be any worse than you living with the chapel's blessing with Owen Bull?'

'Nothing could be worse than life with Owen,' she said vehemently.

'So what is your solution? That we ignore what happened last night? Because I warn you now, Sali, I can't, and I refuse even to try.'

She glanced at the clock. 'The others will be wondering where we are and the dishes aren't even washed.'

'It's more important that we finish this discussion than wash the dishes. Do you really expect me to carry on living in this house, day after day, as if last night never happened?'

'No,' she answered quietly, so quietly, he wondered if she'd really spoken or he'd simply heard what he wanted her to say.

'Then what do you suggest we do?'

'I don't know. Please, Lloyd, I need time to think about what you've said. Time to find out what I feel . . . why are you smiling?'

'Because you are becoming your own person and not a doormat.' He raised her from the chair. 'Come on, sweetheart, I'll help you with the dishes, take you to the bazaar and walk you home. And,' his smile broadened,

341

'begin a courtship that will hopefully result in many, many repetitions of last night. After all your bedroom is next door to mine.'

'I couldn't ... your father ... your brothers ... it wouldn't be right. It would be—'

'Perfect,' he contradicted, 'if you'd allow me to make you my common-law wife.'

She thought of her father and how shocked he would have been if he'd ever discovered that she could contemplate such a thing. 'I'll not live in sin with you, Lloyd.'

'Then we'll just have to carry on sneaking around until you change your mind.'

'I won't change my mind.'

He pulled her close and kissed her. A brutal savage kiss that made her head swim and weakened her limbs. As she reeled helplessly in his arms, he swept her off her feet. 'Your room or mine?'

'Lloyd ...'

'Mine, I think.'

'Do you think you could love me?'

They were lying in Lloyd's bed, Sali's head resting on his chest, his hand stroking her hair.

'I wouldn't be here if I didn't.'

'Enough to live with me openly?'

She looked up at him. 'If I did, that would make me what my uncle and Owen told me I was. A whore.'

'It's just a name, Sali.'

'A name I don't ever want associated with my father's daughter.'

'Given the circumstances, your father would have understood.'

'Would he?'

He stripped the bedclothes away and turned up the lamp. She didn't make any attempt to cover herself and he smiled down at her. 'I want your heart.' He kissed her left breast.

'You have it.'

'And all of your mind that a lover has a right to lay claim to.' He kissed her forehead. 'And your body.'

'You have that now.' She wrapped her arms around him and pulled him close, but he drew back and kissed the flat of her stomach.

'And I want to watch you grow big with my child, because he or she will carry our love into the future. I want to live with you day in, year out, until we grow old and grey together. And if the only way we can do that is in sin as you put it, then that's the way it will have to be.'

'No, Lloyd.'

'I'll wear you down,' he threatened.

'You can try, but you won't succeed.'

'This won't be the last time we'll lie like this.'

'I know.'

'So we sneak around?'

'I love you, Lloyd,' she pleaded. 'Isn't that enough for the moment?'

'It will have to be, if that's all you're prepared to give me, for the moment.' He swung his legs over the side of the bed and pulled her up. 'Come on, woman, we have a bazaar to go to and a son to collect.'

'A son!'

'If it were up to me, I'd adopt Harry and make you both Evanses tomorrow.'

She turned aside so he couldn't see the expression in her eyes.

'If you don't want me to—'

'If it were ever possible, you'd make a wonderful father.'

'And Harry is a son any man would be proud to have.'

'Please, Lloyd, whatever you do, don't mention it to him. The only family life he has ever known has been here with your father, brothers and you. And he's so close to all of you I'm afraid that if it came to an end he would—'

'It won't.'

'If Owen finds us . . .'

'He won't, Sali.' He picked up her clothes and handed them to her, wishing he were as confident as he sounded. First Connie, now Sali, was he destined always to fall in love with women he couldn't marry?

'Tuppence, please.'

'You look blue, Dai.' Lloyd dropped two pennies into the hand of the man sitting behind the card table outside the entrance to the Catholic hall.

'Underneath this coat I'm the colour of a baboon's . . . rear end,' he amended hastily when he saw Sali. 'Here're your tickets, keep them to claim your free cup of tea, Lloyd.'

After the bitter cold darkness of Trinity Street, Sali found the blazing gaslights, noisy crowd, heat and mingling odours of tea, coffee, toffee apples, egg sand-wiches and sweat overwhelming. Lloyd pushed ahead through the crowd but she hung back, surveying the room. Trestle tables had been set up and decorated with garlands of ivy, sprigs of holly, tinsel, and red, green and yellow painted paper friezes. Makeshift poles made from broom handles had been slung above them to support homemade banners and she realised there was little difference between a Catholic and Methodist bazaar. They both had the same kinds of stalls.

White Elephant, Homemade Cakes, Good Used Ladies' Clothes, New Knitted Goods, Ornamental Bric-a-Brac, Household Goods, Toys, Books, Jams, Jellies and Chutneys, Jewels – intrigued by the thought of jewels in a Tonypandy bazaar, she stepped close to the table to see rows of necklaces and bracelets strung from cheap glass beads interspersed with pieces of old-fashioned, tarnished paste.

'See a wedding ring you like?' Lloyd whispered in her ear.

'Ssh, someone will hear.'

'Good God! There's Joey.' Lloyd burst out laughing at the sight of his youngest brother in a white baker's hat and apron, standing behind a stall labelled 'Mouth-watering Homemade Sweets'.

'The sweets are sticky,' Joey snapped, as they approached.

Sali saw that it wasn't just the apron that had amused Lloyd. A sour-faced, middle-aged woman, who looked as though she was about to burst out of her corsets at any moment, was standing alongside Joey.

'And there's me thinking that miracles never happen in Tonypandy. Joey and Victor warned me that you'd be putting in an appearance, Lloyd, but I didn't believe them for a minute.' Father Kelly gripped Lloyd's shoulder and pumped his hand enthusiastically up and down. 'Doesn't Joey look grand in that outfit?' He pushed his hand into his pocket. 'I'll have a pennyworth of that coconut ice there please, Joey.'

Joey ceased scowling at Lloyd long enough to pick up a paper cornet.

'Not with your fingers.' The woman beside Joey rapped his knuckles with a silver spoon before handing him a pair of sugar tongs.

'I see you've your helper well under control, Miss Phillips.'

'I try, Father,' she sighed with a martyred air. 'But like all men, he's more thumbs than fingers and has trouble remembering the rules of basic hygiene.'

'Wasn't it kind of Miss Phillips to offer to man the sweet stall with Joey when Mrs Kavanagh said she couldn't manage without Katie's help with the refreshments.' Father Kelly took a penny from his cassock pocket and handed it to Joey in return for the paper cone. 'Mrs Kavanagh's a dab hand at making the tea, coffee and lemonade, and little Katie is so light on her feet, she scurries around those tables like a wee fairy. No one's had to wait more than five minutes for a cup of tea since she took over the tables.' Father Kelly beamed at Sali. 'And you must be the new housekeeper? Victor and Joey keep singing your praises. I gather you are also the mother of the beautiful boy Victor is carrying around so proudly. I'm very pleased to make your acquaintance. Mrs Jones, isn't it?'

'It is.' Sali couldn't help smiling as she shook the hand of the short, fat priest. He not only looked genuinely pleased to meet her, his eyes twinkled with a glint of boyish mischief that reminded her of Geraint and Gareth.

'Last I saw of them, they were both waiting outside Father Christmas's grotto. I don't know who was the more excited, Victor or young Harry.' He waved towards a stage at the end of the room. Curtains had been drawn across it and an inexpertly painted cardboard sign proclaiming 'Father Christmas One Penny' pinned to the folds. 'It's a long queue, but I'm sure they'll be along soon.' He solemnly presented Sali with the paper cornet. 'That's for bringing a stray sheep back to my fold, even if it is only to the hall for the one night. I know how hard you must have worked to get Lloyd here.'

'I couldn't possibly—'

'Sure you could. And it's by way of a bribe. Victor and Joey say you're a fabulous cook and poor old parish priests like myself always welcome an invitation to a home-cooked meal. Even if we do have to eat it with Marxists.'

Uncertain how to take the priest's sense of humour and his references to Marxism, and confused by Lloyd's smiles, Sali was too bemused to do anything other than take the cornet.

'You matchmaking Joey with Miss Phillips then, Father?' Lloyd asked dryly.

The priest stood back and watched them as they served customers. 'Joey could do worse. She's amassed a tidy bit teaching over the years, or so I've been told. And she's a fine steady woman; an older head might curb some of his wild ways. Now, will you look at that?' The priest shook his head as Joey winked at a well-endowed girl with curly hair who was clearing teacups from the long tables set in front of the stage. 'Something tells me that boy will be saying more than a few paternosters and Hail Mary's when he confesses what he's thinking right this minute about pretty little Katie Kavanagh. Poor Miss Phillips, I think I'll give up matchmaking. There are too many disappointments in it.'

'A lot more water will flow down the River Rhondda before Joey walks up the aisle with a girl, Father.'

'We'll see.' The priest looked Lloyd up and down, 'But there's Victor and you to go first. It's a sin for fine young men like you two not to be married. You have no right to be enjoying life the footloose way you do. Every man needs a bit of misery with which to contrast his happiness and who better to give it to him than a nagging wife?'

'Not all wives nag.' Lloyd glanced slyly at Sali.

'Your mother didn't to be sure, but then she was a saint. So, should I be dusting the marriage service off for you just yet?'

'If I find a woman who'll have me, and that is an "if", Father, we won't be marrying in church.'

'You and your heathen Marxist services.'

'You know full well there's no such thing.'

'I've no doubt that your father is writing one this very minute. I don't suppose there's any chance of you coming to vigil mass tonight? The singing will improve no end if you add your fine voice to the choir.'

'You don't suppose right, Father.'

'What about you, Mrs Jones?'

'I'm not a Catholic, Father Kelly.'

'Don't let that be stopping you. God welcomes everyone in his house even, as I keep telling Lloyd here and his father, heathens. Vigil mass is a nice service, and the singing will be something special, although it would be better with Lloyd. So if you could coax him to change his mind, I'd be grateful.'

'Do you allow just anyone to worship at your church, Father?' Sali asked in bewilderment.

'Anyone who knocks the door and wants to come in.

On two legs that is. We had a dog once, but it bit the organist.'

'Obviously a Calvinist Methodist dog come up from Trinity church to spy,' Lloyd remarked.

'Why the confusion, Mrs Jones?' asked the priest. 'Doesn't our Bible teach us that God has a forgiving nature? I'd welcome the devil himself to a service if I thought I had the faintest chance of converting him.'

'Mrs Jones is used to Methodist ways, Father Kelly,' Lloyd explained.

'Methodists. Ah now, there's a big word.' The priest rolled his eyes and looked heavenwards. 'God in his wisdom has made us practically neighbours in this street and I understand his purpose. We all have to be taught to love our fellow man. And I have learned to forgive the Methodists many things, but not their policy on drink. God would never have created fine whisky if he didn't intend for us to taste a drop or two once in a while. And here comes your boy, Mrs Jones.' He waved at Harry who was sitting on Victor's shoulders clutching a paper cornet and a folded comic under his arm. 'Did you see Father Christmas, Harry?'

'Yes.' Harry grinned from ear to ear as he unfolded his fist. 'And look what he gave me, Mam.' He proudly showed her a penny whistle.

'You are a lucky boy and from that cornet and comic, I can see that Uncle Victor has been spoiling you.' Sali opened her arms and Harry climbed into them.

'Bring Harry to mass in the morning, Victor,' the priest suggested. 'It's a special children's service and it wouldn't surprise me if a few toffees weren't handed out at the end. Tell your father I'll see him later in the County Club, Lloyd, and not to drink all the Christmas cheer before I get there.'

'You look puzzled, Sali.' Victor took Harry's hand, as Sali set him on the floor.

'I've never met a Catholic priest before.'

'Father Kelly isn't typical.' Lloyd laughed again, as the

priest whispered something in Joey's ear that made his younger brother turn crimson. 'We had a right old sourpuss before he came here.'

'*We*' Victor repeated archly. 'Who was it who said, "A lapsed Catholic is still a Catholic"?'

'Probably Father Kelly in hope, after having one too many whiskies with our father in the County Club.'

'He really drinks with your father?' Sali watched the priest work his way through the hall, smiling at the room in general as he slapped men on the back, shook hands with the women, and joked with the children.

'They are close friends.'

'He was wonderful to Mam when she was ill. He called every day to see her.' Victor steered them back towards the sweet stall.

'You can't help liking the man even if you hate organised religion,' Lloyd agreed.

'Do you think he meant what he said about me going to mass tonight?' Sali asked seriously.

'You want to go to mass?' Lloyd couldn't have looked more disapproving if she'd suggested she crawl down a sewer.

'I've never been in a Catholic Church. I'd like to see if they are any different to a chapel.'

'They are,' Lloyd said shortly, 'and Father Kelly will try to convert you.'

'Like he's been trying to convert you and Dad for years,' Victor mocked, lifting Harry up so he could see the sweets on offer.

'You don't know what you're getting yourself into,' Lloyd counselled. Sali watched Joey slip Harry a piece of fudge. 'And priests like Father Kelly are the worst. They are so friendly, amusing and easy to get along with, they seduce people into believing that everyone in the church is just like them. A year from now, the powers in Rome will replace him with a surly old Jesuit, but by then you'll already be halfway to converting, and after that it will be all sin, hellfire, purgatory and damnation. You'll end up being so terrified of God and what heaven might do to you if you don't follow the church's doctrine to the letter, your life will be a total misery.'

'Joey, Victor and Father Kelly don't seem to be living in misery,' she dared to point out.

'Because they take what they want from the church and leave the rest.'

'And you don't think I can do that?' she countered.

The last thing Lloyd wanted to do was undermine her newly acquired confidence. 'You really want to go to vigil mass?'

'I'd really like to,' she reiterated.

'Then I'll come back from the club with Victor and Joey and look after Harry for you,' he relented.

'You mean it?'

'I have a feeling that I'll regret it,' he muttered, 'but yes.'

CHAPTER TWENTY

Sali was happy to walk home alone with Harry, but Lloyd and Victor wouldn't hear of it. They saw her safely to the door, and after promising to return at a quarter past eleven, left her.

Harry was so tired he fell asleep halfway through the first story she read him. After tucking him, Mr Bear and the penny whistle he had insisted on taking to bed with him, under the bedclothes, she went downstairs.

She found it strange to be celebrating Christmas again after three years of being forced to ignore it in Owen's house. The last time she had helped fill stockings had been the month before her father's death when she and Mari had drank half a bottle of sherry between them, while setting presents out under the tree in the drawing room for her family, and beneath the tree in the servants' hall for the staff. It was a ritual she had taken part in every year since she had been twelve years old. Mysteriously, two extra stockings had always appeared on Christmas morning, one for her on the string suspended beneath the drawing room mantelpiece and another for Mari on the brass rail of the iron fireplace in the servants' hall, both packed full of small luxuries courtesy of Father Christmas, whose handwriting bore a strong resemblance to her father's.

She labelled the tins of sweets she had made for Joey, Victor, Lloyd, Harry and Mr Evans, and set them together with the extra ones she had made for Rhian, Connie's family and Megan's beneath the tree. The men's stockings she filled with half ounces of tobacco, pipe cleaners, sticks of shaving soap, boot laces, almonds she had coated with sugar, apples, Spanish oranges and nuts she had bought from Connie. Harry's she filled with nuts, an orange, apple, liquorice root and a bar of Five Boy chocolate. The horse and cart she set unwrapped beneath the tree.

She carried in the Christmas cake, along with plates of iced cakes and biscuits she had baked, and bowls of nuts and fruit, and arranged them on the sideboard. With the gaslight hissing, the fire blazing in the grate, the curtains closed and a pan of sweet chestnuts Victor had brought home waiting to be roasted in the hearth, the room looked warm, inviting and Christmassy.

Not the lavish Christmas of Danygraig House that her father and Mari had orchestrated, she reflected without bitterness, but nevertheless Christmas. And perhaps one Harry would remember as the first he had ever celebrated.

'God rest ye merry gentlewoman,' Victor said, as he and Joey walked into the parlour to find Sali curled on the sofa in the parlour, reading a copy of *Nicholas Nickelby* that she had borrowed from Mr Evans's bookcase.

'Everything looks great, Sali.' Joey reached for an iced cake.

'Before you fill yourself up on sweets, I cut pork sandwiches. They're under a plate in the pantry along with a dish of apple sauce.' Sali marked her page with a small drawing of Harry's, and closed the book.

'Food after, not before mass.' Victor took the cake from Joey and replaced it on the plate. 'I promised Connie, Annie and Tonia that we'd pick them up on the way.'

'We bought beer, sherry and whisky so we can offer callers a drink. The bottles are on the floor at the back of the pantry. Is Harry asleep?' Lloyd came in and sat in one of the easy chairs.

'Yes, and he was so exhausted he shouldn't wake

unless he has one of his nightmares.' Sali returned the book to the shelf. 'I'll just get my coat and hat, and I'll be with you, Victor.'

Mr Evans opened the door of his bedroom as she went into the hall. 'Victor says you're going to mass with him and Joey.'

'If that's all right with you, Mr Evans,' she replied warily, mindful of his reaction to the pullovers earlier.

'It's nothing to do with me where you go in your own time, but as you're intent on visiting a Papist church you'd better have this.' He thrust a finely crocheted silk shawl at her. 'It used to be my wife's. She kept it for best and in case you didn't know, Catholic women cover their heads in church.'

'Mr Evans—'

'You'd better go or you'll be late.'

He went into the kitchen and closed the door before she could thank him, but she felt that she was beginning to understand him. The shawl was an apology, a gesture as big as the man, and she wondered why he found it so difficult to accept gratitude for his kindness.

The service, as Father Kelly had promised, was beautiful. The church was smaller than any chapel she had been in, but the organ would have graced a far larger building. The singing was melodic, the priest's lavishly embroidered robes, the sweet cloying smell of incense and Latin mass exotic after the spartan services of Penuel Chapel. But the thing that impressed her the most was the size of the congregation. The church may have been less than a quarter of the size of the average chapel, but long after every seat was taken, men filed in and stood in the aisles and the back of the church, respectfully removing their caps and making the sign of the cross as they faced the altar. She found it strange that she had never questioned just how many people in Pontypridd and Swansea were Catholic.

Irish lilts mixed with musical Spanish tones and the more familiar pitches of Welsh and English voices as the congregation made their responses. And all around her, people knelt, prayed and sang as if they were actually enjoying the service.

Instead of a sermon, Father Kelly delivered a light, humorous lecture on families and the meaning of Christmas, and when he ended with a couple of lines penned by the poet Thomas Tusser – '"At Christmas play and make good cheer, for Christmas comes but once a year," and remember that's your priest ordering you to do just that' – laughter rippled through the worshippers, something she could never imagine happening in any chapel she had ever visited.

A crib flanking the altar and a beautifully painted plaster model of a blue-robed Virgin Mary holding the child Jesus made it easy for her to pray. But it was a nebulous kind of prayer, directed at a deity far removed from the stern, tyrannical God of her Uncle Morgan's sermons.

She found herself picturing a benign, caring being with a twinkle in his eyes and a sense of humour that matched Father Kelly's, and she prayed that he would take care of her father's soul, bless Mansel wherever he was, and keep her son, all of her family, her aunt, Rhian, Mr Richards, the entire Evans family and herself safe. She didn't allow herself to think from who or what. If God was all-seeing and omnipotent, she didn't need to, and there were people she wanted to block from her thoughts on this holiest of nights. And finally, she asked that he take care of Mrs Evans in heaven and bless her too.

'You will come in for a cup of Christmas cheer?' Connie asked. They were walking down Dunraven Street at a brisk pace to keep out the cold.

'When have you ever known me refuse a cup of cheer, Connie?' Joey replied. They stopped outside her door.

'You, never, but I was asking Victor and Mrs Jones.'

'Not me?'

'I'm not surprised to see you've been practising a pathetic look, given what I've heard about you lately. Come on,' she relented, unlocking the door and leading the way upstairs. She had left the gaslight on low in her drawing room and when she turned it up, Sali saw that the room was furnished in solidly crafted mahogany pieces fashioned in a simple Regency style. The sofa and chairs were upholstered in blue double cloth, woven in a William Morris pattern, and there was a warm inviting scent in the air Sali recognised as mulled wine.

'My grandmother's recipe,' Connie revealed, ladling out glassfuls. She hesitated for a split second when she came to her daughter, then gave her half a glass. 'To all of us.' She gave a brittle smile and raised her glass. 'A happy Christmas and a healthy and prosperous nineteen ten.'

'To us,' they echoed.

When Annie and Antonia brought out plates of ham and chicken sandwiches and apple turnovers, Connie drew Sali aside.

'The boys and Mr Evans tell me you have settled in remarkably well.'

'They are very kind,' Sali answered uneasily, wondering what Connie would think of her, if she knew exactly how 'kind' she had allowed Lloyd to be.

'Knowing my uncle and cousins as well as I do, I think it more likely that you are a born diplomat.' Connie handed Sali a plate.

'They are easy to work for and very appreciative,' Sali replied warily, wondering where the conversation was going.

'You don't find any of them easier to get on with than the others?' Connie fished blatantly.

'Not especially.' Sali was having difficulty keeping her voice steady.

355

'Three young men and a widower, alone in the house with a young widow.' Connie arched her eyebrows.

'Have you forgotten what I told you of my situation?' Sali whispered.

'No, but no one in Tonypandy knows your real situation except me.'

'And Mr Evans and Lloyd,' Sali revealed.

'Oh yes, Lloyd did mention that you'd told Mr Evans and he'd passed the information to the boys.' Connie hoped she'd given Sali the impression that she and Lloyd were *very* close.

'I had to when Mr Evans told me that I could bring Harry into the house.'

'You and your son are both happy there?'

'We consider ourselves fortunate. In return for my services, we have a comfortable home. If you'll excuse me, I am very tired and I have the dinner to cook tomorrow.'

'Annie, Tonia and I will be up straight after mass to help you cook it.' Connie forced another insincere smile.

'You don't have to leave because I am tired,' Sali said to Victor as he picked up his coat and cap.

'It's been a long day for all of us. Joey!' He called his brother, who was engrossed in conversation with Antonia, to heel as if he were one of his dogs. 'See you tomorrow, Connie, Annie, Tonia. Thank you for the sandwiches and the wine.' He kissed their cheeks in turn.

'I'll see you out.' As Connie waved goodbye to them and turned to walk back up the stairs, she found her path blocked by Annie. 'I thought you were a ghost,' she complained.

'Not a ghost. More like a cautionary devil. What are you doing?'

'Nothing.' Connie tried to walk past her, but Annie stood her ground. 'I must see to Tonia.'

'Tonia's getting ready for bed. You can't seriously believe for one minute that you are going to get Lloyd

Evans to come back to you by making that poor girl feel more wretched and guilty than she already does.'

Connie sank down on the bottom stair and Annie sat beside her.

'You told me that you thought you were losing Lloyd before he went to Pontypridd and that was almost ten years ago.'

'I know,' Connie murmured.

'You also told me that Sali Jones was hiding from her husband.'

'She is.'

'Then don't you think that she and Lloyd have enough problems, without you adding to them by trying to hang on to him when your relationship has run its course?'

'What you say always makes sense, Annie.'

'But you don't want to hear it?'

'Not this time.'

'You'll end up making a fool of yourself.'

'I know.' Connie rose to her feet. 'Will you mind?'

'I won't, but you will,' Annie warned and followed her up the stairs.

'So did Father Kelly convert you?' Lloyd asked as he walked into the kitchen on Christmas morning to find Sali and Harry sitting at the table eating porridge.

'You're wearing the pullover—'

'My mother knitted for me. My father told us that you made them up. He gave them to us last night after you went to bed. Thank you for going to all that trouble. We, all of us, appreciate it.'

'It was no trouble. And the service was beautiful, but no, Father Kelly didn't convert me.' She left the table and picked up the bacon and sausages she had placed on plates, ready to be cooked.

'Finish your porridge. I'll have some tea and wait for the others. And you can trust me to pour it myself.' He pushed her hand away as she reached for the teapot but before he poured his tea, he opened the cupboard and removed a brown paper package. 'My father and brothers asked me to buy something,' he looked at Harry, 'to give to Father Christmas for you.'

'Mam says Father Christmas only brings presents for children not grown-ups,' Harry informed him gravely.

'And your Mam is quite right.' Lloyd sat next to Sali and poured his tea. 'But when I was looking for something for your mam, I met a man who knows her and he asked me to give her this from him. It's not really a present,' he said to Sali, 'just something you lost and he thought you'd like to have back.'

Sali untied the string, folded back the paper and stared at her photograph album. 'Mr Goodman had this.' She opened it and ran her fingers over her father's inscription on the flyleaf.

'You did say that he told you a certain person was a good customer.'

'Look, Harry,' she opened the first page, 'that's your grandfather.'

'Can I see him?'

'Only his photograph. He's in heaven.' She turned to Lloyd. 'I'll never be able to thank you enough.'

'I'm just the delivery boy. If you want to thank anyone, it should be Mr Goodman.'

'But I never would have had it back if you hadn't gone there to redeem my ring.' She kissed his cheek.

'You've no need to thank me any more than I have to thank you for my pullover. Now, hurry up and finish your porridge. I hear Joey and Victor stirring and you know what they are like first thing in the morning.'

'Greedy gutses.'

Sali stared at Harry in horror. 'Where did you hear that?'

'It's what Uncle Joey called Uncle Victor yesterday when he ate four cakes in one go in the bazaar.'

Lloyd struggled to keep a straight face. 'There are some things uncles say that shouldn't be repeated to mothers, Harry.'

'And I think some uncles need to learn there are things that shouldn't be said in front of children,' Sali countered, glaring at Joey as he walked into the kitchen.

'A cart! Father Christmas brought me the cart! He knew I wanted it—'

'Yes, darling.' Sali scooped Harry up and sat him on her lap. They were sitting in the parlour opening presents and listening to the strains of 'Hark the Herald Angels Sing' being played by the Salvation Army band stationed on the corner of the street.

'He left another parcel for you, Harry.' Joey handed him the paper, crayons and pencils that Lloyd had bought.

'Let him enjoy the cart before he starts on that and the stocking. Another sherry, Sali? No need to ask if you want more beer, Joey. Refill everyone's glasses before you see to yourself.' Mr Evans sat in the chair next to the fire and knocked the ashes from his pipe against the grate. No one had mentioned the pullovers since Lloyd that morning, but Sali thought it significant that all four men were wearing them. Even Mr Evans had accepted the stocking she had filled for him and the tin of sweets she had made, and she had been overwhelmed by the jewellery casket and watch they had given her and even more touched when a casual remark of Joey's brought the realisation that no one other than Lloyd knew that they had once been hers.

Joey prised open his tin and kissed Sali's cheek. 'You little angel.'

'You are not to eat one of those until after dinner,' his father warned.

'You sound just like Mam,' Joey retorted without thinking.

'Just doing what she'd want me to if she were here,' Billy said evenly. 'That's Connie, Annie and Antonia.' He left his chair as the front door opened.

'I'll get the dinner on the table.'

'Need any help?' Lloyd asked Sali.

'She'll get all the help she needs from us, Lloyd.' Connie walked in, bringing a cold draught of air with her. 'Thank you, Uncle Billy.' She handed him her cape, hat and gloves.

'You brought half the shop with you,' he grumbled playfully, as she set an armful of packages on the sofa where Sali had been sitting.

'Only what I couldn't sell,' she rejoined in the same mocking vein and Sali wondered if she'd ever feel at ease enough with Mr Evans to treat him in such a cavalier fashion. 'Tonia?' she called to her daughter, who came in from the hall with Annie.

Antonia was not as tall as Annie, but even at fifteen was more shapely, and although Sali had never met Connie's estranged husband, the resemblance between mother and daughter was so striking she suspected that Mr George hadn't bequeathed many of his features to his offspring.

'Tonia, arrange the chocolates and candied fruits we've brought on the sideboard and,' Connie frowned at Joey, 'stay away from your second cousin once removed while you do it.'

'Why doesn't anyone trust me?' Joey complained.

'We do.' Annie had already divested herself of her coat and was tying on an apron. 'We just don't trust you around young girls.'

'Victor, Uncle Billy, Lloyd, look after Tonia and keep Joey under control,' Connie ordered, before picking up two bags that Annie had left in the hall. 'Shall we take that bottle of sherry and make a start in the kitchen, Sali?'

Connie complimented Sali on everything; the immaculate state of the kitchen, the table centre she had made from four red candles and a wreath she had woven from ivy, holly and pinecones, the saucepans full of prepared vegetables, the apple sauce, the goose, the chickens . . .

But no matter how hard Sali tried to accept Connie's praise and enjoy the camaraderie of working with her and Annie to produce a good dinner, she couldn't help feeling that something wasn't quite right between her and the woman who had hired her.

'I'll call the men, shall I?' Annie asked, when the meal was ten minutes away from perfection and Connie had set the last bowl of clear gravy soup on the table.

'Please,' Connie and Sali answered together.

'I am sorry, Sali. I keep forgetting that this is now your kitchen,' Connie apologised, in a tone that suggested it was anything but.

'I am only the housekeeper.' Sali knew and felt her lack of status keenly, but she resented the fact that Connie had found half a dozen occasions to remind her that she was merely a servant in the last half hour.

'But a very well thought of housekeeper and employee.' Connie emphasised the last word. 'Gentlemen,' she smiled, as they filed into the kitchen, 'as you see, we've extended the table. Tonia, you sit between Uncle Billy and Victor. Annie, you sit between Uncle Billy and Lloyd. And I'll sit between you and Sali, Lloyd. That way Harry can sit next to his mother.'

'And where am I to sit?' Joey demanded plaintively. 'The coal cwtch or the *ty bach*?'

'Either will do, Joey,' Connie answered. 'But before you go, make sure everyone has a full glass.'

While everyone laughed, Sali intercepted a look between Lloyd and Connie. Lloyd was angry, she was certain of it, and Connie defiant. As Connie sat down she laid her hand on Lloyd's arm and he shook it off. Suddenly Sali knew exactly why Connie was behaving so strangely towards her. Somehow she had discovered that she and Lloyd had become lovers and she was jealous.

'Today went better than I thought it would,' Mr Evans acknowledged when Lloyd left the kitchen to collect coats for Connie, Annie and Antonia from the hall.

'It's been a good eating and drinking day.' Joey cut himself a last slice of cold chicken before Sali cleared it away.

'It won't be if you eat any more,' his father warned. 'You'll burst.'

'Victor will burst before me. You going to the County Club?'

'No. I promised Father Kelly that I'd call in and sample the whisky his brother has sent him from Ireland. Goodnight, Connie, Annie, Antonia.' He kissed each of them and then, to Connie and Sali's amazement, kissed Sali. 'You look about done in, girl, not that it's surprising considering all the extra work you've been doing the past couple of weeks. Don't wait up for us.'

'I won't.'

'We could stay and do the dishes,' Connie offered.

'No, please, it won't take me five minutes.' Sali was polite but firm.

Joey looked to Victor. 'Fancy a quick one down the Pandy?'

'I'm off to Megan's for supper.'

'Any chance of me being made welcome?'

'Not by me.' What Victor hadn't told anyone and Megan hadn't told Sali, was that Megan's uncle and his brothers had made arrangements to visit the Pandy on Christmas evening, and Megan was hoping to get the children to bed early so they could have an hour or two of rare privacy.

'Well, I need a breath of fresh air after all that food.'

'Fresh air, not more beer, Joey?' Lloyd enquired archly, returning with an armful of coats and hats.

'I'll see the girls home,' Joey offered.

'It's all right, I could do with a breath of fresh air too. Real fresh air, so you can escape into the Pandy on the way.' Lloyd helped Annie on with her coat.

'Shall I cut supper sandwiches?' Sali asked.

'If anyone can eat any more after what they've put away today, they have worms.' Mr Evans slipped his pipe into his jacket pocket and went to the door. 'Goodnight everyone, and don't forget what I said about an early night, Sali.'

'Goodnight, Sali, thank you for the dinner.' Connie kissed Sali's cheek.

'Thank you for your help.' Sali found it easier to return Annie and Antonia's hugs than Connie's embrace.

The house fell blissfully silent after everyone left. Relishing the peace, Sali cleared her mind of all coherent thought and washed the dishes, tidied the kitchen and despite Mr Evans's injunction, cut a pile of pork and chicken sandwiches. Wrapping them in scalded clothes, she set them between plates in the pantry.

She swept the hearth, placed an unnecessary guard in front of the fire that had burnt too low to be a risk in the parlour and finally climbed the stairs. Harry was curled on his side around Mr Bear, the horse and cart, tin whistle, paper, crayons and pencils. The bar of chocolate lay on his pillow and Sali moved it on to a chair lest he roll on it during the night.

She washed, changed into her nightdress and slipped between the freezing cold sheets, but sleep eluded her. She preferred to lie back and watch her breath cloud the shadows in the icy room, because every time she closed her eyes, Connie's beautiful face and elegantly dressed figure filled her mind. And now that she knew with a devastating certainty that the warmth of Connie's smile and the love in her eyes were reserved for Lloyd, she felt her heart would break.

Just as she had begun to believe that she could be happy again, the future had been snatched from her. She failed to see how any man presented with a choice between her and her drab clothes and scarred body and the elegantly presented, witty, confident Connie, could fail to chose the latter.

Not that Lloyd even had to make a choice. Mansel had protested that he loved her just as Lloyd had done, but that hadn't prevented him from making love to other women. And for all of Lloyd's assurances that he wanted to live with her for the rest of his life, why should he settle for just her, when Connie was clearly prepared to offer him so much more?

'I'll take a quick look at the Christmas Eve trading figures before I leave, Connie,' Lloyd informed her when they entered her house.

It was the first time Lloyd had told Connie that he was going to look at her books, without first asking her permission and the significance wasn't lost on her. 'Go on into the office. I'll be with you in a minute.' Refusing to meet Annie's disapproving eye, Connie ran up the stairs ahead of her and Antonia and went into her bedroom. Closing the door, she unpinned her hair and brushed it out.

'Mam?' Antonia knocked and walked in.

'It's late, Tonia, you should be in bed.'

'Why don't you want me to be friends with Joey?' Antonia asked plaintively, sitting on the bed. 'Everyone makes jokes about him being a bit of a Don Juan when it comes to girls, but you are serious about not wanting me to see him, aren't you?'

'When you are older you will discover that some men are best avoided,' Connie snapped cryptically, 'and cousin Joseph is one of them.'

'He's funny and good-looking—'

'And an out-and-out womaniser, just like your father. Surely even you have heard that he has a girl in every street in Tonypandy and two in the longer ones. Now, go to bed.'

Her mother rarely shouted at her, but when she did, Antonia knew it was time to retreat. Connie heard her slam her bedroom door, but was too preoccupied by thoughts of Lloyd to consider Antonia's feelings.

She unbuttoned the jacket of the green wool bespoke suit she was wearing and hung it away. The skirt she folded over a chair. She gazed at herself in the mirror for a moment and decided that if she removed her petticoats it would make her intention to seduce Lloyd too obvious. Besides, given his ridiculous insistence that it was over between them, she shouldn't fling herself at him. Men liked uncertainty and the thrill of the chase and if, no, not if, *when* he declared his love for her – again – he would help her out of her underclothes just as he had done on so many occasions in the past.

She slipped on a dark blue silk wrapper trimmed with bands of hand-worked ecru lace, fluffed out her hair, pinched the skin over her cheekbones into a becoming flush and puffed vanilla-scented powder on her nose and above the V of her breasts. When she reached for the blue glass and silver scent bottle on her dressing table she caught sight of Annie watching her in the mirror.

'It's not going to work, Connie.'

Moving slowly and deliberately, Connie unscrewed the top from the bottle, pulled out the rubber stopper and sprinkled French perfume over her neck, breasts and hands. Slipping her feet into a pair of heeled, backless Berlin-worked slippers she swept past Annie and out of the door.

Connie had expected to find Lloyd pacing restlessly around the office as he had done the night he had arrived to tell her that he wouldn't be seeing her privately again. She suppressed a small smile of triumph when she recollected that night. He had been so adamant that there could be nothing more between them and here he was, a couple of days later, alone and waiting for her to join him.

'Sorry I kept you waiting, darling.' She closed the door and reached for the key to lock it.

'There's no need to do that, Connie.'

'Darling, you look cross.'

'Possibly because I am.' There was restrained anger in his calm admission. She chose to ignore it.

'I have a present for you.' She went to the desk, opened

a drawer and extracted a small flat box. She held it out to him, but he didn't attempt to take it. 'Aren't you going to open it?'

'Not until you tell me why you went to such pains to conceal our relationship from my family for thirteen years, only to flirt outrageously with me in front of them two days after I tell you that it's over between us.'

'I didn't—'

'Like you didn't go out of your way to belittle Sali?' His eyes were cold.

'Please, open your present,' she pleaded.

'You first.' He removed a box from his pocket and laid it on to the desk.

'How kind,' Connie prattled nervously, in a vain attempt to pretend that everything was fine between them. She picked up the box and opened the lid. 'How pretty.' She lifted out a gold and blue enamelled lady's fob watch. 'I must thank you properly for it.' She stepped towards him and he stepped back.

'Open it, Connie.'

She pressed the button at the top and the front flew open. The face of the watch was embellished with a butterfly.

'How lovely—'

'Read the inscription, Connie.'

'"A memory of yesterday's pleasures."' The smile faded from her face.

'That is John Donne; the line below is mine.'

Her voice wavered as she read, '"Thank you for allowing me to say goodbye."'

'It appears I was premature in my gratitude. But it *is* goodbye, Connie. Make no mistake about it. I won't be coming back, not again.' He picked up his hat from the desk.

An icy claw of fear closed over her heart, constricting her lungs and making it impossible for her to breathe. She fell back on to the sofa, fighting for air, as the room swung giddily around her.

'Do you want me to call Annie?'

'You can't possibly mean it, Lloyd,' she said finally. 'Not after everything we have been to one another.'

'Goodbye, Connie.' He walked to the door.

'She is married. As married as I am. She can't give you a settled home and family any more than I can. And she's running from her husband. I talked to people in Pontypridd when I went there to buy your present. Sali Watkin Jones is married to a butcher called Bull—'

'You asked questions about Sali in Pontypridd!' He whirled around and faced her. She had seen him angry, but never like this. The savagery of his naked rage petrified her.

'I wanted to find out if she'd told me the truth about herself, and she hadn't, Lloyd,' she babbled. 'Her husband is a respectable man—'

'A respectable man who beat her to a pulp.'

'She was carrying a bastard when she married him. Did she tell you that?' she taunted.

'Who exactly did you talk to?'

'People.'

'What people, Connie?'

She shrugged. 'Just in the shops. I don't know who they were. They said her father had spoiled her. That she'd never had to lift a finger in her life. She was engaged to marry a rich man who ran off and left her for another woman on their wedding day. And Mr Bull had taken pity on her and married her, only for her to present him with a bastard six months later.' Lloyd was watching her intently but when he didn't interrupt, she continued out of sheer nervousness as much as in the hope that she might turn him against Sali.

'They said she was too proud to serve in her husband's shop and after robbing him blind and pushing his idiot brother down the stairs and killing him when he tried to stop her from leaving with the money she had stolen, she ran off with her baby and her husband's sister. Her husband has lost everything, his shop, his business, and it's all her fault. He's been reduced to working for another butcher and renting a room in a pub.'

'Did you tell anyone where Sali was?'

'No one asked.'

'Did you tell them, Connie?' For the first time since she had entered the office, he raised his voice loud enough for Antonia and Annie to hear upstairs.

'No. I don't think so.'

'No? Or you don't think so? Which is it?'

'I don't think so. I had no reason to. I only wanted to find out what people thought of her, Lloyd,' she wheedled, making one last attempt to win him over. 'Let's face it, what do we know about Sali Jones? Only what she told us. I know you admired her father, but you said yourself, you didn't move in the same circles as her. Why can't you see that she's no good?'

'Read that last line on the watch again, Connie, and try to live up to it. And a word of warning, if you ever talk to anyone about Sali again, here or in Pontypridd or for that matter anywhere, or try to hurt her in any way, I'll make you sorry that you ever mentioned her name.'

'Lloyd—'

'I'm doing what I should have done years ago, Connie.' He opened the door.

'You can't marry Sali until she gets a divorce. And I could divorce Albert. All you have to do is ask me.'

'A boy begged you to do that years ago. You said then that it wouldn't work, and you were right. If there was ever anything between us, it's long since burnt out.'

'We love one another, Lloyd,' she cried desperately.

'No, we don't, Connie. We never did. We lusted but we never loved. Do you think love would have degenerated into this?'

'I won't let you go.' She left the couch and threw herself between him and the door.

'If you really loved me you would do just that. In a few short days Sali has taught me that much. Love is about sacrifice and wanting the best for your lover. Please, leave us both with a little dignity, and don't,' he gave her a fixed look, 'ever demean Sali, or try to come between me and her again.' He saw himself out of the house.

Emotionally exhausted, Lloyd walked, oblivious to the families making their way home after visiting relatives, the drunks staggering between pubs, the gangs of boys gathered around the gas lamps playing cards and marbles and their lookouts keeping a watchful eye for policemen who prosecuted anyone caught gambling in the street.

He passed shop windows, stepping in and out of pools of light shed by the gas lamps, without even realising they were there. Connie's face, contorted, ugly in jealousy, filled his mind.

He stood in the square and gazed through the windows of the Pandy watching the men drinking at the bar. Joey was standing with Megan's uncle and brothers at the end nearest the till, pint in hand, chatting to the barmaid.

He remained there motionless for what might have been five minutes or an hour. Only when he was completely calm and in control did he turn towards home – and Sali.

CHAPTER TWENTY-ONE

Lloyd lifted the latch on Sali's bedroom door and peered into the darkness. 'Are you asleep?'

'Yes.'

'You talk in your sleep?' Lloyd stole into the room, closed the door behind him, felt his way to her bed and sat on it.

Sali sat up, panic stricken. 'You can't stay here. Your father and brothers will be in any minute.'

'There's no work tomorrow, so my father won't leave Father Kelly until the whisky bottle is dry and that won't be for hours yet. The Pandy is open until midnight, and as there's no chance that the barmaid Joey is chasing will be free until then, he won't be home until one or two in the morning. And Megan's uncle and his brothers are with Joey, so Victor won't return until they come home and disturb him and Megan.' He struck a match and lit the candle he had carried in from his own room. She was leaning against the brass headboard. Her eyes, dark and enigmatic, reflected the flickering flame, betraying none of her thoughts. 'I've spoken to Connie.' He set the candlestick on the dressing table.

'Why tell me that you've spoken to Connie?'

'Because I thought you'd like to know.'

'Why didn't you say you were lovers?'

'Because you never asked.'

He didn't question how she'd guessed that he and Connie were having an affair and she realised just how close they had become in a few days. Already, there was no need for superfluous words between them. 'I told you about Mansel and Owen. I even told you about my uncle and I've never let anyone know what he did to me. I was too ashamed—'

'The shame is all his, Sali. It wasn't your fault,' he interrupted, reaching for her hand.

'But you didn't tell me about *your* past.'

She looked very beautiful and dishevelled. Her dark hair, which was only just long enough to pin up, fell in a heavy mass of curls to her shoulders. Her silk and lace nightdress was rumpled, the top button at her throat had popped open and he had to fight an impulse to unbutton the row of pearls beneath it.

'Surely you didn't assume that because I hadn't mentioned my past, I hadn't had one? Sali, I am twenty-nine years old next birthday.'

'But it wasn't the past, was it?' she broke in. 'You visit Connie several times a week.'

'Not any more. That night, the first time we made love when I told you we'd have to talk, didn't it occur to you that there was someone I had to say goodbye to before I could make plans for a future with you?' Her hand was frozen and he enclosed it in both of his.

'You haven't visited Connie since?'

'I went to her house tonight because I was angry with her for the way she behaved towards you today. I've told her twice now that it is over between us. I promise you, sweetheart, I won't be going back there and I won't ever see Connie alone again.'

'I don't have the right to ask, but did you love her?' She trembled from more than just the cold.

'I thought I did when I was fifteen.'

'Fifteen!'

He held his finger to his lips. 'Ssh, we don't want to wake Harry.'

'You've been with her since you were fifteen?' she repeated incredulously.

'I started working for your father when I was twenty and I didn't come back until two years ago, so it's been more off than on and to be truthful I think the only reason it lasted as long as it did was force of habit. Both of us found it convenient.'

'I don't understand,' she murmured. 'How can you go to bed with someone because it's convenient?'

'It saved both of us the bother of looking around for someone else. Connie had been living apart from her husband for years when it started between us and, for a few years afterwards I was more concerned with building a career as an engineer than finding a wife. And, just so you understand, it was having sex, not making love. But it took you to make me realise that.' He moved up the bed, pushed a pillow behind his back and pulled her head down on to his chest. 'We've been together twice and both times, and for the only times in my life, I've felt that making love is exactly what happened. But,' he hugged her closer, 'it is also perfectly possible for a man, and I believe a woman, to enjoy the experience in the purely physical sense. You've made me realise that it is like eating a jam tart without the jam, but you have to forgive me, sweetheart, because until us, I had no idea what it could be like with the jam. You said yourself that you didn't know lovemaking could be the way it is between us?'

'I meant it, Lloyd.'

'I know you did.' Kissing her would have been the simplest way to end their discussion. But he also knew that it would take more than a few embraces to heal the wounds that had been inflicted on her by Owen and more especially Mansel. She had a right to be suspicious of men and there were things that needed to be said if they were going to build a marriage, in all but name. His mother had once told him that the only relationship worth having was one based on absolute trust and he sensed that he had yet to win Sali's.

Sali lay against him in the freezing silence, listening to his heartbeat and trying to think past his ridiculous

372

analogy of jam tarts. 'There have been others besides Connie?' she asked finally.

'Yes,' he admitted frankly. 'Why do you think I'm so hard on Joey? I know from my own experience that he's on a merry-go-round to nowhere. I wasn't anywhere near the womaniser he is at his age, but then at his age I had Connie. Later, when I worked for your father, it was different. Before then I used to look at rich people in the same way a penniless boy stands with his nose pressed against a sweet shop window. As a qualified bachelor engineer I found myself invited into houses where my father and brothers would have been kept waiting at the kitchen door. And I wasn't only invited for the sake of the eligible daughters. Some middle-aged, middle-class women have strange ideas about working-class men.'

'So, you've had many lovers?'

'Women,' he corrected.

'How many?' She questioned, dreading his answer.

'Where have you put the block of paper I bought Harry?'

'In his room. Why?'

'Because I'll need at least that much if you want me to make a comprehensive list.'

Suddenly, she realised how ridiculous she was being in questioning his past, especially as he had accepted hers. 'It doesn't matter, does it?'

'No.' He kissed her lips. 'Nothing that happened before we met matters. What's important is what we make of our love and our lives from now on.' He left the bed, unbuttoned his jacket, peeled his pullover over his head, threw off the rest of his clothes and climbed in beside her.

She knew he was right.

'I love you, Lloyd,' Sali murmured sleepily when he woke her hours later by slipping from her bed.

'And I love you. I'll do everything I can to be with you

always. And I'll never, never hurt you, Sali. I promise you that much.'

'I hate block days.' Joey tossed the logs he was carrying on top of the ones his brothers had dumped next to the basement door. Every Tuesday and Thursday, colliery workers were entitled to take home two logs. Painted with numbers to prove they hadn't been stolen and set aside by the workers themselves, they were invariably heavy, but it wasn't their weight that Joey was carping about.

'You've only hated them since Victor started to teach you how to chop kindling.' Lloyd leaned over the bath and dunked his head under water. When he'd thoroughly soaked his face and hair, he lathered a bar of soap and spread it over his hair, neck and face.

'I don't like the way Victor gives lessons,' Joey griped.

'Stop moaning. Bring a block over here and hold it.' Victor pulled out the slice of tree trunk he used as a chopping block.

Joey lifted one of the logs on to the block, gripped the sides and closed his eyes.

'Why close your eyes?' Lloyd rinsed his hair, leaned over the tin bath again and scrubbed the coal dust from his arms and chest.

'One day, Victor is going to miss and chop my hands off, and I hate the sight of blood.'

'I wouldn't risk soaking a log in blood; it wouldn't burn.' Victor brought his axe down sharply and sliced the log neatly in two.

Joey dumped the two halves next to the block ready to be split into kindling and carried over another log.

'I didn't know you hated the sight of blood.' Lloyd rinsed the top half of his body.

'I do, especially my own.'

'You're risking seeing an awful lot of it, considering where you've been courting lately.' Victor split the second log.

'Where?' Lloyd demanded.

'Nowhere,' Joey broke in irritably, forgetting to close his eyes as Victor brought his axe down a third time.

'That's not what a little bird told me,' Victor muttered knowingly.

'Then you can bloody well tell the bird to stop chirping,' Joey snapped. 'It comes to something when a man can't take a walk around his own valley from time to time.'

'Strange how your walks always lead you up to Llan House.' Victor leaned on his axe and waited for Joey to carry over another log.

'If you walk in that direction, the housekeeper will give you a bloody nose. She likes to keep her housemaids close and pure,' Lloyd warned.

'How would you know?' Joey challenged.

'Like Victor, I listen to birds.' Lloyd unbuckled his dust-encrusted trousers, unbuttoned his flies and stepped out of them. He hung them on the nail that held the rest of his coal-blackened working clothes. Stripping off his underpants, he stepped into the bath and lowered himself into the water as much as anyone his size could lower themselves into a four-foot tin bath. 'When you've finished with that, wash my back, Joey?'

After Victor had split the last block, Joey held out his hand. 'Flannel and soap, and move over so I can soak the flannel.'

'Do you think Dad and the others will get anywhere with management?' Victor laid one of the split blocks, cut side down on the chopping block. Swinging his axe in quick, practised movements, he sliced it into two-inch wide sticks.

'I doubt it.' Lloyd answered pessimistically. 'But it's worth a try if it saves us two and half per cent of our wages.'

'Back done.' Joey returned the soap and flannel to Lloyd.

'Take these sticks out to the woodshed, Joey.' Victor

pointed to the pile he'd cut. 'I'll carry the rest up and put them in the wood bucket.'

'What did your last slave die of?' Joey complained.

'The pain I inflicted on him when he wouldn't do what I wanted.'

'When I come back in my next life, I'm going to be the oldest.' Despite his grumbling, Joey piled the sticks in his arms and opened the door.

'Shut it. Now!' Lloyd commanded as needles of rain gusted in on an Arctic breeze, hailing on to his back.

'Joey, go out,' Joey chanted, 'Joey, shut it. I wish you two would make up your bloody minds about what you want me to do.'

'That's your second "bloody" since you came home,' Victor reprimanded.

'There's only us here,' Joey protested.

'The more you swear, the more you're likely to forget yourself in mixed company.' Victor set about the last log.

Lloyd stood up in the bath, wrapped himself in a towel and retreated behind the door. 'You can go now.'

'Kind of you to give me permission to freeze and soak myself, big brother.' Setting his head down against the weather, Joey ran out.

Lloyd tiptoed across the chilly flagstones to the 'clean' side of the basement where they hung their evening clothes. Standing on a rag rug he towelled himself dry, and lifted his underclothes from his peg.

Victor sniffed the air before chopping the last sticks. 'I smell one of Sali's meat and potato pies.'

'I don't know how you do it.' Lloyd pulled on his clean vest and drawers, and heaved his shirt over his head.

'It's just a matter of putting the scents together.'

'Bloody Welsh summers, it couldn't be colder at the North Pole than it is out there.' Joey ran in, rubbing his arms, and slammed the door.

'See what I mean. You're swearing and you don't even realise you're doing it,' Victor lectured.

'Did you close the woodshed?' Lloyd pushed a stud through his collar and fastened it to the neck of his shirt.

'No, I left it open so the rain could give the wood a good soaking.'

'Did you?' Lloyd repeated sternly.

'I shut it and put the latch down,' Joey bit back.

'If you didn't, the rain will drive in—'

'I said I did it.' Joey undressed and hung his pit clothes on the nail next to Lloyd's.

'You're in a hurry,' Victor remarked as Lloyd stepped into his suit trousers, buttoned his flies and buckled the belt.

'It's too bloody cold to hang about down here with Joey opening the door every five minutes.' He pushed his stockinged feet into his clean boots and bent down to lace them.

'Language.'

'Unlike you, Joey, I remember to be polite in company.' Lloyd ran up the stone steps to the kitchen.

Forewarned by Mr Evans that he would be late home from work, Sali had held back the dinner and was checking the pie in the oven when Lloyd walked into the kitchen. He looked around.

'Where's Harry?'

'Next door with Sam. It's his birthday and Megan told him that he could invite four friends to tea. I thought Harry would burst with pride at being one of the chosen.' She closed the oven door.

He grabbed her by the waist, pulled her close and kissed her, a long, loving kiss that left her wanting a whole lot more. Closing his hand over her breast, he carried her down with him as he sank on to his father's chair.

'Your brothers,' she mouthed in alarm.

'Weren't even in their baths when I left the basement.' He slipped his hand beneath her skirt and on to her naked thigh above her stocking top. 'Come upstairs?' His smile broadened, but she knew he wasn't joking.

'You're insane.'

He looked to the stove. 'Nothing needs doing here for five minutes, does it?'

'No, but you know it's never five minutes and how would we explain—'

'I went upstairs to get a book and you were making the beds.'

'They know I make the beds first thing in the morning.' Despite her protest he had already lifted her out of the chair.

He offered her his hand and she took it. Lloyd had taught her many things since the night they had first made love, principally that she couldn't deny him anything he asked of her and she didn't possess the willpower to fight her own need for him, physically or emotionally.

Less than a minute after entering Lloyd's bedroom and locking the door they were making hasty but nonetheless satisfying love. They had both become adept at making the most of their snatched moments, and not even the presence of his brothers in the house could diminish their hunger for one another.

If anything, their lovemaking had become more urgent and more passionate as time passed. It was as though every encounter fuelled the obsession they had for one another. And they had begun to run risks that both of them would have considered insane only a few months before.

Sali only had to think of Lloyd during the day to crave his presence with a longing that drove every other consideration from her mind. No matter how hard she tried to concentrate on housework, she increasingly found herself daydreaming about him, sometimes for minutes, sometimes for an hour or more. She only had to walk into his bedroom or touch his clothes, to start imagining what they would do to one another the next time they were alone. She had begun to wonder if she were going mad, until he confessed that he was finding it just as difficult to keep his mind on his work in the pit.

'I love you.' He kissed her, before gripping the French letter he had used and withdrawing from her.

'Not as much as I love you,' she whispered.

'You might find yourself with an argument there, sweetheart.' He went to the washstand.

'That's the basement door opening in the kitchen.' She leapt from the bed and picked up her drawers.

'You go down first. I'll say I was looking for a book.'

She ran into her bedroom, hurriedly washed, slipped on her underclothes, changed her apron for an overall and carried her apron down the stairs.

Joey and Victor were sitting at the table, glasses of milk in front of them.

'My apron was dirty,' she lied, pushing the blameless garment deep into the basket she kept for the household linen, and 'upstairs' washing.

'Is it pie?'

'Is what pie?' Sali stared blankly at Victor.

'Are we having one of your fantastic meat and potato pies tonight, Sali?' Joey elaborated.

'Are you feeling all right?' Victor questioned, perturbed by her vacant expression. 'You look flushed. You're not coming down with something, are you?'

'It's the shock of tipping hot water over my apron.' As colour flooded into her cheeks, she turned to the stove and lifted the lid on the vegetable pan.

'So are we?' Joey refilled his and Victor's glasses from the pitcher he'd carried out of the pantry.

'Are we what?'

'Having pie,' Joey repeated impatiently.

'Yes . . . yes,' she stammered.

'Beef pie, cabbage, mashed potatoes, gravy,' Victor sniffed the air theatrically, 'apple fritters and custard.'

'Apple turnovers and custard,' she corrected absently.

'Almost right.' Victor grinned at Joey.

'Where's Lloyd?' Joey looked around the room as if he expected him to pop up from behind the furniture.

'I think he went out,' she said quickly.

'He's been a bit odd lately,' Joey mused. 'That's the back door. One of us had better go down and wash Dad's back.'

'I'll go.' Victor left his chair. 'I want to bring the dogs into the basement after he's finished bathing. There's a leak in the kennel roof that I've been meaning to fix, and it's soaking inside. They'll catch their death if I leave them out there in this downpour.' He glanced across to where Sali was stirring the gravy. 'You don't mind do you, Sali? I'll put down newspaper and clear up any mess they make before I put them back in the run in the morning.'

'Pardon?' She stared uncomprehendingly at him.

'Can I bring the dogs into the basement for the night?'

'Yes.'

'Victor's thinking of skinning and jointing them so we can have them for dinner tomorrow,' Joey said, after Victor closed the door.

'He what?'

'Sali, what on earth has got into you?' Joey complained when Lloyd walked in with a pile of books.

'Sorry, I'm a bit preoccupied. Megan came around earlier and suggested that I should send Harry to school after the summer holidays.'

'That's a great idea. It will be good for Harry and it will give you more free time to run classes in the library.' Lloyd set the books down on the window sill.

'What?'

'Everyone says you're the best teacher we have.'

'That's rubbish and you know it.'

'I don't know anything of the kind. The union has been talking about setting up morning and afternoon classes for the afternoon and night shift workers and their wives for some time. You should be teaching more than basic literacy. Geography, literature, history, music . . . What's the matter?' he asked, when she didn't appear to be overly enthusiastic. 'Don't you think people who are desperate to learn but never had the chance to follow a formal education should have an opportunity to better themselves?'

'Of course, but—'

'You obviously love teaching.'

'I keep telling you I'm not qualified.'

'Your pupils don't care. If you go to the library when Harry's in school you can start a morning literacy class for miners on night shift and any of their wives who can spare the time, and from there you can—'

'You are quite mad.' He was so carried away she had to shout to make herself heard. 'One, I am not qualified and two, Harry is not going to school after the summer holidays. He's not even three and a half.'

'He will be by September and it will do him the world of good to get away from your apron strings and play with boys of his own age.'

'You make it sound as if I mollycoddle him.'

'You do.' Lloyd joined Joey at the table.

'I most certainly do not.' Her voice rose precariously. 'He's out now—'

'At a tea party in Megan's.'

'He's with other children, isn't he?'

'Why won't you admit that you keep him too close? He needs to learn to be independent. And if you don't mind me saying so, you wouldn't come to any harm if you made a few more friends.'

'Now I'm friendless!'

'I never said that.' He beamed at her. He had actually provoked her into a real argument. He loved her with all his heart, mind and soul, but his love hadn't blinded him to the fact that she had been so badly scarred by Owen Bull that she had lost confidence in her own opinions as well as her ability to express them. And now she was actually screaming at him. The girl who had been terrified by their family spats was actually quarrelling with him, and it felt wonderful.

'And I suppose you think that Harry should pack his bags and leave home next week,' she retorted, irritated by his smug smile.

'Now you are being ridiculous as well as hysterical.'

His calm only succeeded in infuriating her all the more. 'I am not hysterical or ridiculous,' she yelled. 'Harry is my son and I will decide what's best for him.'

Mr Evans opened the door and walked in with Victor. He looked from Sali to Lloyd. 'What on earth is all the shouting about?'

'Lloyd and Sali were arguing about whether Harry should go to school after the summer holidays so Sali can teach classes in the library during the day as well as the evening,' Joey revealed.

Mr Evans took his place at the table. 'The meeting didn't take as long as I expected, Sali, but there's no rush with the meal. Take all the time you want.'

'It's ready, Mr Evans.' Glad of something to do, she opened the oven door, lifted out the pie and set it on the table. Keeping her eyes averted from the men, she strained the vegetables, mashed the potatoes, poured the gravy into a jug and took her seat beside Lloyd.

'How did the meeting go?' Joey asked, in an effort to fill the silence.

'Much as I expected. We are going back to management with our original offer of a five per cent cut.'

'Which they've twice rejected,' Victor reminded, taking Sali's plate from his father and handing it down to her.

'They say three tries for a Welshman.' His father handed him Joey's plate.

'Why?' Joey asked.

'Because the first two bridges William Edwards built over the Taff at Pontypridd washed away.'

'The third one's standing?' Joey enquired.

'It was the last time I was there. This pie looks even better than usual, Sali.'

'Thank you, Mr Evans.' She was having difficulty in believing what she had just done, not just quarrelling with Lloyd, but shouting and arguing with him in front of his father and brothers. She poked the food around her plate, wishing everyone would hurry up and finish the meal so she could use the excuse of fetching Harry from next door to get out of the house.

'You going out tonight?' Mr Evans asked Victor, noting that he was wearing the navy pinstriped three-piece suit complete with watch and chain that he normally reserved for church.

'I'm taking Megan to the half past six performance at the New Empire Theatre. Harry Freeman and Jennie Dauntley are there this week.'

'You two are only interested in the comedian and the singer?' Joey asked scornfully.

'Who else should we be interested in?' Victor enquired.

'The chorus girls. There's supposed to be a couple of real crackers among them. I'll walk down with you if you like.' Joey made a face at the disapproving expression on Victor's face. 'It's all right, I prefer to sit in the fourpenny pit to the sixpenny circle with the courting couples.'

'Do you mind if I leave the dishes until after I've fetched Harry from next door, Mr Evans?' Sali asked, after Joey split the last of the turnovers between himself and Victor.

'You run this house in your own time, as you see fit, Sali,' he said easily, leaving the table and sitting in his chair next to the fire.

'We could have a quick one in the White Hart before the show,' Joey suggested to Victor. 'Megan is going to take at least an hour to clear up after the party and get the children ready for bed,' he added persuasively.

'You buying?' Victor asked.

'The first round.' Joey handed Sali his bowl and left the table.

'I thought you said a quick *one*, Joey,' his father said.

'So I did.' Joey flashed one of his charming smiles. 'See you all later.'

Lloyd carried his teacup from the table to the sink after Victor, Joey and Sali left. He looked at the pile of dishes, filled a bucket with cold water and set it on the stove to boil.

'Why don't you sit down and give yourself time to digest your meal?' his father said quietly.

'I intend to until the water boils.'

'Sit in your mother's chair,' Billy said, as Lloyd pulled a chair out from under the table.

'Are you sure?'

'She would have hated the thought of us venerating her things as if they were museum pieces.'

'Yes, she would have,' Lloyd agreed shortly.

His father folded the week-old copy of the *Rhondda Leader* that he'd been reading and looked across at him. 'How long do you and Sali think you can keep this up?'

'What?' Lloyd didn't even know why he was asking the question. It was obvious from the way his father was eyeing him that he knew.

'That argument earlier. You were at it hammer and tongs like an old married couple. And the one thing she is right about, is that Harry is her son, not yours. Or would you like to make him yours?'

'I'm fond of the boy.'

'We all are. But much as you're fond of the boy, I'd say you're even fonder of the mother.' Billy pulled his tobacco pouch from his pocket and began to leisurely pack his pipe. 'And in case you didn't know, the floorboards creak between your room and hers.'

'I'd marry her if I could.' Lloyd realised further denial was pointless.

'Would she marry you?'

'If she were free.' Lloyd removed a packet of cigarettes from his jacket, shook one out and placed it in his mouth. 'I suggested she change her name by deed poll, we disappear up to Cardiff in our best clothes, return and announce that we were married there.'

'She wouldn't go along with it?'

Lloyd struck a match, lit his cigarette and shook his head. 'As you and I are the only people in Tonypandy who know that her husband isn't dead, I thought it was a good idea.'

'We're not the only people in Tonypandy who know she isn't a widow. Connie does, and from what I saw at Christmas, she doesn't appear to be all that enamoured with you, or Sali.'

'You knew about me and Connie?'

'Come on, Lloyd. How green did you think your mother and I were? All those evenings you spent down there doing her accounts. Connie has one shop. Granted it's a good one with a brisk trade, but it's hardly a Cardiff department store. Your mother was worried for you. I told her that considering the age difference between you and Connie it was bound to run its course some day. Mind you, I didn't think it would take quite so long.'

'Does anyone else know? Victor—'

'Victor is so wrapped up in Megan, his dogs, horses, garden and rabbiting he doesn't see anything unless it's directly under his nose and sometimes not even then. As for Joey, he's too busy chasing his own women to concern himself with yours. In my opinion they haven't a clue about what went on between you and Connie, but have another argument like the one you just had with Sali, and they'll soon find out about you and her.'

'I hate the way things are between Sali and me,' Lloyd confided. 'I want to be with her day and night.'

'I thought you were.' His father had the grace to smile.

'I mean openly.'

'Then find a way to make that possible.'

'Sali was brought up in the chapel. Even after everything her preacher uncle and husband did to her, she still refuses to live in what she calls sin.'

'That's the chapel for you, founded on guilt and preaching denial, self-abuse and martyrdom as a way of life. There has to be a way out of your problem, boy. My advice to you is find it.'

'Easier said than done,' Lloyd reflected gloomily, then he smiled. 'You approve then?'

'It took me a while to warm to her, but once she stopped shaking every time she was spoken to and the boy moved into the house, she blossomed. If you can get her to acknowledge you publicly as her husband, you'll have done well. Almost as well as I did with your mother.' He puffed his pipe, looked into the bowl and tapped it against the side of the fireplace to empty it. 'Ask her to come to the farm with us on miner's fortnight next month. Two weeks is a long time, there's no saying what might happen. You know how magical the Gower can be.'

'Let me speak to Sali first, she may have other plans.'

'I doubt it. I'm off to the County Club. I'll be—'

'In the library if you're wanted,' Lloyd said for him. 'You always say that. Who or what, is likely to want you?'

Billy tapped his nose mysteriously. 'You have no idea.'

'I don't think you do either.'

'Good luck with persuading her, boy, and if you think me putting my oar in will help, you only have to ask.'

CHAPTER TWENTY-TWO

Lloyd was drying the last few dishes when Sali returned with a flushed, excited Harry.

'Nice hat.' Lloyd tweaked the point of Harry's newspaper Admiral's hat.

'Auntie Megan made it for me. I was at Sam's party. We had jelly, custard and sandwiches and—'

'Far too much cake than is good for one small boy,' Sali chided. 'It's time for bed. Downstairs to wash and use the *ty bach*, Harry.' She opened the door.

'I can go on my own.'

'Are you sure?'

'Sam and the others go to the *ty bach* on their own.'

Sali was just about to tell him that Sam was two years older than him when she saw Lloyd watching her. 'Slow and careful on the steps and don't forget to close all the doors behind you.'

'I won't.'

'You didn't have to do the dishes,' she reproached Lloyd.

'I know I didn't *have* to, but I didn't have anything better to do.'

'I'm sorry about earlier,' she apologised. 'I should never have shouted at you the way I did, especially in front of your father and brothers.' She picked up a pile of dinner plates and carried them to the dresser.

'You may be sorrier than you think.' He handed her the dessert bowls.

'Why?'

'Because my father knows about us.' He took the bowls from her just as she was about to drop them.

'I won't live in sin with you, Lloyd.' It was nine o'clock in the evening. Harry had long since gone to bed and Sali was curled on Lloyd's lap in the kitchen. They had drawn the curtains, turned down the lamp and for once, spent more of the evening talking than making love, but they were no nearer a resolution.

'If you regard us loving one another or making love every chance we get as sinful then we're living in sin now,' he argued persuasively. 'All living openly would do is make our lives easier because we wouldn't have to go pussy-footing around in the middle of the night and my father wouldn't have to listen to floorboards creaking overhead as we tiptoe between bedrooms.'

'He's heard us!'

'There's no need to look embarrassed. He was young once and not too old to remember it. Besides he's a Marxist and we believe in free love.'

'How free?' she enquired suspiciously.

'The freedom to love the person we want.' He hugged her. 'Please, sweetheart, live with me as my wife?'

'I'll think about it.'

'You said that months ago.'

'I know,' she concurred miserably.

'What are you doing for miner's fortnight? Annual holiday, last week of July and first week of August, the only two weeks of the year they allow miners to stay above ground.'

'What are you doing?' It had never occurred to her that the Evanses might leave their house.

'Megan's uncle takes care of Victor's menagerie and we rent a cottage on the Gower from my father's sister. You'll love the place, Sali. It's a short walk from the sea, and next door to a shop and a pub.'

'With a pretty barmaid for Joey?'

'I never noticed the barmaids,' he lied. 'We can go swimming every day.'

'In this?' She fell silent and he heard the rain hammering against the window.

'This is June. It wouldn't dare rain during miner's fortnight. Come with us?'

'I couldn't.'

'You're our housekeeper. We'll need someone to cook for us. Last year when my mother was ill, my aunt hired a girl from the village. Frankly, my stomach wouldn't stand another two weeks of her burnt offerings.'

'If I go, I'll insist on Harry and I paying our own way.'

'I've just asked you to carry on working.'

'I have to pay for our train fare and food and any other expenses.'

'Argue that one out with my father. You'll come?'

'I'll come.'

'Look, Harry.' Sali lifted her son from the back of the wagon that had picked them up at Swansea station and held him in her arms. 'That blue is the sea.'

'We'll teach you to swim.' Victor turned round from the box where he was sitting next to the driver.

'And I can wear the costume Mam bought me?'

'You can.' Sali eyed the women watching them from the doorways of their cottages and hoped they wouldn't think the knee-length swimming costume she had bought for herself too daring. She couldn't imagine any of them stripping off to swim in the sea.

The driver slowed the wagon to walking pace and Joey jumped from the back. He ran to a long, low, pink-washed cottage, opened the garden gate and walked up a short path bordered by clumps of cornflowers and poppies. The door was open. A plump, middle-aged woman appeared in the doorway.

'Auntie Jane, as beautiful as ever.' Joey planted a kiss on her cheek before waltzing her down the path.

'I see you haven't changed, you monster.' She returned

Joey's kiss before pushing him away. 'Hello, Billy, boys. Did you have a good journey down?'

'It was long, as usual, Jane.' Mr Evans climbed down from the wagon and kissed her cheek. 'You look well.'

'I have a few more grey hairs, but I can't complain.'

'The cottage looks good.'

'We've done some work on it. Our Sam is getting married next spring so John and I will be moving out of the big house into here.'

'We won't be able to rent from you next year?' Victor was crestfallen.

'Not from me but John's sister has a little house free. Her mother-in-law died last month, God rest her soul.'

'Most of the farms around here have a small and a big house,' Lloyd explained as he helped Sali and Harry down from the wagon. 'When the eldest son is ready to take over the farm he marries, brings his bride to the big house and the parents move into the little house so they can semi-retire.'

'Mrs Sali Jones, her son Harry, Jane Howells, my sister.' Mr Evans introduced them. 'Sali is our house-keeper.'

'You must have the hide of a rhinoceros and the diplomacy of Solomon to put up with Billy and his boys.' Jane shook Sali's hand. 'I'll show you the cottage while the boys unload the wagon.' She led the way inside. 'This is the kitchen. I've stocked the larder and the boy will be down with the cart in the morning. He'll have fresh milk, eggs, butter, cheese, fruit and vegetables. He sells round the village for us. The baker makes a fair loaf and I've stocked you up with dried goods. I bought you fish for tonight. Billy likes a bit of fish on his first night and it was brought in fresh this morning. But let Victor cook it.'

'Victor?' Sali asked in surprise.

'The boys like to build bonfires on the beach. They roast potatoes in the embers and cook the fish on sticks. Sometimes I think they have never grown up. I've stoked the stove, there's plenty of wood in the shed and the boys know where that is. The parlour's through here.' She walked into a tiny hall and opened the door on a small dark room. 'Not that I've ever known Billy or the boys use it.'

Sali could imagine why, but remained tactfully silent.

Jane walked up the stairs and showed Sali a double bedroom and a small single. 'There are half a dozen beds in the attic. The girl made them all up this morning. She thought we were having one of our fishing parties in, although I did remind her twice last week that Billy and the boys were coming. When Billy wrote and told me he was bringing his housekeeper, I thought you could sleep here. She opened a door in the back wall that Sali had assumed was a cupboard. ' "Servants' quarters". Would you believe it in a house this size? But then, it is two hundred years old.' She pointed to a narrow staircase that ran down the back of the house. 'You might be all right walking down those; someone my size would get stuck. They lead to a scullery behind the kitchen. There's a pump and sink in there. Here you are.' She opened a door on the second landing and showed Sali a small room furnished utility style with a camping washstand and double bed. 'I thought your boy could sleep with you.'

'Thank you, it's perfect.' Sali looked out of the window. Joey was running round the garden with Harry on his shoulders, both of them whooping like Indians.

'I've written to Billy every week since Isabella died, not that I've had many replies. Our Billy was born stubborn and independent, but I was worried about him. Isabella was his life. Then, when I heard from Victor that he was sacking housekeeper after housekeeper, I never thought he'd ever allow another woman in the house and he and the boys were doomed to a life of squalor. I'm grateful to you for sorting him out.'

'I needed a job more than Mr Evans and the boys needed a housekeeper.' Sali unpinned her hat and set it on the bed. 'They have been very kind to me and Harry.'

'No doubt we'll see you up at the farm. Billy knows you're all welcome any teatime. There are horses you can ride and a Shetland my youngest outgrew for your boy. Do you ride, Sali?'

Sali recalled Lancelot, the blue riding habit she'd had made the year before her father died and the rides she had taken with Mansel in the fields around Ynysangharad House. They now seemed part of someone else's life. 'I used to, Mrs Howells.'

'Tell Lloyd or Victor to bring you up. If you'll excuse me, I have a dairy to run that I won't be sorry to hand over to Sam's wife next year. Have a good holiday.'

Sali breathed in the salt sea air and smiled. 'I will, Mrs Howells, and thank you for everything.'

'I'm in Joey and Victor's gang and I'm sleeping in the attic with them.' Harry ran headlong down the attic stairs and barged into Sali as she walked out of the 'servants' quarters' on to the upstairs landing.

'You most certainly are not. You'll pester the life out of them.'

'No he won't,' Victor interposed quietly.

'I can't put him to bed up there all alone at seven o'clock.'

'You won't.' Joey perched Harry on the banisters and held him as he slid down. 'We all keep the same hours here. When we were kids, Mam and Dad let us stay up until they went to bed.'

'Please can I sleep up there with Victor and Joey, Mam?' Harry pleaded. 'There's a lookout post so we can watch for pirates. And if they come we'll fight them off.'

Suspecting that Mr Evans wasn't the only one who knew about her and Lloyd, Sali conceded. 'I suppose so, if you promise to be a good boy and don't annoy Joey and Victor.'

'Yippee!'

'And where did you hear that?'

'Uncle Joey read it to me from a comic.'

It was broad daylight when something hurtling on the bed woke Sali the first morning of the holidays. She opened her eyes to see Harry crouched beside her, covered in sand, dressed in his neck-to-knee damp swimming costume, an ear-to-ear grin on his face as he held a crab by the claw above her head.

'Look what I caught in my net. Uncle Joey, Uncle Victor and me have been up for hours. Uncle Joey says you two are lazy bones.'

There was movement in the bed the other side of her and Sali felt the weight of an arm around her waist. She turned, staring in horror at Lloyd lying beside her.

'Look at my crab, Uncle Lloyd.' Harry shoved it under Lloyd's nose. 'Uncle Victor says I can keep it in a bucket. Do you think crabs eat cockles? I'm going to call it Little Eyes. Uncle Victor says that sounds like an Indian name. Uncle Joey wanted to eat it but I told him it wasn't big enough.'

'It wouldn't make much of a meal,' Lloyd looked from Harry to Sali's horrified face.

'You won't tell Uncle Joey and Uncle Victor that I woke you, will you? They said I wasn't to disturb you if you were still in bed. Uncle Victor said you are going to be my daddy soon, but it's a secret. But even if it is a secret, I thought you'd know, Mam.' He gave Sali a sandy kiss. 'Uncle Joey's frying cockles and lava bread. Shall I tell him to bring some up for you?'

'No, we'll be down as soon as we're dressed.' Lloyd found it difficult to keep his voice steady, but unlike Sali he could at least speak.

'You will tell me when I can call you Daddy, won't you, Uncle Lloyd?'

'That's up to your Mam, Harry.'

'Harry . . .' Sali began.

'That's Uncle Joey calling me. Shall I tell him to lay the table for you as well?'

'Please, Harry.' Lloyd fell back on the pillows and

looked across at Sali, as Harry ran back down the stairs. 'Can he start calling me Daddy?' he asked.

'Nothing's changed. I can't—'

'Everything's changed.' He rolled over and kissed her. 'Every single blessed thing. Please, can everyone finally stop pretending that we aren't a couple?'

'It's strange, for the first few days I felt as though this holiday was endless and now it's over, it has passed in an instant.' Sali and Lloyd were walking hand in hand along the shore. Behind them, the village was a glimmer of distant oil lamps. Waves broke into a froth of gurgling surf over their bare feet. The sea, a vast, dark, glittering expanse, twinkled with the reflected light of the moon and the stars as it stretched to the horizon and beyond.

'And when we get home, it will seem like a dream.'

'That sounds like the voice of experience.'

'It is.' Lloyd kissed her. His lips were warm and tasted of salt. 'I love you and you must admit it has been glorious. Can we go back and announce that we got married here?'

'Give me just a little more time?'

'Sali, can't you see how perfect this is? We've been here two weeks—'

'You need three to call the banns.'

'We could have had a special licence. And now that Harry's seen me in your bed, can't you see how hypocritical this whole thing is?'

'Just a few more weeks,' she pleaded.

'If I gave you all the time in the world it wouldn't make any difference. The chapel has too strong a hold on you.' He couldn't keep the bitterness from his voice.

'It's not the chapel.'

'What then?'

'It's not easy to explain.'

'Try.'

'I'm not even sure I can explain it to myself, Lloyd. I love you more than I ever thought it was possible to love another human being. You and Harry mean everything to me. And being accepted as your wife by your family is a wonderful bonus, but it's not just us, there's my father. I'm not even sure whether I believe in an afterlife or not, but I can't bear the thought of him looking down on me from somewhere and disapproving of what I've become. And there's my brothers and sister. I don't want them to be ashamed of me or think I've committed bigamy. But most of all, there's Owen and Uncle Morgan.'

'For pity's sake, surely you don't give a damn what they think after what they did to you?'

'I would hate for them to be able to say that they were right about me being a whore.'

'I'll give you a month. One month, no more,' he said sternly.

'And then what?'

'I'll announce to the world that we're married and you'll just damn well have to go along with it.'

'Or leave Tonypandy.'

For the first time in two weeks Lloyd and Sali went to bed in separate bedrooms, but Sali couldn't sleep. She tossed and turned to the accompaniment of Joey and Victor whispering in the attic above her. Long after they fell silent, she heard Mr Evans walk upstairs from the kitchen where they had left him reading.

When she couldn't lie still a moment longer, she reached for the candle and box of matches on her bedside table. Slipping out from between the sheets she went to the door that connected the back of the house with the front, opened it as quietly as she could and lifted the latch on the single bedroom. She crept in and stole over to the narrow bed.

'Sali?'

'I couldn't sleep.'

Lloyd folded back the bedclothes so she could climb in. 'Neither could I.'

She lay alongside him. 'What are we going to do?'

'We'll think of something.'

As he pulled her close to him, he didn't tell her that he had already decided on a course of action. He knew if he did, she would only worry and try to dissuade him from carrying it out. But now that he had made up his mind, he was determined to find Owen Bull and demand he divorce Sali. Because if that was the only way Sali would live openly with him as his wife, then that was the way it was going to have to be.

'No one can keep a family on one shilling and ninepence a ton for mined lump coal. Not when a miner's gang can spend half a week shifting muck just to get at the coal in the first place,' Billy Evans said angrily. 'It's scandalous. The Ely miners have every right to strike and Nantgwyn and Pandy are entitled to come out in sympathy with them.'

'I still think they should have given management notice that they were about to strike, if only for the sake of the horses,' Victor interposed.

'And that is why we are holding a strike ballot. You can vote whichever way you want,' Billy eyed all three of his sons, 'but you know what I think.'

'I never thought I'd see the day when we'd go against Mabon.' Joey spooned an extra helping of potato on to his plate.

'He's lost his nerve and forgotten where he's come from,' his father said. 'We have no choice but to back the Ely miners to the hilt. You can bet your last penny that if their management succeed in cutting their wages below the breadline now, our management will be doing it to us tomorrow.'

'Of course they will,' Lloyd said quietly. 'That's why it's so important we show a united front.' He pushed his plate aside. 'I'm late.'

'You've a union meeting again, tonight?' Sali questioned, wondering why he hadn't mentioned it until he'd bolted his dinner and was heading out through the door.

She knew the situation in the pit was serious and she admired him and his father for the stance they were taking, but even so, he had been unusually quiet and abstracted during the weeks since their return. He had spent every Friday and Saturday night in 'special' union meetings his father didn't attend. He hadn't brought up the subject of them living openly together as man and wife once and she found his silence on the subject even more worrying than his constant arguments.

'Can't be helped.' Lloyd hated lying to Sali. 'If I'm going to get the quarter to four train, I'd best be off.'

Joey counted the jam-filled French pancakes on the plate Sali had set in front of his father. 'Twelve,' he announced, 'and as Sali and Harry only ever eat one each and Dad two, that leaves four each for us, Victor.'

'Three.' Sali scooped two of the pancakes on to another plate. 'I'll keep them in the pantry for Lloyd.' She gave Joey and Victor her most severe look. 'And don't either of you two dare touch them.'

'As if we would,' Joey smiled innocently.

Billy closed the kitchen door behind him and followed Lloyd into the hall. 'Would you like me to go to this meeting with you?'

'No. And there's no guarantee it's going to be any more successful than the last few.'

'If it is, be careful,' Billy warned earnestly, 'and not just for your own sake.'

'I will.' Lloyd slipped on his coat, set his trilby on his head, wound his muffler around his neck and picked up his leather gloves.

'If you call into the County Club on the way back, I'll buy you a pint.' His father opened the front door for him.

'I'll try to get back before ten, but don't worry if I'm late. I can take care of myself.'

'I sincerely hope you're right,' Billy muttered under his breath as he watched him walk away.

Lloyd made his way directly to Connie's. He was about

to break his promise to Sali that he would never see Connie alone again, but he'd had an idea earlier that day. One he hoped would finally put an end to his weekend 'meetings'. Uncertain of the reception he'd receive, he pushed open the shop door and went to the counter where Annie and three young boys were serving a small queue of customers.

Annie muttered, 'Excuse me, for just a moment,' to the woman she was serving and called out, 'Can I help you, Lloyd?'

Lloyd had expected hostility, but was taken aback by the venom in Annie's voice. 'I need to see Connie on family business. It's urgent.'

'Privately?' she barked.

'It would be best,' he replied, conscious that everyone in the shop had fallen silent.

Annie opened the door that led to the office and stockrooms and returned almost immediately. She opened the counter. 'Mrs Rodney will see you.' When they were alone in the passage, she pushed her face very close to his. 'If you're thinking of asking Connie to go back to you, don't,' she advised sharply. 'She doesn't need you. She's happier without you than she ever was with you. And I intend to see it remains that way. All you've ever brought her is misery.'

'I only want information, Annie. One minute of Connie's time, that's all.'

'You expect me to believe you?'

'It's the truth,' he assured her.

She hesitated and then moved aside. He went to the office door and knocked.

'Come in.' Connie was sitting in the chair behind the desk, cool, composed and fashionably and elegantly dressed as usual, in an embroidered russet, lambswool gown. 'Lloyd, this is a surprise.' She saw Annie hovering in the open doorway. 'Is there anything else, Annie?'

'No,' Annie conceded mutinously.

'Then would you mind returning to the shop? The

boys' service tends to be sloppy if they know no one is watching them.'

Lloyd removed his hat and closed the door.

'What can I do for you?' Connie appeared indifferent to his presence but Lloyd knew better. She was toying nervously with a pencil, running her fingers along the length of it, from one end to the other.

'Do you remember the last night we talked?'

'I doubt I could forget it,' she answered dryly.

'You said you'd spoken to people in Pontypridd about Sali and her husband. You mentioned he was living in a pub. Can you remember the name of the place?'

She stared at him. 'You are going to look for him?'

'Can you remember the name of the pub?' he reiterated.

'The Horse and Groom. It's at the bottom of the Graig Hill. Handy for the railway station but I wouldn't venture far up the hill if I were you. The miners who live on the Graig are rumoured to be a particularly rough breed.'

'Thank you, Connie.' He replaced his hat.

'You aren't going to kill him, are you, Lloyd?'

'That's not my intention,' he replied evenly.

'You really love her, don't you?'

He turned back from the door to face her. 'With all my heart and soul.'

'In that case, for what it's worth, I wish you – and her – well.'

'After the way we parted, that's worth a great deal, Connie. Thank you.'

'Send Annie in on your way out.' She set the pencil on the desk and picked up a pen.

Lloyd checked his pocket watch as he left the shop. If he was going to make the train to Pontypridd he was going to have to run to the station.

'What did he want?' Annie's voice was full of contempt.

'Just the name of a pub in Pontypridd.' Connie took a

deep breath and faced Annie. 'Seeing him again didn't hurt at all.'

'Do you mean that?' Annie walked around the desk and crouched beside Connie's chair.

Connie struggled to formulate her thoughts. 'But it does feel strange to know that I was deluding myself all those years. I really believed I loved him and now all of a sudden I discover I didn't. In a way that's even worse than losing him. It's having to face all that waste – of evenings, energy, passion – of realising that all the time I was clinging to something completely worthless, we could have been together.' She framed Annie's face with her hands and looked deep into her green eyes. 'I love you.'

'And I love you,' Annie cried in relief. 'More than I can ever prove.'

Connie kissed her gently on the lips. 'Nothing and no one will ever come between us again, Annie. I swear to you. Nothing.'

Lloyd opened the carriage door and stepped down on to Pontypridd station. Checking his cigarette supplies, he called over one of the platform boys and bought a packet of Golden Dawn and a box of matches, before showing his ticket to the collector and running down the steps into station yard. Shaking his head at the cab drivers touting for trade, he left the station behind him and strode on to the Tumble. The square was heaving with people, brakes, wagonettes and the sleekly built carriages of the crache. Elegantly dressed women in fashionable, feather-trimmed picture hats and long woollen coats walked alongside colliers' wives sporting their husbands' flat caps and carrying their babies Welsh fashion, in large checked woollen shawls, tightly wrapped around both of them to leave one hand free to carry their shopping.

Children ran in and out of the traffic, playing chase and hide and seek, and colliers on early shift who had already washed and changed into their suits, caps and bowlers, were filing into the White Hart, Clarence, Criterion and Victoria pubs that lined the square.

Lloyd pulled his watch from his waistcoat pocket and checked the time. It wasn't yet five o'clock. Succumbing to impulse, he jumped on a tram that was heading down Taff Street. He hadn't intended to call on Mr Richards and wasn't sure what he would say to the solicitor if he agreed to see him. But Sali would be grateful for any news of her family, almost as grateful as Mrs James and Mr Richards would be for news of her and Harry.

'Mr Evans, this is a surprise.' Mr Richards left his chair as his clerk showed Lloyd into his private office. 'You did get that cheque I sent you?'

'Weeks ago, thank you, Mr Richards.'

'Please sit down.'

Lloyd shook the solicitor's hand and sat in the chair in front of his desk.

'I hope you invested the money wisely. It was quite a considerable sum.'

'I bought half a street of tenanted houses in Tony-pandy,' Lloyd revealed.

'That will provide you with a good steady income.' Mr Richards nodded approvingly.

'My father has always invested in property. He bought his first houses with a view to providing my brothers and me with our own homes when we married but he now has enough properties to give him a pension when he retires.'

'How are Mrs Bull and the boy?' Mr Richards enquired keenly.

'They are well.'

'You told her you were coming here today to see me?'

'No, Mr Richards, I didn't.' Lloyd shifted uneasily in his chair, unable to meet the man's eyes.

'I sense that something isn't quite right. If she needs anything, anything at all. Money . . .'

'No, it's not that, Mr Richards. I came ... to be truthful I came here on impulse.'

'From Tonypandy to Pontypridd on impulse? I never took you to be an impetuous man, Mr Evans.'

'The impulse landed me here, my reason for coming to Pontypridd was more considered. I am concerned about Sali because she is still terrified of her husband.'

'With good reason, Mr Evans. Are you aware that he has been looking for her?'

'No, but surely he wouldn't expect her and the boy to return to him? Not after all this time.'

'That is precisely what he does expect, Mr Evans.' Mr Richards reached into one of his desk drawers and produced a yellowed copy of the *Pontypridd Observer*. He opened it out, folded back the centre section and pointed to an article.

Lloyd read it.

Owen Bull ... Christmas Eve ... drunk and disorderly ... disturbing the peace ... looking for his wife and son.

'I heard that Sali's husband had lost everything he owned. Yet here it says that his solicitor agreed to pay fifty pounds in fines.'

'Rumour has it that Owen Bull has a stash of money hidden away from his creditors. When the police tried to investigate, he insisted his fine had been paid by an "anonymous benefactor". No one believed him. The police even searched the room he rents, but when they came up with nothing they were forced to take his statement at face value. Did you note the address at which Owen Bull was disturbing the peace?'

'Ynysangharad House.'

'Mrs James's house, and that was the second time Owen Bull went there looking for Mrs Bull and her son. The first time he was bound over in the sum of twenty pounds to keep the peace for a year. I had hoped that the judge would sentence him to a term in prison this time, but Owen Bull's solicitor put forward very convincing arguments. He said that given the time of year, his client had reason to believe his wife and son were in the house. He went on to paint a moving picture of a devoted husband and father whose wife had cruelly deserted him, depriving him not only of her companionship but also that of his son.'

'And the judge believed him?' Lloyd handed back the paper in disgust.

'Unfortunately, but there have been several changes in Owen Bull's life during the last year. He is not considered quite so respectable these days.'

'That's poor consolation for Sali.'

'I agree. But Pontypridd is a terrible town for gossip, Mr Evans. Mr Bull's business closed and he lost his house and shop shortly after the night his brother died and Mrs Bull was admitted to the infirmary. No one wanted to be seen supporting a man suspected of killing his brother and beating his wife.'

'Then he really is bankrupt?'

'He insists he is, but I've heard that he spends every night drinking and gambling. Possibly he paid his fine with his winnings, but he could hardly tell the police that when gaming is illegal.'

'You watch him?'

'His business closed, owing the slaughterhouse and a number of small tradesmen in the town considerable sums of money. Some of those men are my clients. A bankrupt has few friends, Mr Evans. Just about every decent person in the town turned their back on him after his business failed, starting with those in the chapel. Morgan Davies forgave Mr Bull for being drunk and disorderly once, but twice stretched his Christian charity too far. And the Minister didn't like being proved wrong in his evaluation of character. He has become one of Mr Bull's most vicious and vociferous detractors. Mr Bull may have been his senior deacon but his exalted status didn't prevent Morgan Davies from persuading the elders to throw him out. Shortly afterwards the Minister persuaded the town council to demand Owen Bull's resignation as councillor.'

'And Owen Bull now works for another butcher and lives in the Horse and Groom?'

'You are well informed, Mr Evans. How does Mrs Bull like keeping house for your family?'

The ticking of the clock fell, unnaturally loud into the still atmosphere. 'You knew she was living with my family?'

'Not before you visited me at Christmas. I made enquiries. You've no need to look concerned. I was extremely discreet. From what I hear, Mrs Jones and her son Harry are very happily settled in the home of Mr William Evans.'

'Does anyone else know where they are?'

'Only Mrs James and after the scene Mr Bull made outside her house, she understands the necessity of keeping Sali and Harry's whereabouts secret. Which leads me to wonder why you took the risk of coming here to see me today.'

Lloyd removed a packet of cigarettes from his jacket pocket and offered Mr Richards one.

'Try one of these.' Mr Richards turned a cigar box on his desk towards him.

'Thank you.' Lloyd used the cigar cutter Mr Richards handed him and struck a match. 'I hate seeing Sali living in fear, Mr Richards. She told me that she wants to divorce her husband and I would like to help her to do just that.'

'A divorce will be difficult.'

'If it's a question of money, I have savings.'

'If it were that simple, Mr Evans, her aunt would have bought her out of that marriage years ago. There are two problems. First, a woman needs grounds to divorce her husband.'

'The man put her in the infirmary. I've seen . . .' Lloyd only just stopped himself from saying her back, 'her face, weeks after he beat her. Surely that is enough grounds for her to sue him for cruelty?'

'What cruelty? The police report states she sustained her injuries falling against an oven door. Owen could counter sue for desertion, or even worse, restitution of conjugal rights. The judge could even order Mrs Bull and her son to live in any matrimonial home Mr Bull might provide for them and that brings me to the second point. The minute Mrs Bull files suit, Mr Bull will find out where she and the boy are hiding.'

'Then there is no chance of her getting a divorce?'

'I am only a market town solicitor, Mr Evans, more accustomed to dealing with matters of wills, the distribution of estates and the conveyancing of properties than divorce. I could recommend an expert, if Mrs Bull would like to take the matter further. Is that why you are here? To discuss it on her behalf?'

'Not entirely, Mr Richards.' Lloyd left the chair. 'Will you send Mrs James, Sali and Harry's best wishes and love?'

'You said Mrs Bull didn't know that you were coming to see me.'

'She didn't, but it's what she would say if she had known.'

'Mr Evans,' Mr Richards laid his hand on top of Lloyd's as he went to open the door, 'do you intend to confront Mr Bull?'

'Yes.'

'I suppose there is little point in me trying to deter you.'

'None at all, Mr Richards.'

'Then I urge you to be careful, very careful indeed,' Mr Richards cautioned.

'I am a very careful man, Mr Richards.' Lloyd tipped his hat.

Chapter Twenty-Three

The oil lamps in the bar of the Horse and Groom belched black fumes into the atmosphere, which mingled with the pipe, cigarette and cigar smoke, making it difficult to breathe. The room was packed and raucous, the layer of sawdust on the wooden floor saturated with spilt beer and pools of spittle. Half a dozen blousy barmaids, sleeves rolled to their elbows, were working flat out, pulling foaming pints of dark beer. Lloyd pushed his way through to the bar and found himself on the sidelines of an argument as to whether it was better to bring pit ponies up into the fresh air or leave them underground for miners' fortnight.

'They go bloody mad when they come up,' an elderly ostler complained. 'Kicking and biting and not just each other mind, the handlers as well. You get a bite from some of the buggers we have to work with and you know it.'

'What they never have, they never miss,' his companion, who had the height and build of a blacksmith, chipped in philosophically. 'And it's common knowledge they go blind from sunlight when they first come up. That's why they go Doolalley tap. And no sooner do they get used to all the grass, sun and fresh air than they're shoved back down underground. Takes two month's hard work to remind them what they're supposed to do, and those are bloody hard months for the haulage men who are trying to drive the trams. We've had nothing but trouble from the buggers all week. And, I've warned the handlers, there's two weeks to go before they'll become the beasts they were.'

Glad that Victor, who had very definite ideas on pit ponies being allowed to take a break along with the miners, wasn't with him to join in the argument, Lloyd pushed a couple of pennies across the counter and took the pint of beer the barmaid slopped up for him.

The beer smelled of hops, tasted good and strong, and he understood why the pub was full. Leaning with his back against the bar, he studied the room. There were several stained and chipped deal tables and chairs dotted around, but no sign of any gambling. But he hadn't expected a card school to be operating openly, even if the police were prepared to turn a blind eye, no landlord could guarantee that all his customers would remain close-mouthed about it.

'Haven't seen you round here before.'

The man was short, Irish and heavily muscled, but he didn't look unfriendly and Lloyd knew the quickest way to stand out and be noticed in a bar was to drink alone.

'That's because I haven't been in before.' Lloyd held out his hand. 'Lloyd Jones.'

'Derry Leary. So what brings you to Ponty, Lloyd?'

'Used to work here. Came back to pick up some wages I had coming to me.'

'Where do you work now?'

'The Rhondda.'

'Ah.' The man lost interest and sipped his pint.

'I heard a man could find a game here if he wanted one.' Lloyd patted his pocket, 'I have a stake I'd like to double.'

'You a comedian?'

'You don't play poker?'

'That's a mug's game if ever there was one,' Derry said with all the authority of a loser.

'Is there a game to be had here then?'

Derry gave Lloyd a hard look and Lloyd regretted his

direct question. It was a foolish one for a stranger with the height and build of a policeman to ask.

'You a copper?'

Lloyd held out his hands. His nails were pitted with small, black nuggets of coal, his fingers ornamented by blue scars that no amount of scrubbing with soap and water would eradicate. 'Do I look like a copper?'

The man nodded to a door at the back. 'The game's private.'

'How does a man get an introduction?'

'By showing his credentials, Lloyd.'

Lloyd turned to see Connie's husband Albert George.

'I never took you for a gambling man.'

'I like the odd game,' Lloyd refuted, noticing that Derry slunk away when Albert spoke. Connie's estranged husband was immaculately turned out in a striped three-piece suit and long cashmere overcoat, his bowler hat tipped to the back of his head. He smelled of good quality cigars and cologne and Lloyd noticed two gold rings on his fingers. 'You've wandered a fair way out of your territory haven't you? I thought you never went further than the Merlin in Pwllgaun.'

'You know me. Distance no object when it comes to a game with the right stake. Want a drink?'

'I've just bought one,' Lloyd held up his pint.

'That will blow you out. Have a man's drink. Whisky or brandy?'

'Neither, but thank you for asking.'

'Double whisky, Nellie darling,' Albert shouted, 'and one for yourself, keep the change.' He handed her a shilling.

'Ta, Albert, you're a sweetie.'

'I take it you're on a winning streak,' Lloyd commented.

'Every dog has his day or in my case, broken-hearted man. And speaking of heart breakers, have you seen Connie lately?'

'I called into the shop tonight.' It was the first time

since the age of fifteen that Lloyd had been able to talk to Albert about Connie with a clear conscience. He found it a relief.

'And was she as beautiful and cold-hearted as ever?'

'She looked about the same to me, Albert.'

'You're a lucky man not to know about her cruel ways.' Albert took his whisky, winked at the barmaid and leaned on the bar alongside Lloyd.

'So, do I get an introduction to this game?'

'Sure, if you want one, but it won't start much before seven o'clock.'

'Poker?'

'What else.'

'Who plays?'

'Men with a pound stake to put into the pot.' Albert took the plate of pie and mash Nellie handed him. 'You are a darling.'

'Eat it while it's hot, Albert.'

He lifted his eyebrows. 'Don't I always?'

'You are a card and no mistake,' she bellowed.

'I'll eat this in the back. Bring your pint, Lloyd. We can have a chat while we wait for the others to join us.'

The back room was too small for the circular table and half a dozen upright chairs that filled it. A fire blazed in the hearth, and realising that anyone sitting in the immediate vicinity would be roasted, Lloyd opted to sit with his back to the door. Albert sat beside him and after he finished his meal and Nellie removed his plate, players began to file into the room.

Albert didn't effect any introductions and the men barely acknowledged one another. When all six seats were taken, a new pack of cards was produced, taken from its wrapper, shuffled and cut to decide the dealer. Pounds were produced and half a crowns pushed into the centre of the table to start the game. Lloyd flicked his on to the pile and considered that given a day-wage labourer in the pit earned three shillings and two pence, the game could prove catastrophic for any man stupid enough to continue playing a losing streak.

As Albert dealt, Lloyd studied the players. He wished he'd had the foresight to ask Sali what her husband looked like. There were two men with pallid complexions, black-rimmed eyes and blue-scarred hands. Obviously miners. A spiv, smartly dressed like Albert, had soft white hands that looked as though they had never been near a tool. He wondered if the man worked, lived off someone else's back or gambled for a living as Albert did. Could he be a butcher? What kind of hands did a butcher have?

He studied the remaining man. He was short, squat and grossly overweight. The front of his jersey was spattered with food and beer stains. His cheeks hung in fleshy jowls that reminded Lloyd of a bloodhound and his small, round beady eyes were sunk deep in layers of fat. His chest heaved as he breathed heavily and he smelled of sweat and unwashed clothes.

Lloyd couldn't have explained how he knew, but he sensed he was looking at Owen Bull and he found it difficult to remain seated at the table when he recalled the state of Sali's back and her accounts of the beatings her husband had given her.

The game began and continued in a silence that was broken only by conversation relating directly to the cards. Lloyd had played poker with his father and brothers and occasionally in the pubs around Pontypridd when he had lived in lodgings and worked for Harry Watkin Jones. But he had never considered cards as anything more than a way to pass the time. He couldn't understand men like Albert George who became addicted to gambling and allowed it to dominate every aspect of their lives.

An hour passed. The pile of coins and notes in front of Albert grew steadily larger as the piles in front of the other players diminished. The two miners left with their pockets a pound lighter, to be replaced by a couple of heavily built men with forearms the size of Victor's and ruddy complexions that suggested an outdoor life. Possibly farmers or shepherds? All the remaining players, with the exception of Albert, were forced to put up another pound to stay in the game.

Nellie came in and took orders for drinks. Albert had a double whisky, the man Lloyd suspected of being Sali's husband ordered a double brandy, everyone else had a pint of beer.

The drinks were brought and the game continued.

'Too rich for me.' Lloyd threw down his cards after the spiv set half a crown on the pile of money in the centre of the table. He had precisely one shilling and sixpence left of his two-pound stake and he wouldn't have lost that much if he hadn't needed to satisfy his suspicion that the short, squat man really was Owen Bull.

'And me.' One of the farmhands shuffled his cards together.

'I'll see your half a crown and put in a pound.' Albert pulled a note from his pile and tossed it together with the silver into the centre of the table.

'I'm out.' The spiv who had put in half a crown set his cards face down.

'And me.' The second farmhand shuffled his cards together.

'That leaves you and me, Owen.' Albert toyed with a couple of the coins on top of his pile and looked to the man with the food-stained jersey.

Lloyd struggled to look impassive as he leaned back in his chair. He had been right. The man was Owen Bull. He had to be. He was sitting in the same room as Sali's husband. What did he do next? Kill Owen where he sat, or ask him if he'd consider divorcing his wife because he had fallen in love with her?

The idea was preposterous even without Mr Richard's revelations that Owen had convictions for disturbing the peace. Owen Bull did not look like a man who could be reasoned with.

Owen pushed his entire remaining pot into the centre of the table. 'I'll see you.'

'I counted twelve shillings there, Owen, that's not enough to see me,' Albert said softly.

'I'll give you a note.'

'I'm already holding two of yours. I'll not take another.'

'Do you expect me to sit here and let you walk away with that entire bloody pot?' Owen slammed his fist down on the table sending the coins spinning. All the men with the exception of Owen, Lloyd and Albert pushed their chairs as far back from the table as the room would allow.

'I expect you to put enough money down to see me.'

'I'm good for it—' Owen began heatedly.

'Then why haven't you paid off the notes I'm holding?'

'Because unlike you, I work for a living. I haven't had time to go down to the pawn shop.'

'If you have goods worth anything, get them and set them down.' Albert raised his eyes and stared at Owen.

'And as soon as my back's turned, you'll change my bloody cards.'

'Are you calling me a cheat, Owen?' Albert had spoken softly, but Lloyd had never seen his cousin's husband look so composed – or menacing.

'I don't have to get the goods. They're here.' Owen downed what was left of his brandy and thrust his hand beneath the waistband of his trousers. There was something disgusting at the sight of the fat man groping around in his underclothes but Lloyd watched intently until he pulled out a small red velvet bag. 'This is worth ten times as much as the notes you are holding, Albert.'

'Can I see?'

'You can look inside, but no one else.' Owen held out the bag and Albert took it. He opened the drawstring, glanced in, retied the string and set it on top of the notes and coins in the centre of the table.

'Full House.' Owen triumphantly slapped down three kings and a pair of jacks. He leaned towards the pot.

'Straight Flush.' Albert laid down a jack, ten, nine, eight, and seven of clubs.

'You bloody thieving bastard!'

'It was a fair game, Owen,' the man sitting the other side of Albert said firmly. 'We were all watching Albert – and you.'

'He's a cheating, lying . . .' Owen grabbed Lloyd's pint of beer and hurled it at Albert.

Albert moved, but not fast enough. The glass tankard caught him on the shoulder before shattering in a mess of splintered glass and spilt beer on the table. Cards, money and glasses flew everywhere, scattering over the table, chairs and floor as Owen slid across the table on his fat stomach. He tried to grab Albert but Lloyd was quicker. Gripping Owen's wrists, he hauled his hands high behind his back.

'Christ! He's off again. I'll get help.' The spiv ran out the door.

'You all right, Albert?' Lloyd shouted.

'I'll tell you in five minutes.' Albert slumped, ashen-faced to the floor.

'You bloody idiot, Owen, you could have killed Albert.' One of the farmhands went to help Lloyd who was fighting to keep his grip on Owen.

The landlady waded in and slammed Owen soundly across the head with the flat of her hand. 'I said one more time and you're out. Well, you are bloody well out of this place this minute. Pack your traps and go.'

'Where to?' Owen demanded belligerently. The farmhand and Lloyd heaved him off the table and on to his feet.

'I couldn't give a damn so long as you're out of here. Now! You all right, Mr George?' She turned solicitously to Albert.

'I will be when I get off this floor.' Rubbing his shoulder Albert rose unsteadily to his feet and allowed the landlady to help him to a chair.

'Leave quietly, or I'll get Dai the Dead to give you a push.' The landlady glared uncompromisingly at Owen. 'What's it to be?'

'I'll go,' he growled sullenly.

She nodded to Lloyd. 'Release him. Slowly mind, and thump him if he tries anything.'

'You'll not have that bloody bag.' Owen tried to snatch it off the edge of the table where it had been pushed when he had slid across to attack Albert. The second farmhand grabbed it.

'Albert won it fair and square.'

'There's nothing fair and bloody square about a professional gambler.' Owen closed his hand around the man's throat.

The landlady yelled, 'Dai!'

A tall man with arms like tree trunks came in wielding a pickaxe handle. Lloyd dived out of the way, as he aimed it at Owen's head.

Owen crumpled to the floor.

'Carry him out,' the landlady ordered. 'Clear his room and throw his belongings after him.'

'Into the street?' Dai asked.

'No, outside the workhouse. And warn whoever's manning the gatehouse that he's a head case.'

Lloyd watched Dai bundle Owen out of the door like a sack of rubbish. He felt no sympathy for the man, only an immense irritation that he wasn't in a fit state to discuss Sali's future.

'Why do they call him Dai the Dead?' Lloyd helped Albert gather his winnings.

'Because in the day he lays out people in the mortuary and in the evenings he does it here. You going back to Pandy tonight?'

'Yes.'

'Give me a hand to get to the station, there's a good fellow. I feel as sick as a dog.'

'I promise you that your shoulder isn't broken,' Lloyd snapped.

'I don't know how you can be sure. It hurts like hell.' Albert's wince turned into a grimace as he lowered himself gingerly on to a corner seat in the train.

'I've checked it over twice and, working in the pit, I know a broken bone when I see one. All you have there is a bruise. A large one, but just a bruise.' Lloyd took the seat opposite Albert's.

'I feel as though I've been run over by a tram load of coal.'

'If you had, you wouldn't be able to moan and I wouldn't have to listen.'

Lloyd glanced out of the window and stared at his reflection superimposed over the station lights. A few seconds later the guard blew his whistle, a door slammed lower down the train, and the engine hissed steam as it moved slowly along the track. Because they had reached the station an hour before stop tap, the train was comparatively empty and he and Albert had managed to grab a whole compartment.

'Why don't you count your winnings? That should take your mind off the pain,' Lloyd suggested in an attempt to atone for his lack of sympathy. After all, it wasn't Albert's fault that the evening hadn't brought him any closer to finding a solution to the monstrous problem of Sali's marriage to Owen Bull.

'The one thing that I have learned to do over the years is to keep a count as I go along. Give or take a few shillings, I'm ten quid richer than I was before I went into the Horse and Groom tonight and that's without taking Owen's pouch into consideration.' Albert unbuttoned his overcoat.

'That's more than a collier earns in a month!' Lloyd exclaimed indignantly, brushing smuts from his sleeve.

'I use brains not brawn,' Albert bragged.

'Like when you went bankrupt and lost your house, business and Connie?'

'I was younger then.'

'And now you're older, you've had the foresight to bank your winnings for your old age?'

'"Enjoy today, for tomorrow may never come." If you want to take up gambling, you have to learn to live by the gambler's code.' Albert dug into the inside pocket of his jacket and extracted the velvet bag Owen had staked.

'Tonight was a one-off experience.'

'Just because you lost a couple of quid.'

'Which I couldn't afford to lose.'

'You know what they say. "If you can't live dangerously, climb into a coffin."'

'You're just full of maxims today, aren't you, Albert?'

'I never realised you were a misery guts until tonight.'

'Sorry, bad day,' Lloyd apologised.

'If you really couldn't afford to lose the money . . .' Albert put his hand in his pocket.

'It's not that.'

'Then it's a woman.' Albert beamed. 'Good God, wonders will never cease, Lloyd Evans is in love. As I've never seen you make eyes at a girl, I assumed your father had you neutered at birth.'

Stricken by guilt at the thought of his long affair with Connie, Lloyd muttered, 'Drop it, Albert.'

Albert untied the string, opened the bag, delved into it and produced a wide gold bangle embossed with daffodils and leaves. 'Very nice. I'd say quality goods, wouldn't you?'

'My opinion isn't worth much when it comes to women's trinkets, but I'll grant you it looks expensive.' Lloyd thought the bangle too wide and ornate. It was the sort of thing he'd seen middle-aged, middle-class women wearing when they wanted to advertise their husband's wealth.

Albert laid the bangle on his lap and pushed his hand

into the bag again. 'Matching ring and earrings.' He handed Lloyd a heavy gold wedding band and gold earrings fashioned into lover's knots, all wrought to the same design as the bangle. 'They'll look beautiful on Connie, and,' he made a face, 'may make up for the time that I pawned her wedding ring and forgot to redeem it. She would never allow me to buy her another, but then, the ring I gave her was nowhere near as magnificent as this one.'

'Do you think Connie will want to wear another woman's jewellery?'

'What woman?' Albert asked, mystified.

'These things must have belonged to someone before they landed up in Owen Bull's trousers.'

'Someone who didn't have the means to hang on to them,' Albert dismissed.

'Someone whose husband staked the pieces to get him into a game, more like.'

'And not just his wife's pieces either.' Albert tipped the bag upside down and a gentleman's gold pocket watch, diamond studded cravat pin and cufflinks fell out.

Lloyd laughed in spite of his misery. 'I'm not surprised Owen Bull kept those hidden. Show those off after stop tap on the streets of Ponty or Pandy on a Saturday night and you'll never make it to your lodgings in one piece.' He reached over and picked up the pocket watch.

'You think I can't play the gentleman?' Albert demanded indignantly.

'You can play him, Albert,' Lloyd grinned, 'so long as you don't try to be one.'

Too happy with his winnings to take offence, Albert examined the cufflinks. 'These will give me instant credit if I ever hit another losing streak.'

'If?' Lloyd's grin broadened.

'All right, when,' Albert conceded philosophically. 'Some people I can fool, but I know Connie has cried on your father's shoulder about my failings. No doubt he has passed on all the sordid details.'

'Not to me.' Lloyd pressed the top of the watch and the back flew open. 'It's engraved.'

'If it has sentimental value, it would explain why Owen was so reluctant to let it go.'

'It had sentimental value all right,' Lloyd said grimly 'but not to Owen. Look.' He handed over the watch.

Albert read the inscription. *To my beloved nephew Mansel James on the occasion of his reaching his majority, Edyth James, 21 January 1903.*

'Can I see the rest of those things?'

'Why?' Albert asked suspiciously, gathering the jewellery and returning it to the bag.

'Because Mansel James disappeared over four years ago on the night before his wedding and no one has seen him since.'

'Was he wearing this watch?' Albert's eyes rounded in alarm. As a convicted gambler he was no friend of the police, but theft on this scale would warrant a heftier prison sentence than the occasional few days he had served from time to time for unlicensed gaming.

'I'd say it's a safe bet that he was carrying it. Please, may I look at that bracelet and wedding ring?'

Albert didn't hesitate. Scooping everything into the bag, he handed it over.

Billy Evans carried three pints of beer to a secluded table in a corner of the County Club. He set two in front of Albert and Lloyd, and taking the third, he sat on the window seat. 'Have you decided what you are going to do?' He was looking at Albert but Lloyd knew the question was directed at him.

'The police have to be shown these things,' Lloyd said decisively. 'I'm no detective but I'd say that Mr Owen Bull has to explain how he acquired that watch and the jewellery. If I didn't know he was unconscious and safely locked up in the workhouse, I'd go back down to Pontypridd tonight.'

'You show the police those things and I'll lose the lot,' Albert grumbled.

Lloyd gave Albert a contemptuous look. 'How much are those notes you're holding against Owen Bull?'

'Fiver apiece.'

'And how much from tonight?'

'Eight shillings.'

'Leave the bag of jewellery with me and I'll drop ten pounds eight shillings into your lodgings as soon as I have a chance to go to the bank. But I have a condition.'

'What?' Albert enquired warily.

'You tell the police exactly how you came by this bag.'

'They'll arrest me for gambling,' Albert remonstrated.

'Once they see this little lot, they'll have a lot more to worry about than your illegal activities, Albert,' Billy said smoothly.

'Is it a deal?' Lloyd held out his hand.

'It's a deal.' Albert shook it.

'You going to show Sali the jewellery?' Billy asked Lloyd on the walk home from the Club.

'As soon as we get in.'

'If I were you I'd wait until morning. Neither of you will be able to do anything about it until then anyway.'

'I have no right to keep something like this from her.'

'You're hardly keeping anything from her. Just allowing her to get a night's sleep.' When Lloyd didn't say anything, his father added, 'She may take it hard.'

'She's bound to be upset,' Lloyd commented tersely.

'She may be even more upset at the thought of being married to a murderer.'

'All we can say for certain is that her husband was in possession of Mansel James's personal property. He's been arrested twice outside her aunt's house. He could have broken in there and stolen the watch and jewellery.'

'You believe that?' Billy gave Lloyd a cynical look.

'It's a possibility.' Lloyd stopped outside their front door. 'But there's no point in indulging in pointless speculation. Let the police investigate the matter. That's what they're paid to do.'

'Do you want me around when you tell her?'

'No.'

'Well, if the boys are in the kitchen I'll chase them to bed. You'll need somewhere warm to sit if you are going to tell her tonight.'

'Thank you.'

Billy hung up his coat and cap. 'I hope this doesn't change anything between you two.'

'You're not the only one,' Lloyd muttered fervently and followed him into the kitchen.

Lloyd waited until Victor and Joey were in bed before knocking on Sali's door. 'It's Lloyd, Sali, I have to talk to you,' he whispered.

'Now?' Her voice was thick with sleep and he realised he'd woken her. His father was right, nothing could be done about the jewellery before morning, but now she was awake it was too late to change his mind.

'I'll be downstairs in the kitchen.' He walked down the stairs, filled the kettle, opened the hob and set it on the stove to boil, before deciding that tea might not be enough. Opening the cupboard at the bottom of the dresser he lifted out the brandy and sherry his father had bought at Christmas. Both bottles were half full. He was setting glasses on the table when Sali appeared in a long woollen dressing gown and one of the ankle-length, red flannel nightgowns she had bought to replace the flimsy lingerie her aunt had given her.

'What is it?' She looked anxiously at him. 'Did your union meeting go badly?'

'I wasn't at a union meeting. Sit down.' He pulled his father's chair out from the head of the table. 'Do you want sherry or brandy?'

'You're frightening me.'

'I don't mean to.' He poured himself a generous measure of brandy, glanced at her, and poured another into a second tumbler. Setting a glass at her elbow, he sat beside her, took the bag from his pocket and emptied it on the table.

She paled and clenched her fists.

'Do you recognise anything?' he asked gently.

'The cufflinks and cravat pin belonged to my uncle, Aunt Edyth's husband. He left them to Mansel in his will. Mansel knew Aunt Edyth liked him wearing them, so he used them every day, as he did the watch.' She reached out and stroked the pocket watch gently with the tip of her finger but made no attempt to pick it up. 'Where did you get them?'

'Connie's husband won them tonight at cards.' He took her hand into his. 'Owen Bull staked and lost them.'

She gripped his hand so tightly he thought his fingers would break. 'Owen! You went to see Owen!'

'He didn't know who I was. I didn't speak to him about anything other than cards during the game. And, after seeing him trying to tear Albert's throat out tonight in a room full of able-bodied men, I understand why you are afraid of him.'

'He didn't follow you?'

'He was unconscious when we left. The landlady took exception to him trying to kill her customers.'

'But if he guessed that you and I—'

'Think, Sali, how could he possibly have guessed?' He waited a few moments for her to compose herself. 'Have you any idea how he could have come by this?' He picked up the wedding ring.

'No.' She looked at the ring in his hand. 'Mansel and I chose that together, or rather he chose it and because he liked the pattern so much, I went along with him.'

'Have you seen the earrings and bangle before?'

'The last time ... the last time I saw Mansel,' she continued flatly, struggling and succeeding in controlling herself, 'he told me that he had two surprises, which he'd give to me on our wedding night.'

'He had the ring engraved.'

She was shaking so much she knew she would drop it if she took it from his hand. 'Read it to me please.'

He read the inscription slowly and clearly: '"*Mansel and Sali James, 28 July 1906. Brief is life but love is long.*"'

'It's a quote from Tennyson's "The Princess". It was one of my favourite poems before my father died. In those days I was so happy I thought tragedy was romantic.' She remained dry-eyed and unnaturally, terrifyingly calm.

'The bangle is engraved as well.'

'Would you read that to me as well please, Lloyd?'

'It's very personal.' He wanted to hold back, because he already knew what it said.

'Please.'

He didn't even have to look at the words. '"*I love thee with the breath, smiles, tears of all my life! And if God choose, I shall but love thee better after death.*"'

'Elizabeth Barrett Browning, "Sonnets from the Portuguese".'

'I am so sorry, Sali.' He tried to embrace her, but she remained rigid, upright.

'I am all right,' she murmured, very obviously anything but.

'There is no shame in crying.'

'You don't understand, Lloyd. I have done all my crying. For over four years I haven't known what to think. There were days when I honestly believed that Mansel had deserted me because he couldn't bear the thought of marrying me. Now that I have seen his things,' she covered the watch with her hand, 'I know he is dead. He would have never handed any of these over willingly to anyone, especially a man like Owen Bull.'

'He could have sold or pawned them. Owen could have won them at cards.'

'Mr Richards was the last person to see Mansel and he said his wallet was full. Mansel told him that he'd forgotten to put the money he'd withdrawn from the bank for our honeymoon into the store safe. He wouldn't have needed to pawn anything if he'd wanted to get away. If the money in his pocket hadn't been enough, he could have taken more from the safe. He had the keys.'

'What do you want to do about this, Sali?'

'Visit Aunt Edyth first thing in the morning.'

'Go to Pontypridd! You're forgetting I saw Owen tonight. Please, let me go first and alone. Once I am absolutely certain that he is in the police station, I will come back for you. Then you can talk to your aunt.'

'I want to be with her when she sees Mansel's things and she has the right to know they've been found.'

Realising there was no way that he could talk her out of going, and remembering Owen had been unconscious and on his way to the workhouse when he had last seen him, he conceded. 'I'll go with you.'

'No.'

'It's a Sunday. I don't have to work.' He looked keenly at her. 'I won't interfere. You can talk to your aunt in private. All I want is to travel down there with you and sit outside your aunt's door in case that maniac hears that you are in town and tries to hurt you. And, please, for everyone's sake, leave Harry with my brothers and father, just for the day.'

She looked at the jewellery. 'Can I take these things to bed with me?'

'Of course.' He returned everything to the drawstring bag.

'Thank you, Lloyd.' She took the bag from him, left her chair and walked out of the door without a backward glance.

Mansel James might or might not be dead, but Lloyd felt as though he had just lost the woman he loved more than anyone else on earth.

CHAPTER TWENTY-FOUR

'This is not up for discussion, Sali,' Lloyd said tersely. 'We will leave the train at Trehafod and hire a cab to take us to your aunt's house. It's no more than a sensible precaution and before you say another word, how many times do I have to remind you that I saw your husband lose his temper last night?'

Sali bit her lips and stared blindly out of the window of the train, seeing neither terraced houses nor the peaks of the slagheaps piled high on the mountains behind them. She was dreading showing her aunt Mansel's things and she was also missing Harry. It was little consolation that he'd be well looked after. He had been excited at the thought of Mr Evans reading stories to him when Victor and Joey went to church, and going rabbiting with Joey and Victor later that afternoon. She finally turned to Lloyd. 'I want to pay for the cab.'

'Whatever,' he said casually, wise enough not to start an argument. He glanced out of the window. 'We're almost in Trehafod. You'd better drop your veil.'

The cab that took them from the village of Trehafod into Pontypridd crawled at something less than a snail's pace. Sali sat back as far as the seat would allow, glancing out of the window at intervals. Neither she nor Lloyd said a word until they reached Mill Street. She shuddered as they drew near, then to her amazement she saw that the entire area had been flattened right down to the river. Workmen were clearing the rubble and fires burned on the wasteland, stoked by wood ripped from the old outhouses.

'There's no going back, Sali,' Lloyd said quietly. 'Not for you or Harry.'

She sat back and continued to look out of the window. When they reached the burial ground behind Penuel Chapel she noticed a canvas awning had been erected over the grave behind her father's and she covered her mouth with her handkerchief.

'Are you all right?'

'Mr Horton must have died. That is his family grave. His wife was buried the week Mansel and I were to be married.'

'You were close to him?'

'He was the under-manager in Gwilym James. Aunt Edyth and Mansel thought a great deal of him.'

Lloyd gripped her gloved hands. 'I know this is neither the time nor the place but I want you to know that I love you very much and always will.'

'Thank you.'

He couldn't make out her expression beneath her veil. 'No matter what happens, you only have to ask me to do something and I'll do it, whatever it is,'

'I know, Lloyd, and I'm grateful to you. For everything.'

When he had shown her the jewellery, he had felt as though she'd withdrawn to a place where he could no longer reach her. Now he sensed that she was saying goodbye to him.

'I can't get any nearer the house than this, sir,' the cab driver called down to them as he walked his horse into Edyth James's drive.

Lloyd pushed the window down, and looked for signs of someone skulking behind the shrubs and bushes. The drive was packed with cabs, private carriages and a brake. As the cab driver heaved his horse to a halt behind the brake, Lloyd opened the door and jumped down. He pushed his hand into his pocket.

'I want to pay the driver.' Sali opened her purse and gave Lloyd all her loose change. He extracted a couple of coins and passed the rest back to her.

'Thank you very much, sir,' The driver took the money and tipped his hat. Lloyd folded down the steps and helped Sali on to the drive. Taking her by the elbow he walked her quickly and purposefully around the steaming piles of horse manure, towards her aunt's front door. The outer door was open and when Lloyd rang the porch bell, Jenkins opened it on a scene of chaos.

People were milling around, filling the hall. Sali recognised a group of her aunt's elderly friends talking in the corner next to the library door. Maids scurried between the kitchens and dining room with piles of cutlery, crockery and trays of cold food. Two uniformed policemen were sitting side by side on a settle that was far too small for people of their size. A man Sali recognised as the undertaker's assistant was standing in the doorway of the study.

Before she had time to take in all the activity, Jenkins helped her off with her coat. 'Miss Sali, it was good of you to come as soon as you heard the news. But then Mrs Williams and Mr Watkin Jones said you would.'

'My brother Geraint is here?' It said something for the butler's state of mind that he had called her by her unmarried name.

'Mr Watkin Jones has been here since midday yesterday. He has been a great comfort to Mrs James.' The old man looked at Lloyd and despite Lloyd's suit, trilby and cashmere overcoat, he dropped the formal 'sir' that he would have used to address a gentleman and spoke to him as he would have a tradesman. 'Shall I announce you, Mr . . .?'

'I only came to ensure that Mrs Jones arrived here safely. I will be in the hall if you need me, Sali.' Lloyd walked over to join the policemen. If anyone could tell him what was going on, there was a fair chance they would know the most.

Too agitated to notice the butler's condescending attitude towards Lloyd, Sali followed Jenkins.

'Mrs James, Miss Sali is here.'

Sali stepped into the drawing room. Her aunt was half sitting, half reclining in her favourite chair next to the fireplace, Mari sitting on a stool beside her. Mr Richards and the doctor were on the sofa. Sergeant Davies, looking distinctly ill at ease, as he always did in her aunt's drawing room, was perched on a wooden chair close to the door. The undertaker was standing at a respectful distance in the bay window and Geraint was in front of the fireplace leaning on the mantelpiece.

'Sali!' Geraint was the first to reach her. He swept her off her feet and hugged her. 'Mari said you'd come as soon as you heard, but I didn't think you'd dare risk it.'

'You've grown.' Sali held him at arm's length so she could take a good look at him. 'You are so like Father.'

'I'll be twenty-one next week and I want you and your son to come back home.' He scowled. 'Or rather to our home when we have one again.'

Too confused and upset to take in what Geraint had said, Sali glanced around in confusion and clutched the velvet bag in her pocket.

'Sali . . .'

She ran over to her aunt's chair and kissed her cheek. 'Why is everyone here?'

'Because of Mansel.'

'Mansel!'

'Don't you know?' Geraint interrupted. 'When the sexton opened Mr Horton's wife's grave yesterday morning to bury Mr Horton, he found a body lying on her coffin.' He wanted to soften the blow, to make it easy for her, then he saw that she already knew. 'The body was Mansel's, Sali.'

*

'The sexton recognised his hair. No one else in Ponty-pridd had hair quite that colour.' Mr Richards moved on swiftly. Given the precarious state of Mrs James's health, he had volunteered to try to identify the body as soon as he heard that it had been found and Geraint had insisted on accompanying him. Not even twenty-one, Mr Geraint Watkin Jones promised to turn out a very fine young man indeed and he blanched every time he thought of the disservice he had done him and his family.

'The suit he was wearing had his personal label sewn into it and there was his wallet with his initials in gold on the corner.' Geraint picked up the remains of a chewed, cracked, mud and water-stained leather wallet from the sofa table besides Edyth's chair. 'It was empty apart from a photograph of you, Sali.'

'How did Mansel die?' Sali's voice sounded remote even to her own ears.

'There were injuries to the back of his skull, Mrs Bull.' The sergeant spoke for the first time since she had entered the room. 'We think he was bludgeoned by someone who attacked him from behind.'

'Would he have suffered?' Sali turned to the doctor.

'From the fractures in his skull, I think he would have been unconscious in seconds, and dead very shortly after, Mrs Bull.' The doctor hoped that no one beside the sergeant knew that he was speculating. Given the condi-tion of Mansel's body and the length of time it had lain without protection in the earth it had been impossible for him to even hazard a guess as to whether Mansel James had been conscious when he'd been buried.

'There's something else, Sali.' Geraint wrapped his arm around her and led her to a chair. 'They found a pawn ticket beneath the body. Mr Goodman checked his records. It was for a walking stick brought in by Owen Bull.'

'Then you know that Owen killed Mansel!' She looked to Sergeant Davies for confirmation.

'For the moment, all I'm prepared to say is that Owen

Bull is a suspect, Mrs Bull. Apart from the pawn ticket, Mr Bull's half-witted brother dug and filled in Mrs Horton's grave, and everyone in town knew he did whatever Owen ordered him to. Some people even heard him babbling about secret 'night funerals' but didn't realise it meant anything.'

'Iestyn said something to me about a night funeral the morning I married Owen.' Sali fought to keep her emotions in check when she realised that all the time she had been locked up, raped and beaten by Owen, Mansel had been dead, lying in an unmarked grave, and Owen had put him there.

'There's no doubt in my mind that Owen Bull had the opportunity and given that Mr James was carrying a large amount of cash that night, the motive. Every policeman in Pontypridd is out looking for him. We know that he was discharged from the workhouse early this morning, so he can't be far. And you have my word, Mrs James, Mrs Bull, we'll get him and get to the bottom of this.'

'It is poor consolation, Sali,' Mrs James whispered, 'but Mansel died loving you.'

'I know.' Sali went to the sofa table, opened the velvet bag and tipped out the contents.

'Mrs James,' the sergeant approached the sofa table. 'May I take these things and speak to the young man who brought Mrs Bull here? Naturally, I will give you a receipt.'

'You want everything?'

'Not the watch,' he relented, when he saw how firmly she was holding it. 'I know you will keep it safe, but should we charge anyone with the murder of your nephew it may have to be produced in court as evidence.'

'You will find Owen Bull, won't you?'

'I will do everything in my power to make sure that whoever did this to Mr James is apprehended and pays the full penalty for his crime.'

'Thank you.' Edyth watched him gather the pieces together and replace them in the velvet bag.

'Excuse me, Mrs James, Mrs Bull, gentlemen.' The sergeant left.

'When can I bring Mansel home?' Edyth asked the doctor as she sank back on her pillows clutching her nephew's watch.

'Mrs James, I really can't advise you to bring your nephew's body into this house.'

'Of course he has to come home.' Edyth's face was grey, but her eyes flashed with an anger stronger than her emaciated body.

'The coffin will have to remain closed,' the undertaker ventured, looking to the doctor.

'I am old, not stupid, I understand that much,' Edyth snapped. 'Geraint, you will arrange for a service to be held in this house for Mansel and I don't want that fool of an uncle of yours anywhere near here, or the chapel on the day that Mansel is laid to rest.'

'Yes, Aunt Edyth.' Geraint knelt at his aunt's feet and took one of her hands into his, while hugging Sali who was sitting on the stool Mari had relinquished.

'Mr James is being held in the mortuary in the Graig Infirmary pending a full post-mortem, Mrs James, but I could arrange to have the body released to you on the morning of the funeral. Then he can be brought here so he can lie in the hall for a service in the house before being taken to the chapel.'

Mr Richards wasn't a demonstrative man but he could have hugged the undertaker for his solution to what might have proved to be an impossible problem.

'Is that acceptable, Aunt Edyth?' Geraint asked.

She nodded.

'Would you like Mr James buried with his uncle, Mrs James?' the undertaker asked.

'Is there room in the grave for three?'

'There is.'

'In that case, yes. And you two,' she looked from

Geraint to Sali, 'please note that I want to be buried with them.'

'When the time comes,' Geraint added.

She reached out and stroked Sali's hair. 'It won't be long, not now that I know Mansel is with his maker. Will that doorbell ever stop?' she complained peevishly, as it rang for the fourth time in five minutes.

'Shall I ask Mr Jenkins to disconnect it, Mrs James?' Mari asked.

'You do that. And tell him to serve refreshments to those who are here on business and those who have come out of genuine kindness and concern, and to boot all the others out. And on no account is anyone in the house to talk to reporters from the *Pontypridd Observer* or *Glamorgan Gazette*. Not after all the rubbish they printed about Mansel wanting to disappear four years ago.'

'Yes, Mrs James.'

The bell ceased to ring after Mari left the room and the atmosphere in the drawing room gradually calmed.

'You should be in bed, Mrs James,' the doctor advised.

'I am not going into the hall, not with all those people there.' She set her mouth into a grim, defiant line.

'I'll carry you up the back staircase.' Before Edyth could protest, Geraint swept her into his arms.

'You will stay here, in the house with me and Geraint, Sali?' Edyth pleaded after Geraint and the doctor had left her bedroom.

'If I do, Owen might come here,' Sali warned.

'Your brother is staying in the house. Between him, the police and the footmen, Owen Bull will soon be put behind bars where he belongs.' Mari tucked the blankets around Edyth. 'Are you comfortable, Mrs James?'

'Very.' Edyth smiled wanly at Sali. 'Mari has been taking good care of me since you left.'

'I am only sorry that I wasn't here to see it.'

'But you will stay now?' Edyth begged.

'I'll stay,' Sali promised, 'but I have to go back for Harry.'

'He can grow up in his father's house, playing with his father's toys, reading his books . . .' Edyth patted Sali's hand. 'Get him now and I'll see you both later when you bring him back.'

'I'll return as soon as I can,' Sali promised.

'Take the carriage. Mansel's son should travel in style.' Edyth had always been thin, but as she closed her eyes and her features relaxed, Sali could see the skull beneath her aunt's flesh. It was as if the dreadful confirmation of Mansel's death had robbed her of the will to live.

Sali looked back at her aunt and Mari sitting beside the old woman's bed as she opened the door. 'I am glad that we finally found out what happened to Mansel, Aunt Edyth. Terrible as it is, I would rather know than live in uncertainty.'

'At least we can finally begin to grieve for him.' Edyth opened her eyes. 'You promise me faithfully, Sali, you will come back and live here with Mansel's son?'

'I promise, Aunt Edyth.'

'Then I will sleep for the first night since Mansel disappeared. Give me one last kiss.' Sali bent over her and she stroked her face. 'You've grown into a handsome woman, Sal. Grieve, but not for the rest of your life. Mansel wouldn't have wanted that.'

Geraint and the doctor were alone in the drawing room. They looked to the door as Sali joined them.

'I was discussing your aunt's condition with your brother, Mrs Bull. She's had a dreadful shock, she's exhausted—'

'And she has just lost her reason to live.' Sali hooked her arm through Geraint's. 'Today is the first time that I have seen my aunt since I left the infirmary, but I think that now she knows for certain that she will never see Mansel alive again, she is prepared to die.'

The doctor glanced from Sali to Geraint. Realising

from Geraint's bleak expression that he had also accepted Mrs James's mortality, he dropped the jocular, blustering manner he used to chivvy the spirits of the relatives of the terminally ill. 'I believe you are right, Mrs Bull. But if her condition worsens, please send for me. Any time, day or night. I may not be able to help her regain her health, but I can alleviate her pain.'

Geraint offered him his hand. 'We will, Doctor, and thank you.'

'I'll see myself out. No,' he held up his hand as Geraint moved to the door, 'you don't want to face all those people out there until you have to.'

Sali hugged her brother when they were finally alone. 'Despite everything, it is good to see you.'

'And it is good to see you and looking so well. We have all been worried sick about you. Gareth, Llinos and me, as well as Aunt Edyth.'

'And Mother?'

'Is so sunk in laudanum, thanks to Uncle Morgan, that she barely opens her eyes long enough to eat her meals these days,' he said scornfully. 'Thank you for the letters you sent at Christmas. Aunt Edyth asked Mr Richards to smuggle them to us. It was a relief to hear from you. I tried everything I could think of to find out where you were hiding. I suspected Mr Richards knew, but he wouldn't tell us anything other than you and your son were safe and well.'

'Which we were.' Sali sank down on the sofa and he sat beside her. 'As your birthday isn't until next week, I am surprised Uncle Morgan let you stay here.'

'He had no choice. I threatened to take him to court and sue him for mismanagement of father's estate if he didn't. And I still might do just that. He has sold the house.'

'Our house! Danygraig House!' she cried in disbelief.

'To someone who wants to tear it down and build on the site,' Geraint muttered angrily. 'He also sold the

Watkin Jones Colliery to a consortium along with all the shares we owned in other collieries just after Father died.'

'I know.' Sali recalled her outrage after her uncle's argument with Lloyd, when she discovered what he'd done.

Geraint left the sofa and slammed his right fist in his left hand just as he had done as a boy when something had annoyed him. He paced restlessly to the hearth. 'I had a long talk with Mr Richards when I came home yesterday.'

'Didn't you finish university in July?'

'Yes, but one of my friends invited me to go to Italy with him for the summer. Although I applied to Mr Richards for the money to finance the trip, I was surprised when Uncle Morgan didn't try to prevent me from going. His reasons for wanting me out of the way are now all too obvious. He's done just what he damn well pleased with our estate, trust funds and property while I've been away. Mr Richards blames himself for not keeping a closer eye on Uncle Morgan, but it's not his fault.'

'But Mr Richards is our solicitor as well as joint guardian. Surely he could have prevented the sale of the house?'

'He could have if he'd known about it,' Geraint agreed tersely. 'But Uncle Morgan engaged another solicitor to act for him, or rather us, as he's supposed to be in guardianship of our interests.'

'Could he do that?' Sali moved to the edge of the sofa.

'Legally, it's questionable. Mr Richards found out what Uncle Morgan had been up to purely by chance, when the man who has bought our house consulted him about developing the site. The solicitor Uncle Morgan has been using has an office in Cardiff. Mr Richards has already written to him and intends to visit him next week. Although it appears one hundred per cent certain that our dear Uncle Morgan has been selling things he had no right to sell, supposedly on our behalf, to perfectly respectable and well-meaning people. We have no idea of the extent of his dealings.'

'Geraint, you have to go to the police,' Sali broke in urgently.

'If Morgan Davies has taken our money, shares, house, sold them and re-invested the money elsewhere in our name or placed it in the trust fund, he has done nothing wrong except for not informing Mr Richards. And, as Mr Richards pointed out, if we take Uncle Morgan to court for mismanagement of our estate, the legal fees will be prohibitive and all we'd succeed in doing is wasting our own money to no good end.'

'Have you confronted Uncle Morgan about this?'

'Mr Richards and I cornered him in the house yesterday morning. Ten minutes later the sexton came to tell us that he had found a body in the Horton family grave that shouldn't have been there.' He stared blindly into the hearth.

He doubted that he would ever blot the sight of Mansel's remains lying in the earth from his mind. Mr Richards hadn't lied when he'd told Sali that Mansel had been recognised by his hair. But what neither of them would ever tell her or Aunt Edyth was that Mansel's hair hadn't been attached to his pitifully splintered skull.

There had been precious little left, apart from a few rags and dirt-encrusted bones to connect the remains they had lifted from the top of Mrs Horton's coffin with the vibrant, healthy, young man who had courted his sister.

'You're thinking about Mansel, aren't you?' Sali said perceptively.

'Yes. And I could kill Owen Bull . . . and not just for murdering Mansel.' His eyes were moist. 'I heard what he did to you. I even gave Uncle Morgan the slip when I came home on holiday and hid in the doorway of the shop opposite Owen Bull's in Mill Street hoping to catch a glimpse of you.'

'Did you ever see me?'

'No, but I saw the filthy conditions he forced you to

live in, smelled the stench of the river. Saw the work-house clothes he made his sister wear . . .'

'It's over, Geraint. There is no going back.' She unconsciously repeated the words Lloyd had spoken to her earlier in the carriage and for the first time since she had walked out of the infirmary, she actually believed them. In a week Geraint would be in control of their father's estate. Owen was wanted by the police and even if he was innocent of Mansel's murder, which she doubted, he was no longer the respectable deacon her uncle had promoted and protected. No one could force her to return to Owen, not now that Uncle Morgan had lost his hold over her and her family.

And most important of all, she had her independence and a job that paid enough to keep both her and Harry in necessities, if not luxuries. She had Lloyd and the Evanses . . .

She recalled the promise she had made to her aunt to live in Ynysangharad House with Harry so he could grow up surrounded by his father's things. When her aunt was better she would find a way to tell her that she would stay – for a while. But not permanently. The Evanses needed her to run their house – and she needed Lloyd. Desperately.

'I promised Aunt Edyth I would fetch my son and move in here.'

'Where is he?'

'Tonypandy.'

'Tonypandy! Do you mean to tell me that all the time we were searching for you, you were only living in Tonypandy?' He smiled and for the first time that afternoon she saw traces of the boy he had been in the man he had become. 'I imagined Aunt Edyth had sent you to London or North Wales, or tucked you away in a cottage in West Wales.'

'I couldn't risk Aunt Edyth sending me anywhere because I was terrified that Owen would hurt her if he suspected she knew where I was. And Tonypandy was far enough away from Pontypridd for people not to recognise me.' She looked her brother in the eye and braced herself for rejection. 'You do know that Owen's not the father of my son.'

'Frankly, I'd be more concerned if he was.'

'But being Mansel's, he's a bastard.'

Geraint returned to the sofa and wrapped his arm around her. 'He wouldn't have been if Mansel hadn't been murdered.'

'Uncle Morgan said I brought disgrace on all of you. On Llinos . . .'

'I think we've all heard more than enough of Uncle Morgan's pontificating. In time, I might forgive him for selling everything Father spent a lifetime building, but I'll never forgive him for marrying you off to a monster like Owen Bull. When I heard what he'd done I could have killed him. Do you know he wouldn't allow Gareth and me to come home that first Christmas? He ordered the school to send us to a Methodist mission in London so we could see how unfortunates live. I tried to run away and get back here . . .' He looked into her eyes and saw her pain. 'You're right. It is over. I'll order Aunt Edyth's carriage to be brought around and we'll go and get your son. What is he like, Sali?'

'He's three years old and looks exactly like Mansel. He has the same blond hair, blue eyes and smile. He's very bright. I've taught him his letters and he loves drawing, colouring, singing . . .'

'What did you call him?'

'Owen christened him Isaac Bull, but as he never spoke to him from the day he was born, I doubt he would even recognise the name. I call him Harry Glyndwr and we've been using the surname Jones since last August.'

'Harry Glyndwr Jones. A good name. Put in Watkin and it sounds even better.' He rang the bell.

Jenkins opened the door. 'Mr Watkin Jones, sir.'

'Will you order the carriage to be brought around to the front door please, Jenkins. Mrs . . .' He turned to Sali.

437

'Mrs Jones and I are going to Tonypandy to fetch her son.'

'Yes, sir.' The butler hesitated.

'Is something wrong, Mr Jenkins?'

'The person who arrived with Miss Sali has returned from the police station where he has been helping them with their enquiries. He is asking if he can see her.'

'Oh God!' Sali exclaimed. 'I almost forgot he was here. Please, Jenkins, show Mr Evans in.'

'If you wish me to, Miss Sali.' Jenkins's tone suggested that if it were up to him he would show the man the door. He turned his head and glanced at someone standing behind him in the hall. 'If you would come this way. Mrs Jones will see you now.'

That time Sali noticed the condescending inflection in the butler's voice.

'Mr Evans.' Geraint stared at Lloyd in amazement. 'The last time I saw you was the day of Father's funeral.' He looked from Lloyd to Sali.

'I have been living with Lloyd's family, Geraint,' Sali explained. 'It was he who recognised Mansel's jewellery when Owen lost it at cards.'

'You took in Sali and her son, Mr Evans.' Geraint held out his hand. 'I am extremely grateful to you . . .'

'My father, brothers and I are colliers, Mr Watkin Jones, and in no position to take in anyone who doesn't work for a living.'

'I am Lloyd's father's housekeeper, Geraint.'

'A housekeeper!' Geraint whirled round and faced Sali. 'You mean to tell me that you have been working for Father's assistant as a housekeeper?'

'If Lloyd's father hadn't offered me the job, I doubt I would have survived, and I certainly wouldn't have been able to keep Harry with me.'

'All you had to do was appeal to Aunt Edyth, she would have given you money—'

'It wasn't merely a question of money, Geraint. I was

terrified to go to her, even to write to her, and Lloyd and his father—'

'You call one another by your first names! Sali, I accept that Uncle Morgan gave you little choice in the matter of marrying Owen Bull, but to deliberately seek out a home with colliers—'

Jenkins knocked on the door. His shoulders were bowed, tears fell unchecked from his eyes but his voice remained steady and he spoke as formally as usual. 'I am sorry to interrupt, Mr Watkin Jones, Miss Sali. But Mrs Williams has just informed me that Mrs James died five minutes ago.'

She has just lost her reason to live.

Sali's own words came back to haunt her. She had accepted her aunt was dying but dear God, not immediately, and not without saying goodbye.

She rushed past Lloyd, her brother and the butler and ran upstairs. Mari was standing next to the bed.

'It was peaceful, Miss Sali. She never woke up after you left, not once. A few minutes ago she stirred, gave a small sigh and that was it, she was gone.'

Geraint helped the butler to the sofa and poured him a glass of brandy. He looked across at Lloyd.

'Would you call one of the footmen?'

Lloyd held Geraint's look for a moment, then left the room.

Numbed by Edyth's death, Sali was forced to set aside her own grief to comfort Mari, Jenkins, her aunt's housekeeper, maids and footmen, most of whom had spent all their working lives in Ynysangharad House.

Not wanting to entrust her aunt's body to strangers, she and Mari washed Edyth and laid her out. Afterwards, they dressed her in the hand-stitched, beautifully embroidered brushed cotton grave clothes Edyth had made for herself after her children had died. There was a gown

439

that proved too large and long for her shrunken body, a white shawl, a cap with streamers and a pair of fine white silk stockings. When they finished, Sali combed out her aunt's long white hair, laid it over her shoulders and sprinkled it with lavender water before placing the cap on her head.

They changed the sheets and pillowcases and laid Edyth in the centre of the four-poster bed in which she had slept as a bride, and where she had given birth to the children destined to live such short lives.

The light had faded by the time they finished. Sali lit the candles on the bedside tables and sent Mari to get the massive four-foot wooden candlesticks from the dining room. She placed two at the head and two at the foot of the bed.

'Master Geraint asked me to tell you that the undertaker is here, and he'll be leaving soon,' Mari whispered as she returned with more candles for the bedside tables to replace the ones that would burn out before morning. 'But I told him that someone has to sit with Mrs James.'

'You and Jenkins can sit with her.' Sali hadn't intended to sound brusque but she was overwhelmed by the demands being made of her. And there was so much more to be done. She had to apologise to Lloyd for her brother's attitude, fetch Harry, organise funerals for her aunt and Mansel . . .

'We're servants, Miss Sali.'

'Jenkins worked for Aunt Edyth for over sixty years and although you were only with her a year, I could see that she loved you,' she added in a marginally softer tone. 'Geraint and I will pay our respects as soon as we have finished making the arrangements for the funeral. I'll send Jenkins up.' Sali left the room, closed the door and took a moment to remember her aunt, not as she was, lying stiff and cold in her bed, but smiling, happy, full of life and mischievous plans to thwart her Uncle Morgan, just as she had been when she and Mansel had announced their engagement.

She opened her eyes and had a sudden image of Edyth walking down the stairs, her widow's dress trailing behind her, the scent of lavender water clouding her wake, her voice soft, silvery as she called to Jenkins. It was so real, so tangible, she could almost believe she wasn't dead. She placed her hand on the doorknob. It wasn't easy to resist the temptation to return to the room but she squared her shoulders and walked down the stairs into the hall.

If anything there were even more people there than when she and Lloyd had arrived. The maids were clearing the dining room table of leftover food and dishes, and the footmen were moving furniture out of the morning room into the study under the direction of the undertaker's assistant.

There was no sign of the police, or she noted despondently, Lloyd. But Mr Jenkins was standing looking lost and solitary at the foot of the stairs.

'Mr Jenkins? Mr Jenkins?' She had to repeat his name before he gave her his attention and she noticed that his eyes were red-lined, rheumy and glazed with tears.

'Would you please watch over Mrs James with Mari?'

'That is not my place, Miss Sali.'

'I can think of no one more appropriate, Mr Jenkins. You knew my aunt longer than anyone else in the house.'

'If you insist, Miss Sali.'

'Mr Jenkins?'

'Yes, Miss Sali?' He halted on the stairs and turned to face her.

'Have you seen Mr Evans?'

'The person who accompanied you here, Miss Sali?'

'Mr Lloyd Evans,' she elaborated, so there would be no mistake.

'He left the house shortly after you went upstairs, Miss Sali.'

'And he hasn't returned?'

'Not to my knowledge, Miss Sali.'

'You wouldn't have turned him away by any chance, would you?' she demanded.

'Not without direct orders to do so, Miss Sali.'

'And no one gave you those orders?'

'No, Miss Sali.'

CHAPTER TWENTY-FIVE

'Mrs James was quite specific in her instructions regarding her funeral, even down to the number of carriages and the hymns she wanted,' Mr Richards explained. Sali sat on the sofa in the drawing room. Geraint poured her a brandy and topped up his own, Mr Richards's and the undertaker's.

'Aunt Edyth was nothing if not methodical.' Sali sipped the brandy and a weakening wave of warmth swept through her body. She had an intense urge to curl up in bed, pull the blankets over her head and go to sleep. But there was still so much to be done – and seeing Lloyd and fetching Harry were at the top of her list.

'The last time we spoke about these arrangements, Mrs James thought there might not be anyone available from the family to bury her. Circumstances being as they were.'

'Are there any decisions left for us to make, Mr Richards?' Geraint asked.

'If you opt for a double funeral for Mrs James and Mr Mansel James, apart from the inscriptions to be added to Mr Gwilym James's tombstone, no.'

'I think Mansel and Aunt Edyth's names, dates, and possibly "*Reunited in the Lord*",' Geraint suggested.

'Aunt Edyth would approve of that.' Sali agreed, unable to think of anything more appropriate.

The undertaker finished his brandy and left his chair. 'I will arrange for a casket to be brought over this evening. Mrs James wanted to be buried in a coffin identical to the one she chose for her husband. Would you like us to move her down to the morning room tonight?'

'Yes, please,' Geraint answered.

'It is the room closest to the front door, so anyone wishing to pay their respects can do so with minimal disruption to the household,' Mr Richards added for Sali's benefit as he left his chair. 'If you don't want me for anything else this evening, I will leave now and return in the morning. You both look exhausted. It might be as well if you go to bed.'

'I have to go to the Rhondda and fetch my son.'

'Surely not tonight, Mrs Bull? It is nearly ten o'clock,' Mr Richards remonstrated.

'The people who are looking after him have to work in the morning. Besides, I promised him that I would return tonight.'

'I can fetch him for you, Sali,' Geraint offered.

'He doesn't know you.'

'But if I told him that I was taking him to you, surely he would come?'

'No, he wouldn't,' Sali said flatly. 'I have taught him only to trust the people he knows.'

'In that case, I'll tell Jenkins to order the carriage again.'

'Don't disturb him, he's upstairs with Mari and Aunt Edyth. I'll ask one of the footmen to tell the coachman to bring it around to the front door. Goodnight.' Sali shook hands with the undertaker who walked out ahead of Mr Richards.

'My deepest sympathy, Mrs Bull, I know how fond you were of Mrs James.'

Sali clasped Mr Richards's hand a moment longer than necessary. 'Thank you, Mr Richards, and not just for being the first on the scene whenever there is trouble in the family, but also for trying to help me when I was married to Owen. You can have no idea how much your visit to Mill Street meant to me.'

'I was afraid that Mr Bull would hurt you after I left.'

Sali recalled the beating Owen had inflicted on her for offering Mr Richards tea, but said nothing.

'I tried to help you too, Sali,' Geraint protested after Mr Richards closed the door behind him.

'I know, Geraint. It wasn't meant as a criticism. And given that you were only a boy at the time and Mr Richards couldn't do anything to stop Uncle Morgan marrying me off to Owen, or to make my life any easier when I was living with him in Mill Street, it was a hopeless situation.'

'Until you ran away and Lloyd Evans took you in.'

'His father took me in as his housekeeper,' she corrected sharply.

'Lloyd Evans must have loved that. Having the daughter of his old employer skivvying for his family. And don't try telling me you had help in the house. I know how colliers live.'

'Do you, Geraint?' she asked coolly. 'Do you really? Do you know what it's like to work an eight-hour shift, six days a week underground and come up almost too tired to eat and yet scrape up enough energy to go on to evening classes to learn to read and write and all because you went down the pit instead of going to school when you were a child to earn a few pennies that your family desperately needed to survive? Do you know what it's like to try to bring up children on a wage that barely buys enough food for one man and only enables you to rent a hovel without running water? Because there are plenty of houses in Tonypandy that aren't fit for pigs to live in, yet have ten and sometimes more people living in them.'

'My God!' He stared at her in horror. 'Father always said that Lloyd Evans's Marxism would prove to be his downfall and now he's infected you. You've forgotten where you come from, Sali. Along with everything else that Father taught us.'

'You mean his lessons on how to treat our inferiors fairly and justly?'

'Precisely.'

'The working class aren't pets, Geraint. And in general they are not inferior and in some cases a damned sight superior to the middle and upper classes. Now, if you'll excuse me, I'm exhausted and I have to get my son.'

Realising from her swearing that she was overwrought, he said, 'I'm coming with you.'

'Please yourself, but don't mention Lloyd Evans on the way, or go into his house. The Evanses have been my family for the past year and I would hate to have to apologise for my own brother's behaviour to them.'

Sali dressed in her outdoor clothes before going upstairs to see Mari and Jenkins. They were sitting either side of the bed, each sunk in their own grief. She warned them the undertaker would be arriving soon with the coffin, before returning to the hall. After checking with the footmen that Lloyd hadn't returned while she'd been talking to Geraint, she went into the porch. Geraint was already there in his hat and overcoat, waiting. Although the gas lamps either side of the front door had been lit, they were turned down low and the porch and the front of the house were cast in shadow.

'The coachman is taking a long time to bring the carriage around,' Geraint complained irritably.

'It takes time to harness the horses.'

'Sali.' He jerked his head towards the drawing-room window. 'About what happened in there. We are both upset. And on the basis of what I've heard you've been through hell the last four years—'

'We are both upset. Tell me, how are Gareth and Llinos?' She deliberately changed the subject.

'Fine, when I saw them in the summer. You probably wouldn't know either of them. Llinos is quite the young lady and Gareth the young man. They have both settled well in school and they spend most of the holidays with their friends and their friends' parents. But then, Mother isn't in a state to care whether we are in the house or not, and Uncle Morgan never did make much of a home for us. It was bad when Father died, Sali, but it became much worse after you left.'

'Uncle Morgan ... he never ... never paid any particular attention to Llinos after I left, did he?'

'What are you asking?' Even in the darkness of the porch she sensed that he was staring at her.

'He didn't try to hurt her?'

'He hurt you?'

'Beat me when he discovered I was pregnant,' she lied. It was strange how it had been easier to tell Lloyd the sordid details of how Morgan Davies had raped her, than her own brother.

'He tried to beat Gareth once. During the Easter holidays after you left. I broke the walking stick he was using to hit Gareth on his own back, so he beat me instead. I was so ill Mari and Tomas had to send for the doctor. I have no idea what the doctor said to Uncle Morgan but he never touched any of us afterwards.'

'You were badly hurt.'

'The wounds healed. I don't think about it any more.'

Sali knew Geraint was lying. He was no more able to forgive their uncle for beating him than she was able to forgive him for raping her.

'At last,' he sighed, as the carriage rounded the corner of the house. He stepped forward, opened the door and folded down the steps. He was handing Sali inside when a shadow moved in the distance at the bottom of the drive. The horses whinnied and stepped back, rocking the carriage. Sali slipped from the step and Geraint grabbed her as she fell.

'Whoa ... steady ...' The more the coachman struggled to control the team, the wilder they became. The carriage rocked precariously.

Sali recognised the coachman's voice and it didn't belong to her aunt's coachman. She screamed to Geraint, 'Get help from the house ...'

Before Geraint could move, the coachman booted his foot full force into Geraint's face. Geraint crumpled on to the drive. The coachman jumped from the box and hurled himself on top of Sali.

She felt his hands close around her waist and fought with every ounce of strength she could summon, clawing at his fingers and cursing the leather gloves that covered her nails. She tried to kick out at his legs and he flung her to the ground, face down beside Geraint.

He dropped astride her back, and his hands tightened, choking the life from her. She tried to scream, to struggle but the lamplight grew dim and faded into blackness. The smell of wet earth, horse sweat, manure and the scent of geraniums filled her nostrils. The last thing that registered was the pain of the gravel biting into her cheek and lips.

'Sali! Sali!'

Someone was shaking her violently. She wished they wouldn't. She knew that if she moved she would be in pain and she didn't want to be in pain. She wanted to remain where she was, warm, fuzzy and comfortable . . .

'Sali!'

Not comfortable. Her lungs were on fire, every part of her ached, but her back felt as though it had been broken. She tried to breathe but her throat burned. She gulped in air and choked.

'Slowly, Sali, take it slowly. It's all right. I have you, you're safe.'

She was lying on the sofa in the drawing room. Lloyd was bending over her and she was conscious of other people hovering in the background.

'Owen—'

'Owen's gone.'

'You killed him?'

'The police have him.' When Lloyd had prised Owen's fingers away from Sali's throat he had been in a blind, murderous rage. But as soon as the footmen had rushed out to see what the commotion was and restrained Sali's husband, he had been too concerned about Sali to trouble himself with the man. But that didn't stop him from regretting that he hadn't killed him.

'Is Geraint—'

'He's unconscious, but Mari says he'll be fine and we're waiting for the doctor to come and take a look at both of you.' Lloyd refused to address Geraint by name. He glanced at someone standing behind them. 'If her bedroom is prepared, I'll carry her upstairs. Then I'll go and fetch her son.'

'It sounds like you had an eventful time.' Billy Evans poured three small brandies after Lloyd had given him a sketchy outline of the day's events. 'Joey, take this out to the cabman and tell him he's welcome to come inside for a warm.'

'I asked him. He wouldn't leave his cab. He thinks Tonypandy is full of uncivilised striking miners waiting to steal his horse.' Lloyd took the brandy and sat in his father's chair next to the fire.

'How is Sali, really?' His father asked seriously, as Joey went to the door.

'Battered, bruised. But,' Lloyd grimaced, 'not for the first time. I waited until the doctor had examined her. He said that both she and her brother will make full recoveries.'

'And Owen Bull?'

'As I said, in custody. If they don't hang him for the murder of Mansel James, they can hang him for the murder of Mrs James's coachman. The man had been bludgeoned to death with a log taken from the woodpile and his uniform stripped from him. As Owen was wearing everything except the poor devil's blood-stained shirt, the police think he crept up on him when the man was harnessing the horses, killed him, then took his place with the intention of stealing the carriage and getting out of Pontypridd as quickly as possible after losing Mansel James's belongings in that card game.'

449

'You'd think the last place he would want to go to was Ynysangharad House.'

'The butler said the loft above the stable hadn't been used for anything since the coachman moved into the servants' quarters in the house after Mansel James's disappearance. The police held Owen there until the Black Maria arrived the last time he caused trouble at the house, so he knew it was empty. An old lady living alone with her servants – Owen probably thought it was the easiest place to steal a horse. After losing everything he owned in that card game he didn't have the money to buy a train ticket, even if he'd been prepared to risk it. Christ! It makes my blood run cold to think that I took Sali there today. He could have been watching us as we arrived.'

'You weren't to know.'

Victor walked in carrying Harry on one arm, a small case in his free hand.

'Uncle Victor's packed all my clothes.' Harry rubbed sleep from his eyes with his fists.

'Has he now?' Billy held out his arms and Victor sat the boy on his lap.

'What about Sali's things?' Victor asked.

Lloyd finished his brandy. 'I'll pack them.'

'Mam and I will be coming home again, won't we, Uncle Lloyd?' Harry looked wide-eyed and anxious.

'For the moment, the important thing is that you and your mam are together. Now, don't forget anything, and that includes your toys. Uncle Victor and Uncle Joey will help you put everything in bags.'

'The fort and soldiers have to stay. Mam said they were only on loan.'

'Tell you what, Harry, you can loan them in your new house as well. How about that?' Joey opened the cupboard door.

Lloyd went upstairs and walked into Sali's room. He lifted the valise down from the top of her wardrobe.

'You packing everything of hers?' His father stood in

the doorway, watching Lloyd clear her hairbrush and bottle of cologne from the dressing table.

'Everything.'

'You don't think she's going to come back here?'

'No.'

'Lloyd—'

'She's returned to her own kind. That couldn't have been made clearer to me today.'

'Not by her, I know.'

Lloyd placed the last of Sali's belongings into the valise and snapped the sides together. 'Face it, would you be here by choice knowing what's coming to this valley?' When his father didn't reply, he said, 'Ask Victor and Joey if they'll take Harry to Pontypridd.' He slipped his hand into his pocket and peeled a pound note off the roll he had withdrawn from the bank in the hope of bribing Owen into divorcing Sali. 'And give them this to pay for the cab and the journey home. Tell them not to accept a penny from Geraint Watkin Jones.'

Realising Lloyd was adamant, his father took the money on the premise that any overpayment could be sorted out later. 'You will say goodbye to the boy?' he asked, as Lloyd fastened the lock on the valise.

'Of course.'

Billy glanced into the room. 'I'm going to miss her.'

'We all are.' Lloyd brushed past him and ran down the stairs.

Joey picked up Sali's valise and the case containing Harry's clothes from the floor of the cab, went to the door of Ynysangharad House and rang the bell. Victor left the cab and leaned back inside to lift out Harry, who had fallen asleep before they had left Tonypandy. He wrapped the blanket they had taken from Harry's bed closer around him as he carried him to the porch door. They stood in the darkness listening to the sound of bolts being thrown back on an inner door, followed by footsteps and locks opening on the outer door. A footman peered out at them.

'We've brought Harry,' Joey whispered so as not to wake the boy. 'Sali's son.'

The footman stepped back and spoke to someone in the hall. A man came to the door, his face bloody and bruised. Behind him was a short, stout, middle-aged woman who resembled the housekeeper of Llan House so closely, Joey retreated into the shadows.

'I'll take him.' The man held out his arms.

'It might be better if I carried him inside.' Victor sized up the situation and added, 'sir', which his father and elder brother would never have said.

'I think it best the housekeeper put him to bed right away.'

Harry woke, took one look at Geraint's bloody face and screamed.

'It's all right, Harry.' Victor lifted the boy higher into his arms and Harry buried his head in his shoulder. 'Your mam is here.'

'She is too ill to come to the door,' Geraint said, 'Mari, could you take the boy up to Sali's room?'

Her skills honed by years of experience with children, Mari unlocked Harry's arms from around Victor's neck within minutes. 'Come on, darling, I'll take you to your mam.'

Joey waited until Harry and Mari were out of sight before setting the cases he had carried from the cab on to the porch floor. 'These are Harry's and Sali's things.'

'Don't forget Harry's toys, Joey.' Victor tensed, as Harry's screams escalated. Then suddenly they ceased.

'Judging by the silence, my nephew is with my sister.' Geraint continued to block the doorway with his body.

'How is Sali?' Joey returned with the brown paper and string carrier bags of toys.

'As well as can be expected after being attacked, but she is expected to make a full recovery.'

'Will you give her our,' Victor choked back the word love, 'regards, and tell her that we are thinking of her.'

'I will.' Geraint looked down at the cases and bags. 'Take these up to Mrs Jones's room, Harris,' he ordered the footman. He looked at Joey and Victor. 'If you would like something to eat, the kitchens are around the back.'

'We are not hungry.' Joey stared coldly at Geraint.

'You will need money for the cab.'

'We don't need your money,' Joey snapped, losing his temper.

'You will give our messages to Sali?' Victor reminded, taking Joey's arm before he did something they would both regret.

'To Mrs Jones, yes.' Geraint closed the front door before Joey and Victor even reached the cab.

'And what would Master Harry like for breakfast, Miss Sali?' Jenkins enquired, as Sali led Harry by the hand into the dining room.

'What is on the menu, Jenkins?'

'Mrs James's Monday autumn breakfast, Miss Sali – grilled kidneys and mushrooms, sardines, wholemeal scones and fruit.' He pulled out a chair for Harry next to the carver Geraint occupied.

'Would it be a great deal of trouble for the cook to boil Harry an egg, Jenkins? He is used to simple food.'

'Not at all, Miss Sali.'

'You don't have to be so diffident with the servants, Sali,' Geraint reproached when Jenkins had left the room.

'They are Aunt Edyth's servants not ours.' Sali turned to her son. 'This is your Uncle Geraint, Harry.'

Geraint held out his hand to Harry, who shook it only after Sali had prompted him. Sali lifted him on to his chair, took a banana from the bowl on the table, peeled it, placed it on Harry's plate and cut it into chunks before sitting beside him.

'How are you feeling this morning?' she asked her brother.

'How do I look?'

Conscious of Harry shrinking closer to her and realising he was terrified of the bloody bruises on Geraint's face, she wrapped her arm around his shoulders. 'Like you've taken up boxing with professionals.'

'That's about how I feel.' He studied Harry. 'You're right, Sali, he does look like Mansel. But he's going to grow up into a right Mummy's boy if you insist on molly-coddling him the way you are now.'

'He is in a strange place,' Sali reminded, 'and he hates the sight of blood and bruises because he saw so many of them when we lived with Owen.'

Harry looked down at his plate, picked up a piece of banana and slipped it into his mouth.

'You haven't taught him to say grace, Sali?' Geraint asked in surprise.

'What's grace, Mam?' Harry asked.

'Grace is thanking God for the food on the table, Harry,' Geraint answered.

'Uncle Billy says that God doesn't put food on the table, only the sweat of men's labour.'

Geraint pushed his plate to one side and studied his nephew. 'And who is Uncle Billy?'

'Uncle Billy is Uncle Billy,' Harry answered with childish logic before taking a second piece of banana.

'I think you've come back just in time, Sali. You've brought the boy up to be a positive heathen. The sooner he goes to a good school and learns discipline and civilised behaviour—'

'Harry is three years old, Geraint.'

'He needs an experienced nanny to drum some manners into him,' he said sharply.

'A nanny! Geraint, have you no idea how I've been living?'

He pulled the napkin from his lap, crumpled it and tossed it over the debris on his plate. 'Your hands say it all. I've seen kitchen maids with fewer calluses. But you're not living that life any longer and, the sooner you forget about it for your son's sake as well as your own, the better.'

'I have very little money.'

'You're forgetting that you are my sister.' He pushed his chair back from the table. 'Danygraig House may have been sold, but I've already asked Mr Richards to look around for a suitable replacement. It's high time that Harry,' he looked from the boy to her, 'and you, are taken in hand. I have arranged to meet Mr Richards in his office at nine. We will be spending the morning with Uncle Morgan. After the events of last night, I have given Jenkins orders only to admit close friends and relatives to the morning room to pay their respects to Aunt Edyth. There is no need for you to receive anyone.'

'You assume that no one will want to see the wife of a murderer.'

'I am trying to protect you, Sali.'

She looked her brother in the eye but he avoided her gaze. 'You are ashamed of me?' she enquired bluntly.

'Merely minimising gossip,' he countered. 'I will ask Mr Richards to contact Llinos and Gareth at school, so they can return for Aunt Edyth's and Mansel's funeral. Don't delay lunch for me.'

'Mr Davies left after chapel services yesterday evening, Mr Geraint, Mr Richards.' Tomas took their coats and hats.

'But he doesn't believe in Sunday travelling.' Geraint froze as he recalled his uncle's aggressive response to the questions Mr Richards had put to him on Saturday before their interview had been interrupted by the news of the discovery of Mansel's body.

'For where?' Mr Richards enquired, concealing his mounting alarm beneath a professional detachment he had practised for over half a century.

'Mr Davies said it was an emergency. A fellow minister was dying in Cardiff and had asked to see him.'

'He received a telegram?'

'Not that I saw, Mr Richards. When I asked him about the arrangements for moving the household, he referred me to Mr Geraint.'

'No doubt Mr Davies left letters in the study.' Mr Richards tried to sound optimistic for Geraint's sake. 'We'll start there.'

'Look, Harry, here's a whole cupboard full of toys.' Sali opened the walk-in toy store in the nursery and showed Harry shelves crammed with beautifully crafted, expensive toys. She could recall Mansel and her brothers playing with them. There was a far more elaborate and grander fort than the homemade one Joey had packed for Harry and with ten times the complement of lead soldiers outfitted in four painted regimental uniforms, two British, two Napoleonic. She lifted him up so he could see everything. 'You can play with this fort, or this theatre, here's a box of puppets to go with it, and there are lots of wind-up tin toys. I remember those guns. Uncle Geraint and I used to play with them, they fire corks, and here's a farmyard with pigs, sheep, cows, chickens . . . Don't you want to play with them, darling?' she asked, as he shook his head.

'No.' He left the cupboard, walked past the enormous wooden rocking horse and picked up one of the carrier bags Joey had packed. 'I want to play with Uncle Joey's fort.'

He sat cross-legged on the floor and unpacked.

The last time Sali had been in this room was the week before Mansel had disappeared. He was looking for his childhood copy of *Treasure Island*, because he remembered that he'd drawn a picture of her on a blank page at the back of the book. They had found it and laughed at his childish scrawl. But then the room had been dusty and unkempt with scuffed, varnished wallpaper, paint and furniture. Sometime between then and now, Edyth must have called in decorators. The new wallpaper was bright yellow with a teddy bear pattern, the child-scale furniture also new, beech wood ornamented with nursery rhyme figures, and the picture books on the shelves next to the bed looked suspiciously untouched.

She recalled her aunt's words – *He can grow up in his father's house, playing with his toys, reading his books . . .*

It was heartbreaking to think of Aunt Edyth making preparations and plans for them to join her in Ynysangharad House and dying before she saw Harry in Mansel's old nursery.

'When are we going home, Mam?'

Startled, she looked down at Harry. 'Home?' she repeated.

'To Uncle Billy's house.'

'I don't know, darling.' She knelt beside him as he set up the fort and battered tin soldiers the way Victor and Joey had showed him. 'I have a lot of things to do here.'

'But we will go home?' His bottom lip trembled as he looked up at her.

She picked up a photograph of her and Mansel that had been taken the Christmas before her father had died. 'This room used to be your father's, Harry. This is a picture of us together.'

Harry looked at the photograph solemnly for a moment. 'Is he with the angels like Uncle Iestyn?'

'Yes, darling.'

'Do I have to be sad?'

Sali couldn't ask Harry to grieve for a father and aunt he had never known. Not when he had known so much violence and misery in his short life. 'No, darling.'

'Then play soldiers with me,' he instructed practically. 'I'll have the ones with crosses. They will be in the fort, yours will be outside it, and you have to try to take it from my men. We'll have one cannon each. Do you have any matchsticks?'

'Nothing. No papers, no records, just sermons.' Mr Richards slammed the desk drawer.

457

'There's nothing in Father's safe either.'

'Your uncle gave you the key?' Mr Richards asked Geraint in surprise.

'It was open.'

'I think you and I had better get to the bank and check the safety deposit boxes.'

'This is most irregular, Mr Richards,' the bank manager protested. 'As joint guardian, you have access to the bank accounts, but the safety deposit boxes contain sensitive items personal to the family—'

'Mr Watkin Jones and I have just come from Danygraig House,' Mr Richards explained impatiently. 'There is nothing there. No records, nothing. Mr Watkin Jones attains his majority next week and as joint guardian it is my duty to ensure that the changeover is smooth.'

'But Mr Davies—'

'When was he last here?'

'Saturday afternoon. We were closed, but he said it was an emergency and for a customer of his standing—'

'Did he open the boxes?'

'I left him alone with them as usual, Mr Richards.'

'Mr Morgan Davies has been called away on urgent business. So urgent, he didn't even have time to leave a message.'

In the half a century the bank manager had known Mr Richards, he had never seen him panic before that moment. 'I will unlock the boxes for you myself.'

Every safety deposit box was labelled. At Geraint's request the first one the manager opened was marked 'Cash'. It was empty. 'Family Jewellery' contained bills of sale. The atmosphere in the windowless vault buzzed tense and nerve-racking, as the manager lifted the other boxes on to the table. 'Stocks', 'Shares' and 'Bonds' held bundles of neatly tied certificates. 'Property deeds' contained sheaves of papers and 'Bank Books' a dozen books and a few important looking documents.

'If you would like to use my office, Mr Richards, Mr Watkin Jones, you would be most welcome.' The manager took two of the boxes and led the way.

'What's going to happen to us now, Miss Sali?' Mari asked as she carried bed linen into the room Sali had ordered to be prepared for her sister.

'I honestly don't know, Mari. It depends on Geraint. I know he is looking for another house and although I haven't had time to discuss it with him, I presume he intends to stay on in Pontypridd. Mother, Llinos and Gareth have to live somewhere, they will need a house-keeper and I'm sure that you will be the first person they think of employing.'

'Mr Geraint asked how I'd feel about taking the position of nursemaid to Master Harry.' Mari revealed diffidently.

'When did he ask you?'

'This morning before breakfast.'

Sali was furious. She was grateful to Mari for her loyal service to her family over so many years, and especially for the care she had shown her Aunt Edyth and her mother. And given that Mari had spent practically the whole of her life in their employ, their old housekeeper had every right to expect to remain with them. But she felt that Geraint had no right whatsoever to discuss or offer Mari the post of nursemaid to her son without consulting her first.

'I'm sure he meant to talk to you about it, Miss Sali.'

Tight-lipped, Sali muttered, 'I'll discuss it with him when he returns.'

'When I think of your uncle selling Danygraig House—'

'It's done, Mari,' Sali interrupted, not wanting to talk about something that couldn't be changed.

'Are you and Master Harry going to live with Mr Geraint, Miss Sali?' Mari shook a bolster into a case.

'I have absolutely no idea where I'll be living or what I'll be doing a week from now, Mari. At the moment, it's as much as I can do to look as far ahead as tomorrow. There's the funeral tea to arrange, the flowers to order, and after we've done this bedroom, we have to prepare one for Gareth.'

'Miss Sali.' Jenkins knocked the door. 'Sergeant Davies is here. He asked if he could speak to you. I have shown him into the drawing room. Would you like to be served tea?'

'Please, Jenkins.' Policemen always seemed to be able to drink tea at any time of day. 'Serve it right away and tell him I'll be with him shortly.'

'I'll start on Master Gareth's room as soon as I've finished here, Miss Sali.' Mari set the bolster on top of the tallboy and picked up a pillow.

'Harry?' Sali looked at her son who was sitting quietly on the floor in the corner looking at a picture book. 'Will you stay with Mari while I talk to a policeman?'

'Of course he will,' Mari answered for him. 'And as soon as this bed is made up, we'll go down to the kitchen and see if we can find a glass of milk and one or two of the Jumbles I saw the cook making this morning.'

'I'll only be in the drawing room, Harry,' Sali re-assured, 'and as soon as the policeman has gone I'll come and look for you.'

'You haven't done anything naughty?' Harry asked gravely.

'Bless you,' Mari laughed. 'Your mother couldn't do anything naughty if she tried.'

'I won't leave the house without you, Harry.' Sali couldn't help contrasting Harry's present insecurity with the confidence he had displayed only the day before when he had been almost too preoccupied with choosing a book for Mr Evans to read to him, to wave goodbye to her.

'Well?' Geraint asked impatiently after Mr Richards had glanced at all the documents in the deed box and opened one bank book after another, piling them neatly on to the bank manager's desk.

'Payments out of the trust fund set up by your father require two signatures, mine, and after your mother's abdication of her guardianship in favour of her brother, Morgan Davies's. But withdrawals have been made on representation of cheques that I never signed. Also, stocks, bonds and shares have been sold without my knowledge.' He left the desk and opened the door. The manager was standing outside, talking to a clerk. 'Could I see all the cheques that have been drawn from all of the Watkin Jones accounts, starting with the trust fund account.'

'Certainly, Mr Richards.' The manager looked at the clerk who immediately charged off. 'Is there a problem?'

'A serious one.' Mr Richards returned to his chair behind the desk. 'The trust fund set up by Mr Harry Watkin Jones is empty.'

'But of course it is.'

'You knew about this?' Mr Richards was astounded.

'For the past six months Mr Davies has been making arrangements to transfer everything into Mr Geraint Watkin Jones's name in an account in Cardiff. He told us that Mr Watkin Jones was setting up home there and wanted to make banking arrangements in the city.' The clerk knocked on the door and brought in the boxes.

Mr Richards opened the box file and lifted out a sheaf of cheques. The manager walked behind the desk and looked over his shoulder.

'All of those cheques drawn on the trust fund account bear two signatures, just as they should, Mr Richards.'

'The only problem is, neither signature is mine,' Mr Richards stated categorically.

CHAPTER TWENTY-SIX

Mr Richards, the manager and Geraint sat together for over three hours. During that time they examined all the transactions carried out in the last four and a half years in every account that bore the Watkin Jones name. All were empty, their contents transferred into a Cardiff bank account opened in Geraint's name. There was even a specimen of Geraint's signature the Cardiff manager had accepted at face value. But the account held the princely sum of ten shillings, the minimum required to keep it open.

Mr Richards and the manager grew increasingly sombre as they examined the stock, share and bond certificates. Instead of the gilt-edged, national companies Harry Watkin Jones had invested in, all the certificates bore the title 'the Conversion of Savages and Pagans Missionary Fund'.

On paper, the new investments Morgan Davies had made on behalf of his nephew and the family trust fund were worth the same as those made by Harry Watkin Jones. But when the solicitor and manager fell gravely silent, Geraint realised something was terribly wrong.

'What is this "Conversion of Savages and Pagans Missionary Fund"?' he asked, with an escalating sense of dread.

'A scheme your uncle brought to me two years ago'. Mr Richards's hand shook as he returned the stock certificates to their box. 'It was being marketed to potential investors as a honourable, non-exploitive Christian Fund. I refused to allow him to buy shares in it because nothing was known about the people behind it.'

'The company went into liquidation six months ago with losses of over a million pounds.' The manager slumped back, horror-stricken, on his chair. 'The directors have disappeared and as yet, no trace of them has been found.'

Mr Richards's voice was hoarse with the effort it took for him to speak. 'From the evidence here, it appears that your uncle forged my signature to cash in all of your investments and reinvest them in this Christian Fund without your, or my, knowledge or consent. But instead of paying dividends, the company kept demanding further investment to stave off bankruptcy. And that is when your uncle began to throw good money after bad. Judging by the dates on these notes and bills of sale, he drained the cash box and sold your family's personal jewellery to meet the interim payments they asked for. And,' Mr Richards extracted an envelope from the Deeds Box, 'when he could no longer juggle the accounts to make it look as though the dividends on the investments your father had made were being paid, he mortgaged Danygraig House to meet your university fees, your brother and sister's school fees and the household expenses.'

'What about my sisters' and brother's accounts and my mother's annuity?' Geraint was trembling in shock.

'Your mother's annuity and your sister Llinos's dowry went with the trust fund. Your elder sister's dowry was paid to Owen Bull.'

'And Gareth?'

'Under the terms of your father's will,' Mr Richards frowned with the effort it took to recall the exact terms, 'Gareth inherited his gold pocket watch, gold cigarette case, three thousand pounds, the two farms and all the properties he owned in the town of Pontypridd with the exception of Danygraig House. The money and jewellery has gone. The only deeds left that are worth anything are to the two farms and the properties in

Pontypridd that your father bought as investments to secure Gareth's future. I negotiated the rental terms on those leases myself. All are long-term, and the sitting tenants have the right of first refusal should they ever be sold. Your uncle probably thought it would attract too much attention if he tried to mortgage or liquidate them.'

'So Gareth has property.'

'Which he can collect the rents on, but not sell, except at a loss to the sitting tenants and no cash.'

'I will send for the police.' The manager left the office.

'Are you telling me that my uncle has stolen almost everything my father left us?' Geraint demanded querulously.

It cost Mr Richards more than his pride to face Geraint. 'Yes.'

'And my mother, sisters and I are paupers.' Geraint's voice rose even more precariously.

'Yes.'

'Is there any chance of recovering the money?'

'Not unless they find the directors of the Conversion of Savages and Pagans Missionary Fund, and the police have been searching for them for the past six months.'

Geraint laughed hysterically. 'I bet they are a long, long way away.'

Mr Richards felt impotent, duped and shattered. The Watkin Jones's were bankrupt and his professional incompetence was to blame.

'How much are the rents to Gareth's properties worth?' Geraint said sharply.

'Five hundred pounds a year.'

'His and Llinos's school fees come to two hundred a year and that's without extras, and they each have fifty pounds a year allowance. That leaves Mother and me with only two hundred pounds a year between us and no house . . .'

'You are forgetting something, Mr Watkin Jones,' Mr Richards said quietly. 'The properties are Gareth's.'

'I will be his guardian from next week.'

'Are you really prepared to rob your brother as your uncle has robbed you?'

The question hung, unanswered, in the air as they sat in silence, waiting for the police to arrive.

'It is good of you to see me so soon after your aunt's death, Mrs Bull.' Sergeant Davies rose to his feet when Sali entered the room. 'I know how upset you must be. Please, may I offer my condolences. She was a great lady and a generous benefactor to the town.'

'Thank you, Sergeant. I see you have tea, please help yourself to biscuits and cake.'

'The tea is sufficient, Mrs Bull, thank you.'

'Is this a condolence call, Sergeant Davies?'

'No, I thought you'd like to know that your ... that Mr Owen Bull has confessed to murdering not only the coachman but also Mr Mansel James.'

Sali sat in her aunt's chair. 'What exactly does that mean, Sergeant?'

'It means that his trial will be little more than a formality, Mrs Bull, and neither you nor anyone else will be required to give evidence in his defence. Mr Bull has already been transferred to Cardiff jail and his case will be called at the earliest available date at the Assizes. My superiors think it should come up in the next couple of weeks.'

'He will plead guilty? He can't change his mind?'

'When we formally arrested Mr Bull on suspicion of murder in the station last night, he waved his right to consult a solicitor and asked if he could see a chapel minister instead.' The sergeant wrinkled his nose as if the memory was distasteful. 'After speaking to the minister, Mr Bull confessed his sins and proceeded to list them in a manner that was extremely helpful to us. The minister told Mr Bull that if he truly repented, asked God's forgiveness and told us everything he knew, he would be rewarded in this world and the next. Frankly, Mrs Bull, your husband would have been better off asking to see a solicitor. He signed a full and complete statement. Anyone reading it would be left in no doubt of his guilt.'

'What will happen to him?'

'For three murders, Mrs Bull?' The sergeant looked at her in surprise. 'Without a doubt, he will hang.'

'Three?' Sali queried.

'Mr Bull admitted that he threw his brother down the stairs and broke his neck; he also admitted that he beat you and his sister. His extremely detailed confession extends to over ten pages.'

'Thank you for coming in person to tell me about this, Sergeant.'

'Under the circumstances, it was the least I could do.' The sergeant rose to his feet. 'Mr Bull asked me to convey a message to you and Miss Bull. He would like you to visit him in Cardiff prison. If I were you and Miss Bull, I wouldn't feel obliged to do so. But you have until after the sentencing to decide what you want to do. Thank you for the tea, Mrs Bull.' He laid his hand on the doorknob, then turned back to face her. 'I am sorry we couldn't help you before, Mrs Bull. But the force has a policy of non-interference in domestic disputes.'

'So I understood, Sergeant Davies.' Sali gave him a cold smile.

He turned aside sheepishly and opened the door. 'Goodbye, Mrs Bull.'

The days between the sergeant's visit and the funerals passed in dreamlike confusion for Sali. Friends and acquaintances drifted in and out of the house. Geraint and Mr Richards spent hours closeted with the police as the search for Morgan Davies and the directors of the Conversion of Savages and Pagans Missionary Fund widened from Wales to England and Scotland and beyond.

Bitter, angry, his dreams of becoming a gentleman of property and substance as his father had been before him, crushed, Geraint became surly and bad-tempered, a different man.

Guilt-ridden, Mr Richards offered to fund Llinos's and Gareth's remaining education, but immersed in preparations to move their family furniture from Danygraig House into the stable loft at Ynysangharad House and their mother into one of Edyth's spare bedrooms until something more permanent could be arranged, Sali and Geraint were too busy to think of anything except their most immediate and pressing problems.

Ignoring the pleas of Geraint and Mr Richards, and the etiquette that demanded female mourners remain closeted in the house during a funeral, Sali insisted on attending the services and joint burial of Mansel and her aunt. She wasn't sure what the future held for her, but she did know that if she was going to move on, she had first to lay her past to rest.

'Ashes to ashes . . .' Savouring the drama, the minister flung his hands poignantly over the gaping hole. Sali lowered her eyes to the coffins, covered by a profusion of chrysanthemums and dahlias. There were so few flowers available in autumn, and there had been fewer still in January when her father had been buried. She thought wistfully of the roses, anemones and spring blooms that her aunt had loved. And Mansel? She had a sudden vision of him walking jauntily down Taff Street, a white carnation in his buttonhole just like the one he had worn the last time she had seen him.

'Dust to dust . . .' Bending his knees, the minister scooped a clod of damp soil, and circling his arm theatrically over the grave, he opened his hand. The lump of dank earth landed with a thud on one of the coffins below.

Aunt Edyth, Mansel, her father, Iestyn . . . people she had loved, who had loved her, and whom she would never see again. The grim, rain-drizzled scene wavered before her eyes. The entire world seemed grey, not just the tombstones around her and the wall of the chapel. And there was no air. So many people were crowding around, not only in the graveyard but the street beyond.

The attention attracted by Owen's confession and the appearance of Mansel's body after so many years, had brought out not only the press but every curiosity seeker in the town. The minister had been forced to restrict the chapel pews and the graveyard to family, retainers and close friends.

Sali bowed her head and Geraint gripped her arm. Taking a handkerchief from her pocket, she blotted the tears from her eyes beneath her veil.

'It's over, Sali.'

She looked around and realised people were moving away.

'Do you want to throw those flowers into the grave?'

She kissed the two white hothouse roses she held in her gloved hands and threw them down, one on to Mansel's coffin, one on her aunt's.

The crowds parted respectfully. Geraint led her to her aunt's carriage. He helped her in and she leaned back against the padded leather seat.

'Only the wake to go.' Gareth sat beside Geraint.

'And then what?' Geraint said dejectedly. His anger at the loss of his fortune had turned to despair.

'We move on, Geraint,' Sali said. 'We have no other choice.'

'I suppose we don't.' He rapped the roof of the cab with his cane.

Lloyd stood back and watched Edyth's carriage move down Taff Street, a long line of less imposing vehicles following slowly in its wake.

'She would receive us if we went to the house,' his father asserted.

'If you want to go, I won't stop you.'

'And you?' Billy pressed.

'If she wants to get in touch with me, she knows where I am.'

'You said Mrs James was a decent woman. I assumed you'd want to pay your respects.'

'You assumed wrong.'

Billy slapped his son's back. 'I'll buy you a pint in the Clarence. Then we'd better go back to Pandy for that meeting.'

'To plan the strike.'

'We're still talking to management.'

'We won't be after today. We'll be on strike next week and you know it.'

'Probably,' Billy agreed grimly. 'And then God help us all. Management as well as colliers.'

Mr Richards edged his way through the mêlée of mourners, footmen and maids in the hall of Ynysangharad House and tentatively knocked and opened the study door. Sali was sitting with Harry curled on her lap in a leather armchair and they were looking at an album of family photographs.

'I realise you probably came in here to escape the crowds, but would you mind very much if I joined you?' he asked hesitantly.

'I am always glad of your company, Mr Richards.' Sali closed the album and set it on a low table beside her chair. 'Get your picture book, Harry, you can look at it while I talk to Mr Richards.'

'On your lap?' he asked hopefully.

'On my lap,' she echoed. 'Please, Mr Richards, won't you sit down? I could ring for tea or if you prefer, there's brandy, whisky and sherry on the tray.'

'It would be bad form to ask the servants to bring us tea when they are busy serving refreshments to the mourners outside.'

'It would,' she agreed. 'I am afraid I took the cowards' way out and hid in here as soon as I returned from the graveside.' She wondered if Mr Richards had guessed it

469

had been Geraint's suggestion that he, Gareth and Llinos greet the mourners so she could take care of Harry. Her brother had tried to make it sound as if they were doing her a favour, but she knew that while her brothers and sister were prepared to accept her privately, publicly they were acutely embarrassed by her presence. From the way all three avoided any mention of the years that had passed since she had left Danygraig House, she knew they found it difficult to accept the scandal and gossip that had been generated by her pregnancy and sudden marriage to Owen Bull. But Geraint had taken the news that she had worked as a housekeeper to the family of an employee of their father's so badly she doubted he'd ever respect her again.

'If you don't mind, I will help myself to a brandy, Mrs Bull. Can I get you one?' Mr Richards picked up one of the decanters set on a silver tray on a tripod table.

'No, thank you, Mr Richards, but I will have a small sherry, please, so we can toast Aunt Edyth and Mansel's memory.'

'I had no idea Mrs James and Mansel knew so many people.' He poured and handed her a glass of sherry.

'Given the crowds outside the chapel and graveyard, I think every customer of Gwilym James must have come to pay their respects.'

'I am sure that you are right.' He pulled up a chair and sat opposite her, as Harry climbed back on to her lap. 'You two are very close.'

'We are.' She kissed the top of Harry's head. 'I try to spend as much time with him as I can.'

'To Mrs James and Mr Mansel James.' He touched his glass to hers. 'May they rest in eternal peace.'

'To Aunt Edyth and Mansel.' She sipped her sherry.

'Did Mrs James ever discuss her will with you?'

'In a letter to me once. I didn't really take it in.'

'She knew exactly how she wanted to dispose of her estate; the difficulty was in accomplishing it because of the age of her heir. But within certain well-defined parameters, she has managed to leave the bulk of her estate to Mansel's son.' He looked down at Harry who was engrossed in his book.

'But Harry is illegitimate . . . and Mansel . . . there are . . .' She faltered. 'I know he fathered other children,' she revealed abruptly.

'Harry is the only one named in Edyth James's will.' He pulled an envelope from his pocket.

'If you are going to read the will, Mr Richards, shouldn't the other beneficiaries be present?'

'The only other beneficiaries are the servants and, apart from a bequest to Jenkins of five hundred pounds, they will receive relatively minor legacies. I have asked them to assemble in the hall after the mourners have left so I can give them the details.' He opened the envelope and removed the papers it contained. 'I could read this to you or I could explain it. It is a little complicated.'

'I'd prefer it if you explained it to me.'

'Mrs James left her personal jewellery to you for your use in your lifetime, but she stipulated that you cannot sell it, and on your death it is to be passed on to Harry. Everything else she owned, this house, Gwilym James department store, the shares in the Market Company, her other investments and money have been left to Harry and he will come into his inheritance on his thirtieth birthday. Until that time, the businesses and investments will be controlled by a board of twelve trustees, made up of the three senior members of staff at Gwilym James, the two senior directors of the Market Company, two partners from my firm of solicitors, three directors from the Capital and Counties Bank, yourself and Jenkins.'

'Me?'

'And Jenkins,' he added. 'Mrs James settled on twelve trustees because, frankly, she was appalled by the way your uncle commandeered your father's estate. And she didn't even live to see the fraud Morgan Davies perpetuated,' he added bitterly.

'You really cannot blame yourself for what Uncle Morgan did, Mr Richards.'

'I can and I do, but to return to the matter in hand,' he steered the conversation firmly back on course, 'the board is to meet once a month, reasonable expenses to attend the meeting to be drawn from the trust fund, all business and policy decisions to be carried by a majority vote. This house and all its contents belongs to your son, but you can both live in it until he reaches the age of thirty, as can your brother, sisters and mother. I believe Mrs James foresaw a time when you might be called upon to act as the guardian to your family that I should have been. Please,' he protested as she attempted to speak, 'do not attempt to lessen my culpability by making excuses for my deficiencies. However, Mrs James inserted a clause in her will stating that neither Owen Bull nor Morgan Davies can spend a night beneath this roof.'

'Effectively preventing them from stealing Harry's inheritance as they did mine,' Sali murmured thoughtfully.

'Precisely,' he confirmed. 'But the validity of these exclusions are open to question. If, for example, you had wanted to move into this house with Owen Bull—'

'That would have been the *last* thing I'd want to do!'

'Nonetheless, if you look upon it as a hypothetical case, you could, in theory, appeal to the board of trustees, who have the legal right to overturn Mrs James's instructions if they feel the situation warrants it.'

'Please, don't concern yourself, Mr Richards. I have no intention of appealing to the board of trustees to challenge any of Aunt Edyth's wishes.'

'The household expenses, staff wages, the cost of Harry's education, and your and Harry's personal accounts at Gwilym James will be met from another account, which is also controlled by the trustees. My only concern, which I voiced to Mrs James, is that the board might tend to be a little conservative in the investments they choose to make on your son's behalf and in effecting policy changes in the store. But when I consider what Morgan Davies did with your father's estate, that might be no bad thing.'

'No, it might not.' She wrapped her arms around Harry and held him very close.

'Your son will be a very wealthy young man, Mrs Bull.'

'You will be one of the two trustees appointed from your firm, Mr Richards?' she asked.

'No, Mrs Bull, I will not. In view of my dereliction of duty towards your brother, that would not be appropriate.'

'Please, reconsider,' she begged. 'My father and Aunt Edyth trusted you implicitly.'

'A trust that proved entirely misplaced.'

'Uncle Morgan let us down, Mr Richards, not you. Everyone in Pontypridd respects you as a man of integrity and no one knows our family affairs better than yourself. Besides, no one else could have possibly explained the complicated terms of Aunt Edyth's will to me as simply as you just did.'

'I have already resigned from the firm, Mrs Bull.'

'That is a great pity. Please, if you won't sit on the board as a trustee, will you consider a position as my adviser, for Harry's sake?'

He looked at her for a moment. 'If I do, I will only be able to counsel you. I will not even be able to vote.'

'I realise that.'

'And I will not accept any remuneration for my services, not even expenses.'

'If that is what you wish.'

'Then for whatever it is worth, my advice is at your disposal.'

'Thank you.'

'So,' he looked around the room, 'how do you think you and Harry will like living in Ynysangharad House?'

She recalled Harry's repeated requests to go home. 'To be honest, Mr Richards, I am not sure, but I believe that

473

my mother, brothers and Llinos will be relieved. It will solve their most immediate problem.'

'But not all of them.' Mr Richards left his chair. 'If only I could turn the clock back.'

'And do what, Mr Richards? Challenge my uncle to a duel? Accuse him of trying to defraud Geraint before you had any evidence that he was plotting to do so?'

'I should have done something.'

'Don't be so hard on yourself. You are an honourable man accustomed to dealing with honourable men and Uncle Morgan has proved himself to be anything but.'

'You are so forgiving, Mrs Bull. If I may say so, very like your father and your aunt.'

'That is the greatest compliment anyone has ever paid me, Mr Richards,' Sali said simply. 'Please, would you do me a favour and explain the terms of Aunt Edyth's will to my brothers and sister. And would you tell them that they are welcome to live in this house until Harry reaches the age of thirty. After that, any invitation will have to be extended by him.'

'I thought we'd be having something hot after eating cold food all day,' Geraint grumbled as he surveyed the cold collation of smoked fish, meat, bread, cheeses, butters, chutneys and salads the parlour maids had laid out for the family's supper in the dining room.

'The servants have been busy all day, Geraint,' Sali reminded. 'I suggested a cold supper as a way of using up the leftovers and giving the cook a rest after catering for the mourners.'

'I suppose it's your decision to make,' he muttered mutinously, pouring himself a glass of whisky from the decanter on the sideboard.

'And what is that supposed to mean?' Sali enquired frostily.

'That you waltz back after four years away, appoint yourself head of the family, have cosy little chats with Mr

Richards and make decisions that affect all of us without consultation or as much as a by your leave.'

'I haven't made any decisions.'

'Oh no?' Gareth challenged. 'What about you ordering Llinos and me to reject Mr Richards's offer to pay for our education.'

'I didn't order you. I merely said that I didn't think Mr Richards could afford to pay your school and university fees.'

'Whether he can or can't, in my opinion, we should take him up on his offer. After all, he is the one who allowed Uncle Morgan to steal our money, so it's only fair that he should be the one to pay for his mistake.'

'You make it sound as though Mr Richards condoned what Uncle Morgan did, Gareth. He didn't *allow* Uncle Morgan to do anything of the kind. Besides you have lost very little compared to Geraint, and the rents from your properties will be more than sufficient to pay your school and university fees and give you a reasonable living allowance,' Sali said calmly.

'And me?' Llinos demanded plaintively. 'I was to go on to a finishing school in Switzerland to learn French and German.'

'Perhaps you will still be able to. I could ask the trustees for a loan for you.'

'A loan!' Llinos exclaimed.

'Yes, a loan,' Sali repeated irritably. 'If I had the money to replace your dowry I would, but the trustees are not handling my money, they are handling my son's, and I am not in a position to give it away.'

'And how exactly do you expect me to pay it back?' Llinos helped herself to a portion of smoked salmon.

'When you start work after you have finished your education.'

'Work at what?'

'You must have plans . . .' Sali began.

'I had my dowry and Geraint his inheritance. Pass the lemons, Gareth.'

'You were expecting to get married?'

'I haven't accepted anyone, as yet.' Llinos squeezed lemon juice over her salmon.

'I should hope not.' Sali buttered the bread on her plate. 'You are only fifteen.'

'The police could find Uncle Morgan tomorrow.' Llinos cut viciously into her salmon.

'Even if they do, it's unlikely that he will have a penny of Geraint's or the trust fund's money,' Sali pointed out realistically. 'Mr Richards and the bank manager agree that he invested everything in a bogus company.'

'So what are you suggesting? That I find work as a domestic?' Llinos questioned acidly. 'And there's no need to look at Geraint like that. He told us what you've been doing since you left your husband.'

'I am more ashamed of allowing Uncle Morgan to marry me off to a man like Owen Bull than I am of working as a housekeeper to Lloyd Evans's family. But shouting at me isn't going to change your situation, Llinos. Things being what they are, all of you have some hard thinking to do about your futures.'

'What future?' Geraint enquired miserably, sipping his whisky.

'You may have lost your money, Geraint, but you have a home.'

'Your son's home,' Geraint corrected viciously.

'Yours until he is thirty,' Sali reminded. 'Llinos, have you considered training as a teacher?'

'A teacher! Don't be ridiculous. No girl at my school would dream of doing such a thing.'

'I did,' Sali countered. 'And one of my greatest regrets is that I didn't finish my training.'

'That was you.'

'Father encouraged us to be independent. I can't understand how all of you have changed so much in four years. Frankly, if that's what going to boarding schools have done to you, then I never want Harry to attend one.'

'You'd prefer him to go to a council school?' Geraint sneered.

'He may grow up realising that he has to work for a living if he does.'

'I have my rents—'

'Yes, you do, Gareth, but surely you have some ambition beyond collecting them?'

'I was going to use the three thousand pounds to buy land and build a house.'

'You were going to farm?' Sali asked hopefully.

'I was going to employ a farm manager.'

Bewildered by their attitudes, Sali looked from Gareth to Geraint. 'When Father was alive, you both had ambitions. You wanted to be an engineer, Geraint, and you've just graduated from university. You must have considered a career when you were there.'

'I studied English Literature.'

'Why did you change your mind about engineering?'

'Because Uncle Morgan sold the colliery,' he informed her sourly.

'You must have had something in mind when you decided to study Literature,' she pleaded.

'I intended to return to Danygraig House and look after Father's business interests.'

'What interests? The first company Uncle Morgan sold was the colliery company and Father didn't have anything to do with the day-to-day running of any of his other investments. Can't you see that if all of you adopt the attitude that the world owes you a living, Uncle Morgan will have won?'

'In what way?' Geraint replenished his whisky glass.

'He will have destroyed Father's children, as well as his life's work and legacy.'

'So, what are you suggesting, Sali? That you've changed your mind about allowing us to move in here and live off our nephew's charity?'

Sali took a deep breath as she looked down the table. She hadn't known how Geraint would take the news that their aunt had left her entire estate to Harry, but she hadn't been prepared for his rage and bitterness, or Gareth and Llinos's resentment.

'As you are family, it will not be charity. Mother, you and, when they finish their education, Gareth and Llinos, will be welcome to live here rent and household expenses free until Harry is thirty. I am only sorry that I have no money to give any of you.' She braced herself for another outburst, 'So I am afraid that you will have to work to support yourselves.'

'And no doubt you'd like me become a skivvy like you!' Llinos left the table.

'Llinos—'

'You're disgusting. A disgrace to our family. I only wish Father were alive so he could see how low you have sunk.' Llinos left the table and flounced off. A few minutes later, Gareth followed leaving Sali alone with Geraint.

'I could suggest to the Board of Trustees that you be given a position in Gwilym James or the Market Company,' Sali ventured, after a few minutes of strained silence.

'As Mr Horton's son's lackey?'

'You will have to be trained before you can take a senior position, but as family, once you are familiar with the business, I am sure the trustees will offer you a similar post to the one Mansel filled.'

'So I can spend my life working to increase my bastard nephew's wealth.'

She inhaled sharply. 'Thank you so much for letting me know how you regard my son.'

'Deny that Harry is Mansel James's bastard and you deny his right to Aunt Edyth's inheritance.' He refilled his whisky glass with an unsteady hand.

'Not quite. Mansel was her nephew, but I was her great-niece.'

'And you were both her darling favourites.' He emptied his glass with a practised flick of the wrist.

'I am sorry, Geraint,' she apologised brusquely, 'but I cannot do any more for you. As I am sure Mr Richards explained, under the terms of the will, my hands are tied.'

'But you are sitting pretty. Use of Aunt Edyth's jewellery, living expense-free in this house, with all household bills paid and accounts for you and Harry in the store.'

'But no actual money,' she reminded him acidly. 'Will you at least consider my offer?'

'Oh, we'll live here with you to give you and your bastard respectability,' he mocked. 'Between them, Mr Richards and Uncle Morgan have seen to it that we have no choice.'

'Mr Richards—'

'Should have seen what was going on.'

'You probably saw more of Uncle Morgan when you returned in the holidays than Mr Richards did. Did *you* realise what he was up to?' she asked quietly.

'No.' He pushed his plate aside, pulled a pack of cigars from his pocket and lit one.

'The police may still find the directors of the Conversion of Savages and Pagans Missionary Fund.'

'And they may not,' he retorted, refusing to be consoled.

'I am sorry, Geraint. If I had any money I would give it to you, but I don't.'

'When did you get to be so bloody saintly?' He helped himself to another whisky and she fought the impulse to tell him that he had drunk enough.

'I am not, Geraint. But the last few years have taught me to accept things that cannot be changed.'

'We could challenge Aunt Edyth's will. Owen is in prison and likely to be hanged, so there's no risk of him taking any inheritance from you.'

'We?' she questioned.

'Aunt Edyth died before we found out that Uncle Morgan had stolen all my money . . .'

'Do what you want, Geraint,' she said wearily. 'It's been a long and dreadful day. I'm going to bed.'

'For God's sake, Sali.' He downed his whisky and confronted her. 'Have you lost all your pride? We are Watkin Jones's for Christ's sake. People look up to us. We have a position to uphold in the town and for that we need money.'

'Then we should work for it.'

'Skivvying for others as you have done?'

'It is honest work.'

'And you can't wait to get back to it, can you?' he taunted. 'Or is it Lloyd Evans you can't wait to get back to. Dear God, Uncle Morgan was right,' he breathed whisky fumes into her face, 'you are a whore. And a whore to a nobody. A bloody collier—'

'If you force me to chose between living here with you, the way you are behaving right now, and housekeeping for the Evanses I know which I'd prefer,' she shouted, finally losing her temper.

'Then go back to their bloody hovel.'

'I may do just that. But never forget, Geraint. This is my son's house, not yours.' Pushing past him, she left the room.

CHAPTER TWENTY-SEVEN

Sali woke the next morning with a horrible feeling of dread. It wasn't the sick, relentless despair she had woken to every morning in Mill Street, but it was a fear of yet more confrontation with her brothers and sister, the people she should be closest to.

She washed and dressed herself and Harry, and breakfasted with him alone in the dining room. Afterwards, she asked Mari if she would join her in the library so she could pose the question uppermost in her mind.

'Would you mind very much if I asked you to look after Mother again?' Sali studied Mari's face and tried to gauge her feelings.

'I would much rather look after Master Harry.' Mari wrinkled her nose. 'Mrs Watkin Jones has made it clear that she is not happy having to live here and either I've forgotten how difficult she is, or she's become much more demanding since I left Danygraig House.'

'I think Mother has become worse since you left. I spoke to the doctor last week. He has suspected for some time that Uncle Morgan has been giving her far more laudanum than he prescribed. He warned me that it is not going to be easy to reduce her dose, but as her health is badly affected, she needs to cut down drastically and immediately. But with care and patient nursing he is hopeful that it can be done.'

'My care and patient nursing?' Mari enquired dryly.

'You always were good at handling her.'

'And you were always good at dishing out compliments and getting people to do what you wanted them to.'

'If I was, that was a long time ago.' Sali handed Harry a pencil and a piece of paper, as he sat on a chair beside her.

'What about Master Harry?' Mari questioned. 'He will need a nursemaid.'

'Not immediately.'

'You can't possibly look after him with a house this size to run,' Mari protested.

'In my experience of growing up in Danygraig House, it is the housekeeper and staff who run a house this size, not the supposed mistress.' Sali glanced down the list of staff Mr Jenkins had compiled for her that morning. 'Aunt Edyth lived simply for the last few years of her life, but there appear to be more than enough servants to do everything that needs to be done, even with Geraint and Mother living here full time and Gareth and Llinos returning for the holidays.'

'I agree,' Mari said shortly, 'but someone in your position should have a ladies' maid.'

'What position?' Sali scoffed.

'Mother of the heir to Ynysangharad House and Gwilym James.'

'"Mother of" isn't any position at all,' Sali countered emphatically. 'And to get back to my question, will you look after Mother, please, Mari?'

'For you, not for her.'

'You are an angel. Now I can go and see Mr Jenkins and the housekeeper, tell them about your new position, reassure them that no one will lose their job and they can continue to run the house just as they did for Aunt Edyth.'

'You look tired, Miss Sali,' Mari observed, as Sali left her chair. 'You should rest.'

'That is the sort of thing you used to say to me when I was twelve years old and Mother first took to her bed.'

'And you never paid the slightest attention to me then.'

'No, I didn't.' Sali took Harry's hand. 'I have no idea

why I should feel tired. For the past four years I have cooked, cleaned, scrubbed, washed and ironed for sixteen hours a day, and sometimes more, and I didn't feel as exhausted as I do now.'

'Perhaps it's because you haven't given yourself any time to mourn Mrs James – or Mr Mansel,' Mari added quietly.

'I did all my mourning for Mansel four years ago, and every day I was married to Owen Bull. But now, I have Mr Jenkins and the housekeeper to see, letters to write and a list to make of all the things I want discussed at the first Trustees Meeting.'

'And you still think that are going to have time to look after Master Harry yourself, without the help of a nursemaid?'

'For the moment.' Sali smiled down at her son. 'Master Harry always comes first.'

'Do me a favour, Miss Sali?'

'Anything, Mari,' Sali answered absently as she picked up the list of staff.

'Put yourself second.'

'I think I had too much to drink last night, Sali,' Geraint apologised clumsily as he blundered in on Sali in the library.

'I know you did,' she said, without looking up from the letter she was writing.

'Look, until I can sort out something more permanent, we would be very grateful if you allow us to stay here. And despite what I said last night, I do know that it is down to me to find somewhere for Mother, Gareth, Llinos and me to live.'

'I have already arranged everything that needs to be done on the domestic front with Jenkins, Mari and the housekeeper. You will be pleased to know that Mari is going to look after Mother.' Sali signed her name with a flourish at the bottom of the page she'd written, returned her pen to the rack and blotted her letter.

'I am surprised you managed to persuade her. Mother has become impossible since we moved her into this house. And she still flatly refuses to believe that Uncle Morgan has stolen all our money.'

'Mari has always put our family before herself.' She poured him a cup of coffee from the tray the parlour maid had set on a table behind her and handed it to him. 'I suggest you don't put milk in that.'

The significance of her suggestion wasn't lost on him. 'I won't.'

'If you want to help,' she indicated the pile of correspondence on the desk, 'I have only answered a tenth of the condolence letters we received.'

'I'll look at them after chapel. Are you and Harry going to morning or evening service?' He sat at the table.

'Neither.'

'You don't go to chapel?'

'We wouldn't be welcome,' she informed him flatly. 'I was probably only allowed in yesterday for the funeral on sufferance for Aunt Edyth's sake. When Gareth and Llinos come downstairs, ask them what time train they intend taking back to their schools tomorrow.'

'What about Llinos's fees?'

'If the trustees turn down my request for a loan that she can repay, I have a ring Mansel gave me that I can sell. I was keeping it to pay for Harry's education but now his future is assured, I think it important that you, Gareth and Llinos make independent lives for yourselves.'

Geraint left his seat and carried his coffee to the window. He gazed over the fields towards the river and the town on the opposite bank. 'I have considered your suggestion that you ask the trustees to find me a position in Gwilym James.'

'And?' She sat back and looked at him expectantly.

'It would be a start. I'm not saying that I will make a career for myself there, but at least I will earn some

484

money while the police look for the swindling directors of the company Uncle Morgan gave my money to.'

'I will bring it up at the Trustees Meeting tomorrow.'

'Thank you, Sali.'

'Thank my . . . son.' She paused in the hope that he'd remember and feel guilty for calling Harry a bastard.

'We will be living off Harry's charity, but it was you who made the offer and even after the foul way I behaved last night, you haven't made me beg for any favours.'

'You're my brother, Geraint.' She looked him in the eye, but his gaze shifted uneasily from hers. She began to wonder if the life she had been forced to lead for the last four years had created an unbridgeable gulf between them.

An hour before lunch Sali set the unanswered letters aside, cleaned the nib of her pen and screwed the top on the inkbottle. She wanted to write to Lloyd but every letter she had begun had started and ended with 'Dear Lloyd'.

She simply didn't know what to say to him. She even considered writing to his father instead, but felt that a thank you for everything he and his sons had done for her and Harry might sound like a goodbye. And she wasn't ready to say that. Not yet. But neither could she offer any assurances that she would return to live with them.

Eventually she decided to postpone writing until after the Trustees Meeting and she had finished finalising all the domestic arrangements that needed to be made in the house. And there was the question of her mother's health, school fees and finding careers for Llinos and Geraint. Then she had to persuade Geraint to think in terms of finding permanent employment, rather than rely on the police to recover anything of his fortune.

She dressed Harry in his cap and jacket, put on her coat and hat, and picked up the letter she had written to Rhian to tell her that Owen wanted to see them, suggesting that if Rhian could face him, they meet in Cardiff. Refusing Jenkins's offer to post her letter for her or order the carriage, she left the house.

It was a cold, damp, miserable autumn day and a long walk down the drive for Harry, but after they had posted the letter, Sali continued towards Taff Street. No sooner had the melodic sounds from one chapel choir faded as they passed it, than the air was filled with hymns from the next. A few people nodded to her and she returned their acknowledgements, but she knew they were meaningless gestures. Her 'sins' had relegated her to the role of pariah. A position she had reinforced when she had taken the post of housekeeper to colliers. The crache might have flocked to the funerals of her aunt and Mansel in a house her son owned, but no one other than Mr Richards had sought her out and she had overheard Llinos, Geraint and Gareth discussing luncheon and dinner invitations after the mourners had left. Invitations that hadn't been extended to include her.

She stopped outside Danygraig House. The windows and doors were already boarded, waiting for the demolition hammer, and she stood at the gate for a moment, remembering, grateful that there were more happy memories than sad ones. She knew Harry was watching her but she didn't want to burden him with stories of what had been lost. Not when he had so much to look forward to.

Instead she walked up to Market Square and stopped outside Gwilym James. Bored with the window display of women's dresses and household linens, Harry tugged at her hand and pulled her across the cobbled square to the toyshop.

While he studied a display of more elaborate and expensive horses and carts than the one she had bought him for Christmas, she reflected on his future. As Mr Richards had said, he was going be an extremely wealthy young man, but if she told him about his inheritance now, would he end up with the same expectations of a life of 'managing' his investments as Geraint? Or would he strive all the harder to acquire the education and skills he would need to run an organisation that employed people dependent on the wages he could pay?

'Look, Mam, look at that enormous horse and cart full of barrels. I think they are beer barrels.'

'Do you now?' She unconsciously used one of Mr Evans's favourite expressions as she crouched down to Harry's level. 'And what do you know about beer?'

'It tastes funny.'

'And how do you know that?'

'Uncle Joey gave me a sip at Christmas when you weren't looking.'

She smiled. 'He would.'

'When are we going home, Mam?'

'Don't you like living in Ynysangharad House and having your own big bedroom, a toy room and a bath-room?'

'Yes, but it's not like home and I miss the uncles. Do you think you can lift those barrels out of the cart?' he asked with one of his maddening switches of conversation.

'I don't know, darling. We'd have to go in when the shop is open and ask.'

'Can we?'

'We can ask, but I don't have enough money to buy it.'

'I know, but I could see it and touch it.'

'Yes, you could.' She looked at him. What did she want for him? And more important still, what would he want for himself when he was older? If she made the wrong decisions on his behalf, would he end up despising her and being as ashamed of her as Geraint, Gareth and Llinos were?

The idea was even more painful than the thought of losing him to a boarding school in four years' time.

Sali returned to the house to find the sergeant closeted with Geraint in the drawing room.

They've found Uncle Morgan,' Geraint announced.

'His corpse, Mrs Bull. In the river at Taff's Well,' the sergeant elaborated.

Sali sat abruptly in one of the chairs. All she felt was an immense sense of relief that she'd never have to face the man again.

'His pockets were filled with stones.' Geraint poured her a brandy.

'Anything else?' Sali asked.

'Less than a pound in small change. A pair of silver cufflinks, a wallet, a Bible and a hymnal,' the sergeant listed. 'On the basis of the evidence, it appears to be an open and shut case of suicide, but there'll have to be a post-mortem and an inquest. Someone from the family will have to identify the body in order to claim it.'

'Not me.' Sali took the brandy Geraint handed her and laid the glass untouched on the table beside her.

'Mr Watkin Jones?' The sergeant looked expectantly to Geraint.

'Am I right in thinking that if I claim the body I will have to pay the funeral expenses?'

'You are, sir.'

'You are aware that my uncle bankrupted me.'

'Yes, sir. But if no one claims the body, your uncle will be buried at the parish's expense in a pauper's grave.'

'I am afraid I cannot help you, Sergeant,' Geraint demurred. 'I am living on my nephew's charity as it is.'

'Mrs Bull?'

Sali shook her head. 'As Geraint says, Sergeant, we are all living on my son's charity and I am not prepared to ask the trustees of my son's estate to advance burial funds for a great-uncle who has done my family such a disservice.'

'Would you like me to inform you when the funeral is to take place?'

'No, thank you, Sergeant,' Sali said politely.

'Mr Watkin Jones?'

Geraint shook his head. He'd clung to the hope that

the finding of Morgan Davies might lead to the recovery of a portion of his fortune. Now even that slight hope had been dashed, he had no sympathy for the man who had robbed him of every penny of his inheritance. 'When I think of it, Sergeant, my uncle lying in a pauper's grave seems poetic justice, of a kind.'

'I really don't see why you are so insistent on visiting Owen in that place,' Geraint castigated Sali, as Robert the footman, whom Sali had promoted to coachman at his own request, turned the carriage into station square. 'After what he did to you.'

'That is precisely why I do have to see him, Geraint,' Sali interrupted testily, 'because of what he did to Harry and me. I am not visiting him for his sake but my own. I spent four years living in fear of the man. And even when I finally managed to escape, I had nightmares every time I thought of what he would do to us if he ever discovered where we were hiding.' She put Harry's gloves on for him.

'At least allow me to go with you.'

Sali shook her head as the carriage drew to a halt. 'But you could see if the nurse needs help with Mother. If anything, she's become even more difficult in the last month, and the doctor reduced the dosage of her medication again yesterday.'

'Jenkins and the housekeeper can keep an eye on the nurse. I hate the thought of you and Harry in that place.'

'Mari can take Harry to a toyshop or a café while I make my visit. But we'll be together on the train, won't we, poppet?' She gave Harry a reassuring smile as she checked his bootlaces. 'And we'll see Auntie Rhian.'

'She wants to see her brother?' Geraint asked.

'She has as many ghosts to lay as I do. It's strange to think she is still only fifteen. I doubt I would have survived a month of marriage to Owen if it hadn't been for her help.'

'Where does she live now?'

'She works as a parlour maid in Tonypandy.' Sali looked out of the window so she wouldn't see the look on Geraint's face. More than a dozen times during the month since the funeral, he had accused her of being too familiar with the staff and lectured her on 'proper relations' with the servants. She knew he wouldn't recognise Rhian's estimable qualities or her kindness, only her lowly status as a maid. 'Today's her day off and as she's never been to Cardiff, she went in early to look around. I arranged to meet her outside the station at half past three.'

Robert climbed off the box, opened the door of the carriage and folded down the steps.

Geraint alighted first and held out his arm to Sali. As she reached the ground, he muttered, 'Damn it, Sali, I am going with you. And you can't stop me.'

'Not into the prison.'

'Yes, into the prison. But I won't interfere with your visit. I'm not sure how I'd react if I came face to face with the man. In my opinion, hanging is a damned sight too good for him.'

Sali lifted Harry from Mari's arms and set him on the ground.

'I'll get the tickets. As I'm going with Sali, do you still want to come?' Geraint asked Mari.

'I don't want Harry going near that place,' Sali reminded.

'Then I'll get three and a half first-class tickets.' Geraint went ahead to the booking office.

'You can't blame Mr Geraint for wanting to protect you, Miss Sali,' Mari commented, as Sali stared at his retreating figure.

'I don't. My God!' Stunned, she turned her head to see a sea of uniformed policemen thundering down the steps that led from the platforms. What's going on?'

'Police reinforcements down from Tonypandy, ma'am.' Robert broke one of Mr Jenkins's cardinal rules. Servants do not address their betters unless asked a direct question. And in such a case a 'yes or no, ma'am or sir' as required should be the response. If more words were needed, they should be as few and respectful as possible.

'There's trouble in Tonypandy?' Sali's heart was thundering so violently she could barely speak.

'The milkman said this morning that there have been riots there all night. The miners put out all of the boiler fires in the Cambrian Collieries yesterday morning and since then there's been nothing but trouble. Management are trying to run Glamorgan Colliery in Llwynypia with blackleg labour. Fighting broke out between the pickets, police and blacklegs around Glamorgan yesterday. The police forced the picketing miners back into Pandy Square and then they charged in with their truncheons. The miners fought back with everything they could lay their hands on. He said they attacked the Power House and ripped up the railings from around the Glamorgan to use as weapons . . .'

Sali noted the bandages beneath some of the police helmets, and the bloody noses and black eyes sported by a couple of dozen of the officers. 'Has anyone been seriously hurt?' she broke in urgently.

'The police didn't get everything their own way by the look of them,' Robert answered laconically.

'I mean the miners.'

'Dozens, or so the milkman said, but who knows what the truth is, ma'am? The town is full of rumour.'

Fighting palpitations, Sali tightened her grip on Harry's hand, as the police marched out of the station yard in formation. She had never seen so many policemen in her life. There had to be a hundred or more. They filled the Tumble in a tide of blue uniforms within seconds. 'But the police are here now, so the trouble must be over,' she murmured, desperately wanting to convince herself that was the case.

Robert shook his head. 'Looks to me as if that's just one shift coming off duty. From what the milkman said, the government's out to break the strike and as the miners are refusing to accept a pay cut, who knows where it will end.'

'Have all the miners come out on strike from all the pits?' Sali couldn't believe that she had been so wrapped up in her family and Ynysangharad House's affairs as to forget Tonypandy and Lloyd's concerns that a strike would propel the miners into open warfare with the establishment.

'The official strike began a week ago, ma'am. The Coal Owners' Association requested police protection a day later and they drafted in police from all over Glamorgan, Bristol and Monmouth. They say thousands more are coming up from London.'

'Thousands,' Sali echoed faintly.

'So they say, Miss Sali, but there's been so sign of them yet,' Mari interrupted.

'Comes to something when the bloody government send in the police to fight men who are only asking for a living wage so they can feed their families.'

'Robert! You are forgetting your place,' Mari reprimanded.

'It's all right, Mari. Your father was a miner, wasn't he, Robert?' Sali asked.

'And my four brothers. They used to work for your father and had nothing but praise for him, but since your uncle sold out ... begging your pardon, ma'am, Mrs Williams is right. I am forgetting myself.' Bowing to her, he folded the steps back into the carriage and closed the door.

'Why wasn't I told about this?' Sali asked Mari.

'It didn't seem to concern us, Miss Sali,' Mari replied evasively. 'And you've been so busy, what with the Trustees Meetings and settling Mrs James's estate and her personal affairs and seeing to your mother and Miss Llinos's school ...'

'Did Geraint ask you to keep the newspapers from me?' Sali enquired bluntly.

'If I did, Sali, it was for your own good.' Geraint stood in front of her, tickets in hand. 'The train is coming in. We are going to have to move quickly if you don't want to miss it.'

Trying not to stare at the police still flooding down the steps from the platform, Sali grasped Harry's hand. 'Come on, darling, we're all going on a train.'

Rhian was waiting outside the station dressed in a navy blue coat, her blonde hair tucked beneath a matching beret to protect it from the rain.

Sali opened her umbrella, holding it more over Harry than herself. 'Here's Auntie Rhian.'

'You've grown enormous,' Rhian lifted Harry and hugged him. 'And heavy.'

Harry's smile faltered uncertainly.

'He doesn't know me, Sali,' Rhian cried out in disappointment.

'But he soon will once you see him regularly again,' Sali assured her. 'You've met Mrs Williams.'

'I'm very pleased to see you again, Mrs Williams. I've never thanked you properly for getting me a job in Llan House.' Rhian shook Mari's hand.

'You've done well for yourself. From kitchen maid to parlour maid, or so my sister tells me.'

'Mrs Williams has been very kind.'

'My brother Geraint.' Sali crossed her fingers in the hope that Geraint would be polite.

Geraint hesitated for the barest fraction of a second before shaking Rhian's hand. 'I'll get us a cab.'

'Now, darling,' Sali crouched down to Harry's level, 'Mari is going to take you to a toy shop and afterwards you are going to have your dinner in a café, and Auntie Rhian, Uncle Geraint and I will meet you there. Be a good boy for Mari, and this,' she produced a shilling, 'is for you.'

'Silver! For me?' His eyes rounded. His Uncles Joey,

Victor, Lloyd and Billy had slipped him coppers, half-pennies and farthings on pay days, but it was the first time he'd ever been given silver.

'Do you want me to give it to Mari to look after for you?' Sali asked.

He shook his head, took the shilling and tucked it into his glove.

She kissed him and rose to her feet. 'Let him buy whatever he wants, Mari, within reason.'

'I'll remember the within reason,' Mari replied. 'You two girls take care of yourselves in that ungodly place.'

'We will.' Sali took Rhian's arm.

'Your cab, ladies.' Geraint helped Rhian in. Sali took the seat opposite Rhian and Geraint sat beside her. Sali tried to give Rhian an encouraging smile but an image of Owen towering over her, leather belt in hand, came to mind and she froze. The last time she had seen her husband, he had tried to kill her. Throughout their marriage he had beaten, abused and humiliated her. He had stolen her dowry and everything she had owned of any value. She didn't owe him a single thing, so why was she going to see him?

Hardly Christian charity, because Owen and her Uncle Morgan had almost destroyed her faith. Curiosity, because he would be dead soon? Or was she simply seeking reassurance? Would she only finally believe herself free from Owen when she saw him caged in a cell like an animal, awaiting the hangman's rope?

The gates of Cardiff jail towered above them, massive, broad and made from oak thick enough to withstand a siege engine. Sali and Rhian moved instinctively closer to Geraint as he knocked. A smaller door set in one of the large doors opened and a warder emerged. Geraint gave their names and the warder ushered them inside.

Sali found herself in a high-walled, narrow porch. Rain still spattered down on their hats and she realised there was no roof. The warder kept them waiting a few minutes until a second warder appeared. He escorted them across an inner yard, walled in by the same massive grey stone walls as the exterior of the prison, through a door and into the keep of the prison itself.

The atmosphere was dank and musty, the air heavy and foul with the stench of urine, faeces and unwashed bodies. The stink intensified, as they followed the warder down a corridor that led deep into the centre of the building.

Periodically they stopped before a locked door, the warder would speak to the officer manning it and they would be admitted, the clank of locks being turned and bolts pushed home behind them, accompanying their footsteps, as they marched up flights of stone stairs and down further dimly lit passageways.

Finally the warder halted before an open door. Beyond it was an office furnished with a desk, chair and wooden bench. A warder rose from behind the desk and stepped out to meet them.

'Mrs and Miss Bull, sir,' their escort informed him.

'Mrs Bull, Miss Bull, leave your coats, bags, hats and umbrellas here.' The senior officer faced Geraint. 'The request was for two visitors only to see the prisoner, sir. Mrs Owen Bull and Miss Rhian Bull.'

'I am here to support my sister.'

'I will have to ask you to wait here, sir.' He indicated the bench. 'The prisoner has indicated that he wishes to see you ladies separately. However, you can visit him together if you prefer.'

Sali felt intimidated by the sombre surroundings and was terrified at the thought of seeing Owen, although as a prisoner he was in no position to hurt her, but when Rhian grabbed her hand, she sensed her sister-in-law's fears were even greater than hers.

'We'll see him together, Officer.' Sali spoke for both of them.

'By rights you should be searched.' The warder looked

them both up and down. 'Do I have your word that you won't touch the prisoner or give him anything?'

'You have my word,' Sali agreed solemnly.

'You, Miss Bull?' he addressed Rhian.

She nodded, too frightened to speak.

'Follow me.'

They were shown into a small room. A metal door was set into the thick stone wall directly ahead of them. The room was bare except for a plain wooden table and four chairs.

'Sit at the table, ladies. Regulations require at least two officers be present at the interview. However, as you have given your word that you will not try to touch the prisoner, we will remain at a discreet distance.' The warder waited until Sali and Rhian were seated before knocking on the door.

The first thing that struck Sali when the door opened was the size of the cell beyond it. It was roughly the same length as Harry's box room in Tonypandy and no more than four feet wide. The warder spoke to someone inside and a few seconds later Owen stepped out, flanked by two officers. He was dressed in a drab grey prison uniform. His hair had been cropped short and his face was drained of colour. He stumbled as he walked towards the table, and one of his escort gripped his arm above his elbow. He would have fallen if the warder hadn't held on to him and when they drew closer, Sali could see that he was clutching a Bible between his handcuffed hands and was mumbling a barely decipherable prayer.

All Sali could think was how seedy, grubby and pathetic he looked. She could scarcely believe she was looking at the same man who had made her life such a misery. For the first time, she wondered why she had been so afraid of him. She could have done so much more to fight back ... Then she remembered his belt, the beatings he had given her, but most of all the threats he had made about Harry. Had she come to gloat at his downfall? It was a horrifying thought that she had sunk so low.

One of the officers pulled a chair out from the table; the second pushed Owen on to it. When Owen was seated, facing them, Rhian jumped up.

'I can't ... I'm sorry, Sali, I can't ...' She knocked over her chair and fled towards the exit. One of the officers followed her.

Sali raised her eyes and stared at Owen, willing him to raise his eyes to meet her gaze, but Owen sat with his eyes downcast. 'You asked to see us,' she reminded, as the inevitable sounds of the unlocking and locking of the door filled the room.

'The devil led me into temptation and I succumbed. I beg for your forgiveness, Sali. I need your forgiveness ...'

Sali explored her feelings as she listened to his pleas. This man had murdered her lover, an innocent coachman and his own brother. He had made her life a misery, first in Mill Street and later in Tonypandy, when she had never stopped looking over shoulder, fearful that he would discover where she was hiding. He had threatened to harm her son and her aunt ... and now ... to her astonishment, all she felt for him was pity. Logic dictated he didn't deserve it, but then he would never know a love like the one she shared with Lloyd, or experience the unquestioning, trusting devotion of a child like Harry. He had led a miserable, solitary, selfish and brutal life and now he was about to face a death equally savage and lonely.

'I need you to forgive me,' he reiterated, drooling spittle on to the table. 'Please, I am about to meet my maker.' His eyes glazed with fear at the prospect. 'It is your Christian duty—' he said with a trace of his old arrogance.

'You told me I was unfit to be a Christian,' she reminded him softly.

'You had sinned. It was my duty as your husband to correct you and set you on the path to righteousness.'

'By beating, humiliating and degrading me after you murdered Mansel?' she said calmly.

'I didn't mean to hurt him. He had money . . . I was about to lose the shop. Iestyn and Rhian's home . . . He fought back . . .'

'The doctor told me that Mansel died from a blow to the back of his head, Owen. It is difficult for a man to fight back when he's turned away from you.' Her compassion didn't extend to accepting his lies.

'Please, Sali,' he stretched his hand over the table towards her, but she recoiled even before the warder stepped forward, 'I need your forgiveness. You are my wife . . . it is your duty to obey me, for I have truly repented. I have seen the light. I know that God will forgive me if you do, Sali. It is His will that I beg for your forgiveness and in begging, gain his everlasting mercy.'

He was actually enjoying grovelling to her. Sali couldn't bear his self-abasement a moment longer.

'For what you did to me, I forgive you, Owen. For what you did to Harry to blight the first years of his life, I can't absolve you, because it wasn't just me you hurt,' she said simply. 'As for murdering Mansel, Iestyn and the coachman, you will have to ask them for forgiveness when you reach your heaven. I hope for your sake that you do.'

'Sali—'

'Goodbye, Owen.' She rose to her feet and walked towards the door. The warder escorted her out as Owen was returned, still pleading, begging and demanding forgiveness, to his cell.

Chapter Twenty-Eight

'You said within reason,' Mari apologised to Sali, as Harry proudly set out his purchases on the café table.

'Four penny bars of Five Boys chocolate, Harry, don't you think that's being greedy?' Geraint castigated.

'They are for my uncles.' Harry moved one bar to one side of his glass of milk and piled the others on top. 'Uncle Victor, Uncle Joey, Uncle Lloyd and Uncle Billy. And look, Mam.' Oblivious to Geraint's deflated expression, he opened a brown paper bag and removed a box of soldiers. 'New soldiers for my fort on loan.'

'You've wasted your money, Harry,' Geraint reproached. 'The nursery fort isn't on loan and it has plenty of soldiers.'

'He's talking about the fort the Evanses loaned him because I wouldn't allow him to take it as a gift.' Sali smiled at Harry in an attempt to take the sting from her brother's criticism. 'And it was a wonderful idea of yours to get more soldiers, Harry. Now what would you like for lunch?'

'Harry was hungry so we ate early.' Mari pushed her teacup into the centre of the table.

'Sausage and mash and I cleaned my plate.'

'Good boy. Shall we eat?' Sali asked Rhian and Geraint.

Still pale and shaky after her bout of nausea in the prison, Rhian murmured, 'I'm not hungry.'

'I'll have something when we get back to Ynysan-gharad House.' Geraint picked up his coat and hat from the stand where he had hung them.

'Then we'll go to the station,' Sali said decisively.

'I'll carry your parcels for you if you like, Harry?' Geraint offered, in an attempt to appease his nephew.

Harry shook his head and clung to them.

'Give him time, Geraint.' Emotionally drained by the scene in the prison, Sali had an overwhelming longing for peace and quiet. To her surprise she found herself picturing, not the drawing room of Ynysangharad House, but the kitchen in Tonypandy. Harry was playing in 'his' corner with the fort and soldiers, Lloyd and his father were sitting, reading the newspapers and discussing politics at the table, and Joey and Victor were whistling in the basement as they mixed the chicken feed and dog food. The scene was so real, so tangible, she was astonished when the sound of breaking glass shattered it and she saw a waitress bend down to pick up a broken vinegar bottle.

Geraint gave her a penetrating look and shrugged on his coat. 'I'll ask them to send someone to fetch a cab. Rhian's in no state to walk anywhere.'

Paperboys outside and inside the station were shouting the headlines on the newspaper placards.

'War Between Police and Miners in Tonypandy.'

'Strikers Stone Police.'

'Massive Police Casualties.'

'Coal Owners' Association Ask Government to Send in the Troops.'

'A Thousand Metropolitan Police on their Way to the Coalfields.'

'Looks like you left Tonypandy just in time, Sali.' Geraint saw them all into a first-class carriage and slammed the door.

'You're forgetting Rhian still lives there, Geraint.'

'But you're working in a decent house, aren't you, Rhian?' Geraint asked the girl.

'Llan House,' Mari answered for Rhian, who was still white and shaky. 'My sister is housekeeper there.'

Sali bristled in indignation when Geraint said 'decent house'. The inference being that he considered Lloyd Evans's house something other than decent, then she realised that even if she reproached him, he wouldn't understand why. His opinions and outlook on life had been shaped by his boarding school upbringing, just as hers had been by the past few years of her life.

'More police,' Geraint commented, as squad after squad passed their carriage and piled on to the third-class carriages lower down the train. 'They must be expecting more trouble.'

'I've just realised I can't sit with you,' Rhian protested. 'I only have a third-class ticket.'

'I'll pay the difference.' Sali stared at the tall, well-built, helmeted policemen, armed with four-foot cudgels, and thought of Lloyd and all the other miners. And she continued to think, as the train wound its way along the twelve miles of track between Cardiff and Pontypridd.

For more than five weeks she had held back from contacting Lloyd because she had too many other pressing things to do – arrange the funerals, re-allocate the duties of the servants, place her aunt's jewellery in a bank box, settle everything with the trustees, organise a position in Gwilym James for Geraint that wouldn't injure her brother's pride, wait for her mother's health to improve . . .

So many demands on her time to make decisions she had thought only she could settle. Now she realised she had simply allowed them to take precedence. The only choice she had to make was easy, so easy she couldn't understand why she hadn't made it weeks ago. And she didn't even have the excuse of acting in Harry's interest. He had told her what he wanted to do the first day he had spent at Ynysangharad House. Her son wanted to go home and she wanted to be with the man she loved.

'We're almost there.' Geraint left his seat and lifted down

their umbrellas and Harry's packages from the luggage rack.

'I'm not getting out in Pontypridd, Geraint. Harry and I are going on to Tonypandy.'

Geraint whirled round. 'Have you taken leave of your senses?'

'On the contrary, I believe I've just found them.'

'You can't possibly be thinking of going on to Tonypandy. Now of all times. You saw the police get on the train. Heard the newspaper headlines. And don't for one minute think they are an exaggeration. Colliers are a rough breed. You have no idea what they are capable of.'

'Yes, I do. I've been living with four of them for the past year.'

'Did you say that to deliberately annoy me, Sali?' he demanded furiously.

'I told you, Geraint. The Evanses have accepted me into their family.'

'And that's why you think you have to go back there now? Out of some kind of misguided loyalty to them? For God's sake, Sali, you were their skivvy. Paid help like Rhian here.'

'And Mari, Geraint,' Sali pointed out mildly.

'You owe the Evanses nothing,' he railed, refusing to be sidetracked. 'And you have absolutely no conception of what is going on in the Valleys.'

'I have, Geraint, because I know the miners, and Lloyd and his father have told me about their grievances.'

'But Ynysangharad House, the Trustees, the shop, Harry's inheritance ... he needs to be brought up a gentleman if he is to take his proper place in society.'

'The trustees will look after Harry's inheritance and I can go to the monthly meetings just as easily from Tonypandy as Ynysangharad House. The staff, you and Mari can look after Ynysangharad House perfectly well. In fact, probably better than I can. And don't pretend that you, Gareth and Llinos won't be relieved. I know I have become something of a liability. And despite Harry's inheritance, so is he.'

'People need time to adjust, Sali.' Geraint had the grace to look shamefaced. 'In a few years, your marriage to Owen Bull and the circumstances of Harry's birth will be forgotten.'

'And what am I supposed to do while people are forgetting, Geraint? Hide with Harry in the nursery at Ynysangharad House until I am considered "acceptable" by polite society again? Why should I? I am what I am, and if people don't like it they can ignore me as I can them.'

'If you won't consider your own future, consider Harry's. He will be a wealthy and important man.'

'All the more reason for him to be brought up by people who love him and will keep his feet firmly on the ground.' She glanced out of the window. 'There isn't much time, so listen carefully please, Mari. Pack Harry's things and mine and don't forget the toys he brought with him. There's no need to pack anything from the nursery. Ask Robert to send a trunk up by train. This is the address.' She opened her handbag, tore a piece of paper from the back of her diary and scribbled it down.

'Sali—'

'I won't reconsider, Geraint. When things have calmed down in Tonypandy, I will return for a visit. But there is no need to ask the housekeeper to prepare rooms for us, Mari. Harry and I won't be sleeping in Ynysangharad House again.'

'I can't let you behave so foolishly.'

'You have no choice, Geraint.' Sali met her brother's steady gaze. The train drew to a halt. Geraint opened the door, stepped down and offered his hand to Mari. He looked at Sali until the whistle blew, then he closed the door. She went to the window and pushed it down.

'I'm sorry I couldn't be the sister you wanted,' she called after him, as the train drew out of the station.

*

'We're going home, to the uncles?' Harry scrutinised his box of soldiers as the train crawled up the valley towards Tonypandy.

'Yes, Harry.' Sali glanced impatiently out of the window. Every stop at every station along the way had been five times longer than usual. Ten minutes at Trehafod. Half an hour at Porth. Finally the train drew to a halt in sidings.

'Good.'

Sali glanced impatiently at her watch.

'I told Mrs Williams I would be back at six o'clock,' Rhian said. 'What's the time now?'

'Almost seven, but I'll go to Llan House with you and explain that the delay wasn't your fault.' Sali lifted Harry on to her knee. Doors slammed lower down the train and Rhian stuck her head out of the window.

'The police are getting off.'

'There's nothing we can do until we reach the station.' Sali tried to remain calm, but she found it increasingly difficult. 'As soon as we leave the train, grab a brake. I'll pay the extra on the tickets.'

Paying the extra money on their tickets was easily done but there were no brakes or carriages waiting in the rank before the station. The street outside was eerily deserted and silent. Sali and Rhian set out to walk to Dunraven Street.

They had only taken a few steps when they heard the roaring. The swell of thousands of voices raised in anger, accompanied by cries, screams, shouts and the whinny of horses. They turned the corner, stopped and looked on in horror at the scene being played out under the lights of the gas lamps in Tonypandy's main shopping street.

A mass of men and women occupied the street, surrounded on all sides by a thin line of uniformed police wielding batons. Sali stood transfixed.

Whistles were blown and mounted police surged forward, just like their colleagues on foot, swinging their truncheons indiscriminately into the crowd. As their cudgels flailed, the miners fought back, throwing sticks, stones and anything else that came to hand.

Sali saw one of the stones hit a plate-glass shop window. It shattered in an instant. Shards crashed downwards, smashing on the pavement and breaking over the heads of the people in the street. Men piled through the broken glass, grabbing overcoats, hats and shirts from the shop display, tossing them back to others behind them before battering through into the shop itself.

A woman standing beside Sali fell to her knees and began praying. More stones were thrown and more shop windows shattered. Sali felt as though a house of cards was falling, one card at a time, as shop after shop succumbed. First one, then two, then finally all six of Connie's shop windows were destroyed. People swarmed en masse and Sali saw tins, bottles, jars and packages being handed from one man to another. Some were thrown full pelt at the police and their horses. One man was running up the road with an armful of overcoats, another was carrying dozens of umbrellas.

Mr Willie Llewellyn stood in front of his chemist shop and Sali closed her eyes, waiting for his window to receive the same treatment as the others, but the mob flooded post the ex-rugby international's shop in the direction of De Winton Street, bypassing him. Mr Isaac the jeweller stood in front of his shop and fired a pistol in the air, and he too proved lucky.

Feeling she should do something but not knowing what, Sali took a step towards Connie's shop. But even as she did so, she saw there was no way that she would be able to fight her way through the throng to reach it.

'Sali . . .'

'You can't faint, not now, Rhian.' Sali looked down and saw that Harry had wrapped his arms around her legs and buried his face in the skirt of her coat. She picked him up and holding his face against her shoulder, shielded him from the sight of the battle. Mounted policemen charged towards them and she yelled at Rhian.

'Run!'

They charged as fast as they could back the way they had come.

'We'll walk around the back streets,' Sali gasped, as soon as she could draw breath again.

'Mrs Williams—' Rhian began.

'Will have heard what's going on here.'

The side and back streets were full of injured men and women being helped to their houses. As Sali and Rhian turned towards the Evanses house she saw Victor carrying Joey in through the door. Blood was pouring from his head.

Handing Harry and his precious parcels to Rhian, she ran into the house and down the passage after them. Victor didn't ask her what she was doing there.

'Can you look after him?' He lowered Joey into an easy chair. 'I've others to see to.'

Victor was gone before he could answer. She ran to the sink, pumped a bowlful of water and grabbed a teacloth. Kneeling in front of Joey, she bathed his face.

'I'm all right,' Joey mumbled, clearly in a daze.

'Not by the look of you.'

It took her ten minutes to mop the blood from his face and head. To her relief she discovered the cut that was bleeding so profusely was neither as deep nor as long as she had feared. She soaked the cloth in cold water and pressed it to his scalp in an effort to staunch the flow. 'You're going to have a scar on your forehead that will spoil your pretty looks.'

'Women like a man to look like a man, don't they, Rhian?' Joey tried to grin and failed miserably.

Sali turned and saw Rhian and Harry standing behind her.

'I really am going to be fine, Harry,' Joey reassured the little boy, who was struggling to contain his tears and shaking uncontrollably. 'Look, your mam is going to bandage me up as good as new. Why don't you sit on my lap while she does it and you can tell me what you've been doing all the weeks you've been away.'

To Sali's amazement, Harry didn't need any more prompting. Rhian held the compress on Joey's head while she ran upstairs and brought down two of Mrs Evans's linen sheets. She set Rhian to work tearing the sheets into strips while she pinched the sides of Joey's wound together in an effort to stop the bleeding.

'Does it need a stitch?' he asked.

'I think so. We'll have to get you to one of the surgeries.'

'Don't be daft, with all that's going on out there, they are going to be banked up until this time tomorrow. Mam used to sew our cuts herself.'

'I couldn't possibly . . .' Sali bit her lips in exasperation as she released the sides of the cut and blood began to flow again, if anything more vigorously than before.

'Victor will do it when he comes back. He's used to sewing up the horses.'

Victor barged through the door with two more wounded men.

'Why don't you take Harry up to bed and tell him a story, Rhian?' Victor suggested, seeing Harry blanch at the sight of the injured men.

'The beds aren't made up.' Sali pumped another bowlful of water.

'Take him into our room, Rhian, first left at the top of the stairs,' Joey said. 'I'll be up as soon as Victor has seen to this cut and then you can come back down and help Sali.'

The next few hours passed in a hive of frantic activity. Sali brought down more of Mrs Evans's sheets and tore them into strips as Victor brought more and more casualties into the house. She pulled shards of glass from open wounds, swabbed blood with cloths soaked in vinegar, washed and irrigated dirty cuts, smeared goose grease on to the newly cleaned injuries and the gashes Victor stitched with needle and thread from his mother's sewing box. She wound strips of linen around heads, arms and hands, applied compresses of cold water on bruises, and all the while kept the kettle boiling, setting the men who had sustained minor injuries to make tea.

As soon as Joey could move, she helped him to bed. Harry was asleep. Rhian had undressed him down to his underclothes and Sali carried him into Lloyd's room and laid him in his bed until she had a chance to make up the bed in the box room.

'When did you last see your father and Lloyd?' Sali asked Victor. There were only four men left in their kitchen. Megan's uncle, who had a bruised shoulder, two men with cuts in their scalps that Victor had stitched, and a young boy who had sprained his ankle.

He took a deep draught of the tea Megan's uncle had made. 'This afternoon, before the police broke the picket in front of Glamorgan Colliery. They were standing with the other union leaders appealing for calm. A couple of the younger boys started stoning the police, someone ripped up the palings from around the colliery and the police charged and pushed us back into Pandy square.' He raised his face, and she saw that both his eyes had been blacked and his lower lip split. 'Young fools; if only they'd kept their heads, none of this would have happened. But don't worry about Lloyd or my father; it's my guess that the police have kept them safe in the hope that they'll be able to control the mob when they quieten down enough to listen. I'll go back down in a minute to see if I can find them.'

'I'm going with you.' She reached for her suit jacket.

'You're needed here.'

'Rhian can cope, can't you?' Sali didn't even wait for her to answer.

They left the house and walked down the hill. There were even more men and women in De Winton and Dunraven Street than when Sali had arrived, but fewer blue uniforms. The street looked as though a bomb had blasted it. Loot of every sort and description mixed with broken glass littered it from one end to the other. And men were still inside some of the shops, wrecking them.

'Have you seen Connie?' Sali asked Victor.

'She, Annie and Tonia have barricaded themselves into the rooms above the shop. She shouted down to me.'

A man walked past carrying a bale of cloth.

'Sion, think about what you are doing, man,' Victor remonstrated.

'Bastard had it coming to him. Charges top whack for his goods, takes the bloody rent off me every week . . .'

'Sion, you're not thinking straight. If they find that cloth in your house, you'll be going down for a good long stretch.'

'Your family collects bloody rent on the houses you own.'

'And we won't be collecting any more until this strike is settled, Sion. Think, man, there'll be no money coming into this valley for anyone – miners, shopkeepers or landlords – until this is settled.'

'My God.' Sali stared in horror as a solid tide of blue uniformed men surged into the square from the direction of the station.

'There has to be a thousand of them.' Victor leaned against the wall.

'They said in Cardiff that the Metropolitan police were going to be sent here.'

'Go back home, Sali.'

'No.'

'You can't help by staying here.'

'You can't possibly go down there.'

'There's too many boys down there like Joey. They're not bad but they are kids. Stupid hot heads who act before they think. And there are women there. Do you think the police are going to care where their truncheons land? Look after Joey and, whatever you do, keep him in the house.'

Sali returned to find Megan's uncle and the others had left. Rhian had fallen asleep in one of the easy chairs and she covered her with a blanket. She looked in on Joey, he was pale but breathing steadily, and Harry was sleeping peacefully.

In an effort to keep her mind off what was happening, she went into her bedroom. By the look of all the upstairs rooms, they hadn't been cleaned since she had left.

She made up her own and Harry's bed in the box room and carried him into it before stripping and remaking Lloyd's bed. Joey's and Victor's would have to wait until the morning. She dusted and swept the rooms and carried the bundle of linen from Lloyd's bed downstairs.

She changed Mr Evans's bed and gave his room, the kitchen and the parlour a thorough cleaning. She boiled a scrag end of lamb she found in the meat safe, and peeled, cleaned and chopped all the vegetables in the pantry and added them to the broth. Rhian didn't stir. She went down to the basement with the bed linen and found it stacked as high with dirty washing as the first day she had worked there. She set to work, boiling water in buckets and soaking the linen in the baths with soda.

She worked slowly and steadily until the sky lightened and she realised dawn could not be far off. She returned upstairs to see Victor slumped in the easy chair opposite Rhian. She looked at the clock. Six and there was still no sign of Mr Evans or Lloyd. She shook Victor gently, but his eyes remained closed. Exhausted, she uttered a silent prayer for Lloyd and his father, and sat at the table.

'Sali!' She woke with a start and realised Victor was calling her. She rubbed her eyes and looked at the clock. It was eleven. 'Why didn't you wake me earlier?' she mumbled, her mouth dry with sleep.

'Joey's only just woken me. He's taken Harry into the garden to see if there are any eggs. I'm walking Rhian back to Llan House.'

'Mrs Williams will kill me.' Rhian was combing her hair.

'No, she won't,' Sali contradicted her. 'Not if I write you a note.' She took notepaper, pen and ink from the drawer and scribbled a few lines. She folded the note and gave it to Rhian. 'See you on your next day off?'

'If Mrs Williams ever lets me out again.'

'If we go the back way, you can say goodbye to Harry,' Victor said. 'I'll call in the police station and see if Dad and Lloyd are there, Sali. But wherever they are, I'm sure they're fine,' he reassured her.

Sali filled a jug with cold water, went upstairs and washed herself. Realising she and Harry didn't have even a change of clothes, she made a note to ask Victor to call in at the station to see if her trunk had arrived.

She was back in the kitchen, making porridge when Joey came up from the basement with Harry. 'You two must be hungry.'

'I'd prefer a headache powder to food,' Joey answered.

'It won't do much good for a crack on the skull.'

'I suppose not.' Joey sat at the table and Harry climbed on to the chair next to him. Despite her concern for Lloyd and Mr Evans, Sali smiled when she saw that Harry had set out the four chocolate bars he had bought in front of each of the men's chairs. 'I see you have your presents.'

'Harry's promised to help me eat mine later.' Joey ruffled Harry's hair. 'You back for good?'

'Mam said we were coming home.'

'Did she now?' Joey looked at Sali, who was untying her apron. 'Where are you off to?'

'To look for Lloyd.'

'Victor said he would.'

'I can't sit still a minute longer.'

'Let me come with you.'

'You look after Harry and give him his breakfast, I'll be back as soon as I can.'

*

511

Sali walked down to Dunraven Street. A few of the shopkeepers were in the street sweeping up the damage. An enterprising carpenter pushed a handcart down the road heaped high with planks of wood ready to nail across the empty window frames. The police were standing around, confining pedestrians to the pavements, as if they needed to prove that they were finally in possession of the town.

'Please God, don't let Lloyd be dead. Please God don't let Lloyd be dead,' she muttered over and over again under her breath.

Then she heard the steady tread of marching feet. She stood, mesmerised, as a full squadron of armed soldiers advanced up the main street towards her.

The people on the pavements stood in silence facing the road and the troops. She walked behind them, looking at every man tall and broad enough to be Lloyd or his father.

She saw them standing on the pavement in front of the Police Station. She fought her way through the dense crowd until she was close enough to rest her hand on Lloyd's shoulder. He whipped around, the anger in his eyes fading to disbelief when he saw her. His face was grey with exhaustion and there were dark circles beneath his eyes, but when she opened her arms, he swung her off her feet, holding her as though he never intended to release her.

'Megan's uncle said you were here. I thought he was hallucinating after being hit on the head.'

She looked over Lloyd's shoulder at Mr Evans, who was standing beside him. 'From the state of the house, you could still do with a housekeeper.'

'We're strikers, Sali. We can't pay you a penny. I've invested all our savings in houses and I can't ask anyone to pay me rent when they haven't a farthing coming in. God only knows how any of us are going to put food on our tables next week.' His eyes were moist as he stared at the troops.

'We'll manage,' she said optimistically.

'Will we? I never thought I'd see the day Tonypandy garrisoned by soldiers.' Mr Evans turned wearily towards home. 'Talk some sense into the girl, Lloyd, and send her packing.'

'You can't really want to come back here when you have Ynysangharad House,' Lloyd said.

'The house isn't mine, it's Harry's.'

'And he'll need to be brought up a proper gentleman.'

'That's what my brother said. I'd prefer him to be brought up with people who will love and guide him.'

'Sali, my father's right. You have no idea what's coming. The government and the Coal Owners will try to starve the miners into submission. The next few months are going to be hell.'

'Not if we're together.'

'Like my father said, I should send you back to Pontypridd.'

'I won't go, not even if you throw stones.' And there, amongst the wreckage of the main street of Tonypandy, in front of the whole town and a regiment of soldiers, she kissed him.

All Orion/Phoenix titles are available at your local bookshop or from the following address:

Mail Order Department
Littlehampton Book Services
FREEPOST BR535
Worthing, West Sussex, BN13 3BR
telephone 01903 828503, *facsimile* 01903 828802
e-mail MailOrders@lbsltd.co.uk
(Please ensure that you include full postal address details)

Payment can be made either by credit/debit card (Visa, Mastercard, Access and Switch accepted) or by sending a £ Sterling cheque or postal order made payable to *Littlehampton Book Services*.
DO NOT SEND CASH OR CURRENCY

Please add the following to cover postage and packing

UK and BFPO:
£1.50 for the first book, and 50p for each additional book to a maximum of £3.50

Overseas and Eire:
£2.50 for the first book plus £1.00 for the second book and 50p for each additional book ordered

---

BLOCK CAPITALS PLEASE

name of cardholder ....

address of cardholder ....

....

....

postcode ....

delivery address
(*if different from cardholder*)

....

....

....

postcode ....

☐ I enclose my remittance for £ ....

☐ please debit my Mastercard/Visa/Access/Switch (delete as appropriate)

card number ☐☐☐☐☐☐☐☐☐☐☐☐☐☐☐☐☐☐

expiry date ☐☐☐☐   Switch issue no. ☐☐

signature ....

prices and availability are subject to change without notice